Secrets and Lies

By Tempie W. Wade

Secrets and Lies
By Tempie W. Wade

This is a work of historical fiction. While some of the names in this book are the same as real-life historical figures, the actions and words of the characters are strictly figments of the author's imagination and any resemblance to actual events, places, and persons, living or dead are entirely coincidental.

Copyright © 2020 by Tempie W. Wade

UPDTD

Printed in the United States of America.

Print Edition - ISBN: 978-1-7363975-0-3

Digital Edition - ISBN: 978-1-7363975-1-0

For more Information, please visit
www.TempieWade.com

Secrets and Lies

By Tempie W. Wade

Book Six in the Timely Revolution Book Series

"Three things cannot long stay hidden: the sun, the moon and the truth." –Buddha

"Honesty is the best policy." –Benjamin Franklin

Danu (Maggie) — Mother Goddess of Fertility, Motherhood, Wisdom, and Nature

The Dagda (Duncan) —Father God of Wisdom, Fertility, Strength, and Magic

Camulos (Gabe) —God of War

Grannus (Quinn) —God of Healing

Cernunnos (John) —God of Sex and Lust, Protector of the Forest and Master of the Hunt

Toutatis (Alastair) —God Protector of the Tribe

Brigid (Kat) —Goddess of Healing

Lugh (Kendric) —God of Warriors and Justice

Morrigan (Morgan) —Goddess of War, Soldiers, and Fate

Aine (Alanna) —Goddess of Love and Light

Belenos (Steven) —God of the Sun

Aengus (Finley) —God of Youth and Love

1 Chapter One

July 1781
Williamsburg, Virginia

Maggie stared out the window of the nursery, rocking little Steven back and forth in her arms, his eyes almost completely closed now that his tummy was full. She had just finished nursing and was about to lay him down in the crib next to his sleeping brother when she felt Duncan appear in the doorway.

"Need some help?" he whispered, quietly creeping over and kissing his newborn son's head, stroking it lightly as he smiled down at him.

Maggie shook her head and carefully laid the precious bundle next to his brother. She leaned back against her husband and they watched their two angels slumber, both now blissfully lost in peaceful dreams.

Maggie pointed and guided Duncan out into the hall, softly closing the door behind them.

"Where are the triplets?" she asked.

"Downstairs playing with Kat and Alastair. Cora and Cecile are tending them."

"What about Gabe, Quinn, and John?"

Duncan slipped his arms around her waist and looked into her worried eyes. "Making sure that the last of the British army has made their way out of town. They have been standing guard on this side of the fog line all morning just to make sure things are progressing along nicely."

He stroked Maggie's face that still showed signs of concern.

"Do you think anyone will come here to look for Pennington and his men?" she asked nervously.

"Nay!" he replied gently. "Not that they will find us even if they did. We all have full Fae powers now, and nothing will be able to cross that line without one of us letting it in. No one can hurt us now, remember?"

Maggie sighed and laid her hands flat against his chest. "It's a little difficult to get into that mindset after years of worrying, and this whole immortality thing is taking some getting used to."

"Ye will get no disagreement there, my love. This is new territory for all of us. Personally, I am still trying to come to terms with the fact that I was dead two very short days ago."

Maggie embraced him tightly, rested her head on his shoulder, and whispered, "That is not something I ever want to think about again."

They both turned when the sound of voices drifted up from the foyer below. Slowly, Maggie and Duncan made their way over to the landing and leaned over the rail to see that Gabe, Quinn, and John had returned.

"How did things go?" Duncan called down.

"There are a few stragglers here and there, but for the most part, the army has cleared out," replied Quinn.

"Did anyone attempt to find their way to the house?" asked Maggie as they started to descend the staircase.

"If they did, we never knew it," replied Gabe. "The coast seems to be all clear."

"Personally, I think we can breathe a collective sigh of relief," added John, and he led the group toward the drawing room.

Maggie and Duncan took the chairs nearest the children while Gabe and Quinn sprawled out on the sofa. John helped himself to a drink before choosing a chair next to Maggie and Duncan to watch the babies play.

"Are they being good today?" Maggie asked.

"They are always good," answered Cora. "Honestly, they are the happiest babies I have ever seen."

"Cora is right," added Cecile. "They never fuss about anything." She looked warily toward Maggie. "Speaking of fussing, shouldn't you be in bed? You did just give birth to two babies a few days ago. It is too soon for you to be up and about!" she fretted.

"I am feeling perfectly fine," replied Maggie, reaching down to pick up Morgan, who had toddled over to her. John knelt to gather up Alanna, who had crawled over to him and was pulling up on his leg. As he looked for a place to set his drink down, Cora moved quickly to take the glass from his hand.

"Let me get that for you," she said with a smile.

"Thank you, Cora," he said graciously, trading his glass for the baby.

"So many lovely ladies in this one room," remarked John, before kissing the top of Alanna's head and lifting her up in the air, making her giggle. "How could a man ever choose between the lot of you?"

Maggie took notice of the fact that Cora's gaze was somewhat fixated on John, and that a slight tinge of pink had appeared on her cheeks. Just as she was wondering what that was all about, Maggie caught sight of Cecile, who was watching John with a smirk as well, seemingly enjoying the view from her seat.

That's odd. It must be my imagination.

John shifted Alanna over to one arm, and she rested her chin on his shoulder as he rose from his chair. As he did, a tiny bit of barely noticeable drool dripped down onto his shirt. Just as Maggie was about to point it out, Cora sprang to his side and pulled a handkerchief from the front bodice of her dress.

"You have a little something there," she said to John. "Please, allow me to get it for you."

Before he could respond, Cora began to blot the area on his shoulder, while she casually placed her other hand flat against his back. After spending an unusually extensive amount of time on that one spot, John, still holding Alanna, looked down at her peculiarly.

"I think you got it all," assured John. "Thank you, Cora," he smiled.

"It was my pleasure," she said, her hand leisurely lingering, having slipped from the middle of his back down quite a bit lower. "Is there anything else I can do for you?"

John looked at her strangely. "No—but thank you for asking."

Cora nodded her head, her hand still touching him as if she were not ready to leave his side.

John turned, sat back down in the chair and shifted Alanna to his knee so he could bounce her.

"Can I get you another drink?" asked Cecile sweetly, and moved nearer to where John was.

"Nooo—I am good," he replied, drawing out his words, clearly confused by the attention.

"How about something to eat?" offered Cora, sensually stroking his back before Cecile came over to do the same.

He looked back and forth at the two of them uncomfortably as everyone else in the room stopped to watch the rather odd exchange.

"Umm—ladies, I really don't need anything at all. I am fine, I assure you."

Maggie stood, still holding Morgan. "Cecile, Cora, why don't you take the babies upstairs?"

They both frowned, expressly deflated, and reluctantly moved to gather the triplets, Kat and Alastair following them out of the room. Once they were gone, Maggie turned to John.

"What the hell was that all about?" she demanded.

"I haven't the foggiest notion," answered a somewhat bewildered John, glancing toward the doorway.

"John! Have you been flirting with them?"

"No, of course not! They are both married women. I have no idea what brought that on," he shrugged, "Perhaps, they are feeling neglected by their husbands and looking for a little attention."

Maggie cut him a sharp look as Hettie ducked in and announced that dinner was ready.

Hettie was still putting food on the table when the group meandered into the dining room. After John took his seat, Hettie leaned over to set a plate on the table before him, lightly brushing against him as she did. She then looked at him as if she had just seen him for the very first time.

"You look mighty handsome today," she said softly, sporting a bashful grin.

"Thank you," replied John, laying his hand over on hers, "and you, my dear Hettie, are devastatingly beautiful, as always."

Hettie giggled and put her arm around his shoulder to pull him tightly against her. Just as Hettie loosened her grip, one of her hands slid discreetly out of sight, causing John to jump just a bit, startled, yet pleasantly surprised, before his face broke into a rather wide grin. He looked up at Hettie, who winked back at him flirtatiously before turning around.

Maggie and Duncan exchanged astonished looks with each other, and with Gabe and Quinn who had witnessed the exchange, as well. Once Hettie was out of the room and back in the kitchen, Maggie leaned across the table and whispered, "Did she just grab your—?"

"Indeed, she did," he chuckled, "and I must say, I cannot say I disliked it."

"What on Earth?" asked Maggie, quieting herself when Hettie came back into the room.

Hettie set the final plate on the table and leaned over John again, this time purposefully brushing against his back with her rather ample bosom. She rubbed his shoulder with her hand and said, "If you need anything at all, you just let me know," before going back into the kitchen.

Gabe propped his elbow up on the table and rested his chin in his palm with a dumfounded expression on his face.

"What in God's name was that all about? What is it with you and the women in this house today? They can't seem to keep their hands off you."

Maggie raised her hand as if she were in elementary school and had something to say to the teacher. "For the record, *I* have not grabbed any part of his body today."

Duncan took her hand. "And it had better stay that way," he teased and kissed it. He thought for a few seconds, then looked at her oddly. "What do ye mean ye haven't grabbed him *today*?"

"Maybe the God of Lust and Sex is affecting the people around him more than we know," suggested Quinn.

"*Could* that happen?" questioned Maggie. "*Would* that happen?"

"Fae are known for enamoring humans," answered Duncan after giving it some consideration, "and a few possibly more than others. It would make sense the one with dominion over lust and sex would come across a bit stronger, I suppose."

Maggie turned to John and wagged her finger. "You had better be careful where, and who, you *rub off* on now that you are fertile. I'm sure Hettie is well past the point of wanting any babies."

John smirked at Maggie and rubbed his chin, seeming to enjoy the entertaining turn the conversation had taken.

"So, women are just going to fall at John's feet everywhere he goes now?" questioned Gabe.

"Now, that *would* be interesting," teased John.

"I guess we will see," said Duncan, taking a plate of food and passing it around.

"Well, since that is one of your abilities, you should be able to grant it to people, in theory, right?" asked Maggie and took a piece of bread.

"Yes, he should," said Quinn. "Just as ye can grant fertility, he should be able to create desire."

7

"Want to test it?" asked an all-too eager John with a big grin on his face. "I can try it with you and Duncan if you like."

"Don't waste your time and energy," Gabe scoffed good-naturedly. "Those are the *last* two in this world who need it."

"What about you and Quinn?" offered John, turning to Gabe.

"I don't think we need it either," Quinn smiled adoringly at his husband, took Gabe's hand in his, and kissed the back of it. "Besides, I doubt it would affect us since we have all been turned to Fae."

Duncan waved his fork around in the air. "Quinn is right. If one god or goddess could affect another in such a way, as ye can imagine, it would become total chaos. There is a reason they were not allowed to meddle in each other's affairs."

"We still have so much to learn," Maggie sighed, "and we need to figure it out before the children are old enough to be given their abilities. It would help if we knew what we were doing first."

"We will get things sorted out," assured Duncan, rubbing her leg reassuringly under the table.

She placed her hand over his. "I certainly hope so!"

John decided to pay a visit to the village that night since he had not been for a few days.

After the children were asleep and everyone had left for the evening, Maggie and Duncan slipped down to the hot springs. They stripped and stepped into the pool.

"Best gift ever!" exclaimed Maggie, sinking to her shoulders in the warm water.

"Indeed!" purred Duncan and snaked his arms around her waist, a seductive expression on his face.

"So, tell me about this Dagda," she said with a curious smile on her face and wrapped her arms around his neck.

"Well," Duncan planted a light kiss on her shoulder, "the Dagda is a father, as ye know, and a magician who holds rein over wisdom, agriculture, strength, and even fertility."

"Fertility?" asked Maggie teasingly. "Are you trying to cut in on my action, mister?"

He tossed back his head and laughed. "Nay, but it might explain how we ended up with a set of triplets and twins."

"You may have a point there!" She grinned and kissed him.

"What do you make of all of this with John?" she asked as Duncan ran his eyes and his hands sensually over her backside.

"I think John can take care of himself," he growled. "Tonight, I have my own needful desires I have every intention of satisfying," he said and lost himself in her.

2 Chapter Two

Two days later, David Percy found Maggie and Gabe in the drawing room, working at the desk.

Wringing his hands, the man was obviously upset. "Maggie, I need a word with you."

"Of course, David," she said and stood, leading him over to a chair. His face was bright red, streaked with tears, and it was apparent that he had not slept at all the night before. She glanced over her shoulder at Gabe curiously as he moved to pour the distraught man a drink.

"David! What is the matter? Has something happened?" she asked, as Gabe handed him the glass.

"It's Cora," he replied, his voice cracking. "She has asked me to petition for a divorce."

Maggie and Gabe exchanged dumbfounded looks.

"Why on Earth would she do that?" asked Gabe.

David looked down into his glass, another wave of emotion overtaking him, the tears now flowing freely.

"She has stated she has fallen hopelessly in love with another."

Maggie laid her hand sympathetically on David's shoulder. "Oh David, I am so sorry."

"Wait!" exclaimed Gabe, suddenly, completely confused. "Who is this man she has fallen in love with?"

David looked up at Maggie. "John!" he exclaimed and broke into a pitiful sob.

Maggie thought she must have heard wrong.

"Did you say —John?" Maggie shook her head. "No! David, there must be some mistake. There is no way she and John are involved. He would never have an affair with a married woman."

He leaned forward with his forehead in his hands. "She insists she wants to leave me to be with him."

"Maggie is right," agreed Gabe. "She and John could not possibly be together. I don't understand why she would say such a thing."

"Because she does not want to be with me anymore," he whispered pitifully and wiped his tears with his hand.

Maggie put her arm around him in hopes of comforting the poor man, who was beside himself and completely undone, while raising her eyebrows quizzically at Gabe with a shrug.

"I love her so much, Maggie. I do not know how I shall live without her. I had no idea she was so unhappy, and out of the blue, just yesterday, she broke the news to me." When he leaned against her and bawled, Maggie rubbed his back in a vain attempt to console him.

"David," she said and patted his shoulder, "let me talk to Cora and find out what is going on here. I am certain there must be some sort of misunderstanding."

"Would you?" he asked, lifting his gaze, hope sparking in their depths.

"Yes!" she said and smiled reassuringly. "Now, why don't you let Gabe take you back to your house and get some rest while I get this mess resolved?"

He dragged his sleeve across his face and stood. "Thank you, Maggie. I knew I could count on you."

"Come on, old chap," said Gabe and guided him toward the door, glancing over his shoulder at Maggie, baffled by the turn of events.

Maggie held up a pretend bottle as if she were chugging it, indicating to Gabe that it was probably best to just get the poor man drunk.

Gabe nodded in agreement.

Once they were gone, Maggie called Hettie into the foyer and asked her to come along with her to find Cora, who was in the side yard minding the babies.

"Cora!" called Maggie. "I need to see you inside. Hettie will watch the children while we speak."

The nanny came to join her and followed her into the drawing room.

Maggie leaned against the desk and motioned Cora to a seat.

"Your husband just left a few moments ago, and he is extremely upset because he thinks you want a divorce. I told him there must be some mistake."

Cora looked down, a guilty look on her face. "Oh no, he is right," she said softly.

"Cora, I thought you and David were very much in love with each other."

"We were... we are..." she stuttered. "I still care for him a great deal— I just find I desire another more."

"John?" Maggie asked, wincing slightly.

The young woman hung her head and nodded.

Maggie sighed. "Have you and John been seeing each other away from the house?"

"No, ma'am."

"When, and where, have you been alone together?"

"We haven't—not yet anyway," replied Cora quietly.

Maggie folded her arms, perplexed. "Has John made unwarranted advances toward you? Because, if he has stepped out of line, I will handle the matter immediately."

"No, ma'am!" she protested. "He has been a perfect gentleman."

Maggie scratched her head. "I think maybe you should explain to me exactly what is going on here."

"Well," she stated, "the other day when we were in the drawing room with the children, and I brushed the spot from his shirt, I felt something stir deep within me I have never felt before, and I am sure he did as well. It was as if I had seen him for the first time. I only know that I must be with him, no matter what the cost."

Maggie held up her hand. "So, that's it? That's the only contact you two have ever had."

"Well yes!" Cora nodded. "But the feeling was so strong neither of us can possibly deny it."

"I don't suppose you have mentioned your feelings to John?"

"Oh no, ma'am! I wanted to get the divorce first, but of course, I know he must feel the same. Love that strong is undeniable."

Oy!

Maggie rubbed her forehead with her palm. "Thank you, Cora. You can go back to the children and, please, send Hettie back inside."

"Yes, ma'am," she said and left the room.

Maggie sent out a mental message.

Duncan, please come to the house.

On my way, my love.

Maggie was still leaning against the desk when Hettie came back into the room.

"Everything alright?" asked the housekeeper.

"No! Cora thinks she is in love with John, and she is planning on leaving her husband for him," answered Maggie, moving to the side cabinet and pouring herself a large drink.

"Cora and John?"

"I know, it's ridiculous, isn't it?" said Maggie and downed her whisky in one shot.

"It sure is!" Hettie laughed heartily. "That girl has taken leave of her good senses, especially since John is *my* man, and he and I are the only ones who are going to be together."

Maggie slowly lowered the glass and stared at Hettie in disbelief. "*You* and John?"

"Yes! A man like that needs a woman who knows what she is doing," she replied, "and I *know* exactly how to please a man."

Oy! Oy!

Maggie blew a few loose strands of hair out of her face. "Hettie, Duncan and I will be out for the afternoon. Please make sure the children are seen to."

"Yes, Maggie," she said and left the room as Duncan came around the corner.

"Ye needed me, my love?"

"Oh boy, do I? We have some major problems to sort out!"

They saddled the horses and Maggie explained everything to him as they rode towards the tribe.

"She actually asked David for a divorce? Och! The poor man!"

"I know they love each other, and that Cora is just not thinking clearly. At least we know now John is indeed affecting the people around him."

"What are we going to do about it?" asked Duncan.

"There has to be some way that he can control it or tone it down. I guess we need to check the books and see if we can find any answers," she answered with a long sigh.

Once they reached the village, they went straight to John's longhouse. Maggie knocked loudly on the frame of the entryway but became aggravated when she received no response. She pushed open the door and stormed in when she perceived some faint noises coming from inside.

"Maggie! Wait! John is probably not alone!" warned Duncan and grabbed for her arm, but he was unable to stop her before she marched in and flung open the bedroom door.

Duncan was right—John was in bed surrounded by four completely naked, overly amorous women.

Maggie shielded her eyes with her hand and pointed towards the door.

"Everyone out!" she ordered, much to the chagrin of the desirable ladies draped across John's bed.

"Maggie! What the bloody hell are you doing?" he demanded, strategically pulling a blanket to cover himself, displeased by the interruption.

"GO!" she shouted.

Each woman stopped to thoroughly kiss John as they crawled out of his bed, which he greedily took the time to reciprocate. Once they were all gone, he leaned back against the headboard, two fingers to his temple and a vexed expression on his face.

"What is this all about? Why did you make those women leave? I was just getting started—" Suddenly, his face broke into a devilish grin. "Unless *you* want me all to yourself."

"Nay, she does not!" roared Duncan and appeared behind her.

John simply laughed.

Maggie picked up his clothes off the floor and tossed them onto the bed.

"Get dressed, Romeo! We need to have a long chat."

Maggie and Duncan waited by the fireplace, while John gathered himself. He came out of the bedroom, pulling his shirt over his head, and walked over to pour himself a drink.

"What is so damned important that you had to interrupt the deliciously sordid afternoon I had planned?" he asked and raked his hand through his hair. "I was just getting warmed up."

Maggie folded her arms and glared at him. "Cora has asked David for a divorce."

"That is unfortunate!" John took a seat, leaned back, and splayed his legs. "I am extremely sorry to hear that, but I don't see what that has to do with me."

"She is leaving him for *ye*," added Duncan.

John lowered his glass. "For me? I don't understand."

"Apparently, you are 'lust-dusting' all the women on the estate," said Maggie dryly.

"Lust-dusting?" asked John, amused. "I have done no such thing, even though I am not exactly sure what that means."

"It means all of these women are falling under your spell as the God of Lust and Sex," explained Duncan, "and ye do not even realize ye are doing it."

Maggie nodded and took the chair next to him. "The scent of sex is rolling off you, and regular women are powerless against it —even Hettie is being affected."

"Hettie?"

"She thinks you need a woman who knows how to please you, and that she is that woman."

John tilted his head thoughtfully for a moment, as if he were considering the possibilities.

"Oh, come on!" Maggie smacked his shoulder. "This is serious."

John laughed at the serious expression on her face. "I will simply tell Cora *and* Hettie there is no future for us —problem solved."

"I don't think it will be enough," said Maggie worriedly. "Cora is convinced she wants you, and there is nothing more dangerous than a woman trying to get a man she really desires."

"Unless it is someone trying to get in the way of a woman trying to get who she really wants," clarified Duncan solemnly.

"So, what do you suggest we do?" asked John.

"Come back to the house with us and let's see if there is anything in that book of yours that will help," answered

Maggie. "In the meantime, lay off the women until we figure this whole thing out, and by the way, you reek of stale sex."

John lifted his glass to his lips as Maggie swatted at his shoulder again. "What were you doing with four women anyway? I warned you about where you put *that*," pointing towards his lap.

John looked down, then back up at her. "But, my dear Maggie, I am completely innocent. In fact, I was ambushed."

Maggie and Duncan both raised eyebrows at him, expressions of disbelief filling their faces.

"I was!" he exclaimed, affronted, and looked to Duncan for help where there was none. "I rode back into the village and before I could get off my horse, two women came out to greet me. They pulled me towards the house, and by the time we got to the door, two women had turned into four, and I was completely devoid of clothing from the waist up."

Maggie narrowed her eyes at him, trying to decide if he were making it up.

"The next thing I knew, I was in my bed and so were those same four half-dressed women —touching every part of my body." He took a sip of his drink, a devilish smirk crossing his lips. "What was I supposed to do?"

"Tell them to leave?" griped Maggie. "Come back to the house? Run away? All of the above?"

Duncan shook his head. "I am not sure that would have worked," a grave tone in his voice.

"Thank you!" said John, raising his glass in a toast to Duncan. "You see, Duncan understands."

Maggie wrinkled her nose at Duncan while shooting him a disapproving look. "Don't encourage him!" she scolded.

Duncan moved next to Maggie. "Nay, ye do not understand. Fae, other than an occasional visit from Finn, have not walked the Earth in a very long time. When they did, the humans who were around them were affected by them in good and bad ways, and always to the extreme, but that was from just being around *one* Fae at a time. People in the Colonies have never encountered such power and now, suddenly, there are five of us, plus the children, in one place. We may be creating an abundance of these emotions just by being here."

Maggie rubbed the bridge of her nose. "Why just John?"

"We don't know, in fact, that it *is* 'just John'." He kissed the top of her head. "Lust may be only the beginning, and since it is such an extreme emotion, it would naturally be the first one to surface. We have only been Fae for a few days, and this might be a taste of what is to come. We will need to keep a close eye on what is going on around us."

Maggie turned to John. "I think we should keep you in sight at all times for the foreseeable future."

"Maggie, I had no idea you liked to watch," he taunted.

She slapped his chest again, this time harder. "You are taking your new job entirely too seriously."

Duncan smirked. "In his defense, he may not be able to help it. We cannot assume that going from mortal to Fae overnight will not change us in some ways. If the essence is latching on to what is already there, it may be amplifying what is truly inside all of us."

"I don't think that it has me," she pointed out.

"Aye, but ye were already half-Fae, and your inherent goodness has always been there at the forefront, so there wasn't much change to take place. The rest of us, however, may be a completely different story."

Maggie made a face and groaned. "This was never going to be simple, was it?"

"Nothing else ever has," her husband snarked, "why should this be?"

3 Chapter Three

Gabe and Quinn were waiting at the house when the trio returned.

"Where is David?" asked Maggie.

"Sleeping it off in his bed. The man took one drink of whisky and was out cold," divulged Gabe before turning to John. "There's our homewrecker." He leaned in closer to his old friend before taking a step back and waving his hand in front of his face. "Good Lord man, you need a bath. You smell like you have spent the day at a French whorehouse."

"I will take that as a compliment," declared John with a chuckle.

"Don't!" quipped Maggie, leading them all into the drawing room and pulling the doors closed behind them.

Once they were alone, Gabe and Quinn were briefed on what was happening.

"First things first," said Maggie, "we need to get this whole thing with Cora and David straightened out."

John nodded. "I will have a word with her immediately."

"Ye should probably take a bath first," warned Quinn and raised his knuckles to his nose to block the smell. "If ye speak with her with another woman's scent on ye like ye have now, it may not go well."

"More like the scents of *four* women," mumbled Maggie disgustedly.

"Four!" exclaimed Gabe incredulously. "Seriously, John? What the hell, man?"

John shrugged. "Can we get past the numbers, please, and move on to the more important issue at hand?"

Maggie moved to the doors and opened them to call out to Hettie.

"Will you set up the bath in our bedroom for John, please?"

Hettie smiled. "I sure will. Will he be needing someone to scrub his back for him?" she asked, giddy at the prospect.

Grimacing, Maggie groaned. "NO! Will you just take care of it, *please*?"

Hettie nodded and was off.

Maggie sensed the babies were about to wake up for a feeding, one of the new things she could do now that she had been transformed into the Mother Goddess. She turned back to the room.

"I will be in the nursery." Stopping to wave her finger in John's direction, she added, "Keep him out of trouble, will you?"

"We will do our best," replied Duncan.

Maggie quietly opened the door to the nursery. Finley was starting to stir ever so slightly. She untied her top before carefully picking him up just as his eyes fluttered open.

"Hello, sweetheart," she said and settled into the rocking chair with him. She was singing softly when she heard a soft tap at the door.

"Come in," she called out.

"Mind some company?" asked Gabe.

"Not at all!"

He stopped to peek on Steven, who was still asleep before pulling up a chair next to her.

"You really were born to be a mother," he whispered and smiled as he watched them.

"On many levels, it seems," she said, looking down at Finley. "Is John getting cleaned up?"

"He is indeed," he paused and eyed her warily. "Want to talk about it?"

"About what?"

"Whatever is bothering you. You seem a little — flustered, I suppose would be the best word —with John's recent activities, I mean."

She glanced away, looking towards the window. "I don't know what you mean."

"Oh, I think you most certainly do," he said and leaned on the arm of the chair, closer to her. "I know you a little too well, Mags."

"Was he always like this?" she asked after a moment of silence to gather her thoughts. "I mean, I know John has always kept a woman or two around to meet his needs, but I thought he was more discreet and discriminant about it before, wasn't he?"

Gabe bobbed his head side to side as he pondered the question. "John does seem a bit different these days—

and it does appear he has embraced his new status with a great deal of added enthusiasm."

"Duncan thinks it may be the Fae essence making him that way, intensifying what was already there."

When Gabe heard Steven wake, he stood, moved to the crib, and picked him up to rock in his arms. "And that bothers you?"

"Everything about this new situation bothers me," she said and laid Finley against her shoulder, lightly patting his back. "For God's sake, Hettie thinks *she* is the woman who should be in John's bed pleasuring him."

"Hettie?" gasped an astonished Gabe.

"Oh, yes!" Maggie nodded. "She informed me of it right after Cora's little confession."

"Good God!" he exclaimed and smiled down at Steven.

"If every woman on this estate starts to feel the same about him, we will have a serious issue on our hands," she pointed out.

Maggie stood and laid Finley, who had drifted off to sleep, back down in the crib before taking Steven to nurse.

Gabe gave Maggie a good once over. "How are you doing? You did just give birth, lose your husband, raise him from the dead, kill his murderer, and become the leader of the Fae— all in one day, I might add."

"Oh yeah, I almost forgot about that. It feels a lot longer than just a few days ago." Maggie touched Steven's face. "Honestly, I am just grateful to have all of my children, and all of you, safely in this world."

Maggie looked up. "Do you think the army will come looking for Pennington?"

"I don't think they would even know where to start," he reassured her. "In all of the confusion with their departure, it may be days, or even weeks, before they realize he is gone, and they will have no idea where to begin the search." Gabe leaned in closer, laying his hand on her leg. "It's not your fault. He was a madman, just like his brother, and if you hadn't stopped him, he may have hurt a great many more people."

Maggie placed her hand over his. "I know."

John stripped down and stepped into the tub of hot water. He sighed, closed his eyes, and leaned back to relax— only to feel a pair of hands on his shoulders, catching him off guard. His eyes flew wide open, and he was stunned to see Cora standing there in the room with him, wearing nothing but a smile.

"Mind if I join you?" she asked.

"Yes, as a matter of fact, I do mind!" John held out his hands in a blocking gesture. "Please, put your clothes back on!"

"Why would I do that, silly?" she asked and stepped into the tub before he could stop her.

"Now, Cora," he warned, "you cannot be in here!"

"I think I already am," she said and giggled, positioning herself on her knees and resting her hand on his thigh. "You are such a desirable man," she purred and eyed him lustfully.

He caught her hand and pushed it away, but she used her other to trace his arm all the way up to his face.

"You must cease this immediately! You are a married woman!" beseeched John, taking hold of her by the wrists and trying to move her away from him.

"I have asked him for a divorce. I am all yours now." She leaned in for a kiss as he reclined back, trying to get as far away from her as he possibly could, causing water to slosh out onto the floor.

"Maggie! Duncan!" he called out in desperation. "I could use some assistance in here!"

Maggie and Gabe were watching the twins sleep when they heard John's cry for help. They exchanged puzzled looks before rushing into the hall, meeting Duncan just outside of the bedroom.

"What's going on?"

She led the way into their bathroom. Maggie was the first one to the door and was stunned, and rather unamused, by the scene playing out before her.

John was in the tub, with Cora sprawled atop him, her arms wrapped around his neck, trying her best to have her way with him. John's eyes were wide, his arms flailing and reaching out from the side, silently pleading for help as Cora smooshed her lips to his.

"Cora! John! What the holy hell is going on in here?" demanded Maggie.

Gabe and Duncan managed to get past her to see for themselves, both immediately covering their mouths with their hands to conceal the amusement on their faces.

Maggie strode into the room and snatched a towel from the hook, holding it out as she averted her eyes. "Cora! Get out of that tub this instant!"

Cora looked back at John, and hesitated slightly, before finally grabbing the towel, a look of annoyance on her face. As the young woman stepped out, Maggie noticed Duncan and Gabe being thoroughly entertained by the antics. Shooting them evil looks, they quickly turned their heads to the side and pretended to have not seen anything.

Cora wrapped the towel around herself, and looked down, seemingly contrite.

"Get dressed and meet us downstairs!" ordered an enraged Maggie.

Cora nodded, but as she walked by John, she let her hand drop so she could sensually trace along his shoulders with her fingers.

"We will finish this later," she bent and whispered quickly before scuttling out.

Duncan and Gabe turned their backs and stepped aside, giving her a wide berth to pass.

As soon as she was gone, Maggie looked down at John, who had now laid back in the tub with his hand pressed to his cheek, drumming his fingers against his face.

"What happened?"

"I honestly have no idea. I was just sitting here, relaxing, when she appeared out of nowhere, without any clothes on. I tried to get her to leave, but she jumped into the tub before I could stop her."

"Oh, for goodness sake!" fussed Maggie, rubbing her forehead. She grabbed another towel and threw it at him on her way out. "Finish your bath and meet us downstairs."

Maggie stopped when she reached Duncan and Gabe who were trying to go unnoticed. "Enjoying the show?" she asked, her voice dripping sarcasm. Seizing each by the arm, she pulled them in front of the doorway. "You two stand guard until he is done and don't you dare let any more women near him."

She brushed past them with a huff and went down to the drawing room, grabbing a bottle of rum on the way, and chugging it before plopping down on the sofa.

Cora was the first to arrive, taking a seat on the sofa next to her.

"Who is watching the children?" asked Maggie.

"Cecile and two of the other women who have been helping out," she said downcast. "I am so sorry for what happened. I don't know what came over me." The young woman started to cry. "You and Colonel Asheton have been so good to me and I love you all so much. Please don't send me away!"

Maggie turned the bottle up again before standing to pace the floor.

John, Duncan, and Gabe finally appeared, as did Quinn who had been in the kitchen. Maggie met them at the door.

"Cora!" said Maggie as she shoved him in her direction. "John has something he needs to say to you."

The young woman raised her head, smiling through her tears as John moved unsurely to stand in front of her. "Yes?" she asked, hopefully, smoothing back her hair.

John folded his arms in a stern manner. "Cora, there is nothing between us. There never has been and there never will be," he said firmly. "You need to go back to your husband and tell him this was all a terrible misunderstanding."

She looked up at him, tears still on her eyelashes, distraught. "You can't mean that! Surely you feel what this is between us?"

John shook his head. "You are mistaken— I feel nothing."

Cora stood and tried to take his hand. "But I desire you above all else and all others. I love you —I must have you!"

John took a step back, holding her at arm's length. "You need to understand that is never going to happen. You have a husband who loves you very much and you need to go back to him at once."

Cora shrank back as if she had been punched in the gut. "I see," she said, deflated and stared down at the floor. She turned, unsure of what to do, then headed for the door.

"Cora, wait!" called Maggie, but she was gone before she could catch up with her.

Maggie came back into the drawing room and turned the bottle up again as she collapsed on the sofa. "Well, that went well," she remarked sarcastically.

John sat down next to her and took the rum for a swig of his own.

Gabe placed his hand on Quinn's shoulder. "Come on! We will go after her."

"Hopefully, she went home to make up with David," suggested Maggie.

"We will find her," assured Quinn.

After they were gone, Maggie turned to Duncan. "The babies have been fed and are asleep. If you will check on the rest of the children, John and I will go downstairs and see if we can figure out a way to tone him down a bit."

"Alright! That sounds like a plan!" Duncan came over and slowly kissed her. "I love ye."

Maggie sighed and touched his face. "I love you too."

4 Chapter Four

An hour later, Maggie and John sat in the collection room, searching for answers.

"I had no idea this book would have sexual positions in it," he said with a roguish grin. He pointed to one page. "Is that even possible?" he asked.

Maggie rolled her eyes as he turned to the next.

"Oh, I am definitely trying this one," he mumbled to himself and focused on the details, tapping the side of his head, lost in thought.

Maggie slammed a different book on the table angrily, startling him. "Can we please focus on the task at hand?" she asked. "This is turning into a major problem, in case you haven't been paying attention."

John sighed and leaned back against his chair, his fingers interlocked behind his head, regarding her intently. "You used to be a great deal more fun, do you know that?"

"And you used to not take four women to bed at once," she muttered under her breath as she sat down, aggravated and blowing out a hard breath.

"Is that what is bothering you?" he asked sincerely. "You don't like to see me with other women?"

"I am a happily married woman," she stated resolutely and sighed, her face resting in her hand on her propped elbow as she looked over the other books on the table.

"I am well aware of that, and I respect what you and Duncan have together. I would never do anything to jeopardize that relationship, but with that being said, it doesn't mean seeing you two together doesn't sting a little bit every now and again," he said softly and honestly.

Maggie closed her eyes. "Did our time together actually mean anything to you?" she asked quietly, "or was I just another notch on your bedpost like all the other women you take to bed?"

"Oh Maggie!" His face softened and he leaned forward to take her hand. "Of course, it did. It meant more to me than you will ever know. Please don't allow my dalliances with other women to be any indication that my time with you was not something special. That is simply not true." He stroked her hand with his thumb and looked down. "In fact, if you and Duncan had not married, as soon as this war was over, I had every intention of making haste straight to Virginia for you. My only regret is I didn't do it sooner and missed my chance." He kissed her hand tenderly.

Maggie reached over to touch his face and smiled sweetly at him.

"Oh John! Your 'lust-dusting' doesn't work on me, you know," she said, and a slow grin spread across her face.

"Damn!" he cursed and chuckled. "It was worth a try."

She shook her head and laughed. "It is good to know, however, that our time together meant as much to you as it did to me," she whispered.

"It did indeed," he said seriously and kissed her tenderly on the cheek. Pulling his book back over in front of him, he cleared his throat and asked, "What were we looking for again?"

Duncan descended the staircase and came over to join them.

"All of the children are safely back in their rooms. Which reminds me, we need to start the house addition as soon as possible." He moved to Maggie's side and kissed her. "Having any luck?"

"Depends on what you are looking for," John smirked, sliding the book over in Duncan's direction, opened to one of the more interesting pages with graphic drawings.

Duncan raised an eyebrow. "Is that even possible?" he asked and tilted his head to the side for a better look.

"Only one way to find out," John grinned.

He and Duncan exchanged a mischievous look while Maggie rolled her eyes upward and lifted her chin to the ceiling. "Good Lord give me strength. You two are like teenage boys getting ready for a panty raid."

They both stopped to look at her strangely.

"What's a 'panty raid'?" asked John.

"Never you mind!" Maggie let out a deep sigh. "We have found no way to put a cap on John. There is absolutely nothing in any of the books about it."

"It makes sense there wouldn't be," said Duncan. "These books belonged to Fae who were Fae since the time of their existence. They never knew what it was like to *not* have their powers, so why would they write anything down about how to use something that came as naturally to ye and I as sleeping and breathing?"

Maggie chewed on her lip. "I can control the fertility aspect of things. I can will it, grant it—direct it, if you will—just the way we do the fog. What if John can redirect what he is putting out there as well?"

"I am not sure I understand," said John.

Duncan looked to Maggie, taking her meaning. "Aye! While ye might not be able to stop what comes from ye, maybe ye can spread it out to others, so to speak, and water it down in a way."

"Really?" asked Maggie. "You think John needs to spread even more of himself around out there?"

John burst into laughter.

"Nay, my love," Duncan grinned, "but what if he could send it into a couple, for example, who had diminished sexual interest in each other, causing them to reignite what they have lost over the years?"

"Like Cora and David?" she asked, hopefully.

"Exactly!" he acknowledged. "Over time, I suspect we will all get a better handle on how this works, but ye must remember, we are only days into this. There is no reason to believe we should have a grip on how anything goes. In the meantime, we are on a trial and error basis."

"You think it will work?" asked John.

"I'm not sure we have any other choice," replied Duncan. "We all stand to lose a great deal if those two decide to go their separate ways. They know far too many of our secrets, not even counting the new Fae ones."

A short while later, Gabe and Quinn joined them.

"Did you find Cora?" asked Maggie.

"Aye," answered Quinn. "She is at our house with Kat and Alastair. We told her she could stay the night."

"Making any progress?" asked Gabe as he looked over the opened books on the table.

"We have a theory," mumbled Maggie, somewhat unconvincingly. "We think maybe John can "lust-dust" Cora and David, hopefully redirecting some of whatever he is dripping all over the place."

"That sounds extremely messy," commented Gabe dryly.

"And very unromantic," added John.

"Suddenly romance is your thing?" Maggie remarked.

He shrugged. "No need to be classless about it."

"Perhaps Maggie can give ye some tips on how she does what she does," suggested Duncan.

"When I first did it, I didn't even know I was doing it. I merely stated the intent and it happened."

"That was because ye were already half-Fae," said Quinn. "John will have to work a bit harder at it."

Maggie looked back at John. "Just close your eyes, feel it flowing inside you, and then say what you want to happen. We will get Cora and David in the same room tomorrow, give it a try, and hope for the best."

The next morning, Quinn brought Cora up to the house with the children while Duncan went to find David. Maggie and John remained in the kitchen as Quinn sent Cora into the dining room for breakfast.

"I am not sure I can do this," whispered John nervously.

"You will be fine." Maggie took him by the hand and rubbed his arm. "You just need to concentrate on the task at hand."

Maggie peeked around the corner and saw that Duncan had escorted David into the room with Cora. When she saw him, Cora got up to leave, proclaiming she did not want to talk to him, but Duncan physically blocked the door to prevent either of them from leaving.

He sent Maggie a message. *Better get on with this.*

Maggie turned to John. "Okay, close your eyes and concentrate. Feel the energy flow throughout every fiber of your being."

John nodded and shut his eyes. He held up his hand and willed the desire to go first into Cora, and then into David. As he began to focus, Maggie started to see a noticeable shift in the air that appeared to ebb and flow like an invisible stream.

"You are doing it," she whispered encouragingly. "Keep going."

Just as the wave of energy hit Cora, Hettie walked up directly behind John —and pinched him on the rear. When she did, John's concentration broke and the line flowing into Cora shifted to the left —and straight into Duncan before John righted himself to send it back across to David.

"Shit!" Maggie took a step forward for a better look, not realizing she had stepped into the flow herself— the one now focused on David.

David turned to look at her, a wide smile spreading across his face. It was the same stupid grin now planted on Cora's face, only she was staring at Duncan.

"Oh fuck!" mumbled Maggie.

"What's wrong?" asked John. "Did it not work?"

"Oh, it worked," replied Maggie, watching David cross the room to her. "Just on the wrong people."

David made his way over to Maggie, smoothing his hair as he moved. "Maggie, you look absolutely stunning today," he called out and smiled.

"Hello, David," she replied, rather unenthusiastically.

Maggie looked over her suitor's shoulder to see that Cora had snaked her way over to Duncan, her hand now on his arm.

Duncan looked back at Maggie, a horrific expression on his face.

Maggie folded her arms, irritated by the new set of circumstances they now found themselves in.

What happened? What went wrong?

Hettie grabbed John's ass, and now you and I are the ones who are screwed.

David had begun to ramble on about something or another, but Maggie didn't hear a single word he said.

She looked back at John, whose face was completely devoid of color, looking a bit like he was about to vomit.

"Perhaps we could talk in the drawing room," said David.

"Huh?" asked Maggie.

"A word alone in the drawing room, perhaps?" repeated David who had managed to take both of her hands in his.

Maggie attempted to pull them free. Finally, after some work, she managed to disengage several of his fingers. "Wait for me in there," she pointed. "GO! NOW!"

David nodded, kissed the hand that he was still grasping, and went to wait for her.

"I don't know what happened," mumbled John, in disbelief.

"Hettie's ass grabbing shifted the stream and you hit the wrong people," she stated.

"How do I fix it?" he whispered desperately.

"I wish I knew." Maggie stomped across the dining room to Duncan. Cora had backed him against the wall and was now sensually fondling his chest.

Duncan had placed his hands on her shoulders, careful not to touch her inappropriately while attempting to push her away, but she was more than a little persistent.

Maggie grabbed Cora from behind and spun her around. "The babies need attending upstairs. GO! NOW!" she ordered.

Cora looked longingly at Duncan, who had taken the opportunity to take refuge behind his wife.

The nanny let out a sigh, longingly. "Yes, Maggie," she said before leaving the room.

Gabe and Quinn came into the dining room as she went into the foyer.

"How did it go?" asked Gabe.

"Well, the good news is that Cora is no longer desirable of John," revealed Maggie sarcastically.

"And the bad news?"

"She is lusting after my husband—and David after me."

"What?"

Quinn looked to John for an explanation.

John covered his mouth with his hand and looked down at the floor. "Hettie distracted me in the middle of all of this and things went sideways —literally."

"Any idea how we fix this?" inquired Gabe.

Maggie shrugged. "I am going to send David back home." As she started towards the drawing room, she pointed to Quinn and said, "Go downstairs and check Finn's book to see if there is anything to correct situations like this. I will be right back."

Maggie found David sitting in a chair and he rose as soon as she entered the room. "Maggie! There you are. I have missed you."

"Yes, David," she said with the roll of an eye.

He smiled. "I want to thank you for your help yesterday. You were a great comfort to me, and I cannot tell you what it means to me personally."

"You are quite welcome, David. I hope you and Cora will be able to work things out soon."

He looked down. "I do not think that is going to happen. I will be filing the petition for divorce this afternoon. It is best for all parties concerned."

Maggie reached out and touched his arm. "Please don't. I know Cora loves you very much and she does not want this."

David looked down at her hand and before she knew what was happening, he had taken Maggie by the shoulders and pulled her into a kiss.

Immediately pushing him away, she exclaimed, "David! I am a married woman!"

"Don't worry, Maggie, I won't tell Duncan. It can be our little secret. You know very well that I am the soul of discretion."

Maggie put her finger to his lips. "There will be NO secret because there will be nothing to tell. Nothing is going to happen between you and I, let me make that perfectly clear."

"But Maggie," he tried to lean closer, "I am filled with such desire for you. If I cannot have you, I do not know what I shall do."

Maggie began taking steps backwards as he took ones forward, matching her step for step as if they were dancing a tango. She was stopped by the desk when she backed into it, trapped. Maggie frantically felt around behind her and realized the week's books for the shipping company were still there. Picking them up, she forcefully swung them around, planting them squarely against his chest.

"The books! I need you to take these—to your house—and go through them —thoroughly. I think there are some discrepancies and I cannot concentrate on anything else until they are reconciled."

He looked at her strangely but gathered the ledgers to his chest.

"Please David—for me. It would please me very much."

He smiled. "Of course. I will take care of them. I will do anything for you."

Maggie took him by the shoulders, turned him, and firmly guided him to the front door.

"They need to be done this instant. Don't come back until you have gone over each and every detail. In fact, it may take several days." She pulled the door open and shoved him outside.

He turned. "A kiss before I go?" he asked, hopefully.

Maggie swung the door closed in his face, leaned her back against it, and blew out a long breath.

"It's going to be a long fucking day," she said to herself.

Maggie went back into the dining room.

"What did ye do with your admirer?" asked Duncan.

"I sent him back to his house with the books for the week. That should keep him busy for a little while." She pointed at Gabe. "You need to keep Cora occupied as well— and far away from my husband."

"I will send her down to the school with the children for the day and tell Alastair to keep her there," he assured.

"Good! The rest of us need to go to the collection room with Quinn and try to figure this whole mess out."

5 Chapter Five

Two hours later, they each had a volume in hand, going through the pages and looking for anything that might help them with their current predicament.

"According to Finn's book," Maggie pointed at a page, "the god or goddess who casts the spell, and Finn, are the only ones who have the ability to reverse it."

"So, John can indeed fix this," said Gabe.

"In theory," she affirmed.

"And ye," added Duncan.

Maggie looked at him strangely. "Me? Why would you think that?"

"Ye took Finn's place as leader, and he did gift ye his book, so it would stand to reason ye would have that power as well."

Maggie shook her head. "No, I don't think so."

Duncan moved to stand behind Maggie's chair. "It is no mistake he made ye the leader of this new generation. Given the amount of children we have to raise, and everything that could go wrong, it would be prudent to have a safeguard in place to undo what damage might be done, wouldn't ye say?"

"You really think so?" she questioned.

"He wouldn't have given ye his tome if ye weren't able to use it," he said and kissed her on the top of the head.

She leaned back to smile up at him. "This whole "God of Wisdom thing" looks mighty good on you. It's pretty damn sexy too."

He leaned down and sensually kissed her lips.

John cleared his throat. "Does it say exactly *how* to undo it?" he asked.

"No," she shifted to look back down at the page, "but I would guess it is the same way you cast it, just in reverse."

"So, who do we try it on first?"

After checking on the babies, the five of them went down to the school. Alastair was in class with the other children, while Cora was helping in the community kitchen and watching Kat while she played with some of the younger ones. Kat immediately ran up to greet them as soon as she saw them, along with several of the other children who came over to see Duncan, whom they had grown to love greatly. Maggie and John slipped into the side entrance of the kitchen, out of sight, to find Cora.

"There she is," said Maggie when she came around the corner. "Are you ready?"

"As I will ever be." He stretched out his fingers and shook them before looking over his shoulder for good measure. "Watch my back this time?"

"You can bet your ass I will!"

Cora's face lit up with anticipation when she caught a glimpse of Duncan through the window. She wiped her hands on her apron, before taking it off, and patting down her hair.

John closed his eyes and focused once again, sending out the invisible force, catching her just as she was about to reach the door.

The woman was still smiling, and looking out at Duncan, when John's 'whammy' slammed into her. Her smile slowly started to fade. She blinked, moving her head as if she were shaking off a dream, and looked around the room as if she had forgotten something. After a few moments of looking dazed, she shrugged and went back to helping the ladies who were cooking.

"Think it worked?" he asked.

"Only one way to find out," answered Maggie.

She called for Duncan with her mind, and they watched him cautiously enter the dining area, carrying two children in his arms who Maggie was convinced he was using as human shields. Quin and Gabe followed with Kat, a few steps behind in a precautionary manner as backup.

"Hello, Cora?" he said when she came back into the room.

"Hello," she replied. "Is there anything I can do for you, sir?"

"Is there anything ye *want* to do for me?" he asked, drawing out his words.

"No," she answered with a peculiar look on her face, "I don't believe so."

A relieved Duncan smiled. "Good! That is good news indeed!"

Cora gave him another odd look, shrugged, and went back to what she was doing.

Maggie patted John on the back and let out the breath she didn't realize she was holding in.

"It worked, thank goodness! One down, one to go."

The following morning, David returned to the house where he found Maggie in the drawing room alone at her desk working.

"Good morning, Maggie," he greeted her, an impish grin on his face as he peeked around the corner.

"Oh, good morning David."

He made his way over to where she was seated. "I completed the books. Everything is in order and has been filed away."

"Thank you," she said, hoping a good night's sleep had somehow straightened him out.

He leaned across the desk. "Now, about that kiss."

Obviously not.

She looked up at him, laid down her quill, and steepled her fingers. "You want a kiss?"

"Yes," he grinned, "I do. I have been looking forward to it all day and night."

She pushed her chair back, stood and planted her hands flat on the desk. "Alright! Close your eyes first."

He did as he was told, smiled, and puckered up his lips.

Maggie reached out her index finger and touched him right between the eyes. "This is not the girl you are looking for. Go back to your wife." She sat back down in her chair and stared at him as his eyes fluttered open. "Are you alright, David?"

He blinked, then looked around as if he didn't know where he was. "I... uh...what was I saying?" he asked, thoroughly confused.

Leaning back, Maggie smiled. "You were saying the books are all in order."

"Oh yes," he straightened his coat, "all is well."

"Thank you, David," she said.

"Of course!" He looked towards the hall. "Have you by chance seen Cora today? I feel the overwhelming urge to see her."

"Why don't I get her for you?" she suggested and stood. "Wait right here."

Maggie left the room, closing the doors behind her. She held up her index finger and looked at it. "That was easy," she said before blowing on it and returning it to an imaginary holster on her hip.

"John!" she called.

He and Duncan appeared from the dining room.

"Yes?"

Maggie went over to them. "David is in the drawing room and I have removed whatever you hit him with. I am going to get Cora. You wait until you get a clear shot, then hit them at the same time— and make sure no one else is anywhere near them when you do." She turned to Duncan. "Make sure no one distracts him."

"Understood, my love!"

Maggie went upstairs and found Cora with the babies. "Cora, you are needed in the drawing room. I believe...umm...Gabe wishes to speak with you," she lied.

"Yes, ma'am."

Maggie leaned over and watched from the top of the stairs as Cora made her way down and into the room with David. As soon as they were alone together, John slipped over to the door, closed his eyes, and worked his magic. Maggie could see the stream flow from his hands and into the room before peeking inside, and turning to look up at Maggie, he gave her a thumbs up.

Thank goodness.

She descended the stairs, Duncan meeting her at the base.

John was still looking inside the room, a big grin on his face. "I think the divorce may be off," he announced over his shoulder. He suddenly rushed to their sides, barely avoiding David and Cora, who stumbled out into the foyer, embraced in a passionate kiss, tugging at each other's clothes.

Maggie cleared her throat loudly. "Everything alright?" she asked when they finally noticed the others standing there.

"Forgive us, Maggie," murmured David, looking up with his lips still pressed to Cora's. "We thought we were alone."

"I take it the two of ye have reunited?" asked Duncan.

"Oh, yes!" replied Cora. "I am not sure why we ever wanted to be apart."

"Neither am I," said David, gazing adoringly into her eyes.

Maggie came to stand between them, taking them each by the arm. "Why don't you go home and spend the rest of the day there? As a matter of fact, take the rest of the week and have a second honeymoon."

"Yes!" David readily agreed. "That is actually a wonderful idea."

"Have fun!" she said as she shoved them out the front door, waving.

"Think they will stay together?" asked John.

"They will now!" Maggie pushed the door closed with her foot. "In about nine months, they won't have any other choice."

"You didn't!"

"Oh, I most certainly did."

6 Chapter Six

The first week of August, the addition onto the house began. Joshua had drawn up plans to add an extra wing off the side of the drawing room, ones that specifically would not interfere with the main house during construction. The days were quite warm, so Maggie and some of the ladies in the house took the babies outside whenever the weather permitted.

They were out in the side yard one afternoon when Onyx came galloping at a high rate of speed around the corner. As soon as he saw Maggie, he started to whinny and paw at the ground, indicating she should follow him. Maggie instinctively knew something was terribly wrong.

"Cora, Cecile—watch the babies," she said, scrambling to her feet. She rushed behind the big black horse, following him to the stables. As soon as she reached them, she could hear someone groaning in pain.

Onyx waited for her to catch up so he could show her exactly where she needed to be.

Maggie recognized the voice. "Harm!" she shouted.

A louder moan was her only answer; she rushed inside to find Harm lying on the ground.

"What happened?" she demanded and dropped to her knees next to him.

"I was shoeing one of the newer horses when he became upset and kicked me."

Maggie pulled up his shirt to see his ribs were already swollen, blue and black, obviously broken, and blood was spilling from his head. She looked around only to see they were completely alone.

She called for Duncan in her mind.

Where are you?

Helping Joshua on the addition. What's wrong?

Get to the stables! Harm is badly hurt!

On my way.

"Hang on Harm, help is coming."

She dabbed at his head with the hem of her gown and tried to keep him alert by getting him to talk. "How did you manage to cut your head open?"

"It must have happened when I fell," he heaved, "Ms. Maggie, I am having an awful hard time breathing."

"I know," she cradled his head, "Duncan is on his way. We will get you to your house shortly." She tried to distract him from the obvious pain he was in. "You know, you have Onyx to thank. He came and got me."

"How did he know? He won't nowhere near here," he gasped.

"Well, you know Onyx, Harm. He is smarter than your average horse."

Onyx whinnied, alerting Duncan to where they were. Duncan, John, Joshua, and Abel rushed in.

"What happened?"

"One of the horses kicked him. He's got broken ribs at the very least. We need to get him to a bed."

The men moved to pick him up and they very carefully carried him out of the stable. Harm's house was nearby and closer than the main house, so Duncan ordered them in that direction.

Maggie called out to Onyx, patiently waiting by the stable door. "Go find Quinn and bring him back."

Onyx dipped his head in acknowledgement and galloped off.

Once they reached Harm's house, they got him into bed and helped him out of his shirt. His ribs looked worse than before, and the cut on his head was bleeding excessively. Harm had stopped speaking altogether and was now drifting in and out of consciousness.

Maggie poured clean water in a bowl and found some rags to clean up the cut on his head, holding pressure to it to stanch the bleeding.

"I sent Onyx for Quinn," said Maggie to Duncan.

"What can we do?" asked Joshua.

"Let Hettie know what is going on and where we are."

Joshua and Abel left for the house.

"What should we do?" asked Duncan.

"Quinn should be able to heal him when he gets here," she whispered.

John looked on worriedly. "You think he really can?"

Maggie carefully wiped the blood off Harm's face. "He is the God of Healing. I know he hasn't tried yet, but this is as good a time as any."

The cold water on the wounded man's face brought him around just a bit and caused him to roll his head back and forth, calling out Hettie's name in his delirium.

Maggie looked back at Duncan and John, frowning when she heard some of the words spilling from his lips.

About a quarter of an hour later, Quinn and Gabe finally appeared at the front door.

"What the bloody hell is going on, Maggie?" demanded Quinn. "That blasted horse of yours almost took the skin off my neck when he grabbed me by the collar with his teeth."

"We need your help! Harm has been injured badly."

Becoming serious, Quinn rushed to Harm's bedside, taking a seat on the edge of the bed.

"One of the horses kicked him in the ribs, and he cut his head open when he fell."

Quinn started examining him. "Has he been out the whole time?"

"Just since we moved him here," replied Duncan. "Ye need to heal him."

"I don't know if I can," whispered Quinn, unsure of himself.

"Yes, you can!" commanded Maggie, turning to look him in the eye. "Being the God of Healing is no good if we cannot use the abilities that come with it to help the ones we love. Don't think about it—just do it!"

Gabe moved to his side and placed his hands on his shoulders encouragingly. "You can do this. I know you can. I have complete faith in you!"

"How?" he asked, his voice full of uncertainty.

"The same way Kat did for Gabe," declared Maggie. "Touch him and make it happen."

Quinn nodded and placed his hands over Harm's ribs. He closed his eyes and focused intently on the injuries, until a small white glow appeared from his palms, growing in size as Quinn directed the flow into the patient's torso.

"Is it working?" asked Maggie anxiously as she chewed on her thumb.

"Give him some time," whispered Duncan into her ear and wrapped his arms around her waist to calm her nerves.

Quinn moved his hands, along with the light, from Harm's ribs up to the man's head and over the gash. They were all amazed to see the cut on his head start to slowly close before their eyes.

"I think he's figured it out!" Gabe smiled, pride in his husband evident in the wideness of it.

After Quinn was finished, Harm's eyes fluttered open. He looked around to see a roomful of people staring back at him hopefully.

"Wh...what happened?" he asked.

Maggie moved to pour him a glass of water. "The horse kicked you in the stables. Don't you remember?"

She and Quinn helped him to sit up and sip the water. When he was finished, he ran his hand down his side. "I do remember. Shouldn't I be hurting though?"

The two exchanged wide-eyed looks, not taking into account how they might explain his miraculous recovery. "Quinn gave you something for the pain," covered a quick-thinking Maggie.

"Aye," agreed Quinn. "You should rest for a couple of days so ye can heal."

"But I feel perfectly fine," he proclaimed.

"That's the medicine," lied Maggie. "Just let it do its job."

The door burst open and they all turned to see Hettie rush inside. "Is Harm alright?" she demanded.

"He will be fine," replied Duncan. "Quinn attended him, and he just needs to rest for a while."

Hettie went over to stand next to John. "Are you sure?" she asked warily.

"Yes," assured Maggie, "he will be as good as new in a few days. He just needs to take it easy."

"Thank the good Lord!" exclaimed Hettie and turned to John, unexpectedly embracing him tightly, her hands finding their way to his butt cheeks, and giving an inconspicuous squeeze.

"Hettie!" John cried out, pretending to scold her. "You are so bad," he whispered in her ear with a smirk.

Hettie grinned back at him and gave him a little wink before turning to address Maggie. "I just made a big pot of soup. I will bring some down and we will keep an eye on Harm."

"Thank you, Hettie. That's mighty kind of you," said Harm.

Maggie looked over at their patient, who was looking at Hettie doe eyed. She looked back at Hettie, who didn't even notice he was gazing at her —and got the distinct feeling there was something far more to it.

He has a thing for her.

Duncan picked up on her thoughts and looked back and forth between the two of them, seemingly drawing the same conclusion.

So, it would seem.

"Hettie," said Maggie, "why don't you stay with Harm and look after him? We need to get back to the children. I will send Cecile down with the soup."

Hettie looked a bit puzzled. "Alright, if you want me to."

"I do!" Maggie grinned. "Harm, if you need anything, just send word."

"Thank you, Ms. Maggie."

"Aye, I will check on ye in a bit," said Quinn as he stood.

The others moved to the front door, but Maggie slipped her arm around Hettie. "Make sure you take good care of him."

"You know I will, Maggie."

Once they were all outside, Maggie and Duncan's faces betrayed them. They embraced with huge smiles on their faces.

"What's that all about?" asked Gabe, wagging his finger between them.

"Harm is sweet on Hettie," announced Maggie.

"What?" John seemed confused.

Duncan nodded. "Hettie has no idea."

John turned back towards the front door. "Huh!"

"Jealous?" Gabe teased John and slapped him on the back.

"Maybe a little," quipped John, "but I like Harm a great deal and he and Hettie would be perfect for each other."

Onyx appeared from the side of the house, looking to Maggie for an update on his friend.

"He is fine, Onyx." She walked over to the horse and rubbed his muzzle. "He will be up and around for you to harass in no time."

The horse seemed most pleased by the news.

Maggie leaned her head against him. "Go easy on him for a couple of days," she whispered.

Hettie tended to Harm until he was feeling better and he was back in the stables three days after his accident, claiming to feel better than he had in years.

Onyx kept a keen eye on him the first few days, as did everyone else.

Maggie found Hettie in the kitchen one day after breakfast. She pulled up a chair while Hettie cooked.

"How is Harm feeling?" asked Maggie.

"He seems to be fit as a fiddle," replied Hettie while she concentrated on chopping vegetables.

"It must have been all of your good cooking!" Maggie smiled.

"I reckon it didn't hurt none!"

Maggie propped her elbow on the table with her face in her hand. "What do you think of Harm?"

Hettie continued to look down as she worked. "What do you mean? I like him fine. I have known him a long time."

"How *well* do you know him?" she fished.

The woman stopped what she was doing to look at Maggie, putting one hand on her hip. "What are you getting at?"

Maggie shrugged. "Harm's a man, you're a woman, you are both about the same age…"

Hettie narrowed her eyes. "Are you asking if we have ever— courted?"

"Have you?" she asked nonchalantly.

"What makes you think we *would* have?"

Maggie dropped her arm, smacking it on the table. "I think Harm likes you."

"Well, I like him fine, too," said Hettie, confused. "We have worked beside each other for many years."

"No Hettie, I mean he *likes* you— as in the way a boy likes a girl."

Hettie went back to chopping. "You need to lay off the rum. It's done gone to your head."

"No, I don't think it has," Maggie smirked, "but for curiosity's sake, if he did— how would you feel about it?"

"Don't matter, 'cause he don't," she turned to get something from behind her, "besides, I am too old for that."

Maggie laughed. "You are never too old for *that*."

Maggie was sitting in her chair at her desk, reclined back, looking up at the ceiling when Duncan came in.

"What are ye doing?" He came over and kissed her.

"Trying to figure out how to play matchmaker."

"Are ye looking for a new husband?" Smiling, he leaned against the desk, his arms folded.

"Never!" She ran her hand over his hip, seductively. "I meant Hettie and Harm."

Duncan shot her a disapproving look.

"Oh, come on," she said and scooted up on the edge of the chair. "Everyone deserves to find love and you are never too old."

"Ye are starting to sound like a true Fae— meddling in the affairs of humans."

Maggie wrinkled her nose. "A little helping hand never hurt anyone." She stood, grinned, and reached down to stroke him.

He laughed, placed his hands on her hips, and eyed her with desire as his body responded. "Well, I guess I can't argue with that logic."

"No need trying," said Maggie breathily, biting at his lips playfully and with some urgency.

Duncan turned her until her back was against the desk facing him, wrapped his arms around her buttocks, and lifted her, so she was sitting on the edge— the two so completely absorbed in each other they didn't take the time to close the doors. He reclined her back until she was sprawled out on the desk, pushed her knees up, and raised her skirts.

She closed her eyes and let out a delightful sigh as he started at the bend of her knee and licked his way all the way up to her sweet spot, arching her back and crying out his name as he brought her over the edge with only the tip of his tongue. As she gripped the sides of the desk, her body still in orgasmic spasms—they heard Gabe angrily shout, "For the love of GOD, close the fucking doors! There are children in this house!"

They both erupted in laughter when they heard Gabe slam the pocket doors shut. Duncan raised his head, a desperate look of need on his face.

"Well, the doors are closed, and I see no need to stop now. Besides, I don't think I could if I tried."

He crawled atop her on the desk, undoing his breeches as he moved, and slid inside her, pumping hard and fast, until they both lay sated and breathless, tangled up in each other's arms.

"Gabe sounds a little pissed!" remarked a breathless Maggie with a chuckle.

Duncan pulled her tighter to him. "He won't give us too much grief, especially after I walked in on him and my little brother in the collection room the other day. I saw more of Quinn's arse than I ever thought I needed to."

As they both lay there laughing, they heard a sudden creak, a crack, a pop— and found themselves in the middle of a pile of splintered wood. The desk they'd been lying on had taken all it could take and had collapsed in on itself in a heap. They laughed even harder as they picked little pieces of wood out of each other's hair.

"I think we need a new desk!"

"Aye, and a sturdier one," agreed an amused Duncan.

They were still laughing when they came out of the drawing room. Searching, they located Gabe and Quinn in the dining room.

"You two need to watch yourselves," scolded Gabe. "Anyone could have seen you."

Duncan walked over and picked up an apple from a bowl on the sideboard, biting into the crisp fruit and leaning one hip against the edge.

"The way ye and Quinn were looking out in the collection room the other day?" Duncan grinned. "Ye two should watch yourselves," he said mockingly, "anyone could have seen ye."

Quinn dropped his head and shook it with a smirk.

Gabe turned to glare at Duncan, an awkward look on his face. "You couldn't have made yourself known?"

"I didn't want to interrupt!" Duncan laughed, slapping his brother-in-law on the shoulder. "That would have been rude and ye both were otherwise occupied."

Maggie went to pour herself a drink but found the decanter empty. "I will be right back," she said, stopping to plant a lingering kiss on Duncan.

He sighed aloud, before picking another piece of wood out of her hair.

Gabe good-naturedly rolled his eyes at their display of affection.

Maggie entered the kitchen to find Hettie smoothing her hair and straightening her dress. She jumped a little, startled, when she saw Maggie. "Oh Maggie! I didn't see you there."

Looking at her oddly, Maggie walked to the cabinets and took a bottle of rum down from one of the shelves. "I needed a refill," she said, shaking the bottle back and forth.

"I'm sorry," apologized Hettie. "I will restock everything."

"I've got it," said Maggie as she came over to her, "and avoid the drawing room. There is a bit of a mess in there. I will get Duncan to clean it up and put a new desk on the project list."

Hettie folded her arms and raised an eyebrow. "A new desk?"

Maggie cringed. "Yeah, the other one was old —and rickety."

"It was as solid as stone the last time I cleaned it," scoffed Hettie.

"'Was' being the key word," mumbled Maggie.

The housekeeper shook her head disapprovingly. "Ain't no wonder we got so many babies around here."

Maggie wrinkled her nose and waved her hand in Hettie's direction. "Are you going somewhere?"

Hettie looked down and ran her hand over her midsection. "Oh, yeah! I thought I might take some food down to Harm since he is so busy in the stables."

Maggie grinned slyly. "I think that is a wonderful idea." She sat the bottle of rum on the table and went back over to the shelf, looking over the labels. She settled on a bottle of wine and took it down. "Why don't you take this with you? Harm will like it— and you might, too."

Handing her the bottle, Maggie offered, "As a matter of fact, why don't you take the rest of the afternoon off? We can fend for ourselves."

Hettie looked down in deep thought. "Well, I reckon it would be nice to be out of the house for a bit."

"Go!" urged Maggie. "What are you waiting for?"

"You sure?"

"Yes!" Maggie smiled and shooed Hettie out the door. "Enjoy your afternoon."

Maggie returned to the dining room humming a lively tune.

Duncan took notice. "What are ye so happy about?"

She popped the cork out of the bottle. "Hettie is going to see Harm. There may be hope for them yet."

7 Chapter Seven

Three days later, Maggie sat on a blanket outside with the triplets, watching Gabe and Alastair practice with their swords. Duncan came out to join them, taking a seat next to her before Kendric crawled over onto his lap.

"Gabe is better than he has ever been," remarked Maggie, watching them with curiosity.

"Well, he is the God of Soldiers and Swords now."

"He is also doing a wonderful job teaching Alastair. He is so patient with him."

"Aye! He and Quinn are both wonderful fathers." Duncan made faces at Kendric, making the boy laugh out loud.

"Speaking of good fathers," said Maggie, leaning over to kiss him on the cheek.

"I never thought I would love being a father as much as I do. Of course, I never even thought about being a father until I met ye." He smiled and returned her kiss.

Maggie caught sight of a movement around the side of the house—John and Kitchi. They waved to Maggie and Duncan as they went to join Gabe and Alastair. As soon as Gabe handed Kitchi a sword, John left them to their lessons and came to join them.

"Good morning!" said John as he bent over and picked up Morgan.

"Morning!" Maggie nodded her head in the direction of the others. "What is Kitchi doing here?"

"He is taking sword lessons with Gabe."

"Really?"

John nodded. "Gabe offered to teach him and actually, several of the other boys are interested as well, if Gabe would like to take on a few more pupils."

"Who better to teach them than the God of Swordsmanship?" noted Duncan. "It will be good for them to learn."

Maggie looked back across the lawn. "They could not ask for a better instructor."

"Gabe is loving it," added Quinn, coming up behind Duncan. He smiled and waved at Gabe who waved back in return. "He is really in his element."

"I think that is great!"

Duncan handed Kendric to Maggie and she looked at him strangely, following his gaze to see Harm trying to get his attention. "I will be right back."

Maggie watched them closely as they talked, especially when she noticed Harm looking upset and rather disturbed. "I wonder what that's all about?"

Her husband returned a few moments later with a grave look on his face.

"What's wrong?" she asked as he sat back down.

Duncan sighed. "Harm asked Hettie to marry him."

"That's wonderful news!" exclaimed Maggie excitedly.

"It would be if she had not turned him down."

"Oh no!" Maggie's cheerful mood faded. "Why?"

"She didn't say. Maybe ye can find out?"

"Hold my baby!" Maggie handed Kendric back to Duncan. "I will be right back."

Maggie located Hettie in the kitchen giving instructions to the women who helped in the manor. Catching their attention, she motioned the other ladies out so she could speak to the housekeeper in private.

"Hettie!"

"Yeah, Maggie?"

She pulled up a chair. "Got anything you want to tell me?"

Hettie shook her head. "No, I don't think so."

"Get any interesting proposals lately?" she pressed.

Hettie gave no response and turned around to stir a pot boiling on the fire.

"Why did you turn Harm down?" she asked. "I thought you were fond of him."

"Well, I am, and I would have said 'yes'," Hettie straightened up and faced her, "but it wouldn't be right to marry Harm and keep John on the side."

Maggie lowered her head and raised both of her palms to her forehead, feeling a sudden headache about to come on.

Fuck!

"You turned Harm down because of John?"

"Well, yes. I need to be right here for John when he gets tired of playing games with these girls who are chasing after him, and he figures out he needs a *real* woman."

Maggie shook her head, let out a deep sigh, and got up to leave.

Returning to the side yard, Maggie went right up behind John and grabbed him by the back collar of his shirt. "Go fix, Hettie!" she ordered, pointing toward the kitchen.

John looked up at her, confused. "What are you talking about?"

Maggie smacked him on the back. "She turned Harm down because of you."

"Really?" asked Duncan.

"There has got to be a way to stop this and make you less desirable to women," huffed Maggie.

John shrugged. "What can I say?"

Maggie growled at him. "This is all your fault!"

"What do you want me to do?" he asked.

"I don't know! 'Lust-dust' the two of them or something!"

"Maggie," cautioned Duncan, "he has to be careful with that. If he hits people with it who aren't meant to be together, it can cause major problems, as we all well know."

"I know, but Hettie said she would marry Harm if she wasn't waiting for John."

"There is a love potion in the book I have," offered Quinn, hopefully. "That might break whatever hold John has over her."

"Again, we must be cautious about meddling," warned Duncan.

"I think this is a chance we need to take," she said, stopping to think for a moment. "I think we should try Quinn's potion. If John hits Hettie and Harm too hard with *his* 'stuff', one of them may break a hip at their ages."

Quinn brushed off his breeches as he got up. "I will go downstairs and find the recipe."

"I will go with you," she said. "I will send Cora and Cecile for the babies."

"Nay!" said Duncan, holding Kendric up in the air. "I will stay with them. I don't get to spend nearly enough time with them."

Maggie's heart warmed and she smiled. Leaning over, she kissed him sweetly. "I love you so much!"

"I love ye too!"

Quinn pulled down his book from the shelf and brought it over to the table. He flipped it open and thumbed through it until he found exactly what he was looking for. "Here it is. A few ingredients, an incantation, and they both have to drink it."

"Is it really that simple?" asked a wary Maggie.

"As simple as anything else Fae-related is."

Maggie grimaced. "Yeah."

"Besides, it will be a chance to test it for Ben," he said with a wink.

"About that— let's keep it between us," she whispered, chewing on her fingernail. "Duncan doesn't need to know about it."

"Keeping secrets from my brother?" he teased.

"You know how he is. He would get all upset, and we see how well that worked out last time."

"Aye, ye have a point." Quinn looked down, skimming the page with his eyes. "I can have this ready in a couple of hours."

"Well, let's give it a go."

Quinn turned to Maggie who was eyeing a particular book on the table. "Have ye opened it?"

Maggie exhaled sharply and ran her fingers lightly over the cover. "No," she replied softly.

"It *is* rightfully yours, and I expect she wouldn't mind too much," he said gently.

"I know," she scrubbed the spot between her eyes. "but I am still not ready to look in my mother's book. I am not sure I ever will be."

Quinn put his arm around her shoulders. "If, and when, ye decide to, and if ye want me to be here with ye, I will be."

She leaned against him as he hugged her. "I know. Thank you, Quinn."

He kissed the top of her head. "Of course. Anything for my favorite sister-in-law."

"You mean your *only* sister-in-law?" she teased.

He laughed. "That too!"

Two hours later, the five gathered in the drawing room.

"How do we do this?" Maggie held up the corked bottle for a closer inspection.

"They must ingest it, then immediately lay eyes on each other," explained Quinn.

"We are probably going to have a hard time getting them in the same room at the same time," pointed out Duncan.

Maggie agreed. "So, I will somehow get this stuff into Hettie, and you two will be responsible for getting it into Harm."

"They just have to be close to each other when they drink it and at around the same time," clarified Quinn.

"Okay," said Maggie, and she handed Duncan a bottle of rum after pouring two glasses for herself. "I will corner Hettie in the kitchen, while you two get Harm outside of the kitchen door. We will meet somewhere in the middle."

As soon as Maggie left the room, Duncan spun around to face Quinn. "How sure are ye this potion is going to work?"

Quinn shrugged and flipped his hand back and forth. "Eh?"

Duncan shook his head disapprovingly at his brother, popping the cork out of the rum bottle and holding it for Quinn to pour the mixture in as Duncan swooshed it around. "Well, here goes nothing."

They located Harm out by the stables— the man looked utterly miserable when they went over to greet him.

"How are ye doing, Harm?" asked Duncan when he stood next to him.

"I don't know," the man replied, downheartedly, his eyes fixed on nothing on the ground.

"Well, there's nothing like a little rum to make ye feel better," suggested Quinn enthusiastically and offered Harm the bottle.

"Oh, I don't drink much," he admitted and pushed it back.

"I think it's a good time to start," proclaimed Duncan, and laid his hand over on Harm's shoulder. "Nothing like trouble with a woman to make ye take it up."

Harm eyed the bottle nervously when he caught a whiff of the pungent odor. "That smells kind of strong."

"It will help," insisted Quinn.

The horseman thought hard for a moment and finally shook his head. "Oh, why not?" He accepted the bottle and turned it up, coughing when the alcohol splashed against the back of his throat.

Duncan patted him on the back. "Ye alright?"

"Just not used to it," croaked Harm and wiped his mouth with his sleeve.

Putting his arm around the man's shoulder, Duncan steered him towards the kitchen door. "Ye know, it occurred to me, Harm, that maybe ye aren't fighting hard enough for Hettie. Women like it when men get all fired up on their behalf."

"Aye," added Quinn. "They like to feel like there is no other woman in the world ye want to be with."

Duncan shot him a 'how would you know' look behind Harm's back.

Quinn threw his hands up in the air and shrugged.

"Ye need to let her know how much she means to ye." Duncan spoke directly into Harm's ear.

Harm took another swig from the bottle. "Is that what you did with Ms. Maggie?"

"Oh aye!" Duncan smiled, glancing towards the house. "I swept her right off her feet and I never let her forget she is the only woman there will ever be for me."

Harm sighed. "Do you think that would work?"

"Aye!" said Quinn. "Ye should march right in there and tell her exactly what ye think and how ye feel."

The horseman looked back and forth between them. "Maybe y'all are right." He took an extra-long drink from the bottle and threw it to the ground with a marked determination. Sucking in a deep breath, he started towards the door and at the same time, the alcohol swiftly hit him full force — and he fell flat on his back with a marked 'thump'.

"Bloody hell, Harm!" mumbled Duncan, as he and Quinn reached down to help him stand up.

"I must have tripped," he muttered, looking around.

"He's drunk on three sips?" whispered Quinn, pulling him to his feet.

"Come on, Harm. We'll help ye. Ye need to stay awake long enough to tell Hettie how ye feel."

Harm leaned against them as they helped him to the kitchen door.

"Are ye ready?" asked Duncan.

"Ready for what?" asked a sloshed Harm, looking around, his eyelids heavy and smacking his lips.

"To tell Hettie how ye feel!" reminded Quinn.

"Oh yeah! That!"

Duncan shook his head and cracked opened the door. He and Quinn exchanged 'what the hell' looks behind Harm's back as they simultaneously shoved him across the doorway.

"Christ be with ye, man," offered Duncan.

Quinn screwed up his face. "I sure hope that potion works!"

Duncan cocked his head to the side. "I just hope he can stay on his feet long enough to get into the house."

Maggie went into the kitchen and sat down at the table with two poured glasses of rum, one with the potion.

"Hettie, have a drink with me. It's been one of those days and I hate to drink alone."

Hettie eyed her with suspicion, her hands planted on her hips. "Since when do *you* hate to drink alone? Ain't never bothered you before."

Maggie set the glass in front of her. "You and I both deserve a break today."

Hettie thought for a moment before picking up the glass.

"Cheers!" Maggie held up her glass and watched Hettie take a good, long sip.

"That is good stuff," she said with a smile.

"Yes, it is," replied Maggie, looking down at her own drink. "You would really have said 'yes' to Harm if it weren't for John?"

Hettie nodded her head and pulled up a chair. "Yeah, I suppose I would have. I sure do miss having a man in my bed."

Maggie looked at her with an astonished look on her face as Hettie finished off her rum.

"Missed?" she asked, curiously. "Who's been in your bed, Hettie?"

"I was married once before," she confessed.

Maggie got up, took down a bottle of rum from the shelf and refilled Hettie's glass. "When was that?"

Hettie sighed. "I was young— just twenty— and we were lucky enough to have a few good years together."

"Hettie! I had no idea you had been married before. Why have you never mentioned it?"

"It was so long ago, and it never came up."

"What happened?" Maggie sat back down.

"Some of the new slaves who were brought to the estate were sick with a fever when they got here. Micah caught it from them. I got it too, but I got better. He didn't."

Maggie laid her hand over on Hettie's. "I am so sorry, Hettie."

She smiled and patted Maggie's hand. "You would have liked him. He was a good man— and we broke a few pieces of sturdy furniture too," she winked.

Making a face, Maggie burst into laughter. "Good to know!"

A wistful gleam appeared in Hettie's eyes. "Ain't nothing like having a man in your bed who knows what he is doing," she grinned, "but I don't have to tell you that!"

"No argument there, sister," said Maggie and raised her glass.

They sat there for the next few minutes giggling about men until all of a sudden, Harm burst through the door, staggering drunk, Duncan and Quinn close behind him, holding out their hands willing him to stand and ready to catch him if needed. Harm tried to straighten up, before slumping over again. Duncan winced, unsure if the man would stay on his feet or not. Harm pulled his shirt down tight, pointed his finger at Hettie, and stopped to collect his thoughts.

"What are you doing?" demanded Hettie and stood, smelling the alcohol on him. "Are you drunk?'"

Maggie looked at Duncan, incredulously.

How much did he have?

Three swigs. The man's not a drinker.

Harm shook his head and pointed at her again. "I love you, wo— woman and I intend to make you my wi— wife!" he proclaimed loudly. Taking a step to the side, he almost fell, but Duncan moved swiftly to right him. "Thank— you!" he slurred and nodded to Duncan.

"You're welcome!" Duncan chuckled, steadying him.

Harm looked back at Hettie. "We are get — getting married!" he pronounced emphatically while pointing at the floor. "And I won't take no for — for an answer. I lo— love you and you are the only woman for me— every life of my day— day of my life— sweep your feet off."

Hettie scratched her head, trying to decipher his words. Maggie lowered her gaze and lifted her hand to her lips to conceal her amusement.

Duncan smacked himself on the forehead with his palm.

Maggie could hear his thoughts and she was quite sure what she heard were swear words in Gaelic, the hilarity making her entire body shake from the laughter she was desperately trying to hold in.

Harm attempted to stamp his foot but lost his balance and swayed a bit. Quinn caught him, pushing him back up.

"Thank you!" Harm nodded to Quinn.

"You're welcome," said Quinn and grinned back.

Harm looked at Hettie with complete and utter love in his eyes. "What do you say, woman? Will you marry me?"

Hettie took a few steps towards him and gazed into his eyes, her face melting into a goofy, lovey-dovey smile. "Oh! I reckon I will." She reached out, grabbed him by the shirt, and pulled him into a kiss.

Harm's knees buckled and Duncan and Quinn rushed to each grab an arm to hold him in place. When Hettie pulled back, he grinned, turned to Duncan and then to Quinn, who were still supporting him, and bobbed his head back and forth. "She said 'yes'! She said 'yes'!"

"I heard!" Duncan laughed.

"Congratulations! Ye did it!" said Quinn.

Maggie hugged Hettie from behind, laying her cheek flat against her back. "I am so happy for you," she whispered.

They all watched with fascination as Harm proceeded to completely pass out. Duncan and Quinn each took an arm and wrapped it around their necks.

"We'll just take him home and put him to bed. We can tell him what happened and celebrate tomorrow," suggested Duncan with a wide smile.

While they hauled him away, Maggie happily wrapped her arm around Hettie's waist. "Looks like we have a wedding to plan!"

Two weeks later, Hettie and Harm were married in a beautiful ceremony in the garden at the estate, surrounded by all the ones they loved, along with Onyx, who had appointed himself as best man. Hettie wore a lovely blue brocade gown Cecile made especially for the occasion. It was followed by a grand reception at the community kitchen —the women had spent the week preparing for it. The wine flowed freely, and the entire day turned into a lively celebration for all to remember.

"Hettie looks so happy," Maggie said to Duncan, leaning against him, watching the bride and groom greet their guests.

"Aye, and so does Harm. Do ye know we actually had to tell him the next morning he even asked her? He had no recollection from the previous night."

"Well, there's a lot to be said for alcohol." Maggie fiddled with the collar on his shirt. "Worked pretty well for us that first night, as I recall."

"Aye, it did," he growled and pulled her against him for a kiss.

"Think they will like it?" she asked and looked back at the newlyweds.

Duncan followed her gaze. "I think so."

"Think they will like what?" asked Gabe as he, Quinn, and John came over to join them.

"Maggie and I paid a visit out to the waterfall yesterday. We are loaning the longhouse to them for their honeymoon."

Maggie smiled. "I actually hit it with a little Fae magic. It is now completely covered in a canopy of living roses and we left some candles around the rocks."

"Sounds very romantic," replied Gabe.

"Especially after I give them *my* wedding present!" John smirked, devilishly.

Maggie narrowed her eyes at him.

"Don't worry," John waved her off, "I will just hit them with a little bit, so they don't hurt themselves. Although, we may not see them for a few days."

"How can you hit them with a "little" when you can't control it?" asked Maggie, suddenly overly concerned about Hettie and Harm.

"I will do it from far away," he teased, a naughty look on his face.

She wrinkled her nose at him in response.

"I suppose I can always heal them if they do get hurt," remarked Quinn and sipped his wine.

When the time came for Hettie and Harm to leave, they were more than a little surprised to see the small carriage hooked up for them and Onyx was the horse pulling it. Maggie had decorated it with flowers and instructed Onyx to take them to the waterfall. She would send him back the next day to bring them home. Maggie pulled Hettie off to the side just as they were about to leave, and they embraced.

"I love you so much, Hettie! I know you and Harm are going to be incredibly happy together."

Hettie wiped away a few tears that had slipped down her face and kissed Maggie on the cheek. "I love you too, Maggie, and I am not sure how, but I think I have you to thank for Harm and me being married today."

"Just be happy and enjoy your honeymoon!" said Maggie, with a sniffle.

"Where are we going?' asked Hettie, eyeing Onyx uneasily.

"It is a special place to me and Duncan. I hope you and Harm enjoy it as much as we do. It is all set up and ready."

"I am sure we will," said Hettie and embraced her again.

Harm took her by the hand, before giving Onyx a suspicious look.

"Are we safe riding with him?" whispered Harm, pointing his thumb back towards the beast.

"Yes!" replied Maggie loudly for Onyx to hear. "I have told him to behave himself. He will get you where you are going without any foolishness or he will answer to me."

Onyx turned his head back and appeared to snicker wickedly at them as Maggie cast him a 'behave yourself' look.

"Be off ye two." Duncan held out his hand and motioned toward the coach, helping Hettie up as Harm followed behind. He closed the door and smacked the side of it twice to let Onyx know they were ready to depart. The happy couple waved at everyone gathered around to see them off.

"Hettie!" called Duncan suddenly as they pulled away. She craned her neck around. "Don't let Harm drink any rum tonight. Ye want him 'upright' for the wedding night," he yelled and laughed.

She winked at him with a flirtatious grin.

Gabe, Quinn, and John came over to stand next to them as they watched them go. Just as they were moving out of sight, John raised his hand and smiled, carefully aiming in the direction of the coach as it disappeared into the sunset.

Duncan slipped his arms around Maggie from behind. "Today was a good day."

"Yes, it was," she said and turned to face him, "and tonight is going to be even better," she smirked.

"Oh, I like the sound of that."

8 Chapter Eight

September 14, 1781

Maggie held tightly to Duncan's hand so as not to lose him in the rapidly growing crowd. Nearly the entire town had come out to greet their newest and most famous visitor. A sense of hope and anticipation, combined with a certain amount of uneasiness, filled the air and could be felt by everyone on the streets.

Duncan turned to smile at her, his richly colored golden eyes glittering in the sunlight.

They all had the same color eyes now, apparently a side effect of becoming a full god or goddess. It only added to his sexiness—if that was even possible.

Maggie was lost in the sight of him when he held up his hand and pointed. She turned to see the entourage they had been waiting for coming down the street.

Gabe and Quinn pushed their way through the crowd just in time to join them.

"Popular man," noted Gabe, looking around.

"With good reason," replied Maggie.

They watched as the line of horses rode past them at a canter; their riders modestly nodding at the townspeople as they passed —some smiled back, others remained stone-faced and silent.

While Maggie knew how this war would end, the people around her did not, and an uncertain future made for difficult times.

The four of them stood just outside the home of Mr. George Wythe, and as the town's newest visitor's horse approached, the man pulled to a complete halt when his eyes fell upon Maggie.

"Mistress MacGregor," his voice called; he dismounted and came over to greet them.

"General Washington," she smiled, "welcome to Williamsburg."

He held his hand out towards the house. "Please, come in and join me." The General escorted her inside, Duncan, Gabe, and Quinn following behind.

"General, allow me to introduce my husband, Duncan, my brother-in-law, Quinn, and Colonel Gabe Asheton, a name you already know."

The General took the time to greet each of them individually as a volley of his advisors started to fill the house, attempting to pull the man in several different directions. He offered Maggie an unspoken apology, along with a weary, rather aggravated expression on his face.

Maggie's chuckle was soft. "General, we know you are otherwise engaged. Our home is just outside of town and we would be honored if you would escape to join us for dinner tomorrow afternoon. I believe I owe you a tour of our estate."

Washington took her hand and smiled warmly. "Mistress MacGregor, nothing would please me more."

He lifted Maggie's hand to his lips and kissed it. "I shall be happy to see you then."

"We look forward to it," she replied, and they departed.

"He is a frightfully busy man," remarked Duncan when they stepped outside.

"I am afraid that poor man will barely see another moment's peace for the rest of his life." Maggie looked around the town. The British army had left its mark and it was truly heartbreaking.

"It's only going to get worse, you know," she said with a sigh, her eyes drifting to the Governor's Palace as Duncan slipped his arm around her waist. "When the battle breaks out, the governor's residence will become a field hospital. In the future, they will exhume over a hundred fifty American soldiers from behind it, and in December of this year, it will burn completely to the ground."

"But from its ashes, a great town will be rebuilt in the future, to teach the history of the beginning of this nation," he whispered, kissing the top of her head.

A sadness filled her voice. "That doesn't make watching it like this now any easier!"

"Come on," said Duncan, "John is waiting for us at the tavern."

"Do you think it is safe for him to be in town?" asked Gabe as they dodged residents on the street. "I mean, Washington does know his face well."

"Washington believes John is dead and he doesn't exactly look the same as he did back then. We can brush it off if he does recognize him. After all, everyone watched Major John André hang in Tappan."

They made their way into the tavern, and Maggie groaned when she saw John had four women surrounding him at the table. Gracie greeted them as they came in.

"Maggie!" The woman leaned in for a hug. "We have missed you around here."

"I have missed you, too, Gracie! How are you?"

"Better now that the British are gone and good riddance to them all. They were not kind or generous with their coin while they were here." Gracie pulled back. "How are the babies?"

"Wonderful! Our house overfloweth."

Gracie smiled when Gabe came over and kissed her on the cheek. "Hello, Gracie."

"Oh, I have missed you, too, Colonel! Let's get all of you a table."

"We already have one," said Duncan, pointing to John.

"One of yours, is he?" asked Gracie with a glance over her shoulder. "I should have known he was a MacGregor when he walked through the door." Gracie turned to stare at John, a little sigh escaping her as she bit her lip— her gaze lingering longer than was socially acceptable.

Maggie rolled her eyes. "Rum punch for me."

Gracie's concentration finally broke. "Oh, of course! I will bring it right over."

They went to the table and Maggie shooed the women away. "I am sorry, ladies, but we need these chairs."

The women expressed their discontent, but John made it up to them by taking the time to seductively kiss each of their hands before their departure—and the ladies swooned.

"Stop it!" said Maggie and swatted at him. "You are drawing attention to yourself." She took the seat next to him and Duncan took the one on the other side of her.

"You know very well I can't help it," he argued while sporting a sly smirk.

"You are going to end up with some kind of disease they haven't even invented medicine to get rid of yet," she berated, settling into her chair.

"Careful," warned Gabe sarcastically, leaning in, "or Maggie might just give you an 'infection' from the whorehouse the way she did Quinn and I at the last party we attended."

John laughed and Maggie screwed up her face at Gabe. "You can't let that go, can you?"

"No, I don't believe I ever will," Gabe chaffed.

"I really must know the rest of that story," insisted John.

"Later! When there are less people around." Maggie winked.

"Did you locate him?" asked John, changing the subject.

"Yes, and he will be joining us for dinner tomorrow." Maggie watched for Gracie and her rum punch.

"In that case, I shall make myself scarce."

"I am not sure you need to," she replied and squeezed his hand. "You look very different than you did back then, and the entire world believes you are dead."

"We'll see," he simply stated in order to placate her.

Gracie came over with their drinks, sporting a huge smile for John, which he reciprocated. "Are you going to introduce us?" she asked, hopefully.

"Yes, of course. This is John MacGregor, Duncan's cousin. John, this is Gracie."

John stood and bowed to her, a mischievous look in his eye. "It is a pleasure to meet you," he said and took her hand.

Gracie giggled and her face turned bright red as she stared adoringly into his eyes.

Maggie admonished him with a look and shook her head.

"Gracie," Duncan took charge, "we will all be needing dinner."

Gracie turned her head, but not her eyes— they were still fixated on John. "Did you say something?"

"Dinner?" parroted Maggie and waved her hand over the table. "We need to eat."

"Certainly," she said, reluctantly pulling back from John and slowly making her way to the kitchen, glancing back over her shoulder every so often.

"Can't you turn that off?" fussed Maggie.

"Even if I could, why on Earth would I want to?" teased John as he leaned over and kissed her on the cheek.

"Oh, I don't know! Maybe because you are causing women to lose their ever-loving minds?" she chided. "Perhaps because we don't need to draw unnecessary attention to ourselves given all that has happened?"

"Have ye tried to control it?" inquired Quinn, genuinely curious.

"I haven't really attempted to." John thought for a moment. "Do you think I could?"

"Ye should be able to," replied Duncan, stroking his chin. "It would probably take a great deal of focus and practice, but there is no reason ye should not be able to in time."

"Either that or we lock you in the cellar," mumbled Maggie dryly. "I think we have some chains down there that will hold you."

John cocked his head in contemplation. "I find myself strangely intrigued by that suggestion—as long as I have company, of course," goaded John.

The next day, the household bustled with activity, preparing for their special guest. Maggie walked around nervously, making sure everything was in order.

"For the love of God woman, will ye calm down?" Duncan grabbed her around the waist. "Everything is fine."

"Are you certain everyone on the estate is aware they need to be on guard?" she questioned.

"Aye! Ye are overthinking this."

"Duncan," she sighed, "we never have guests here because we have so much to protect, and the one guest we do have coming, is going to be the first president of this country. I just want things to go smoothly."

"They will," he reassured her, "and if it doesn't, we will have Quinn brew up a potion to erase his memory."

Maggie thought for a moment. "Does he have one of those? Because we should probably keep a few bottles of that around at all times just in case anyway."

A knock at the door interrupted them. Maggie blew out a deep breath as Hettie appeared from the kitchen to answer the door.

"Go on into the drawing room." Hettie shooed them away. "At least try to pretend you know how proper folk act," she scolded.

Maggie and Duncan scooted into the drawing room where Gabe and Quinn were already waiting.

"Is John coming?" she asked.

"I don't think so. He doesn't want to take any unnecessary chances," answered Gabe. "He knows how much this means to you."

Maggie and Duncan were waiting anxiously when Hettie appeared around the corner.

"General George Washington— and his guest," she announced, unable to contain the excitement on her face.

Washington appeared in the doorway.

"General!" Maggie went over to welcome him. "We are so happy you could join us."

He bowed and accepted her offered hand, pausing when he caught sight of her MacGregor ring, but regaining his composure so quickly no one took notice. "My dear, Mistress MacGregor, the pleasure is all mine. I am simply happy I was able to sneak away from the war for the afternoon." He kissed her hand. "And I hope you don't mind I brought along a special guest I believe you are rather well-acquainted with, if I am not mistaken."

They all looked to the doorway as Wyatt's smiling face appeared.

"Hello, Aunt Maggie!" he called out and went over to greet her.

"Wyatt!"

She laughed as he joyfully wrapped his arms around her, picking her feet up off the floor.

"And, all of my favorite uncles," he exclaimed, warmly greeting each of them.

"This is an unexpected surprise!" declared Gabe as they embraced tightly. He pushed his nephew back and patted his face. "You're not in trouble, are you?"

Washington laughed. "Not in the least. Young Wyatt has become a valuable asset to our army. We are in your debt for sending him to us."

"Really?" replied an astounded Maggie. "I must say I am impressed."

"Where is Uncle John?" he asked eagerly. "I have so much to tell him."

Duncan clasped his hands together. "He had some urgent matters to attend and, unfortunately, he is unable to join us for dinner."

Wyatt seemed disappointed but recovered quickly. Anxiously, he inquired, "So, is it a boy or a girl?"

"Two boys!" Maggie grinned.

"Twins?" asked a stunned Washington. "In addition to your triplets? My goodness, you must be the busiest woman in all of Virginia."

"We have a great deal of help."

"When can we see them?" asked Wyatt, excitedly. "I have missed the babies and Kat and Alastair more than you can ever imagine."

"I am sure General Washington didn't come all the way out here to see a houseful of children," said Maggie with a smile.

"Oh contraire," the General refuted, accepting a proffered glass from Quinn. "I would love to meet them."

"They are all finally napping now, but I will be happy to introduce you later."

They enjoyed a lively, relaxed dinner, speaking of anything and everything except the war. When dessert was brought out, Kat rushed into the room, playfully squealing and laughing, with Alastair close on her heels.

"Katherine Hannah Spencer Asheton!" reprimanded Gabe through gritted teeth, giving her a stern look and standing to catch her. She dodged her father causing

Quinn to get out of his seat to head her off. She reversed course and ran to hide behind Washington's chair.

"I am sorry, Father," said an out of breath Alastair, who had stopped to lean over with his hands on his knees. "I tried to keep her busy, but she got away from me."

"Hello, cousin!" Wyatt said and grinned.

As soon as the little girl saw him, she ran and leapt straight into his lap.

"General, allow me to introduce my cousin, Kat."

Washington smiled, amused. "It is very nice to meet such a charming and engaging young lady."

Kat grinned and leaned against Wyatt's chest, sucking her thumb.

"Please forgive the intrusion, General," apologized an embarrassed Gabe, "I am afraid the children sometimes overwhelm their nannies because they are rapidly being outnumbered by them. I will take her back upstairs."

"Never apologize for the sound of healthy, happy children in a home, Colonel. They are indeed a blessing."

"Allow me to introduce my son, Alastair," said Quinn, placing his hands on the boy's shoulders.

Alastair bowed to the General. "It is very nice to meet you, sir."

Washington dipped his head. "It is a pleasure to meet you as well, young man."

Gabe went to take Kat, but she clung firmly to Wyatt, burying her face against his chest. "Kat!"

"It's alright, Uncle Gabe. I will take her up."

Wyatt stood, still holding on to Kat, who had locked her little arms around his neck tightly. "Pardon me, General."

Wyatt started out of the room, Gabe and Alastair following close behind. "Pardon me as well, General," said Gabe, "It seems I need to have a little chat with my daughter."

"Certainly," nodded Washington, thoroughly enjoying the entertainment.

Just as they returned to their dessert, Maggie caught sight of Hettie frantically waving a towel in the air from the kitchen and pointing. Maggie smacked Duncan's leg under the table just as Kitchi's face appeared over Hettie's shoulder. They stared for a moment with wide eyes as their guest slowly turned to follow their gaze.

Washington looked down into his glass, back to Kitchi, then leaned towards Maggie and whispered, "Is your port a great deal more potent than I realized, or am I really seeing an Indian standing in your doorway?"

Maggie sighed and laid down her fork. "The answer would be 'yes' to both your questions."

She motioned Kitchi in, resigned to the fact her hopes for a smooth dinner had gone completely out the window.

"General, meet Kitchi. He belongs to a tribe that resides on the edge of our property."

"You have an Indian tribe here?" he asked incredulously.

"Yes. We maintain a great friendship and peace with them."

Kitchi stepped into the room, looking down and shuffling his feet.

"What can we do for you, Kitchi?" asked Maggie.

"John needs your help," he said quietly.

"What's the matter?" Duncan laid his napkin on the table.

Kitchi winced. "You need to come because there is some trouble with the men over the women."

"Oh, for God's sake," mumbled Maggie, and leaned her head down with her hands covering her face.

Duncan and Quinn were already out of their chairs.

"Please, excuse us, General, I think this is a matter we need to see to with some urgency," said Duncan. "We will return shortly."

Washington nodded and looked oddly after them as they left. He turned back to Maggie and leaned in again. "Does this sort of thing happen often during dinner?"

Maggie downed her drink. "More than you would think. Welcome to the mayhem that is 'Beechcroft'. There's no place like home."

Washington chuckled softly and took his glass in hand. "I must say, I envy you. I greatly miss the chaos of home, and I look forward to being in the thick of it once more."

Maggie topped off Washington's glass and then her own. "A toast to home, then," she said, and they clinked glasses.

"I am actually grateful for a few moments alone with you," he said as he pushed his plate away and reclined back in his chair. "I was hoping we would get a chance to speak privately."

"Let's retire to the drawing room, shall we?" she suggested and moved her seat back to stand.

Washington took a chair in front of the fireplace and Maggie brought over two fresh glasses and a bottle. "How do you feel about rum, General?"

"I am rather fond of it," he beamed; she handed him a glass that he held up for her to fill.

She poured herself one and sat down across from him.

"Major Tallmadge sends his regards, by the way." He watched closely for her reaction.

Maggie looked down into her glass. "I trust he is well?"

"He is— and, rest assured, his broken heart will heal in time," he said sympathetically, seemingly reading her thoughts. "You should really stop blaming yourself for moving forward with your life. I am certain he would not want you to feel guilty for finding some happiness in this world."

Washington leaned back and crossed his legs, stroking his chin. "I have no doubt he will find someone as well when this war is over."

"I know. I made him promise he would," she half-smiled, "and he will honor it."

"Above all, he *is* a man of his word," agreed Washington and sipped his drink.

Maggie regarded the man, knowing there was a burning question on his mind he wasn't sure if he should ask or not.

"A matter of weeks," she said out of the blue.

"Pardon?"

"It will be over in a matter of weeks, at least the main fighting part of it. The formalities of ending the war will take a little while longer to sort out."

He stopped mid-sip, then lowered his glass slowly. "How is that possible?"

"Yorktown is the key. Cornwallis will be there and forced to surrender in a few short weeks as long as you keep the pressure on him."

"It can't be," he said, shaking his head in disbelief. "It isn't possible."

"But it is. As I have told you before—you must stay the course. There are still difficult times ahead, but, as with anything worthwhile, there are always growing pains in the beginning."

Washington sat in silent contemplation for a moment before he raised his glass in her direction. "What I wouldn't give to know what you know."

Maggie laughed. "Be careful what you wish for, General. Sometimes, it's not all it's cracked up to be."

The General sipped his drink and regarded her. "I couldn't help but notice that lovely ring on your right hand," he remarked. "It appears to be very special."

She held it up for him to see and smiled. "It is. This is the crest that belongs to Duncan's family. I had them made for all of us as a symbol of our unity."

Gabe joined them in the drawing room before Washington had the chance to inquire further. "Again, please forgive me, General."

"Nothing to forgive, Colonel," he replied.

"Where is everyone?" asked Gabe.

"John was in need of some urgent assistance, so Duncan and Quinn went to see to him." The expression on Maggie's face spoke volumes. "Where's Wyatt?"

Gabe winced. "Kat refused to let him leave. I think he has missed her as much as she has missed him, so he is spending some time with her. If I know my darling daughter, by now she has him fully committed to a tea party for the rest of the afternoon."

Gabe took a seat and turned toward Washington. "Speaking of Wyatt— is he really doing all that well for you or are you just being polite?"

"Yes! Nathaniel Gardiner took him under his wing and within a few short weeks, he was handling patients all on his own. Gardiner said he was the fastest learner he had ever seen. Wyatt has saved a great many lives and you should all be enormously proud of him."

"That is good to hear," said a relieved Maggie. "We were a little worried about him finding his way for a while."

"He speaks very highly of all of you, and I understand the way he met his 'Aunt Maggie' for the first time was quite the adventure," Washington smirked, "It never ceases to amaze me what a remarkable woman you truly are."

Gabe smiled and laid his hand over hers. "Yes, she is."

Maggie set down her drink. "I think I owe you that tour. Up for a ride, General?"

"I thought you would never ask!" said a pleased Washington and stood.

"Gabe, care to join us?"

Grimacing, Gabe shook his head. "I think maybe I should check in with Duncan and Quinn in the event they need some assistance."

Maggie and Washington chatted on their stroll to the stables where Onyx was already waiting for them.

"Is this the remarkable beast I have heard so much about?"

"The one and only! General, meet Onyx."

Washington approached and stepped to the fence to greet the horse. Onyx was on his best behavior, for once, standing tall, looking proud and regal for their special guest.

"He is truly a magnificent creature. Wherever did you find him?"

Maggie rubbed his mane. "He sort of found me, and we have been inseparable ever since."

"Major Tallmadge told me all about him, but the stories do not do him justice."

"He is definitely one of a kind, thank goodness. I am not sure the world could handle more than one of him."

They mounted their horses and Maggie gave General Washington the ten-cent tour of the place. He was fascinated at how well the estate ran and how abundant things were. He was even more impressed by how self-sufficient they had become.

Maggie avoided the areas that would have raised suspicions, as everyone played the parts they were assigned when unexpected visitors showed up. By the time they arrived back at the main house, Duncan, Quinn, and Gabe had returned. They were in the drawing room with Wyatt and all the children.

Washington's eyes widened with amazement and delight when he saw them all together. "You are truly blessed here," he whispered to Maggie.

"We are indeed," she replied.

After a few more drinks and spending some time with the family, Washington announced the time had come to return to town. He gave Wyatt leave to spend the night and to return in the morning, but Wyatt insisted he had patients to get back to, promising to visit as soon as he could.

Maggie and Duncan escorted them to the door.

"General, we are truly humbled you joined us," said Maggie. "I hope we can do it again very soon."

"My dear," he said as he took her hand, "I am the fortunate one to get to spend the afternoon with you and your family. Thank you and I hope when this is all over, you and your husband will visit Martha and I at Mount Vernon and allow me to repay the kindness."

Maggie smiled. "I would like nothing more; I would love to meet your bride."

They bid him good evening and watched them leave. As soon as they closed the door, Maggie leaned against Duncan. "Do I even want to know what's going on with John?"

Duncan grinned. "Oh aye, I think ye will want to hear this."

9 Chapter Nine

After the children were taken back to the nursery, Maggie took a seat and Duncan brought her a large drink. She took a massive gulp. "Okay! Let me have it. What happened with John and the tribe?"

Duncan and Quinn exchanged amused looks as Duncan related the story.

"When we got there, John was in the middle of the village surrounded by most of the tribe's men. It seems they were rather upset by the fact all of their women only wanted John, and not them, whenever he was around."

"Are you kidding me?" asked Maggie, her eyes wide.

"Mingan was attempting to calm them down, but it wasn't working. It seems they were all too frustrated by their 'unmet needs' to care," added Quinn.

"They were angry enough to drag him down to the river and drown him," Duncan laughed, "Mingan managed to send word by Kitchi and stall them until we arrived."

Maggie pressed her palm to her cheek, her mouth forming an 'O'. "So, what happened?" she finally managed.

"After speaking with the other men and Mingan, we all came to the agreement it would be best if John came back to the house to live for an extended amount of time," replied Gabe. "We managed to sneak him in and hide him downstairs while Washington was still here."

"For crying out loud," Maggie sprawled back in the chair, "what are we going to do about him? This is getting ridiculous."

"I don't know," Duncan shook his head, "but we should probably figure out something soon."

Maggie stood up. "I think I should probably go talk to him."

Duncan grasped her hand. "I can't believe I am saying this but go easy on him. He has had a rough day."

Maggie found John in the collection room, leaned back, staring into the fire, nursing a bottle. He was so focused on the flame, he didn't hear her come in.

"Are you alright?" she asked, wrapping her arms around his neck from behind the chair, pressing her cheek to his.

He laughed softly and laid his hand over hers. "I am fine."

Maggie stepped to his side and pulled up a chair to sit close to him. "What are we drinking?"

Looking down to read the label, he held it out for a better look. "I'm not sure, but it tastes a little like a peach I had while I was in Charleston, for some reason."

"Ah!" Maggie took the bottle from his hand. "That would be schnapps, and I am particularly fond of it." She turned it up. "Oh, that's good. In my time, you would take this and mix it with orange juice and a little vodka. It was called a 'hairy navel' and it was delightful." She closed her eyes. "You know, it's the little things I miss the most."

"What else do you miss about your time?" he asked, always enthralled when she spoke of the future.

"The food," she sighed, "not that I don't love Hettie's cooking, but things like pizza, Chinese takeout, and chocolate."

"What's pizza?"

She held her hand open, palm up. "It is like a crunchy bread crust with tomato sauce, cheese, and meats on top that is baked. You eat it with your hands, and it is divine."

"And Chinese food?"

"Noodles with chicken and vegetables on a bed of fried rice, along with egg rolls stuffed with cabbage that comes with a sweet sauce you dip them in." She licked her lips and groaned. "I can almost taste it now."

"That sounds— interesting." he said and took the bottle back for another drink.

Maggie leaned her head back on the chair. "I also miss music, soft beds, hot showers, and massages. Oh, what I wouldn't give for a two-hour massage at a day spa."

"What's that?" he asked and handed her back the bottle, leaning closer.

"You lay on a table, under a sheet with nothing on and another person rubs you down in oil from head to toe."

John looked intrigued. "Now, that sounds like something I would like."

Maggie swatted at him. "It's not sexual—it's just — relaxing. It clears your mind."

"Same thing," he teased.

Maggie looked him over. "Duncan told me what happened. I'm sorry. I know how much you like living with the tribe."

John flipped his hand. "Don't give it a second thought."

"I feel some responsibility for the difficulty you are having."

He furrowed his brow. "What on Earth are you talking about? You had nothing to do with the actions of the men there."

Maggie rubbed her temple. "I know, but I turned you into a Fae and all of this—desire you are oozing—it is because of that."

He took her hand and kissed it. "Maggie, you saved my life from the hangman's noose and gave me a wonderful gift to boot. Do not apologize for that. All these pesky details will get sorted out eventually. Besides, I get to spend eternity with you, and because of that, I am indeed a fortunate soul."

She squeezed his hand. "As much as I appreciate you saying that, we do need to find a way for you to control the effect you have on women. It could get us in a great deal of trouble if we are not careful."

John nodded in agreement and Maggie took another sip of the bottle before returning it to him.

Maggie and John were well on their way to being drunk, heartily laughing when Duncan found them.

"What's so funny?" he asked as he came up behind Maggie's chair.

"Maggie was just telling me about some things from her time. I am not sure what to believe."

"Oh, it's all true," assured Maggie. "2018 is a wild time."

John looked to Duncan. "Maggie tells me there are places called 'strip clubs' where women dance almost naked, up on a stage— on a pole, of all things."

Maggie burst into laughter at the look of excitement in John's eyes.

Duncan dragged over a chair next to Maggie. "How do they balance on a pole?"

Maggie giggled. "They don't! They dance around it and use it to hold them up while they get men—you know, 'excited'. Some of them can even hold themselves upside down by their ankles."

Her husband raised an eyebrow. "What else do they do?"

John slid up on the edge of his seat. "Tell him about the 'lap dances'."

"Aye, tell me about them," Duncan leaned on the arm of her chair, propping up his elbow with his chin resting on his palm, completely engrossed in the conversation.

"Well, men will sit in a chair while the woman comes over to dance, and she uses her body to bump and grind against his lap to arouse him, but they don't have sex. It's just to get the men all worked up." She looked back and forth between them. "Surely, they do the same thing in whorehouses here."

"Oh, they do," responded John, "but they don't leave the men 'hanging', so to speak."

"What's the point of starting something ye don't intend to finish?" asked Duncan, confused.

"Because the men pay them to do it."

Duncan scratched his chin. "They pay them to *not* have sex with them?"

Maggie scrunched up her face, suddenly wondering about it herself. "Well, paying for sex isn't really legal in most places and I guess some men just like to watch? Or they need the help before they go home to their wives? I don't know." Maggie winced and threw up her hands. "I am afraid I am not explaining this very well."

"Oh, I think we get the point," Duncan smirked, "but feel free to demonstrate later if ye like."

Maggie reached over and pulled him into a kiss. "Oh! Maybe I will."

John raised his hand with a stupid grin on his face. "May I watch— for the sake of reference, of course?"

"NO!" they replied in unison.

"Besides, it's not like you need any help getting all worked up," said Maggie.

John leaned back and softly chuckled. "No, I suppose I don't."

Maggie and Duncan retired that night as soon as all the children were asleep.

John settled into the guest room, which would be his new home for the foreseeable future.

Duncan stretched out in the leather armchair by the fireplace in their room, his shirt and boots off, his legs splayed out wide. Maggie poured them each a whisky and handed one to him while he watched her with a mischievous look on his face.

"What?" she asked, playfully.

"I am waiting for ye to show me how this whole 'lap dance' thing works."

"Oh, you are, are you?"

He stroked his chin. "I have been looking forward to this ever since ye mentioned it earlier."

Maggie shrugged and poked out her bottom lip, feigning disappointment. "But I don't have any music."

"I'll hum any tune ye like," he whispered, as he ran his hand up her thigh and wantonly smacked her behind.

She pushed his hand away. "You can't touch the ladies when you are getting a lap dance, *sir*. The ladies can do whatever they like, but not the other way around."

"I am not sure I can abide that rule," he teased, using his finger to trace the nape of her neck and down to tug at the front of her dress.

Maggie thought for a moment. "Oh, that might be a problem," she taunted, and an idea came to her, "but I may be able to remedy that."

She looked around the room, until her eyes fell upon what she was looking for. Setting her drink down, she went over and took his belt off the hook, before coming back to stand in front of him.

"What are ye going to do with that?" he asked curiously.

She took his glass from his hand and set it on the table next to hers. "Making sure you 'don't touch'," she smirked, looping it and smacking it against her palm.

Duncan's eyebrows shot up.

Maggie leaned down and kissed him, pulling his right arm up and slipping the belt over it. She moved behind him and took his other hand, slipping it in the loop so his hands were tied behind the chair.

"Maggie! What are ye doing?"

She came back around and pressed her finger to his lips. "Shh! Let me do things my way tonight. You might just like it."

He eyed her warily with a suppressed grin on his face. "Alright, do with me what ye wish, my love."

"Oh, I will," she purred and pulled at his bottom lip with her teeth.

Stepping back, she winked at him and slowly started to remove her dress in a sexy striptease, stopping when she was down to only her shift. Duncan seemed to be thoroughly enjoying the show given the size of his rather large erection. She moved closer to him, running her finger all the way down his chest, then up to his mouth, pushing it between his lips. He sucked on her finger with his eyes locked upon her, as she closed her eyes and moaned in delight. She pulled her finger out, then used it to trace back down his chest and stomach to the part that needed the most attention.

It was his turn to groan when she turned around and backed up against him, gyrating and grinding her hips on his lap, enjoying the feel of his pressing need.

"Christ, Maggie!" he murmured.

She turned to face him while pushing down her shift and brushed her bare breasts against his chest. His eyelids had gone heavy and he drifted into a dreamy state, his breathing becoming more labored. Maggie placed her hands on his thighs and kissed him, which he gratefully accepted and reciprocated greedily. She pulled back, just out of his reach, then dropped to her knees. After unfastening his breeches, she leaned down to have a taste of the part of him she desired the most. As she went down, she felt the chair lift off the floor slightly, pulling against his tied hands.

"No, no!" she warned breathily and wagged her finger. "No touching or I will stop."

He rested his head back against the chair, trying his best to control himself. "Do ye have any idea what ye are doing to me?" he hissed through his teeth.

"I think I have a pretty good idea," she purred and went back to focusing on the task at hand. She moved her head up and down until Duncan could control his lustful need no more.

He snapped the belt that bound his hands clean in half and reached down to scoop her up in one swift move, making her 'whoop'. His lips fell upon hers, crushing her body and taking her breath away as he carried her over to the bed. He was inside of her in an instant, pumping hard and holding her in place with his kiss until he spilled inside of her.

As they lay entangled with one another panting, she giggled. "You cheated!"

"Aye, I did," he laughed, "and ye will have to find something a hell of a lot stronger than that belt to hold me next time."

"Oh, you want me to do it again?" She raised up on her elbow.

He turned to face her. "Oh aye, I think I do, and I will repay the favor when ye least expect it." He rolled her underneath him and took his time making love to her again, assuring all her needs and desires were completely fulfilled. As dawn approached, they lay lazily wrapped in each other's arms.

"You know what I miss?" asked Maggie, stroking his chest.

"What?" he asked dreamily.

"The beach at the house in Scotland. I have such fond memories of it."

Duncan laughed softly. "I seem to recall a few that stick out in my mind as well."

"That night we lay under the stars talking, and then the night you asked me to marry you were some of the best times of my life."

He rolled over to pull her tightly to him. "My favorite memory of that beach was after ye said 'yes' to my proposal."

Maggie closed her eyes, picturing the scene in her mind. "Oh, that was a pretty good one, too." She grinned. "I wish we were there right now."

They were embraced in a kiss when a sudden 'whooshing' sound surrounded them out of the blue and a rush of wind picked them up— just before dropping them with a collective 'thump'.

"Oww! What the hell?" Maggie rubbed the back of her head and felt the sting of sand on her backside.

"What the hell, indeed?" asked a dumbfounded Duncan, rolling over on his back to sit up and look around.

Maggie slowly raised up on her elbows and was astonished to see they were no longer in their bedroom, but in front of the loch at the stronghold in Scotland, lying completely naked on the sandy beach. "Am I dreaming?"

"If ye are, then we both are," replied a flabbergasted Duncan.

"How?"

"Ye said ye desired to be here," he pointed out, "and, so here we are."

Maggie turned to him. "So, we can just wish ourselves to places now?"

"It would certainly seem so. Finn could do it —why not ye?"

Rolling over on her stomach, she pushed up on her arms to see the house was lit up. "Should we go inside?"

"It would be rude not to," he said and stood, brushing the sand off his body and holding out his hand, "besides, it will be good to see Mother and my brothers."

Maggie took his hand and after he helped her up, she looked down. "Umm —we don't have any clothes on."

Duncan took notice as well and laughed. "Well, this should be an interesting homecoming. Won't Mother be surprised?"

They made their way up the path and slipped in the side kitchen door. Duncan looked around the room as he held Maggie's hand, who was behind him. He ducked and dodged, waiting until he saw no one around, before pulling her over to the cabinet in the corner that held extra linens for the bedrooms. Taking out two blankets, he wrapped one around her and the other around his waist, holding it in place with one hand.

"At least we can get in the main part of the house now," he chuckled.

"Your mother is going to freak out."

They giggled like teenagers as they snuck through the house and into the library, laughing at the absurdity of their current situation and appearance. They opened the door, thinking they were home free but were mortified to see Lady Aurnia sitting on the sofa, serving refreshments to five young women dressed in white robes.

"Hello, Mother," said Duncan, the smile slowly fading from his face.

Lady Aurnia's eyes grew wide at the sight and appearance of her son and daughter-in-law, standing in front of her company with wicked smiles on their faces, sand in their hair, barely covered by blankets, obviously fresh from lovemaking. She rolled her eyes and stood. "Hello, son."

The five women who were sitting in the library rose, formally bowing and falling to their knees, before Maggie and Duncan.

Lady Aurnia looked at them oddly before looking back at Maggie, who was frantically pulling the blanket to her body tighter.

"We bow before the Goddess Danu," said the one who seemed to be in charge.

"What? Where?" asked Maggie, looking over her shoulder to see who they were referring to and came to the conclusion they meant her, so she held up her hand.

"No! No! No!" Maggie wobbled over to them, trying not to trip on the blanket before bending down to the closest one to her, while attempting to keep herself covered. "Please, don't! I am not a goddess."

Duncan cleared his throat.

Actually, ye are.

You aren't helping.

The woman lifted her head with a puzzled look on her face.

"Please! Stand up!" begged Maggie.

The women slowly stood, unsure if they were doing the right thing.

A stupefied Lady Aurnia watched the scene before turning to Duncan. "What are ye two doing here?" she finally asked.

"It's a long story," said Duncan, putting his arm around his mother and leaning close to her. "Who are these women?" he whispered.

"They say they were guided here," she replied.

Duncan and Maggie stared back at Lady Aurnia in disbelief.

Lady Aurnia quickly took Duncan, then Maggie, by their arms and pulled them out into the hall. "Excuse us for a moment," she called over her shoulder, "I will be right back."

Once they were away from the women and alone, Lady Aurnia turned to them both. "What on Earth is going on? How long have ye been here, why do those women think you are a goddess, and for the love of God, where are your clothes?"

Maggie scratched the back of her head. "We just recently arrived."

"We were in our bed at home a quarter of an hour ago," clarified Duncan.

"Ye were what?" asked Lady Aurnia, suddenly deeply concerned.

"There are a few things we need to tell ye," said Duncan and kissed his mother's cheek.

"Maybe we could tell you while we borrow a few things?" suggested Maggie.

Lady Aurnia looked them over. "Oh aye, that might be a good idea," she said before leading them upstairs to her bedroom.

Lady Aurnia produced one of Duncan's father's tartans from a drawer and handed it to him before she went to her wardrobe to find a dress for Maggie.

"Where are my brothers?" he asked.

"They are out doing some early morning training on the edge of the woods. They will be back shortly," she replied and handed Maggie a gown.

Maggie and Duncan both stepped behind the screen to dress and explained to Lady Aurnia the details of their newfound god and goddess status.

"Ye were dead?" asked Lady Aurnia as Duncan came to stand next to her. She touched his face. "Oh, my sweet boy."

He kissed the palm of her hand. "Aye, but I am perfectly fine thanks to my remarkable wife."

Maggie stepped from behind the screen as Lady Aurnia gave her a good look over.

"The baby?" she asked, anxious when she saw Maggie was no longer pregnant.

"Babies!" Maggie smiled.

"Twins," added Duncan. "Two boys! Steven and Finley, both healthy and braw lads."

Lady Aurnia laughed and hugged them both. "Oh! I cannot wait to meet them!" She looked to Duncan. "Ye named one of them Finley?"

"Aye!" he said and folded his arms. "By and by, can ye tell me why ye picked that particular name for me?"

"It was the name of the man who introduced me to your father. A truly kind, older gentleman who, come to think of it, I haven't seen since. Why do ye ask?"

Maggie and Duncan exchanged looks.

"I guess Finn was in our lives long before either one of us knew it," said Maggie, dryly.

Duncan made a face, before shaking it off. "The women downstairs, Mother, who are they?"

Lady Aurnia folded her arms. "Worshipers of the Goddess Danu from the island of Hiort."

"I don't understand," said Maggie.

"There are still pockets of people all over who practice the olden ways," explained Duncan. "They revere the Fae but remain hidden and guarded since the spread of the Church. They practice mainly in the woods where no one will find them, but I know nothing of ones from an island."

"It seems they are from an ancient order," elaborated Lady Aurnia. "I had no idea these particular women even existed or what brought them here to us. They were just telling me their story when ye arrived."

Maggie sighed. "I expect we had better hear what they have to say."

As they descended the stairs. Logan, Reade, and Evan burst through the front door, shoving each other and carrying on as brothers do.

"The three of ye have been slacking off on training day, no doubt!" announced Duncan rushing down to greet them.

"Duncan!" exclaimed Logan and they embraced.

Duncan repeated the same massive hug with Reade and Evan.

"We don't have such a ball-buster to keep us in line anymore," teased Reade.

Maggie and Lady Aurnia exchanged amused looks when Logan noticed her.

"Maggie!" He came over and picked her up off the floor in a huge hug. He looked down at her. "Ye look wonderful! The baby?"

"Ye all have two new nephews," proclaimed Duncan with his arm still around Reade.

"Where are they?" asked Evan. "We want to meet them and the triplets. It is well past time!"

"They aren't here," replied Maggie.

Logan's face suddenly became grave. "Ye wouldn't have left them without good reason. What's wrong?"

Lady Aurnia motioned towards the dining room. "We should talk. Let me check on our guests first."

"What guests?" questioned Reade, looking back at his mother.

"Worshipers apparently," Maggie shrugged.

A befuddled expression crossed Evan's face. "Wait! What?"

They waited for Lady Aurnia to return, before moving to the dining room and updating the brothers on what had been going on.

"Ye are now Danu?" Reade asked in utter disbelief.

"And Duncan is the Dagda?" added Evan, pointing at his brother.

"Well, not exactly!" Maggie scratched her head as she tried to explain. "We are our own versions of them. According to Finn, it picks up on what is already within you."

Logan leaned back laughing. "And John is Cernunnos! How is that working out for him?"

"The female half of the estate will not leave him alone," scoffed Maggie, "and the male half of the estate isn't too happy about it. We are spending most of our time trying to keep relationships intact."

"Mingan should be very happy." Lady Aurnia hid a sly smirk behind her hand.

"Aye, he is!"

"Good thing he is not here with those women. We would never get him out of here," added Maggie, sarcastically. "Speaking of which, we should probably speak with them."

"Aye!" agreed Duncan and put his arm around her.

10 Chapter Ten

They moved to gather in the library with the five young women, who all stood together in a close circle. When Maggie entered the room, they turned to face her.

"Goddess," greeted the one in charge as they bowed their heads in unison.

"It's Maggie," she corrected. "Just call me Maggie."

"But ye are the Goddess Danu," she looked to Duncan, "and, ye are the Dagda? Isn't that correct? We can feel the power emanating from ye."

"So, I am told," replied Duncan dryly.

"He is also my husband," said Maggie, rubbing his shoulder.

Their leader nodded her head in acknowledgement. "I am Rozem, the head priestess of our order." She turned to the other women and formally introduced them. "This is Enid, Shanley, Noni, and Rowena."

Maggie looked over at the lovely young women. Rozem was the tallest of the three, with beautiful long dark hair and very deep, green eyes. She couldn't help but notice a certain amount of pride and determination in each calculated move these women made, reminding her of the stories of the Amazon warriors from Greek mythology.

Lady Aurnia introduced the rest of the family as the women stood firm.

Folding her arms, Maggie moved closer to them. "Maybe you should explain who you are and exactly why you are here."

Rozem gave a short nod. "I am the leader of a sect of all women who are born to serve the Goddess Danu. We live on the island of Hiort in a place much like this, secretly hidden away in the mountains. Our home is bountiful and provides everything we need to live in peace away from all others besides the few locals who inhabit the lower part of the island. We are also protected by a great mist such as the one that ye have here, so we are kept completely hidden. A few weeks past, we felt a shift of some sort as our protective barrier began to dissipate and our food sources began to wither."

"A few weeks ago, ye say?" questioned Duncan.

"Aye," replied Enid.

Maggie and Duncan exchanged knowing looks.

At the same time we were turned.

And about the time Finn left.

"We had no choice but to leave," explained Shanley. "Our home was no longer sustainable."

"What brought you here specifically?" inquired Maggie.

Enid stepped forward. "I am the prophetess of our order, and I received revelation saying our time was done there and our services were needed here."

"Needed?" asked a concerned Duncan. "For what reason?"

"For the Goddess in whatever way she sees fit or desires," replied Rozem. "For protection, for spells, for sacrifice —whatever ye call upon us for. Rest assured, we have remained 'pure' in case it was required for some purpose as well."

"Pure?" Evan cocked his head to one side. "Ye mean ye have never…?"

"Wait! All of ye are virgins?" interrupted Reade, a stupid boyish grin on his face.

Maggie and Lady Aurnia both slapped him in the chest at the same time.

"Forgive my son's atrocious manners," said Lady Aurnia as she cut him a scathing look. "He spent too much time in the stables with the hounds as a child and I am afraid it shows."

"Why would you do all that?" questioned Maggie. "Why would you live your life waiting for a goddess to come along and use you?"

Rozem appeared visibly confused, seemingly unsure of why she needed to explain this. "It is what we were born to do, what we were marked for." Her tone shifted to one of respectful suspicion. "How do ye not know of us?" she demanded. "Our order is ancient and have worshipped ye always. Have ye not heard our prayers?"

"I am kind of new to all of this, on many levels." Maggie shrugged.

"What do ye mean by 'marked'?" inquired Lady Aurnia.

Rozem turned her perplexed gaze from Maggie to the elder woman. Pulling her hair back from the nape of her neck, she revealed a small birthmark, in the shape of an unusual circle. "Each female child who is born with this mark is sent to the order at the age of seven years by their family. We are raised by our fellow sisters and trained to be who we are, while being taught the old ways and rituals."

Maggie held up her hand. "I'm sorry! Did you say people give up their children at seven years old to a bunch of strangers they know absolutely nothing about?"

"Aye," affirmed Rozem, readjusting her hair. "They never see their birth families again. It is a great honor and privilege to be blessed with such a child and to be able to give your daughter to the order."

"Like hell it is!" shouted Maggie angrily. "What kind of parent gives up their little girl to become a human sacrifice at that age?"

The young women looked around at each other, uncertain of what to think of Maggie's outburst or how to react.

Duncan moved to her side and gently slipped his arm around her, resting his hand on her hip. "Maggie," he whispered softly, "ye must remember things are sometimes different than what ye are used to —ye know better than anyone. These people have been doing this for as far back as their history records and well beyond that."

Maggie closed her eyes and laid her hand over on his, trying to calm herself.

"Why have we never heard of ye?" asked Logan.

The one called Shanley was the one to answer. "Our order lives in secrecy with our *only* purpose being to serve the Goddess; others would have no reason to know of us and, besides, we have little to no contact with the outside world, or men for that matter —it, and they, only corrupt."

"Then, how do ye find the children?"

"We stand watch over the area below our home during the spring solstice. The girls are born only into certain families who are true believers in the ancient ones— the secret passed down by word of mouth for generations. They are brought and left on the island on that day, however Rowena was the last one to come to us nine years ago."

"And there are *no* men where ye are?" clarified Reade.

"No!" replied Rozem, seemingly irritated by the question. "Why would we ever need them?"

Evan and Reade exchanged excited looks.

"I am afraid you have wasted a trip, ladies," said Maggie suddenly. "There is no goddess to worship or serve here."

"The divination was very clear," insisted Enid. "We ARE needed here for some purpose, and the fact our home is withering away to nothing is proof of that."

Rowena interjected, trying to be helpful. "Perhaps the Dagda has needs ye are too busy to attend?"

"Aye," agreed Shanley. "His appetite for women is known to be ferocious. Surely, ye have far more important things to do than to bother with satisfying his carnal needs. We are capable of seeing to that," she stated, matter-of-factly.

Maggie turned to face Duncan, narrowing her eyes at him. "Does the Dagda have any particular 'needs' not being satisfied?"

Duncan raised his eyebrows and swallowed hard. "Absolutely not! The Dagda is a happily married man and all his 'needs' are very well tended by his wife." He leaned forward and kissed her on the nose. Looking over at the women, he declared resolutely, "NO ONE will ever be taking her place in that regard, let's make that perfectly clear."

"And it had better stay that way," mumbled Maggie with a wry grin.

"I don't know why you are here," said Maggie, turning back to the women, "*We* are not even supposed to be here ourselves because our home is in America. We aren't even sure *how* we got here." She shrugged. "I don't know what to tell you. I think you should go and find your real families—the ones who brought you into this world. Get married, have children if that is what you want, just go and be happy. You owe your life to no one except yourselves, least of all a Fae."

The women looked around at each other confused and clearly disturbed.

"Evan and I can escort ye," offered Reade innocently. "We would be more than happy to see ye home."

"Nay, ye will not!" Lady Aurnia smacked him on the back of the head. "Not unless ye plan on marrying one of them."

Shanley folded her arms and glared at Reade. "Why would we need an escort from two men of all people? We are more than capable of taking care of ourselves. We train each day for it."

Lady Aurnia turned to the young women. "All of ye must be tired. Ye will stay here and rest until we have figured things out."

"Thank ye," said Rozem, grateful for the invitation. "That is very kind of ye."

Lady Aurnia stepped into the hall, called for Flora, and instructed her to show the women to some of the extra rooms.

"Dinner will be ready soon. Ye can rest until then."

"What the hell?" asked Maggie, once their guests were out of earshot.

"Who even knows anymore?" Duncan moved to the table of whisky.

"I knew there were pockets of people here and there who still worshiped the old ways, but I had no idea a group of women on an island with a protected home even existed," confessed Lady Aurnia as she took a seat. "Much less, ones born just for use by the Fae."

"There is a great deal we have been in the dark about," Duncan handed Maggie a poured glass, "but what we do know is that something definitely compelled them to leave their home."

"Speaking of home," Maggie paused to down the whisky, "we should probably figure out if we can get back the way we came or if we need a ship. No one knows we are gone."

"If ye *can* come and go as easily as ye did earlier, perhaps ye will consider bringing my grandchildren over for a wee visit," suggested Lady Aurnia hopefully.

"Aye," said Duncan, moving to kiss his mother's cheek, "as long as we can do it safely."

"So, how are we going to do this?" asked Maggie.

Duncan came over and wrapped her in an embrace. "Well, we were like this before," he smiled.

"And naked," Maggie pointed out.

"Oh, come on!" complained Logan and rolled his eyes. "Do ye two ever take a break?"

Maggie winked at her brother-in-law and leaned against Duncan's chest. They each closed their eyes and thought of their bedroom. Upon hearing the same 'whoosh', they felt the breeze against their faces and landed in their bed, still wrapped up in each other's arms.

Maggie peeked with one open eye. "We're home!" she announced.

"It seems we are!" Duncan kissed the side of her head.

They got up and checked on the babies, who were all still sound asleep. Sauntering back to their bedroom, Maggie turned to Duncan. "Would you rather share your bed with five virgins tonight?" she teased.

"God no!" he exclaimed, slipping his arms around her. "Five women who have never been with a man before? That sounds more like a nightmare. Besides, why would I want them when I have a goddess right here —and she knows how to give 'lap dances'." He groaned and kissed her thoroughly.

"Good answer!" She laughed and kissed him back. "You really are the God of Wisdom."

11 Chapter Eleven

The next morning after breakfast, Maggie and Duncan called Gabe, Quinn, and John into the drawing room and told them about the previous night's adventure.

"All ye had to do was think about it, and ye were there?" Quinn was genuinely confounded.

"It was almost too easy," replied Duncan.

"Do you suppose the rest of us can do it?"

"I don't know!" Maggie chewed on her bottom lip. "I suppose? Why don't you try it? Close your eyes and concentrate on..." she looked around, "...the side garden. See if you can do it."

"Alright!" Quinn stood up, closed his eyes and blew out a deep breath readying himself. Scrunching up his face, he focused —but nothing happened.

Duncan walked over to him, then around him looking him over. "Are ye thinking hard enough?"

"I thought I was," he replied, "but how would I know?"

"Good point!" Duncan waved his hand. "Try again."

Quinn closed his eyes and cleared his thoughts before seeing his destination in his mind. This time, his body faded out slightly, then shimmered back in, but he was still there.

"Whoa!" Gabe exclaimed and took a step back.

"What happened?" asked Quinn.

"You became dim, then bright again," replied John, fascinated; he came over and poked his chest with his finger to see if he was really there.

Quinn frowned at him.

Duncan looked to Maggie, puzzled. "We weren't even trying last night."

Maggie nodded and came over to join them. "We were also together. That may have had something to do with it."

"And naked," noted John with a smirk. "Maybe you should try it that way!"

"I think not!" said Gabe to John, wagging his finger at him. "You know, I am not even sure I trust you around my husband the way you have been behaving lately."

John gripped his shoulder good-naturedly.

"Maybe you just need practice," suggested Maggie. "See exactly where you want to go in your mind."

Quinn nodded, closed his eyes once more, directing all his energy into the task at hand —and vanished completely out of their sight.

"Where did he go?" asked John, spinning around.

"The garden," called out Quinn as he came back through the door, grinning. "It worked."

"Well, that can certainly come in handy in a jam," noted Gabe.

Quinn came over to stand with his husband, placing his hand lovingly on his lower back. "Aye, it will."

John clapped his hands together. "Now back to the matter of these women —what do you think that is all about?"

"No clue!" Maggie exhaled sharply. "I told them to go live their lives and forget about serving the Fae."

"Do you think they will?"

"Of course not," she replied and plopped down in a chair. "That would be far too simple, and never mind the fact they have been brainwashed from birth to think they solely exist to serve a race that has not been seen in forever."

"Why do ye think they were guided to the Scotland house?" asked Quinn out of the blue. "I mean, I could understand if they were guided here to the Colonies, if they were destined to serve ye, where we actually are, but why there?"

Maggie and Duncan exchanged uneasy looks.

"That is a good question," pondered Duncan aloud. "Do ye think they were, or will be, needed *there* for some reason."

"Maybe I will take a quick flip through Finn's book and see if there is anything about the order in there," Maggie stood, "since it is fairly thick, I have not had a chance to go through everything."

"I think Gabe and I are going to go practice transporting ourselves to other places," said Quinn, turning to John, "ye want in on this?"

"I thought you'd never ask."

After Maggie left the room, John leaned close to Duncan and whispered, "So, did you get that lap dance last night?"

"Indeed, I did!" Duncan smirked.

"You...um...going to tell me about it?" pressed John.

"Nay, I am not!" Duncan winked and slapped him on the back. "I am just going to let ye wonder."

John shook his head, disappointed. "You are absolutely no fun."

Two hours later, Maggie sat at the table, leaning over Finn's book.

"Aha! I found it!" she exclaimed.

Duncan came to lean over her shoulder.

"This text says several women are chosen —born each generation specifically to serve gods and goddesses, and they carry a miniscule amount of Fae blood in their veins. They are to remain pure in case a virgin is needed for a spell, a blood sacrifice, or as a concubine." Maggie leaned back and looked up at Duncan. "Surely my mother did not keep female concubines?"

Duncan shook his head. "Not that I have ever heard of. I suspect the order started out serving all the gods and goddesses and eventually just moved to worshipping one over the years. Since they are all women, it would make sense they singled out Danu, the Mother Goddess, as the specific one to worship."

"They did blood sacrifices?" she asked, her voice strained.

"Not all of them, but there were one or two who demanded it in tribute. Those were the days when the Fae were many, and their power ruled supreme."

A detestable expression appeared on her face. "I'm not sure which would be worse —being a sacrificial virgin or a forced concubine."

Duncan kissed the top of her head. "They do not see it that way, my love."

"Well, they need to learn to see things a different way," she insisted. "We cannot let those women waste their lives like this —taking away little girls at the age of seven— Duncan, it's barbaric. I can't imagine giving up one of our children like that."

"Well, ye have the power to change it since ye are the one in charge now."

"And I will!" she vowed, flipping the pages. "I also found this." She pointed to a specific paragraph. "It seems that being able to move from one place to another is indeed an ability of the Fae. It is called 'shimmering' and we can go wherever we like without the need of a ship anymore. It also means we can visit your mother more often."

Duncan smiled and slipped his arms around her. "I like the thought of that."

"Me too, my love!"

A noise from behind them caused them both to look up. Gabe, Quinn, and John all came from the direction of the underground pool, laughing and soaking wet, leaving a trail of water behind them as they walked.

"What happened?" asked Maggie as she stood.

Quinn had taken off his shirt and was wringing it out. "We were trying to surprise ye by landing here in the collection room," he chuckled.

"We missed!" Gabe chortled.

"Well, practice makes perfect, although you should be more careful. You might end up in a rock somewhere," warned Maggie.

"Find anything?" asked John, pulling the ribbon from his hair so he could shake it loose.

"The women are who they say they are," replied Duncan.

"So, what next?" asked Gabe sitting down. Taking off his wet boots, he poured the water out and set them aside to dry.

"We send them back to their families and stop this craziness of tearing little girls away from their parents. People should not be bred to serve other people. It's ridiculous."

"Yes, Maggie," Duncan slipped his arms around her, "but they were very young when they were taken to the order and chances are, they do not even remember who they are. The only family they have now are each other and sending them to places that they know nothing of would be cruel."

"Ye are forgetting that someone, or something, did guide them to the house in Scotland for a reason," added Quinn. "There are no coincidences."

Maggie sighed. "Either way, we need to return to Scotland and speak with them."

12 Chapter Twelve

Three days later, Maggie had Cora, Cecile, and Hettie, along with one of the wet nurses, come over to watch the children for the day while their parents paid a visit to 'town' and by that, meaning Scotland.

John looked at the group apprehensively. "Do you think the rest of us can actually do this?"

"We did it and without even trying," replied Duncan. "There is no reason the rest of ye should not be able to."

"Just the same," suggested Maggie, "maybe we should hold onto each other?"

"Ye are right," agreed Duncan. "It wouldn't hurt."

Maggie slipped one arm around Gabe's mid-section and the other around John's. Duncan took Quinn by the shoulder, then placed his hand on Maggie's waist.

"Ready?" he asked.

"We'll see!" She winced and instructed them all to focus on the beach in Scotland. The now familiar 'whoosh', wind, and 'thump' came before they all found themselves standing at their intended location.

"Everyone in one piece?" she asked cautiously.

"Other than my stomach being in my throat?" John coughed, his face a bit pale.

"Yes, it is a bit like being turned inside out," added Gabe, leaning over with his hands on his knees, gulping in a few deep breaths.

"Really?" Maggie touched Gabe on the back. "Duncan and I didn't experience anything like that."

Duncan looked over at Quinn. "How about ye?"

Quinn held his arm around his mid-section. "I don't think I will be eating anytime soon."

Maggie and Duncan exchanged worried looks.

"Maybe it just takes some getting used to?" offered Maggie with a grimace. "It's not like it will kill you— you *are* immortal after all."

After they had pulled themselves together, the group walked up the path to the main house. They located Lady Aurnia and the other MacGregor brothers in the library.

"My boys!" she exclaimed when she saw them, coming over to hug them together, then to Maggie and Gabe, and after everyone had been properly greeted, the other two brothers were introduced to John.

"Did ye bring the bairns?" asked Lady Aurnia.

"No, I am afraid not. We are still getting this traveling thing down and we want to make sure they won't be harmed before we try it with them," replied Maggie.

"Of course!" Lady Aurnia was visibly disappointed but understanding. "Ye must keep them safe, no matter what."

Lady Aurnia pulled Maggie over to the sofa. "What are ye doing here?"

"We came about your guests," answered Duncan.

"Och! Those women!" scoffed Logan. "They are nothing but a disruption to this household."

"I don't know," Evan grinned, "I wouldn't say that. I rather enjoyed seeing them fight stripped naked to the waist."

"Seeing them what?" Maggie gasped.

"It seems they train the same way we do," clarified Reade, "only they remove part of their clothing to do it, so it doesn't get in the way."

"Ye try getting men to practice when there are topless women running around all over the place," grumbled Logan. "It's damn near impossible!"

"Are they any good?" goaded Quinn and nudged Gabe, entertained by Logan's complaining.

"They are excellent," noted Reade. "I have never seen anything like it, but they do tend to get a little angry when the men stop to gawk at them —and there is also the matter of the men not appreciating being told bathing once a week isn't nearly enough."

"The sooner those women leave, the better!" fussed Logan, draining the glass of whisky in his hand.

"Careful, Brother," said Duncan, slapping Logan on the back, "ye know what happened when the last woman caused a disruption around here." He beamed at his bride.

"Aye, I finally got grandchildren," mumbled Lady Aurnia to Maggie while casting a sideways glance at her other sons.

"Where are they now?" asked John. "I should very much like to meet them."

Maggie pointed at him warningly. "Those women are virgins, and they damn well better stay that way."

John scrunched up his face at her.

"Off practicing more rituals, no doubt," replied Reade. "They do those in the nude as well."

"Your lives sound positively miserable," retorted John sarcastically and took a seat on the sofa on the other side of Duncan's mother.

"I think it is nice to have more women around the house," proclaimed Lady Aurnia. "And by the way, ye all *could* stand to take baths more than once a week. Women like their men to smell good—like John here." She laid her hand on John's leg, much to his surprise and delight. Lady Aurnia leaned closer to him and inhaled deeply. "What *is* that marvelous scent ye are wearing? It is absolutely divine."

"Scent?" Maggie found herself suddenly extremely interested. "What scent?"

"The one coming off of John."

She stood up and went around to John's other side, taking in a deep breath. "You are absolutely right! There is something there. It's very slight, but it *is* there. What does it smell like to you?"

Lady Aurnia closed her eyes and smiled. "It is the scent of a man, freshly washed, but not too clean as to take away his personal scent— with a hint of mint— and something sweet, but I am not sure what it is. What does it smell like to ye?"

"I smell something sweet as well, but I can't place it either."

John leaned his head back and grinned as the two ladies got as close as they possibly could to his chest, each placing a hand on him as they pressed their noses to his neck.

"Of course!" exclaimed Maggie, recalling something from a biology class. "It's pheromones."

"What are 'pheromones'?" Duncan grabbed Maggie by the waist and physically pulled her away from John, who winked at him in return.

"It's something the body puts off during sex. It's what attracts animals to each other during mating season, but people can give it off as well. It is what makes couples desire each other— and John reeks of it."

"It does seem to be getting stronger," said Lady Aurnia, and she touched his arm.

John leaned in her direction and smiled warmly, gazing directly into her eyes.

Lady Aurnia was now completely enthralled.

"NAY!" growled Duncan, lunging forward and shoving them apart. He planted his finger on John's chest. "Ye keep your hands and your other filthy body parts away from my mother! Understand?"

"Duncan!" scolded Lady Aurnia. "What is the matter with ye?"

Maggie took Duncan's arm and pulled him away.

"John is irresistible to women. We have been trying to figure out a way to tone him down, but, so far, we have been unsuccessful. It is starting to become a problem."

"A problem for *you* maybe," muttered John.

"It will be a problem for ye if ye touch my mother!" warned Duncan sternly.

John was chuckling softly to himself when Rozem came into the room. She stopped suddenly when she realized there were guests and bowed. "Goddess, ye have returned."

"Maggie! Call me Maggie!"

Rozam nodded and looked around, surprised. "Ye have brought others?"

As soon as John saw Rozam, he stood. "I am John," he said and formally bowed.

"Ye are Cernunnos," she said, looking him up and down.

Maggie pointed to Gabe and Quinn and introduced them.

"Camulos and Grannus. It is an honor to meet ye all."

"How do ye know who they are?" asked Duncan.

"I just do," said Rozam. "We, who are of the order, all do. We feel it as a part of who we are."

Maggie cleared her throat. "We would like to speak with all of you."

Rozem nodded. "I will get the others."

Maggie noticed John watching Rozem intently as she left. She leaned down and placed her hand on his chest. "In all seriousness, I really need you to control yourself around these women," she whispered. "We have enough issues right now."

"I will be on my best behavior," he promised but with his eyes still on the doorway.

Maggie placed her hand on his face and turned it, so their eyes met. "John! I mean it!"

The ladies returned as Logan, Evan, and Reade made themselves scarce. Maggie had them all take seats and stood before them.

"Ladies, I don't know how things were done before, but as we understand it, the five of us are all that are left of the Fae. None of us need you for anything, so you are just wasting your time waiting to serve us."

Duncan came to Maggie's side. "Are ye five all who are left of your order?"

"Aye! Our numbers were once in the hundreds," said Enid. "This is the fewest we have ever had as far as our records show."

"So, what do you do there all day?" asked Quinn.

"We live! We have our chores that contribute to the community and we worship, we study, we train, we do what must be done," answered Shanley.

John was fascinated. "And there are no men there?"

"No, none at all."

"How interesting," he replied, stroking his chin, frowning, when he caught Maggie cutting him a look.

"My suggestion to you is to go live your lives the way you wish and be happy."

"Forgive me Goddess," interrupted Noni, "but what makes ye think we are not living the way we wish? I can assure ye, we were all extremely happy where we were."

The five women nodded in agreement.

"Don't any of you want to have families of your own or to go out and see the world?" asked Maggie.

"We do not want for anything," replied Rowena.

Maggie folded her arms and sighed. "Do whatever you want to do, but don't sit around wasting your lives waiting for us to call upon you."

"I am afraid we cannot," insisted Enid firmly. "Whether ye know it or not, we were sent here because ye need us for some reason, and we will not leave until that need is fulfilled."

"I don't understand," Maggie now exasperated, "no one here has sent for you."

"Enid is our prophetess. Her visions have never been wrong," persisted Rozem. "If she says we are needed here, then we are. Make no mistake. Why else would our home be dying?"

Lady Aurnia stood. "Ladies, why don't ye go get cleaned up for dinner? It should be almost ready."

The women stood and filed out of the room as Maggie collapsed in a chair. Duncan moved behind her and rested his hands on her shoulders.

"Maybe they are indeed needed here," pondered Quinn. "Stranger things have happened. Look at us."

"Quinn is right. There are no coincidences with the Fae, a lesson we have learned the hard way," agreed Duncan and kissed the top of her head.

"What do we do?"

"We wait and see what happens," said Gabe. "What else can we do? They don't appear to be going anywhere because they have nowhere else to go."

"Well, for the time being," Lady Aurnia stood, "I am just grateful to have all my boys and my daughter-in-law at one table for a meal. Let's go sit down and enjoy our time together."

"I am interested in hearing more about your home," said John to the group of women as they broke bread.

Rozem wiped her mouth. "The house is much like this one, only we do not have a village inside the gates. Our walls encompass the entire estate to prevent any unwanted guests. We grow our own food, keep animals for meat and milk, and we have been blessed with the most glorious fruit trees to provide a great abundance."

"How do ye spend your days?" asked Duncan.

Noni put her fork down. "We are each assigned chores needed to keep our home running. Some of us garden, some tend the animals, while others cook or teach the younger girls. After the mid-day meal, we worship, we practice our fighting skills and after supper, we do the things we like to do."

"Like what?"

Enid smiled. "I personally like to write poetry. Shanley likes to design and build things to simplify our work. Rowena likes to paint. We all have our own individual tastes."

"Your fighting skills are quite remarkable," mentioned Lady Aurnia. "Where did ye learn?"

"Shanley is our instructor," answered Rowena. "She is an excellent teacher."

"I was taught by the one before me. Many of our skills are passed down. We always train with the one who was before."

"Like an apprenticeship," affirmed Quinn.

"Exactly!" Rozem smiled. "We have done things that way for generations."

"You mentioned records before," said Maggie. "Do you have a library, as well?"

"We do," replied Enid. "It is mainly composed of stories of the old ones, records that have been kept, herbal remedies, and things to help us along in life."

"Much like the ones we have," murmured Logan and glanced over at Duncan, with some concern on his face.

Gabe sipped from his glass and set it aside. "I am most curious. Exactly what led you here?"

"When I receive revelation," explained Enid, "it is after I go into a meditative state. Sometimes, when I come out of it, I find I have written things down. The map to your home was one of those things."

Duncan noticed Maggie looking down at her plate, picking at her food. He slid his hand over on her thigh and she looked up at him with a forced smile.

What is it?

I just have a bad feeling.

Duncan laid his napkin on the table and pushed back his chair. "If ye all will excuse us, I would like to take a walk down by the water with my wife before we have to leave."

He stood, offered his hand for Maggie and helped her up, before escorting her outside. He slipped his arm around her waist once they were alone under the stars. "Tell me what's bothering ye, my love."

"Someone, or something, definitely sent them here— it's the reason that concerns me and it's not like we have anybody we can ask."

"Are the the women themselves worrying ye?"

Maggie shook her head. "No! I think they have been completely honest with us, and I genuinely believe they only want to help."

"Agreed. Maybe Finn's magic was protecting them and when he left, so did it. It may be as simple as that."

Maggie stopped when they reached the shoreline. "Somehow, I doubt it, and I don't like it when I don't know what I am dealing with. Heaven knows, we are all completely out of our element with this whole Fae thing."

Duncan cupped her face with both his hands. "Ye worry too much." He brushed his lips lightly against hers and pushed the hair back from her face.

"Old habits die hard, I suppose," she whispered, before letting out a sigh.

Later that evening, after promising to return in a few days, they bid farewell to the family and shimmered back to Virginia in time for the babies' late afternoon feeding.

After putting them down, Duncan found Maggie in the collection room rummaging through some of the books.

"What are ye doing, my love?" he asked, as he came to join her.

She looked up from her seat, pulling her hair back. "I am trying to figure out why these women showed up at the stronghold. They seem convinced they were sent for a reason."

"Having any luck?" he asked and leaned against the table.

"No!" She slammed the book shut. "It's not fair, Duncan! Finn went off and left us with all of this and with no clue of what we are supposed to do. We are floundering here." She closed her eyes and leaned back in the chair, covering her face with her hands. "I wish, more than anything, we had just one person here who knew what the fuck was going on!"

"I know!" He pulled her up from the chair and into his arms. "We will figure it out."

They were in the middle of a long, lingering kiss, when a blood-curdling scream was heard from upstairs. They rushed up the staircase and into the foyer, hearing loud voices and the sound of someone frantically shouting as they moved.

Nothing could have possibly prepared them for what they were about to see next.

Gabe, Quinn, and John stood with their backs to them, as Gabe urged someone to calm down. Maggie and Duncan pushed by him to see what was going on. What they saw was a woman on her knees on the floor, looking up, terrified at the three men surrounding her. Maggie's eyes fell to their unexpected guess and the blood drained from her face. Extending her arms behind her, she steadied herself against Duncan. He reached for her but was unable to catch her before she fell to her knees. Before he could ask what was wrong, Maggie managed to choke out one word that left them all completely stunned and speechless—

"Mom?"

13 Chapter Thirteen

Maggie reached out for the woman before her, convinced what she saw was merely a hallucination.

"Mom?" she repeated, her mind in disbelief but her heart hoping against hope.

"Maggie?"

The woman slowly held out her hand as if in a dream state. They stared at each other for a few long seconds before scrambling over to each other and embracing, sobbing onto the other's shoulder.

Duncan, Gabe, Quinn, and John all exchanged dumbfounded looks before staring down at the two women on the floor.

"Did she just say 'mom'?" whispered Gabe.

"Mom? Is it really you?" Maggie pulled back and touched her face with both hands, afraid if she let go, she might disappear before her very eyes.

"Maggie!" Tears streamed as she looked her daughter over, "You're alive!"

Ana Bishop wiped the wetness from her daughter's face before hugging her again.

"How are you even here?" posed Maggie.

"Where exactly am I?" questioned Ana.

"You are in my home —in Williamsburg."

"Williamsburg? Ye live in Williamsburg?" Ana pulled back a little dazed. "That can't be. Why wouldn't ye tell us or come to see us? Surely, we would have seen ye. Maggie, I don't understand. What is going on? Where have ye been all this time."

"I don't understand either Mom, nor do I care. I am just happy to see your face," she laughed through the tears. "I can't believe you are here." Maggie looked concerned and touched her mother's shoulders. "You *are* here, aren't you? I'm not dreaming or having a nervous breakdown or anything like that." She looked up at the others. "Do you see her as well? You do, don't you?"

"Aye!" Duncan smiled and knelt, touching her back gently. "We all see her."

Maggie laughed and kissed him before he looked to Ana.

"It is very nice to finally meet my mother-in-law."

Ana looked at him oddly, then back to Maggie in bewilderment.

Gabe cleared his throat. "Whisky and some privacy may be in order." He pointed toward the drawing room.

"Yes! YES!" exclaimed Maggie while Duncan helped her up.

John offered Ana his hand and helped her to stand as she studied her surroundings.

Maggie took her mother around the waist, led her into the next room and to the sofa. Once seated, Maggie refused to turn loose of her hand.

Gabe offered Ana a full glass of whisky, which she gratefully accepted.

"Mom, I want you to meet everyone. This is Duncan MacGregor, my husband."

"I recognize ye from the portrait," she acknowledged. "Although, it is nice to meet ye in person."

Maggie pointed. "This is Gabe."

He stepped forward and bowed. "It is certainly a pleasure to meet you."

"This is Quinn, Duncan's brother, and John, Duncan's cousin. Everyone, this is my mother, Ana Bishop."

Ana downed her drink in one shot, set the glass on the table, and looked at Maggie.

"Can ye kindly explain to me exactly what the hell is going on here? Fifteen minutes ago, I was sitting in a chair in my house, before hearing a strange sound and everything going black. I woke up on a strange floor to find my missing daughter, whom we presumed dead, very much alive and living in the same town?"

Maggie took her other hand. "We are in the same town, just not in the same *time*," she said with a wince.

"What? What do ye mean by that? Maggie, have ye been drinking?"

"No," Maggie picked up Ana's glass and handed it to Gabe to refill, "but *you* probably should be."

Duncan moved to Maggie's side. "There is no easy way to say this and, I know this will come as a shock to ye, but this is the year 1781."

Ana moved her gaze around to all of them before letting out a nervous laugh. "Really, Duncan is it? This is not the best time for jokes. Ye have been keeping my daughter away from me, and I don't find it the least bit amusing. We thought she was dead, for God's sake."

Maggie looked up and Duncan, then back to her mother. "He is telling the truth, Mom," she said softly. "In 2018, I passed out on that beach in North Carolina and woke up in the year 1765. I didn't leave you and dad on purpose. I would have never in a million years done that to the two of you, and you know I would not have intentionally stayed away —I didn't have any say in the matter."

Ana blinked, trying to find words. "Ye expect me to believe this nonsense, Maggie?" she whispered and stood up. "I am your mother, and I deserve a better explanation than some absurd, made-up lie."

Maggie rose. "Take a good look around, Mom. Does this look like anything from 2018 or whatever year you just came from?" Maggie waved her hand around the room. "LOOK HARD!"

Ana exhaled sharply before turning to scan the room, looking at the house, at the people, their clothing and the furnishings —no light switches, no fixtures, nothing modern. With a perplexed expression on her face, she closed her eyes and listened. There were no sounds of cars, planes, trains, or anything else running, inside or outside of the house. Slowly, she walked over to the window, pulled back the curtains and gazed out as a nagging, gut feeling from somewhere deep inside told her Maggie spoke the God's honest truth.

Maggie went to join her. "I would have never left you and Dad like that, and if there was any way to have contacted you, I would have done it. In your heart, you know I love you both too much to do something like that to you, Mom."

"How is this possible?" she muttered.

"Oh, Mom," she said and put her arms around her, "that's an awfully long and complicated story." Maggie led her back over to the sofa.

"What do ye recall of the Fae legends?" asked Duncan.

"The Celtic Faerie Tales?"

Duncan nodded.

"They are the stories ye tell children before ye put them to bed."

"Not quite," Maggie whispered and patted her hand.

Gabe stepped over with her refilled glass and handed it back to her. "You might need this," he smiled.

Maggie looked to Duncan. "How do I explain this to her without her memories?"

"What do ye mean?" asked Ana, accepting the drink gratefully. "I have lost no memories."

"Yeah, Mom, you kind of have."

Quinn drummed on the table with his fingers. "It may be a good time to open that book ye have been avoiding, Maggie."

"Aye," agreed Duncan. "Maybe something will ring true if she hears it?"

"I'll go get it," offered Quinn and he disappeared.

"What book?" demanded Ana, "and why are ye talking about me as if I am not here?"

"Mom, what do you remember about your father?"

She shrugged. "I loved him very much. He gave me that beautiful necklace I passed on to ye."

"But that's *all* you remember."

Ana thought for a moment as she searched her mind. "It is."

"Doesn't that seem strange to you? Of all the memories of your life, you only have that *one* of your father?"

Ana blinked hard and stared at Maggie. "I never really thought about it before."

Quinn returned and handed the book to Maggie.

"Mom, you don't remember because your memories were taken from you when you fell in love with Dad and gave up your Fae powers as the Goddess Danu to be with him."

Ana reached forward and felt Maggie's forehead. "Sweetheart, are ye unwell? Do ye have a fever?"

"I am perfectly fine!" Maggie handed her the book. "This once belonged to you."

Ana set down her glass and accepted the tome, looking it over and running her hand across the cover. "I have never seen this before in my life," she disagreed.

"Open it, Mom."

Ana looked back down at it, before slowly turning to the first page and silently skimming it. "Is this some sort of elaborate joke ye are setting me up for? Am I being 'punked'?"

Ana pointed at the first page.

Taken aback, Maggie looked down and read the forgotten language, which apparently her mother could still comprehend as well. Somewhat in shock, she pulled the book onto her lap for a better look and scrutinized the top of the first page.

"Fucking son of a bitch!" she exclaimed.

"Margaret Bishop! Watch your language!" her mother scolded.

"Margaret?" Duncan looked to his wife with the corners of his mouth twitching up. "Your name is Margaret? We are married with five children, and I did not know this about ye?"

"I hate that name!" she mumbled. "Don't ever call me that!"

She looked up from the book. "I suppose you were right, Quinn. I should have opened this a little sooner."

"What is it, *Margaret*?" asked Gabe, with a wink.

"I will turn you into a wart covered toad for real and it will make that whorehouse infection look like a walk in the park!" she threatened. Gabe laughed softly and indicated for her to continue.

"The first page is a spell to restore memories to a Fae goddess who has had them taken away."

"Truly?" Duncan peered over her shoulder.

"Well, that should make explaining things simpler," supposed John.

"What do you say, Mom? Do you want your memories back?"

"I haven't lost any memories, Maggie, so I don't know what ye are going on about."

"How do you know, Mom? If you have *lost* your memories, you wouldn't remember, now would you?" Maggie scrunched up her face and read the words aloud.

They all watched with utter fascination as a small white light rose from the middle of the page, up into the air, and straight into Ana's eyes.

When it was done, Ana blinked a few times, before shifting her gaze to Maggie, as if seeing her for the first time, reaching out to touch her face.

"Son of a bitch! What the fuck did my father do now?" she spouted off.

"Ah! Now I see where Maggie gets that colorful language from!" declared Gabe.

Maggie and Ana both turned to glare at him with the same dirty look.

"And that same irritated expression, as well," John was quick to point out.

"I take it your memories have returned?" inquired Quinn hopefully.

"Aye," she nodded and reached across to pick up the glass of whisky before downing it in one shot before explaining. "When I decided to leave behind the Fae life for Maggie's father, I slipped that spell in my book just in case it was needed for some reason. I guess it is a good thing that I did."

She held up her glass in John's direction and shook it for him to refill. "Maggie, why did my father pop ye back to 1765? Did he even give ye a reason?"

"Yes. He said I needed to save the MacGregor family. If I hadn't been in the right place at the right time, the entire line would have been wiped out in a single night."

Ana frowned. "That would have indeed been a problem," she pondered, standing to pace the floor. "Why didn't he send ye back home afterwards?"

Maggie smiled up at Duncan and he slipped his hand into hers. "The MacGregor line needed to carry on. Duncan and his brothers are the last of the Fae blood on Earth."

Ana watched the two of them and understanding bloomed across her face. "I see. Where is Father anyway?" she asked, looking around.

"He said he needed to rest and take a 'slumber'. Not permanently, just for a bit."

Ana downed her third glass, genuinely confused. "He left with no Fae to watch over things?"

"That's not 'entirely' true?" Maggie replied, timidly.

A thought suddenly occurred to Ana. "How did *I* end up here?"

Duncan tightened his grip on Maggie's hand. "I think it may have happened when Maggie said she wished there was one person here to help guide us on our paths as Fae gods and goddesses."

Ana's face paled and she took a closer look at Maggie and then around at the others. "Dear God, ye are all full Fae!" she exclaimed. "He turned ye."

"Technically," said Maggie, standing and moving next to her mother, "he turned *me* in order to save Duncan and I turned the rest of them with the abilities he bestowed upon me."

Ana took Maggie's hands in hers. "He made ye the leader of a new generation of Fae, didn't he?"

Maggie nodded. "He said it was needed to save the future of the world."

"Well, he's not wrong, sweetheart. I'm sorry, Maggie, that ye were thrust into this without any warning or any prior knowledge of what I once was. It must have all come as quite a shock to ye."

Maggie bobbed her head. "I survived, but I have missed you and Dad so much." Her eyes flew wide open. "Oh my God, Dad! He will be frantic." Maggie looked to her mother, excitedly. "Can I wish him here, too?"

Ana closed her eyes and squeezed her hand tightly. "Oh, Maggie, were that ye could," she said softly, sadly. "Your father passed away a couple of months ago."

Maggie's hand flew to her mouth and her body slumped.

Duncan rushed and caught her, helping her to the sofa, and pulling her against him as she sat in a state of shock.

"How?" she managed to get out.

Ana brushed away a few of her own tears. "It was a stroke. He went peacefully in his sleep. I'm so sorry, baby."

Maggie rested against Duncan. "I guess I just always thought in the back of my mind, that somehow, some way, I would see you both again. I'm sorry, Mom. I know you must miss him terribly."

"I do," she said softly, "and more than ye will ever know."

Cecile appeared at the door to the drawing room. "Pardon me, Maggie, but the babies are ready to nurse."

"Babies?" Ana's ears perked up.

"Aye," said Duncan with a smile. "Ye have a few grandchildren."

"Really?" she grinned.

"Maggie and Duncan have been very busy," explained Gabe.

"Come on, Mom," Maggie wiped her face with her sleeve and stood, "it's time to meet the next generation."

Maggie rocked Finley, while her mother admired little Steven in her arms.

"He looks so much like your father!"

"I think so too!"

"Twins! How wonderful!" proclaimed Ana.

"They go nicely with the triplets," smarted Maggie.

Ana laughed aloud. "Ye have triplets as well?"

"Yes! They are outside with the nannies— Kendric, Morgan, and Alanna."

"Oh, Maggie! I can't believe it."

"Yeah, we don't half-ass anything around here," she smirked.

"Ye are very happy, aren't ye?" she asked and took one of the other rocking chairs.

"I am—now. It was an interesting few years there for a while." Maggie filled her mother in on everything that had happened since 1765.

Ana sat dumbfounded as she listened. "My daughter, the Revolutionary War spy, rubbing elbows with George Washington and other body parts with Benjamin Tallmadge. I daresay your father would be proud —and probably a little disturbed."

Maggie chuckled. "I'm just grateful Dad dragged me to all of those museums growing up. It saved my ass in more ways than one."

They put the twins back down and went outside to meet the triplets. Hettie and Cecile were keeping an eye on them while they played.

"Hettie, Cecile, I want you to meet someone," said Maggie, leaning into Ana. "This is my mother, Ana Bishop."

"Your mother?" exclaimed Hettie. "But I thought…"

Ana intervened. "We were separated and had no idea where the other one was until recently, but we are together now."

"I see," said Hettie, glancing over at Maggie. "Well, I know Maggie is happy to have you here. Your daughter is something special. You should be proud of her."

"Aye, I am." Ana turned her attention to Kendric, Morgan, and Alanna. "Oh, my beautiful grandbabies," and she kneeled to greet them.

Ana was still sitting on the ground enjoying her grandchildren when Duncan came out to join them; Maggie met him halfway across the lawn.

"How are things going?" he asked, slipping his arm around her waist and kissing her forehead.

"It's been an interesting day, to say the least," she said and turned to watch her mother.

"I think that is an understatement if I ever heard one," he grinned, and they strolled over to the children.

"What do ye think?" Duncan asked Ana.

"I think I am over the moon to be here," she replied, happily bouncing Morgan on her lap.

Suddenly, a loud, unholy 'neigh' from the side of the house caused them all to pause and turn to see what was happening. Onyx was galloping hard, straight towards them, and in a hurry.

Ana set Morgan down and climbed to her feet, a look of pure joy erupting on her face. She moved to position herself directly in his path, placing her hands on her hips; he halted just as he reached her, stopping mere inches from her before lowering his head. Ana reached for him as Onyx lightly butted his head to hers. "My dear old friend," she smiled through misty tears, "I have missed ye so much. We have been apart for far too long."

Onyx enfolded her into a hug the same way he always did Maggie.

Ana rubbed his muzzle and laughed with delight. "Have ye been with Maggie all this time?"

The big horse nodded and appeared to smile proudly.

"I should have known," she whispered and scratched his ear. She kissed him on his nose. "Thank ye for looking after her. Ye are indeed a true and faithful friend."

Maggie strolled over and touched her lightly on the back. "He was here when I first woke up in North Carolina," she explained in a low voice, so only Ana would hear. "He has been my constant companion and he has always had my back."

"Just as he always did mine!"

After a late supper that night, they ushered Ana down to the collection room. Her eyes widened with amazement as she looked around, taking in the scene. "Well, Father outdid himself on this, didn't he?"

"We were rather surprised by it," said Duncan. "Especially with the underground springs."

"Springs?" she asked. "Like the ones in Scotland?"

Gabe offered his arm and escorted her around, giving her the full tour before finding her a seat.

"It was a departing gift," said Maggie; she and John brought glasses over for everyone.

"Where do ye suppose he actually went?" asked Quinn.

Ana scoffed. "If I know Father, he is probably holed up somewhere in the future in a Vegas hotel room with three hookers, an unlimited supply of whisky, and watching home-improvement shows on the television."

Maggie nearly spat out her drink.

"What's a 'hooker'?" asked Duncan.

"A prostitute," replied Maggie.

"Finn's Fae Fuckery!" Duncan gloated, wagging his finger at her. "Ye see, I told ye so."

It was Ana's turn to choke on her drink, laughing.

"Do they do 'lap dances' as well?" questioned John with anticipation.

Maggie bobbed her head back and forth. "You would be surprised what some of them will do for the right price."

"I wish to know all about it!" and a mischievous gleam appeared in John's eye.

"Good Lord, Maggie!" exclaimed Ana. "What have ye been telling these men?"

"They wanted to know about the future, so I enlightened them."

Ana shook her head. "So, tell me," and sipped her drink, "what was it that ye needed help with that ye wished me here for to begin with?"

"Oh, with everything that happened today, I almost forgot," said Maggie. "It seems a bunch of women from the island of Hiort showed up at the stronghold in Scotland saying their home was dying and they were guided there for some reason. They also claim to be your worshippers."

"Well, that *is* an interesting twist." Ana pondered the information as she finished off her drink.

John rose to refill it, smiling at her as he did.

She looked up, bit her lip, and returned it with a devilish one of her own, watching him from behind intently as he moved away.

"MOM!" exclaimed Maggie when she took notice.

"He is the other issue," declared Duncan.

"What's the issue?" she asked, never taking her eyes off John.

"Cernunnos over here is 'lust-dusting' every woman he comes into contact with," replied Maggie. "We need to find a way to neuter him before he breaks up every marriage in Colonial America. Heaven knows, just keeping the couples on this estate together has been enough of a task in itself."

"That sounds terribly uncomfortable," remarked John, sitting back down and unconsciously covering himself protectively.

"Lust-dusting?" Ana snickered. "That's a new term for it. I seem to recall the same problem with the original Cernunnos. Ye will learn to control it with time. It will take a great amount of concentration and practice for now, since ye are all so new to things, but soon, it will become second nature and ye will do it without even knowing it."

Maggie waved her finger in a circle at John. "You are starting lessons tomorrow."

John blew her a kiss in return.

"Back to the women in Scotland," said Quinn.

"Oh yes! The order the women of Hiort are from is as old as the Fae themselves. They were originally put into place to serve as human companions for the Fae, very highly regarded as the privileged among mankind, who were chosen for such an honor, some of them even allowed to bear the children of the Fae gods. Over the years, a few of the gods and goddesses would come to use them for more nefarious reasons, so Father decided to make a special place for them on Hiort to personally protect them and to give them the means to take care of themselves. I came to care for them a great deal, so I became a frequent visitor, and I found myself spending a lot of time with them. As the other Fae decided to slumber, the order's worship shifted from all the Fae, to just me, because I was the only one they ever saw and listened to their prayers. I wanted to make sure they were safe, so I spent time teaching them how to protect themselves. They carry a small amount of Fae blood, already making them stronger than most men and they were very eager to please."

"Why would they receive revelation to go to the stronghold and from whom?" asked Gabe.

"It would have had to have come from Father before he left, and as to why, I am not sure —unless..." she trailed off, lost in her own thoughts.

"Unless what?"

"How many McGregor men are there?"

"Quinn and I have three brothers, plus John, who is from the same family, Quinn's son, Alastair and our bairns. That would be it." Duncan ticked off on his fingers, wiggling his thumb several times for the children.

"How many women are there in the order?"

Maggie sighed. "There are only five."

"Five?" asked a stunned Ana. "The last time I was there, nearly a hundred existed." She scratched her head. "If ye say Father's main goal was to make sure the MacGregor and Fae bloodlines are extended, perhaps he sent them for that exact reason."

"You think Finn sent them to get pregnant?" Maggie was somewhat disturbed by the thought.

"Well, even Father is not *that* crude," Ana replied dryly, "but, if he had a hand in their unions of love the way he did yours and Duncan's..."

Duncan and Quinn exchanged an amused look before bursting into a boisterous bout of laughter. Duncan had to give himself a minute before he could even speak. "Ye think Finn sent our brothers the loves of their lives? After all the hell they gave me, this is the best news I have heard all year!"

"Knowing Father better than anyone here, that would be my best guess," she commented, grinning behind her glass.

Gabe looked to the brothers. "Lady Aurnia is going to be thrilled!"

"He probably has someone in mind for all of ye as well," claimed Ana, pointing around the room.

Gabe and Quinn stopped laughing abruptly and looked at each other.

"Um, Mom," Maggie cleared her throat, "Gabe and Quinn are 'together'. They were married in a Fae ceremony by Lady Aurnia."

"Oh!" she exclaimed holding up her glass. "Well, 'congratulations' to ye both." She turned to Maggie. "And, good on Lady Aurnia for being such a forward-thinking woman. I always liked her very much."

"Ye know our mother?" inquired Duncan.

"Not officially, but I have kept an eye on all the MacGregors over the years."

"What if we decide we don't *want* just one woman?" John waved from his chair. "I have no desire to settle down."

Ana winked at him with a wicked smile.

"Could their reason for showing up be that simple?" asked Maggie.

"Ye have met your grandfather! What do ye think?" Ana slapped a hand on the table, laughing.

Maggie cut her eyes over to Duncan. "Actually, that does sound exactly like him, doesn't it?"

"If that is the case," mentioned Quinn, "this might not be such an easy thing. Our brothers were not too keen on those women the last time we were there."

Maggie cringed. "You are right —Logan was downright hostile."

Ana smiled. "How do ye think passion gets ignited, my dear? It has to start with some sort of spark."

"At any rate," said Duncan, "we will need to go back and perhaps for a little bit longer this time."

Gabe sighed. "That would involve leaving the children."

"Would it?" Maggie cocked her head. "Mom, is it safe to shimmer with the babies?"

"Of course, dear. They have Fae blood, and they will be just fine."

"So, we can take them to visit Mother," stated an incredibly pleased Duncan.

"You can go as well, right Mom?" asked Maggie.

"I don't see why not as long as I am holding your hand, and ye will it. I may not have my powers, but I do still have Fae blood. Besides, if ye can pull me through time, a trip across the ocean should be a piece of cake."

Maggie looked around. "I guess we are going to Scotland for an extended stay."

Later that night, Maggie knocked on her mother's bedroom door, holding an armful of gowns.

"Mom, I brought these for you. The jeans and t-shirt might stand out a bit."

Ana laid them across the chair. "Thank ye, sweetheart." Her mother took her hand and pulled her over to sit on the bed.

"How are you doing, Mom? Today has been a bit crazy."

"Maggie, I cannot tell ye how delighted I am to be here with ye and my grandchildren." She cupped her face. "I never thought I would see ye again and to find ye now, after all this time, so happy— I cannot express the joy it brings to my heart."

"I have missed you so much, Mom! Not a day has gone by when I didn't wish I could pick up my phone and just call you— and Dad." Tears started to drip down her face.

"I know. I miss him too, baby!" said Ana and pulled Maggie to her, stroking her hair.

"Was it worth it?" she whispered.

"What?"

"Giving up immortality for a few, short human years with Dad?"

"Absolutely! I would do it a thousand times over again for the time I had with ye and your father. I have no regrets for what I gave up because I gained so much more in the bargain. Ye are such a gift to me, Maggie. Don't ever doubt my love for ye and your father." Ana kissed Maggie's forehead. "Now, go to bed and get some rest. I am not the only one who has had a long day."

Maggie laughed and stood. "I never thought I would say these words, but it's good to hear you order me around again. Good night, Mom."

"Good night, baby!" she smiled.

Maggie stopped at the door. "I'm really glad you are here."

"Me too!"

Duncan was sitting in one of the chairs in the bedroom when she returned. She went to him and he pulled her down onto his lap.

"Is your mother all settled in for the night?"

"Yes," she whispered, resting her head on his shoulder.

"How are ye holding up with all of this?"

Maggie shrugged. "I am thrilled to have my mom back. Never in my wildest dreams did I think I would, but my Dad…." she trailed off, and a flood of tears erupted from her eyes.

Duncan slipped his hands around her and pulled her tight. "Let it out, my love," he said softly.

The dam burst, and Maggie sobbed into his chest, too upset to say the words aloud. *I miss Daddy so much!*

"I know," he said and tightened his hold on her, whispering soothing Gaelic words into her ear. He held her until she was too exhausted to cry anymore, before gathering her up and carrying her to bed, spending the rest of the night comforting her.

The following morning, Gabe found Ana down by the stables, visiting with Onyx.

"Good morning," he called as he and Alastair approached. "Hello, beast," he muttered to Onyx, who proceeded to huff an acknowledgement while enjoying an apple from his former mistress.

"And good morning to both of ye! What brings the two of ye out so early?"

"School," derided Alastair, unenthusiastically while scratching his nose.

"Yes, and you should get to it!" Gabe smiled and squeezed his shoulders.

"Alright, Father," he groaned before he ran off to find his classmates.

"I suppose somethings never change with time, like a child's intense dislike of school," Ana chuckled as she watched him go. "Maggie loved to learn but hated the idea of having to attend class. Somedays, it was a true battle of wills."

"I absolutely believe that about her. Maggie can be quite stubborn when she wants to be."

"Is the school here on the estate?" Ana inquired.

"Oh, yes. Allow me to show you," he said with a wave of a hand, and they walked in the direction Alastair had just gone. "How did you sleep?"

"I kept waking up thinking I was dreaming," she sighed and smiled. "I actually pinched myself a few times to be sure all of this was real."

"Where are Maggie and Duncan?" he asked.

"I think they are sleeping in late this morning. Maggie is probably trying to get over the shock of my appearance— and she is still terribly upset by the news of her father's passing."

Gabe clasped his hands together behind his back. "You seem to be handling the change fairly well."

"Yes, well, after my memories returned— let's just say, this is nothing out of the ordinary," she laughed. "In fact, it is actually more like the norm."

"If you say so, although I am not certain I shall ever get used to it."

Ana looked over at Gabe. "Ye and Maggie have a rather special relationship, don't ye."

"We do, and it is one I am grateful for each day. Maggie and I have been the greatest of friends since the day we met. She knows more about me than anyone, even Quinn, and she loves me despite it."

Ana stopped. "There is one burning question I have no explanation for — ye are not a MacGregor, and ye do not have Fae blood, correct?"

"That's right."

She gave him a puzzled look. "How were ye made into a Fae god? The only way that could have happened was if someone gave up being one."

Gabe offered her arm and she accepted. "I have you to thank," he said and patted her hand where it rested against his. "Finn contained your Fae essence in your necklace, and Maggie gave it to me, so Quinn and I could remain together."

Ana smiled at him, nodding as understanding washed over her, and they continued to walk. "I knew that ye seemed so familiar, but I could not for the life of me place why. That explains it."

"I hope you don't mind," he whispered and leaned in.

"Not at all. From what Maggie has told me of ye, I think she made an exceptionally good choice. My daughter has an excellent head on her shoulders."

The village and the community kitchen came into sight, and Ana stopped; Gabe felt her tense.

"What is it?" he asked.

"Please, tell me Maggie does not keep slaves — not my daughter!"

Gabe had to chuckle. "Quite the opposite. All the people here are here because they want to be. Maggie has taken them in, protected, and cared for them. Here they are paid a weekly wage, are given their own homes with acreage, with the freedom to come and go as they please. Each person who finds their way here has Freedom Papers waiting when, and if, they ever ask, but not one person ever has. Maggie makes sure they, and their children, are educated, taught trades through apprenticeships, or can learn whatever they want. She keeps them safe above all else, and they are happy and content here. We are all one big family, and it is a much better way to live than what awaits them off these grounds. The same goes for the Indian village on the edge of the property. They were nearly decimated before Maggie came along, and now they thrive because of her good heart and generosity."

Ana sighed and smiled. "*That* sounds more like my Maggie."

"You did an excellent job raising her. You should be proud."

"Thank ye," she said softly, "and thank ye for looking after my girl when I could not."

Gabe chuckled. "I am afraid she has taken care of me far more than I have taken care of her. Your daughter is a wonder, and fearless when it comes to protecting the ones she loves."

"She is a bit headstrong — she gets that from me— but her heart, that all comes from her father."

"I'm sorry for your loss," offered Gabe. "It must have been difficult to lose them both."

"It has been, but now I have my Maggie back and a whole slew of grandchildren to help fill that void. I just wish Steven could be here to see them as well."

A few days after spending some much-needed time together, Maggie and Ana gathered the entire family, along with all the children, and went outside to get Onyx. The house staff had been told they were traveling and to not bother coming to the main house that day. Within minutes, they were standing on the beach in Scotland.

"I have missed being able to do that," said Ana, stopping to stretch her arms above her head and taking in a deep breath of fresh air.

"Well, this trip went much smoother," announced John.

Ana let her gaze drift to the water. "The more ye do it, the easier it gets. It will be like that with all your Fae powers. They will also get stronger as time goes on."

"Are we really back in Scotland?" asked Alastair, taking in everything around him.

"Aye we are, son!" Quinn smiled and ruffled his hair. "Why don't ye and Kat run on ahead and surprise your grandmother?"

Alastair took Kat by the hand and they ran off towards the house.

Maggie turned to Onyx. "Go behave yourself and don't break anything."

He nodded and was off on his own adventure.

They took their time wandering up the small hill to the back entrance of the house and found Lady Aurnia in the hall happily chatting away with Alastair and Kat when they came inside.

"Oh, my babies!" she exclaimed, beaming, and kissed Duncan before taking Finley from him, then moved to kiss Maggie and greet Steven. "Such fine bairns!"

Quinn, Gabe, and John all took turns kissing her on the cheek. John lingered a bit, forcing Duncan to warn him off with his eyes.

Maggie motioned her mom over. "Lady Aurnia, I want you to meet someone. This is my mother, Ana."

Lady Aurnia gave Maggie a bemused look, then turned to Ana. "Your mother? How is that possible?"

"We will explain everything once we are settled."

Lady Aurnia's face split into a wide grin and she grasped Ana by the hand. "It is indeed a pleasure to meet ye."

"The pleasure is all mine," said Ana. "Maggie has told me so much about ye and I cannot wait to get to know ye better."

"Come in and sit down!" Lady Aurnia herded everyone into the library so they could all relax and visit while Maggie filled her in on the past few days' events.

"That's quite a story," her mother-in-law finally said. "Ye really think that's why these women are here?"

"It's the only thing we can figure," offered Maggie.

Lady Aurnia couldn't contain her giddiness at the prospect.

"Mother," cautioned Duncan, "I think it's best if we let nature take its course and not try to force anything. We should probably not even mention it to the others in case we happen to be wrong."

"Of course son, whatever ye say," but the excitement remained in her eyes.

"I hope you don't mind if we stay a few days," said Maggie.

"Like I would let ye leave when ye just got here with the children."

About an hour later, the rest of the MacGregor men wandered inside. After lots of hugs and greetings, they came over to take possession of the babies, getting to know their nieces and nephews better.

"Where are the women?" asked Maggie.

"Off communing in the woods, baring their teeth to the moon — who knows?" grumbled Logan, disgustedly. "Let's just appreciate the fact they are somewhere else at the moment."

Maggie covered her face to conceal her amusement.

"Actually," corrected Lady Aurnia, "they took their horses out for a ride. I sent them to the warm springs to relax, and they should return before dusk."

"At least we will get a peaceful supper," said Reade. "Logan and Shanley can't make it through one minute of the day without starting an argument of some sort."

"What do ye disagree about?" asked Quinn.

"What DOESN'T that woman disagree about?" complained Logan.

"Ye sound very frustrated, Brother," goaded Duncan, "or is there something else I detect in your words?"

Logan furrowed his brow. "What do ye mean by that?"

Duncan shrugged. "The last time I was tied up in knots like that, I ended up married to the love of my life."

His brother scoffed. "Well, don't ye worry. I loathe that woman, and I wouldn't be with her if she were the last woman in Scotland."

Duncan cut his eyes over at Maggie.

I detect a little note of something.

There is a fine line between love and hate.

The rest of the day was spent together as a family with the MacGregor brothers and Lady Aurnia making a fuss over the babies, Kat, and Alastair, while giving Maggie and her mother some time alone together.

Maggie and Ana found themselves in the collection room. Ana stood in front of her own shield on display, slowly reaching out to touch the metal.

Maggie hugged herself and inclined her head. "That is pretty impressive."

"That was from a long time ago," whispered Ana, lightly tracing the pattern with her fingers.

"I was completely enamored by that the first time I saw it," said Maggie, slipping her arms around her mother's waist. "Now, I know why. Duncan even had our wedding rings engraved with the pattern," and she held out her hand to show her.

"This shield belongs to ye now, sweetheart!"

Maggie shook her head. "I don't have a thing to go with it," she teased, took her mother's hand, and led her over to two chairs. "Mom, I need to ask you something."

"Anything, dear."

Maggie leaned forward in her chair, clasping her hands together in her lap. "What exactly am I supposed to do as a Fae goddess? I mean, I know carrying on the MacGregor line is important, but Finn said I was needed to save the world. I don't know what that entails."

Ana took her hand. "Maggie, ye are already doing everything ye need to do. Your job as a Fae is to give mankind a helping hand, and ye are already changing the world. The people on your estate, for instance—look at what kind of lives they would have had if ye had not come along. Who's to say one of their descendants, because of your loving care, doesn't go on to cure cancer or invent a way to prevent global warming, all because ye took in their great, great grandmother and gave her a better life? Ye may have already saved the world and ye don't even know it. Darling, ye have the best soul of anyone I know, so just keep doing what ye are doing by helping people when ye can and spreading some of that inherent goodness ye have around. A simple small act of kindness on your part can dramatically change someone's life and future for the better."

"That's pretty much what Finn said."

"My father, as King of the Fae, has the unique ability to see throughout generations — past, present, and future. I have no doubt, though his ways a bit unorthodox, he knew exactly what he was doing."

"But Mom, by the same token, a simple act on my part can change things for the worse. What if I do something that throws history completely off track?"

"Sweetheart, ye know the basics of history, so ye will know if something jumps too far off the rails, and ye will be there to correct it."

Maggie groaned. "No pressure there."

"Ye will be fine." Ana settled back in her chair. "Have a little faith in yourself. Lord knows I do."

Later that evening, Maggie sat in front of the fireplace in the library, nursing Steven with Duncan sitting by her side, holding Finley, when they heard the women come through the front door. Slowly, they made their way into the room.

Rozem was the first to notice them. "Goddess, ye have returned!"

"With the children," added Shanley, a huge smile spreading across her face.

"It's Maggie, and yes, we have all of the children with us."

The women gathered around to look at the twins, taking time to make over them.

"How were the springs, ladies?" asked Duncan.

"Quite refreshing," said Enid.

"It was a lovely day for a ride," added Rowena.

Shanley looked at Finley with a look of longing in her eye. "I know I have no right to ask, but may I please hold him?"

"Of course," said Maggie, "but he may get a little fussy because it's time for his supper."

"I don't mind."

Duncan stood and showed her how to hold his head in the crook of her arm and she carefully cradled him, her face beaming. "He is beautiful," she murmured, staring down at him and touching his little nose.

Maggie and Duncan exchanged hopeful looks.

Noni peeked over her shoulder at Finley. "We never get to see babies. They are so— tiny."

"They get bigger," assured Duncan.

Movement at the doorway caught Maggie's eye. It was Logan, standing quietly watching Shanley with an odd, yet peaceful expression upon his face.

Look at the doorway.

Duncan glanced up and followed Logan's gaze.

Would ye look at that?

At about the same time, Finley decided he had waited long enough for his next meal, starting to kick his feet and complain loudly. Shanley attempted, in vain, to bounce him and settle him down.

Logan's tranquil face rapidly shifted to one of concerned annoyance. "Ye are doing it all wrong," he criticized gruffly and stomped across the floor, Finley growing louder with each step. "Give him to me!" holding out his hands.

"No!" exclaimed Shanley, turning her back to him, clutching the baby tighter to her breast. "I just got him."

"Aye and listen to him. He obviously doesn't like ye. I will take my nephew now, if ye don't mind!"

Shanley turned again. "I DO mind."

They continued to argue until Maggie finished up with Steven. "Logan, how about you take Steven from me, and I will take Finley so he can eat? He will be much more content after that."

Logan glared at Shanley but reached for Steven, taking him in his arms and speaking sweetly. Maggie accepted Finley from Shanley, settling him comfortably to her breast to nurse.

"This is how ye hold a baby," whispered Logan in a contemptuous tone, "and they don't like to be bounced so much."

After a little more back and forth bickering, Rozem quieted Shanley, and the women excused themselves to leave the room.

Logan sat down and spoke to Steven in a gentle, soothing manner. "Women are a pain in the arse," he said to the baby. "Avoid them at all costs. Your Uncles Quinn and Gabe are the only men who have figured this out. Ye should listen to them because they are smarter than all of us."

Maggie and Duncan chuckled to themselves.

"Ye seem to take some issue with Shanley," prodded Duncan.

Logan huffed. "That woman would argue with the devil himself. As a matter of fact, the devil would kick her out of Hell just to not have to listen to her mouth."

Maggie winked at Duncan. "I think she is a lovely woman."

"Ye would!" he mumbled. "All of ye blasted women stick together."

14 Chapter Fourteen

The following day was training day, so Maggie, John, Lady Aurnia, Ana, and Shanley stood off to the side to observe the men practicing while the other women took over watching the children. Gabe, Quinn, and Duncan were steadily disarming a line of men, one after the other — the God of Swordsmanship showing off his skills— none of them even breaking a sweat. Maggie smiled at Duncan, who was obviously delighted to have a sword back in his hand.

Shanley paced back and forth with her hands behind her back, shaking her head, watching the actions of another set of men practicing. Unable to control herself any longer, and after watching Logan knock one of his own men on his backside for the third time, she marched over to them and yelled at the man on the ground.

"Ye must conceal your weaknesses! He notices every little thing ye favor, like your wrist for instance. Ye have been injured before, and the stiffness prevents your full movement," shouting at him, "If ye cannot conceal it, ye must find a way to use it to your advantage."

The man looked down at his wrist, confused by her astuteness as everyone else stopped to watch the exchange.

A perturbed Logan pointed his sword in her direction. "I can train my own men, if ye don't mind. I don't need your help."

Shanley stepped closer to him. "Obviously ye do, because if ye were training them the right way, this man wouldn't be on his backside as we speak," she spat.

Logan's face turned red. "My men will not be taking advice on battle fighting from *women*," he bellowed.

The woman narrowed her eyes. "Then your men better get used to being knocked on their arses." She turned on her heel and headed straight for the house.

Throwing his sword to the ground, Logan let out an angry roar to the sky as Duncan came over to him, placing his arm on his brother's shoulder.

"She's right ye know," he pointed out.

Logan growled at Duncan with a murderous look in his eye, then stomped over to the water bucket.

Duncan glanced over at Maggie and winked. *Ah! What a glorious day it is! She's really getting under his skin. So I noticed. I think I will go have a chat with her.*

Maggie found Shanley on the sofa with one of the books from the library in her hands. "Are you alright?" asked Maggie, sitting down next to her.

"Why wouldn't I be?" she replied, curtly.

Maggie shrugged. "It seems Logan has you a bit flustered."

"I don't know what ye mean," she said, burying her face in the opened book, trying to look disinterested in all matters concerning the man.

Reaching over, Maggie took the book from her, flipped it over and put it back in her hands. "It's easier to read if it's right side up."

Shanley clenched her teeth and slammed the book shut. "I don't know why he makes me feel so...so..."

"Passionate?" suggested Maggie. She casually leaned closer to her. "The MacGregor men tend to make you feel all sorts of wondrous things."

Shanley turned to Maggie, an abhorrent look upon her face. "Are ye insinuating..."

"...that you are having feelings for Logan?" she finished. "I am not insinuating it. I am flat out saying it."

"I can think of no good use for that man," she fired back, her face now bright red.

"Oh, I can!" Maggie smirked. "Especially, if he's anything like his brother in bed."

Shanley's eyes flew wide open. "I would never be with him — even if he were the last man in Scotland."

"Never say never," cautioned Maggie rising and starting towards the door. Once she was in the hall, she heard the unmistakable 'thud' of a book hitting the wall with an extreme amount of force behind it.

Maggie chuckled to herself.

Oh yeah! This poor girl has got it bad for Logan!

Maggie waved to Duncan when she rejoined the others.

"What was that all about with Logan and Shanley?" asked Lady Aurnia.

Maggie winked; her mother-in-law's face went from concerned, to surprised, then to excited. Her jaw dropped and she looked over at Logan who was still fuming from their earlier words. Lady Aurnia grabbed Maggie's arm and whispered, "Truly?"

"So it would seem, though neither of them seems to know it yet."

"We need to get to work," she said with a gleam in her eye.

"What are you ladies up to?" asked John, suspicion lacing the words.

Lady Aurnia linked her arm in John's. "Working on getting me some more grandchildren."

"This should be interesting!" Ana grinned, took John's other arm and they all went back into the house. Shanley had left the room, so they settled into the library to strategize. John poured drinks for Maggie, Ana, Lady Aurnia, and one for himself.

"How are we going to get them together?" asked Lady Aurnia.

"Alcohol worked pretty well for me and Duncan," Maggie offered. "We know there is something there, we just need to bring it out and help them see it."

"I can help bring 'something' out," proposed John.

"I don't think that is the best of ideas, at least not until you can control it a little more."

"I have an idea!" Lady Aurnia went to the side door, opened it, and called out to the men. "Alright boys! Dinner will be ready soon. All of ye off to the loch to get cleaned up so your stench doesn't run us away from the table. We will bring some clean clothes down to the water for ye."

Maggie looked at her strangely as she closed the door.

"I think that will be a good job for you and Shanley," her mother-in-law encouraged.

"Oh!" The plan dawned on Maggie. "I think you might be right."

Maggie tapped lightly on Shanley's bedroom door with her free hand.

"Yes, Goddess?" the young woman answered when she opened the door.

"Oh, for goodness sake, it's Maggie, and I was wondering if you could assist me with something."

"Anything!"

Maggie removed a few tartans from across her arm and handed them over. "I need help taking these to the loch. The men are getting cleaned up after training and they require fresh clothing. Would you be so kind?"

"Of course," agreed Shanley and gathered them up. "I want to apologize for my behavior earlier," she said as they walked. "I don't know what got into me."

Maggie looked down and pressed her lips together. "The MacGregor brothers tend to have that effect on women. Duncan and I had a fairly rocky start ourselves."

"Ye and the Dagda? But ye two are perfect for each other."

"We butted heads quite a bit in the beginning, but that's how you know there is something there. You don't feel emotions that strong about someone you don't care about."

"I wouldn't be so sure about that," Shanley muttered.

After they made it outside, something made Maggie glance back towards the house. Lady Aurnia, Ana, and John were at one of the windows looking on curiously.

Maggie smiled when Shanley caught sight of Logan and stopped cold in her tracks; the man was wet and barely covered from the waist down by the water. Maggie also noticed a glint of desire in her eyes as she continued to stare at him.

All the MacGregor men, and Gabe, were busy washing themselves when they reached the shoreline.

"We brought you some clean clothes," called Maggie.

"Did ye now?" Duncan grinned and walked towards her, stopping when the water was just slightly below his waist.

"The last time you walked out of this water like that, you ended up with a wife," reminded Maggie.

"I remember it very well," he smiled and reached for a tartan.

She held it up, just out of his reach, waving it playfully, before pulling it back and then tossing it to Gabe. "I will be curious to see you in that, Gabe," she said with a flirty glance back at Duncan.

Quinn reached under the water, smacking Gabe's behind. "Aye, so will I!"

Gabe came out of the loch and wrapped it around him as Maggie handed one to Quinn, who did the same.

Gabe fiddled with the unfamiliar fabric. "I never thought I would see the day when I was trying to figure out how to put one of these on."

"There's a trick to it." Quinn came over to help him. "I will teach ye— upstairs," he kissed his husband, "and maybe a few other things if ye are interested."

Gabe caressed Quinn's cheek lovingly. "Oh, you know me. I'm all about learning."

Evan and Reade took ones from Shanley and covered themselves as she turned away, nervously.

"Ye can look if ye like. We aren't bashful around here," assured Evan with a grin.

They laughed as Shanley's face went beet red even though her eyes were still averted.

The men on the beach went into the house, leaving only Duncan and Logan, who had gone further out in the water.

Maggie stepped into the loch to her ankles and held up another tartan, just shy of where Duncan stood.

"Oh, ye want to play games, do ye wife?"

"Do I?" she asked flirtingly. "I do like games!"

"Aye, I think ye do!" He walked out of the water, completely nude, grabbed her around the waist and dragged her into the pool.

"Duncan!" she squealed and tried to push him away, but he held firm.

"Now, look at me!" she said, shaking her head and giggling.

"Oh, I am," he growled and kissed her. "Your trousers are all wet now. We are going to have to take them off to dry," he said devilishly and slipped his hands down to cup her bottom.

Maggie sighed and leaned her head against her chest.

As much as I like that idea, I think we should leave Logan and Shanley alone.

Duncan cast a quick look over Maggie's shoulder to see Shanley standing on the beach, a vexed expression on her face, tapping her foot impatiently while holding out the tartan for Logan.

I'm not so sure about that.

Maggie turned around and winced.

Any ideas?

"Alcohol worked for us," he whispered.

She playfully smacked his chest. "That's exactly what I said!"

"I do not have all day," they heard Shanley shout.

"THEN GO, WOMAN!" yelled Logan. "No one asked ye to stand there all day."

"Fine!' She balled up the tartan and threw it into the water. "There's your dry clothing," she called out before turning and stomping back to the house.

"Well, it isn't very dry now, is it?" Logan roared back, snatching it from the top of the water. "Damn women!" he mumbled, shaking it out and wrapping it around his waist before walking out of the loch. He turned toward Maggie and Duncan who were watching the scene unfold. "Can't ye send these women back home already?"

Maggie shrugged. "There here for a reason?" she offered unconvincingly.

Logan huffed and stormed off as Maggie and Duncan looked at each other before bursting into laughter.

Duncan kissed Maggie, letting out a seductive sigh, sliding his hands inside the backside of her trousers. "Well, at least we are alone now," he growled.

"Not quite," she whispered and turned her gaze to the window. She held up her hand and waved to their mothers and John, who were all pressed to the glass, smiling and waving back.

"Oh, for crying out loud," he bemoaned.

Maggie cupped his face and kissed him. "Come on. Let's get ready for dinner. I know you are starving."

"Oh, I'm starving alright," he said, following her out of the water, "but, not for food."

Duncan roguishly chased Maggie back into the house and up to their room to change into dry clothes. Maggie stripped off everything as soon as they were in their room and was pretending to sift through some dresses she had on the chair when Duncan came up behind her, lightly planting kisses on her back.

"They will be waiting for us for dinner," she teased.

"I'll be quick," he whispered and pulled her against him, his urgency apparent.

She turned to face him. "How quick?"

"Let me show ye," he said, sitting down on the edge of the bed.

Maggie climbed atop him, and slowly impaled herself upon him. They both let out satisfied moans as she took him all the way inside and in a matter of minutes, they were both sufficiently satisfied— for the time being anyway, laughing and kissing.

"Was that quick enough?" He tugged at her lip with his teeth.

"Maybe a little too quick," she pouted. "But I will let you redeem yourself later."

"Oh, I definitely will," he said, smacking her behind as she bounced off to get dressed.

They could hear Shanley and Logan arguing as soon as they reached the top of the stairs and the pair continued to disagree all the way through dinner, despite everyone's eager attempt to change the subject.

After the meal, their argument grew even louder. The others quietly departed the dining room to retire to the library, leaving them to continue their quarrel alone.

"Goddess, allow me to apologize," offered Rozem, shame making her pale, pacing the floor, pressing her hand to her face. "Shanley has never acted like this before. She rarely loses her temper and never to this extent. I don't know what has gotten into her."

"It's alright. Why don't you and the rest of the women go check on the children for me? I need to speak with the family alone."

"Of course."

Reade turned to Evan. "Maybe we should go help with the bairns."

Duncan's head snapped up, shooting them puzzled looks.

"Why are ye so surprised, Brother?" asked Evan. "We like being around our nieces and nephews. They are like little people, but even more entertaining."

It was Lady Aurnia's turn to stare at them dumbfoundedly. "Ye know ye can have your own, right?" she pointed out. "It's not that difficult."

As soon as they were gone, Maggie turned to her mother and glanced toward the door. "How sure are you these women were sent here for the reason you think?"

Ana shrugged. "A solid ninety-eight percent."

Maggie looked around at the others. "What are the odds on Logan and Shanley being meant for each other?"

"Oh, they are," assured Duncan, dryly. "They are far too much alike to NOT be meant for one another."

Chewing on her thumb, Maggie looked at Duncan, unsure of herself. "But are we positive?"

Ana let out a deep sigh. "Maggie! Ye are the Queen of the Fae. The answer is already within ye. Just ask yourself."

"What?"

"Darling, ye have the ability to see situations unlike anyone else. Stop thinking like a human and start acting like a Fae. Listen to what's already inside of ye."

"Mommm...I don't know how," she whined, exasperated, plopping down in a chair. "I told you, we are completely lost. None of us know what we are doing. We have been winging it at best, and we get far more wrong than we do right."

"Stop doubting yourself!" Ana took her daughter's hand. "Close your eyes."

Maggie didn't move.

"Margaret!" she said, threateningly in her best 'mom' voice.

Maggie huffed, giving her mother an annoyed look, before straightening up and shutting her eyes. "Pretend there are two of ye. One is your human self, standing in front of the other, your goddess self. Do ye see it?"

She nodded. "My goddess self has a throne and a crown."

Duncan chuckled quietly into his hand as everyone else grinned.

"Alright," continued Ana, "now, still your mind and have your human self ask your goddess self the question."

Maggie sat quietly for a few moments before a slow smile spread across her face. Her eyes popped open. "Is it really that easy?"

"Yes, and before ye know it, ye won't even have to ask. The human and goddess will combine, and your answers will come as naturally as breathing."

Maggie stood and hugged Ana. "Thanks, Mom."

She turned to John, confident. "Hit them with the 'lust-dust', but just a tiny bit. The love is already there, they just need to see it."

"Maggie, are ye sure about unleashing John?" Duncan moved to her side.

"I am. They are meant to be together— there is no doubt in my mind—they just need a little help to see it." Maggie looked to John and motioned with her head.

He started out of the room with everyone else close on their heels, but they stopped at the doorway to the dining room just out of sight.

"No one touch John's ass," whispered Maggie, spreading out her arms protectively behind him, causing Ana and Lady Aurnia to look at each other and shrug.

John held up his hand and started the wave, sending it to them until they were both within the stream. As soon as it hit, the arguing abruptly ceased.

They all watched anxiously to see what would happen next.

It was NOT what they were expecting.

Logan raked everything off the dining room table as Shanley rushed into his arms. Franticly, they kissed, desperately tugging at each other's clothes as Logan lifted her onto the table.

"It worked!" John seemed rather pleased.

"A little too well. You hit them with too much!" scolded Maggie and her eyes flew wide open. "We have to stop them!"

"Why?" demanded an affronted John.

Maggie turned to glare at him. "Because she is a virgin and her first time should not be on a dining room table?"

Lady Aurnia winced. "Oh, ye are right!" and she pushed Duncan inside the room. "Stop them!"

"Me? Why me? I didn't do it. Let John clean up his own mess."

"So Shanley will want to have sex with John, as well? Because it's every woman's dream to have two men take her innocence on the dining room table her first time?"

scoffed Maggie sarcastically and pointed. "GO! Hurry up!"

Duncan turned to see Shanley's skirts already pushed up around her waist— and Logan lifting his tartan.

"Oh, for fuck's sake! Whoa there, brother!" he called out with his hands held up, crossing the room in a hurry.

"GET OUT!" growled Logan.

"Yes, get out!" added Shanley with her lips squished against Logan's face.

Duncan rushed over, inserting himself between the two. "Brother, ye cannot take this woman's maidenhead on the table where we just had dinner."

"Then I will take her upstairs to my bed!" he spat and tried to brush Duncan off, who stood firm.

"Not until ye wed her!" ordered Lady Aurnia, hurrying into the room, not wanting to let a good opportunity pass by.

"Stay out of this, Mother!"

"I will not!" she chastised with her hands on her hips. "This woman is under my roof and my protection. I will not see her — violated— without the benefit of marital vows."

"Then, marry us and leave us be!"

"Is that how you ask a girl to be your wife?" interjected Maggie, personally offended for Shanley as she went to her side and yanked her skirts down. "The woman you love deserves better than that."

Logan covered his face with his hand and looked to the ceiling. "Christ almighty! Can ye all just go away?"

Quinn and Gabe walked over to join them.

"Maggie is right," fussed Quinn. "Ask the lass the right way. She may not *want* to marry ye?"

"On one knee," added Gabe and pointed at the floor, "like a true gentleman. After all, a lady only gets proposed to once."

Ana and John hung by the doorway, both thoroughly enjoying the show.

"Fine! I will ask her, and then I will take her upstairs," he said through gritted teeth.

"That sounds good to me," encouraged an impatient Shanley.

"Nay, ye will not," scolded Lady Aurnia. "Ye will take her on your wedding night the way ye are supposed to or ye will not at all."

"Maggie and Duncan didn't wait until theirs," he argued.

"But I was not a virgin," clarified Maggie and scrunched up her face. "I'm afraid the horse was already long out of the gate on that one."

John turned to lean his forehead against the wall, his laughter now uncontrollable.

"I am not waiting!" shouted Logan.

"We could marry ye tonight with a Fae ceremony," suggested Lady Aurnia, innocence beaming from her face.

"Fine!" Logan straightened up and raked his hands through his hair.

"You need to ask her," nudged Maggie and pointed to Shanley, who had lain back on the table with her hands interlocked behind her head staring up at the ceiling while the debate over her virtue continued.

Logan closed his eyes and blew out a deep breath. He pushed Duncan aside, took Shanley's hands and pulled her up, before dropping to one knee.

"Will ye marry me this very night?" he asked, very sweetly with a look of love on his face, "so my family will go away and leave us in peace to our own business."

"Yes, I will," she accepted before taking his face in her hands and greedily kissing him.

They spent the rest of the day getting Shanley ready for her wedding at midnight. Lady Aurnia located a somewhat suitable, but plain, gown and they all helped her to prepare.

Maggie, Lady Aurnia, and Ana were helping Shanley while the rest of the women were preparing the chamber for the ceremony.

"Are ye nervous?" asked Lady Aurnia.

"I am about the wedding night," replied Shanley, truthfully.

"Ye will be fine!" Ana smiled reassuringly.

"What will it be like?"

"If he's anything like his brother, you won't be able to walk tomorrow," mumbled Maggie behind her hand.

Ana's face showed her approval.

"Like father, like son," murmured Lady Aurnia holding up her own hand and nudging Maggie with a sly wink.

A knock at the door interrupted them. "It's Duncan."

Maggie walked over and cracked it open. "Hello, my love."

"Hello yourself," he said in a low, sexy voice and kissed her. "Logan wishes to speak with ye."

"With me? Why?"

Duncan glanced warily over at Shanley. "He has a few questions he was hoping ye could answer." Maggie seemed bewildered, so he clarified with a mental message.

About virgins.

"Oh, for crying out loud!" she exclaimed. "Seriously? He's asking me?"

Everyone stopped what they were doing to look at her.

Duncan cleared his throat and she remembered the said 'virgin' in the room. She turned. "I will be back shortly." Picking up a bottle of whisky from the table, she handed it to Shanley and pointed to her mother and mother-in-law. "Drink lots of this and heed their advice. You will be fine."

Offering a warm smile as she went, she followed Duncan into Logan's room where the sounds of a lively discussion had carried out into the hall.

"You can't be brisk or crude about it," John was saying. "You have to take your time— be gentle and understanding or neither one of you are going to have a good night."

"I say just get it over with," professed Reade. "The sooner the better."

"Absolutely not!" disparaged Gabe. "Just remember, if you traumatize her, she will never let you touch her again and forty or fifty years is a long time to sleep in a frigid bed."

Maggie stood in the doorway, eyeing the group as she listened to the conversation, hardly believing what she was hearing. "Oh dear God in Heaven! Is this what men talk about on their wedding day?" She took John's glass of whisky from his hand. "You wanted to see me?"

"Aye!" Logan welcomed her in. "I need your advice on how to handle a virgin."

Maggie rubbed the bridge of her nose and screwed up her face. "Why are you asking *me*?"

"Well, Gabe said ye were the expert on virgins."

Maggie turned to glare at Gabe, who was shaking with laughter while holding up his hands protectively, preparing himself for retribution.

"Really?" she asked wryly.

"Well, you were one at one time," he snickered, "weren't you? And you *have* been the undoing of at least one man I know of."

Maggie slapped his chest with her hand.

"Technically, I won't be officially deflowered for a couple of centuries," she snarked dryly and looked to the others. "Why aren't any of you giving him advice?"

Duncan stepped behind her and kissed her shoulder. "Because none of us have experience in that regard."

Maggie turned to Duncan. "You don't? Not one? Ever?"

"Nay, my love. I always preferred older women — before I met ye, of course," he clarified.

Maggie turned back around. "None of you either?"

They all stared blankly down at the floor.

"Gabe, Penny was one when you were married, wasn't she?"

"She was," he nodded, "but, considering I am married to a man now, I may not be the best one to offer guidance," he pointed out and took a swig of whisky.

She looked to John. "Surely, you have, of all people."

"Without getting into details, let's just say I prefer women who know exactly what they are doing, and leave it at that."

"Are ye going to help me or not?" pleaded Logan. "Or do I need to ask Mother?"

"Nay!" the MacGregor men all shouted simultaneously.

Maggie hung her head. "What do you want to know?"

Logan waved his glass around in the air. "I just want to know how to please her without causing her pain. She hasn't so much as been around a man, much less done anything else. I don't want to frighten her off."

Maggie noticed a whiskey bottle on the table. "Hand me that, Quinn." She took it from him and downed half of it in one gulp.

Duncan attempted to wrest the bottle from her. "Maybe I should hold on to this."

She held it tight to her chest. "Wedding night advice on virgins always requires alcohol."

"She would know!" quipped Gabe.

"Look, just take your time, be attentive, and take your cues from her. She will let you know what she likes and, if you are doing things right, she won't even notice, or care, about the little bit of pain that goes with it. Besides, I gave her plenty of whisky, so she will be fine." Maggie held up her hand. "Oh, for a happy marriage in general— resist the urge to argue with her. Just say, 'yes dear' to everything. You will be much better off."

"That sounds like the best advice ye will ever get, Brother," agreed Duncan and laughed.

Logan nodded. "Thank ye, Maggie."

"You're welcome," she said and left the room.

Maggie went downstairs to grab more whisky, and found Rozem, Enid, Noni, and Rowena all sitting in the library, talking to each other.

"Everything ready?" she asked on her way to the liquor cabinet.

"Aye," said Noni without looking up. "The altar has been prepared for the ceremony."

Maggie noticed they all seemed a little down, so she picked up two bottles and moved to join them. "Why is everyone so glum? Aren't you happy for Shanley?"

"We are very happy for her. This is what she genuinely wants," answered Enid. "We are just wondering what will become of us. Ye have said we are not to worship ye, but that is all we know. Shanley is taking a husband, but we don't know what to do with ourselves."

Rowena wrung her hands. "We don't even have a home anymore."

Maggie sat down. "What do you *want* to do?"

Noni shook her head. "That's the problem— we don't know."

"How old are you?" Maggie asked her.

"Rowena and I are both sixteen."

Maggie leaned forward. "It's perfectly normal that you don't know what you want to do. You are still young, and you should be having some fun."

Rozem was noticeably quiet.

"Rozem? Is there something you would like to do?"

The woman nodded and looked at the floor. "The past few days with your babies have made me selfishly want a family of my own."

Enid took Rozem's hand and whispered, "If ye are selfish, sister, then so am I, because I want the same thing."

"That is not selfish, and if it is what you want, then do it."

"We would need to fall in love for that," pointed out Enid.

Maggie pulled out the cork of the whisky bottle, took a big sip straight from it, and leaned back in the chair. "Lucky for you, I know of two single MacGregor brothers whose mother would love for them to fall in love, take wives, and have enormous families. You just need to convince them of it."

Rozem and Enid exchanged excited looks.

"How do we do that?" asked Rozem.

Maggie took another swig. "You had better leave that to me. Let me see what I can do." She waved the bottle in the air. "Why don't all of you go spend some time with Shanley? I am sure she could use the support from her sisters right about now."

The women eagerly departed as Maggie polished off the bottle.

Great! Now I must convince two more MacGregor men they need wives they don't want.

Duncan found Maggie an hour, and a bottle and a half of whisky, later.

"Here ye are," he said as he came up behind her and kissed the top of her head. "What are ye doing?"

"Trying to figure out how to play matchmaker," she replied, staring straight ahead, balancing the partially filled bottle on her leg.

He pulled up a chair next to her. "Who are we trying to marry off *this* time?"

"Rozem and Enid have decided they want husbands as well, and I was thinking, given all we have learned, Reade and Evan might be the perfect candidates."

"Do ye now?" Duncan chuckled. "Do my brothers happen to know?"

She rolled her eyes. "Of course not! The men are always the last to know. Besides, after some internal meditating, I am convinced Finn matched them as couples just like he did Logan and Shanley, and you and I— they just need to figure it out for themselves."

"Why don't ye just let things happen naturally?" He took the whisky bottle and had a drink for himself.

"You know your brothers — that will take forever."

He sighed. "Ye might be right. What's your plan?"

Maggie shrugged. "I dunno. I was just going to wing it."

"Oh good! What can possibly go wrong?"

A few minutes before the ceremony, Maggie, Lady Aurnia, and Ana were looking over the altar room.

"I think everything is ready," said Maggie, glancing around one final time.

"There is just one more thing!" Lady Aurnia handed Maggie a book.

Maggie held it up. "What's this?"

Lady Aurnia and Ana exchanged a smile.

"We discussed it and decided the Queen of the Fae should conduct this ceremony," proclaimed her mother-in-law.

"Me?" asked Maggie, taken aback. "Why me?"

"Yes, ye!" said her mother. "Ye are Fae royalty and a blessing from ye will seal the union unlike anything else."

Maggie looked down, before setting the book on the table. "I don't know, Mom. I don't feel much like a Fae queen."

"Ye will, sweetheart. These things just take time. Now, ye should put on something more appropriate for this wedding."

Maggie looked down at her gown. "What's wrong with this? I didn't really bring much else to wear."

"Maggie! Stop acting like a human!"

She put her hands on her hips. "Mom! It's kind of the only way I know how to act."

"Oh right, I keep forgetting." Ana took her daughter by the shoulders. "Just imagine yourself in something else, and that is what ye will be wearing."

"Just like that?" asked Maggie. "It's that easy?"

"Hello? Ye are the Queen of the Fae— a magical being who can wish things up." Ana waved her hands up and down her own body. "Case in point, your mother from the future?"

"Oh, right! I keep forgetting," she replied sarcastically. "So, what do I pick?"

Ana thought for a moment. "Something ethereal, befitting a queen."

"Like 'Freddy Mercury' Queen or 'Beyonce' Queen?"

Ana rolled her eyes. "Like a Celtic Queen! Something gold, shimmery, and sexy. Think of what Duncan would like."

"He prefers me naked," she mumbled.

"It's true!" Lady Aurnia nodded in agreement.

Ana smirked. "Well, give him something to look forward to taking off."

"Excellent idea!" Lady Aurnia said to Ana. "Maybe we will get some more grandchildren out of it."

"Oh, that would be nice," agreed Ana, putting and arm around Lady Aurnia's shoulder, the two ladies having become close over their short time together.

Maggie wagged her index finger. "Don't get your hopes up. You two have five children from me and Duncan. Consider our 'grandbaby making' obligations fulfilled."

The two grandmothers both made faces to express their disappointment.

"Alright!" Maggie sighed and put her fingers to her temples, rubbing them as she tried to pull something together in her head. She closed her eyes and imagined herself in a dark gold, body-hugging dress that had a see-through shimmery overlay giving it a more flowy look. She felt the fabric form around her body before opening her eyes and looking down. "Holy crap! It worked!" She looked up. "How's this?" she asked, holding her arms out in her best model pose.

"It's beautiful!" said Lady Aurnia, walking around Maggie for a better look, pulling the fabric out to rub it between her fingers.

"Very nice, Maggie!" cheered her mother. "Now, more importantly, let me see the shoes."

Maggie smiled, held up her index finger in a 'wait' motion, closed her eyes and imagined herself in a pair of 4-inch strappy gold-glitter stilettos. She opened her eyes and pulled up the hem of her dress to show them off.

"Impressive!" marveled her mother.

"Mom, I can't believe it," she said excitedly, "I can wish up jeans and t-shirts anytime I want. Do you have any idea how much I have missed old, comfy t-shirts?"

"Of all the gorgeous things ye can come up with, that's what ye want?"

Maggie rolled her eyes. "Mom! You have no idea how uncomfortable eighteenth-century gowns are, especially in Virginia in July. Seriously, why do women willingly wear this stuff? Especially when air conditioning hasn't even been invented."

"Well, just be careful, dear. You don't need to bring too much attention to yourself," warned her mother.

"Wait! Can I do this for others?" she asked, suddenly.

"Yes, ye can since ye have Father's powers."

"Oh!" Maggie smiled as she closed her eyes and wished her mother and Lady Aurnia into two beautiful new modern gowns.

They each looked down, then at one another, and made over each other like schoolgirls.

"Oh my!" exclaimed Lady Aurnia, holding out her arms. "I have never felt anything so wonderful— and light."

"Ye always did have magnificent taste, sweetheart," complimented Ana.

Maggie looked up the staircase. "I think we should give Shanley a little 'something, something' special for her wedding day and her bridesmaids some dresses that will turn a few MacGregor men's heads."

"I like that idea!" encouraged Lady Aurnia.

Maggie took them both by the hands and shimmered them into the bride's chambers.

A short time later, Maggie sent a message to Duncan. *Get Logan and the rest of the men down to the chamber. We will be along shortly.*

Aye, my love.

Once the men were in place, Maggie shimmered into her spot as officiant of the ceremony.

Duncan's eyes went wide, his face lighting up when he saw her in the dress.

Everyone else stopped to admire her as well.

"My God!" he exclaimed as he went to her side, took her hand, and kissed her cheek. "Ye look — well, there are no words."

Maggie cupped his face and kissed him on the lips. "I am just embracing my 'inner goddess'."

"I must say, I like the looks of her, and I can't wait to get this off of ye," he whispered, caressing her behind.

"And I am looking forward to it."

Lady Aurnia and Ana were the next to come in; the men were delighted to see them all dressed up. The women of the order followed, and Reade and Evan both developed big, stupid smiles on their faces when they caught sight of Rozem and Enid in long, flowy empire dresses that put all their best 'assets' on full display. Judging by their reactions, Maggie would be performing two more ceremonies not long after this one.

Shanley appeared in the doorway, in a stunning modern mermaid style gown, clinging perfectly in all the right places. Logan only had eyes for her, and it was apparent to everyone in the room, the two were indeed meant for one another.

Maggie conducted the ceremony, and everyone cheered as the bride and groom kissed.

As soon as the ritual was over, Logan and Shanley hastily excused themselves, and headed straight upstairs to his bedchamber, barely able to contain themselves to make it that far. Everyone else stayed behind to celebrate; the alcohol flowed freely.

Reade and Rozem were getting to know each other better as were Evan and Enid.

Noni and Rowena decided to go up and check on the children, claiming to just want to watch them sleep, both having fallen head over heels in love with the babies.

"You look pretty spectacular there," Gabe came over to kiss Maggie on the cheek.

"I do, don't I?" she grinned, "It's nice to be dressed up in something so pretty and flowy for a change."

"You really do look like someone who stepped straight out of a dream," marveled John, looking her up and down.

Duncan cleared his throat while giving John a warning look, who just grinned in response.

"That dress only needs one more thing," called her mother, who seemed to be searching for one of the Fae items on the wall.

"What are ye looking for?" questioned Quinn. "Perhaps I can help ye find it."

Ana sighed. "There should be a small gold chest here somewhere, but I don't see it."

"The one engraved with the lovely flowers?" asked Lady Aurnia.

"Yes! That's the one!"

Lady Aurnia pointed. "It's in the small alcove on the side wall. Duncan, would ye get it for her, please?"

Duncan set down his drink. "Certainly." He returned with it and placed it on the table.

"Yes!" Ana's face lit up. She touched it gingerly before opening it.

It turned out to be a rather large jewelry box. Ana pulled out two gold arm cuffs engraved with the same pattern on her shield. She put one on each of Maggie's upper arms. "As the Fae Queen, ye should always be dripping in gorgeous things."

Maggie ran her fingers over them, admiring the workmanship. "Mom, these are beautiful!"

"They were my favorites," she said and took a step back for a better look, "but, I must admit, they look far better on ye than they ever did on me."

"I can't take these!" Maggie started to take them off.

Ana prevented her, embracing her daughter. "Ye can, and ye will. They belonged to my mother, the original queen, and now they belong to ye, along with everything else in this box."

"Why *did* the original queen leave?" inquired a curious John.

"Living forever gets old. For the first few centuries, it's interesting enough to observe mankind, and the next few centuries, ye make it more intriguing by joining in with them, meddling in their affairs," she smirked, "but after a while, it becomes tedious. Father and I were never bored because we were always the two who were closest to mankind. We would interact, even live with them, something the others just didn't bother with after a while, but Mother never really cared for mortals as much as the rest of us and, before long, she grew tired of Father's shenanigans more than anything else."

"Like what?" asked Maggie.

Ana winced. "Father would always take the side of mankind when they quarreled, which was quite often, mostly because of his fondness for human women. His appetite was much like John's," she said, winking at him, "and my mother may have been Fae, but she was also a very jealous wife. The original continental land break— one of their first big arguments."

Duncan turned to Maggie. "I'm glad we don't argue."

"They would have their little squabbles, then make up and tolerate each other for a while, before the next big blow up rolled around. However, the last one they had was over a human woman Mother found out about. In that case, Father had fallen deeply in love with her, and even took a mortal form to live a human lifetime with her. They had been together for a few years and had two children. When Mother found out, she was so angry, she appeared at their home and killed his lover, along with their children in front of him. She also cast a spell preventing him from bringing them back. Father was beside himself and disappeared for a great long while. Mother brushed it off and waited for him to return to her so they could makeup as they always did, but he never came back. When she realized he was truly finished with her— that is when she decided to take the eternal slumber."

"Wow!" said Maggie softly, looking at Duncan as he took her in his arms.

"That will never happen to us, my love," he assured and kissed the side of her head.

"I hope not!"

Ana smiled at their display of affection. "No, I don't believe it will." She closed the chest. "At any rate, this is all yours now."

"Mom, it's your stuff. Don't you want to keep it?"

She touched Maggie's face. "My dear, I can't take it with me when I go."

"Go? Where are you going?" asked Maggie nervously.

"When I die," she clarified.

"Oh!" Maggie said softly and shook her head. "But you have Fae blood, so I can make you immortal again. You can stay here with us."

"Ye could, but then I wouldn't get to be with your father in the next life, and the thought of never being with him again is just not an option for me. I will happily go when my time in this world is done."

Maggie leaned against Duncan. "I know the feeling."

"But I am not going anywhere anytime soon," said Ana. "Aren't we supposed to be celebrating anyway?" She changed the subject in an attempt to lighten the mood.

"Indeed!" agreed John, handing Ana a fresh glass.

The next two hours were filled with lively merriment. Once Duncan decided he could stand it no more, he leaned over and whispered to Maggie, "Time to get that dress off ye."

"It is, isn't it?" she teased and wrapped her arms around his neck, staring into his eyes. "Good night all," she called, never breaking her gaze, and shimmered them to their bedroom so they could be alone.

Duncan bit his lip as he looked her up and down. "Have I mentioned how beautiful ye look tonight?"

"Oh, you like this old thing, do you?"

"Indeed, I do! It shows off all the curves I love so dearly. Now, exactly *how* do I get it off?"

Maggie turned around and held up her hair. "That's the great part." She reached around and pointed to the zipper. He took the tab, fiddled with it until he figured out how it worked, and pulled it all the way down until the dress fell away into a pool on the floor at her feet.

Duncan slipped his hands around her waist. "That is ingenious." He kissed the back of her neck and took notice of the bra and lace panties. "What are these?"

Maggie turned back around so he could get a better look. "This is called a 'bra', and you will be seeing more of them since I am able to wish them up now. It keeps me from being so 'jiggly'," she giggled as she shook her shoulders.

"As much as I adore the 'jiggle'," he teased, "I find myself fond of this as well." He traced the top of the very low-cut bra with his finger before replacing it with his lips. He slipped his hands down. "And this?"

"Oh! These are called 'panties' and they are what women wear instead of shifts."

"I have to say, I think I will like the future." He reached around, cupped her buttocks, and lifted her onto the bed.

That's when he noticed her shoes. He looked closer, fascinated and amused. He slipped one off and examined it. "Interesting!" he said as he tossed it unceremoniously over his shoulder and onto the floor.

"The pole dancers wear them," she informed him.

"Oh," he said and removed the other, tossing that one over his other shoulder, before crawling on top of her. "Well, if ye think ye are getting me all worked up without finishing the 'job', ye have another thing coming."

She pulled his face to hers. "I wouldn't dream of doing that."

The following morning, Maggie found Ana and Lady Aurnia in the library enjoying some time with Steven and Finley.

"Here they are," she said as she came in. "It's almost their breakfast time."

Lady Aurnia bounced Steven on her knee. "We stole them away early."

"Where are the triplets?"

"Noni and Rowena took them outside with Alastair and Kat to play," replied Ana.

"They are really good with them, aren't they?" asked Maggie, undoing her top.

"Aye, they are," said Lady Aurnia and handed her Steven, who was starting to fuss. "Especially since they have never been around wee ones before."

"Anyone seen the newlyweds this morning?"

"Did ye expect to?" Lady Aurnia giggled.

"Not if Logan is anything like Duncan!" Maggie laughed.

The ladies looked up when Noni and Rowena came into the room.

"Good morning," said Maggie. "I thought you were with the children."

Noni and Rowena came to sit down looking resentful.

"Their uncles stole them away from us," complained Noni, her face full of disappointment. She and Rowena's expressions suddenly shifted, and they exchanged a nervous look. "But it gives us a chance to speak with ye."

"About what?"

"Well," Rowena fiddled her thumbs, "we were wondering if ye might need some help with the babies—in America."

Noni nodded. "Ye asked what we would like to do, and we would like to stay with your family and help ye, if that is agreeable to ye. Since Rozem and Enid want to marry, it would not be fitting for us to remain here. We really have nowhere else to go."

"You want to come with us and become nannies for the children?"

"Ye know we would be very loyal and discreet," added Rowena. "They are special, and it may be wise to have someone to watch over them who knows exactly who and what they are, especially as they get older."

Maggie scratched her forehead. "I am not going to lie; we could use the help and they are already doing things that are not normal. So far, we have been able to cover, but it is only a matter of time until someone notices."

"It would be prudent to have someone around who would not be fazed by those strange things as they get older," agreed Ana.

Maggie eyed the young women, seeing in their faces how much they wanted to go. "Let me speak with Duncan, but I don't see why not."

"Thank ye, Goddess— I mean, Maggie," corrected Rowena excitedly.

"Aye, thank ye!" Noni smiled, relieved. "Ye will not regret this."

15 Chapter Fifteen

Two weeks later, Rozem and Reade, and Enid and Evan were married in a double ceremony. A week after that, they all shimmered back home with two new additions — Rowena and Noni.

Hettie immediately took a liking to the girls, taking them under her wing, and teaching them everything she knew. They, in turn, fell in love with Hettie, and she became a mother figure to them both.

True to their word, Maggie and everyone on the estate stayed to themselves during the next few months and as far away from the war as they could.

In October of the same year, General Washington would take Maggie's words to heart, putting all he had into Yorktown, making it the last major battle of the Revolutionary War. On October 19, 1781, the surrender ceremony would occur, even though the formal end of the war would not come until the signing of the Treaty of Paris in 1783.

Shortly after they returned from Scotland, one evening after the children were in bed, Maggie gathered the Fae gods and her mother in the collection room for a meeting.

"There is something we need to discuss." She paced in front of the fireplace. "Now that Duncan's brothers have taken wives and, those wives have Fae blood, we need to consider making them the offer of becoming gods and goddesses."

They all sat silent.

"I know we didn't really have any say in the matter of being turned," she continued, "but they do and, if I am not mistaken, their children will have abilities just like ours."

Ana nodded. "Aye, they will, but their children will only become gods and goddesses if ye choose to turn them, just like yours."

"Aren't we putting the cart before the horse?" asked Quinn. "Maybe we should let them *HAVE* children first."

"Yes, but this is a decision we cannot take lightly," said Maggie, sitting on the arm of Duncan's chair.

"Technically, your mother can be turned as well," John pointed out to Quinn and Duncan.

"That's not the only issue," fretted Maggie. "There is the matter of the collection in Scotland and the stronghold, but also, we cannot stay here for the next several hundred years. People will start to notice we are not aging. We need somewhere we can go to, and live for a period of time, before we come back as our descendants. If we have other gods in Scotland, we can simply swap houses for a few years, so the others will have somewhere to go, as well, while the collections are being watched over."

"In addition, there is one more thing to keep in mind," added Ana. "Everyone in this room, and the children upstairs, are destined to be major gods and goddesses. If ye turn the brothers in Scotland and their wives, they will be minor ones and not have the strength and abilities that all of ye do. Neither will their children. It's just something to remember."

Duncan took her hand. "I agree with Quinn. I think we should wait a bit and get a handle on this ourselves before we start turning others. We have some time." He pointed at John. "After all, we might end up with someone who can't control themselves like this one over here."

John stroked his chin and smirked. "My dear Duncan, there has never been, nor will there ever be, another like me."

Everyone burst into laughter.

"Besides," said John, "I am getting things under control. Ana has been graciously working with me, and I am developing a better handle on things, so to speak."

"You have, Mom?" asked Maggie, surprised.

"Aye! I figure I might as well be useful while I am around, and John is right, he is getting there. It just takes some practice."

"So, we wait and see what happens with the family in Scotland," declared Maggie.

"Since we are bringing up issues," said Quinn, "Gabe and I discreetly shimmered into town this morning. Williamsburg is overrun with soldiers and the wounded. We found Wyatt tending them, and he, along with the other surgeons, are vastly overwhelmed."

"Not to mention the fact the town is running short on everything, especially food," added Gabe. "I think we need to step in."

"Absolutely!" agreed Maggie wholeheartedly. "Pull whatever stores we can manage from here and send Captain Russell with the ships to gather from other places. I will start to make some trips out to restore parts of the land that have been damaged. Winter in Williamsburg is going to be hard on the citizens with the soldiers here."

"They need more than that!" Quinn looked down at his hands. "I want to go to the hospital and help. I have the ability to heal the sick and wounded just by touching them, and I can't stand by and do nothing when so many are suffering."

"But ye can't," disagreed Duncan. "We cannot draw attention to ourselves here, and if everyone suddenly makes a miraculous recovery—"

"Yes, but what good is being Fae if we can't help out a little?" Maggie looked to Quinn. "Do what you can that does not draw attention, and let the medicines do the work on the others. Just be discreet. We cannot have people suspecting anything out of the ordinary."

"Understood!" Quinn appeared grateful for the support.

"Alright then," conceded Duncan, "we can start gathering things in the morning."

Maggie leaned against him. "And I will go down and check with Mingan to make sure they don't need anything."

"I can do that," offered John.

"I think you should give it a little more time," replied Maggie. "Let the men get laid a few more times so their memories fade just a bit."

Ana looked back and forth between them, baffled. "What on Earth?"

"John ruffled a few feathers with the men in the tribe," answered Duncan, and took a sip of his whisky. "Frustration is a terrible thing."

"Oh, I see!" Ana smirked. "I will go with ye," she said to Maggie. "I would like to meet them after all ye have told me about them."

The following morning, Maggie and Ana rode Onyx together to the tribe.

Ana patted his neck. "I have missed our rides, old friend."

He whinnied happily in response.

"You know, you two can go out anytime you want, Mom."

"I know, I just feel like I might be overstepping a bit. After all, I am not 'Danu' anymore."

Maggie slipped her arms around her mother's waist from behind and laid her cheek against her back. "No, you are even better. You're my mom."

"Oh, sweetie! I am so glad to have ye back!" She pulled Maggie's arms tighter around her.

"So, tell me about ye and John," said Ana out of the blue.

"Tell you what?" asked Maggie innocently.

"Ye two have slept together." A statement, not a question.

Maggie scrunched up her nose and made a face her mother could not see. "That was a long time ago, before I met Duncan," she explained. "He helped me through a difficult time when I lost Ben and the baby I was carrying."

Ana turned her head and looked over her shoulder. "That man is in love with ye, Maggie."

"He knows we can only be friends," said Maggie softly. "I will never want another man over Duncan."

"Then, stop keeping him on a leash like a little puppy dog."

"What do you mean?" she asked, affronted. "John is with one or twelve women every time I turn around. He isn't hard up for comfort, and it's not like he tries to hide it."

Ana looked ahead. "Because he sees it gets to ye, and he knows it would not get to ye, if ye didn't have feelings for him. That, and as a bonus, it chaps Duncan's arse."

Maggie closed her eyes. "I do love John, Mom, but in a much different way than I do Duncan."

"Then stop giving him a hard time for being with other women, so that he can move on with his life."

"I don't mind him being with another woman, it's just that there are so many of them."

"Maggie, it is not your place to judge his decisions and as long as he sees it bothers ye, he will continue to hold out hope. Besides, he IS the God of Sex and Lust — what do ye expect? It IS what he does by nature."

Maggie sighed. "I suppose you are right. I guess I thought maybe he would settle down a bit when I granted him fertility."

"Ye did what?" exclaimed Ana, astonished.

"He thought he was sterile, so he came to me and asked me to do it for him. I thought maybe he had someone special in mind, and that maybe he really wanted to be a father."

"Or, maybe he thought being a father, the way Duncan is, would make him more appealing to ye," suggested Ana.

"No, he wouldn't— would he?"

Ana shrugged. "Who knows for certain? Men in love lose their minds and do strange things."

Maggie shook her head. "At any rate, he was staying with the tribe at the time when Mingan was begging for help repopulating, and so were the women for that matter, so I figured, what could it hurt?"

"Ye might want to consider trying to find him some condoms," replied Ana, dryly.

"Wait! Are they a thing yet?" asked Maggie, suddenly interested in the answer.

"I don't know. Ye are asking the wrong one."

Maggie looked up from the trail when the tribe came into view. "You know what, now I am just downright curious. I am going to have to find out the answer to that question."

As they rode into the village, the children came running out and greeted them as they dismounted.

Ana smiled, watching them all come to hug Maggie.

"Hello, Maggie," called Mingan, as he approached, waving.

"Hello, Mingan! It's good to see you. Come meet my mother, Ana Bishop. Mom, this is Mingan, the chief here."

Mingan's face lit up. "It is nice to meet the woman who brought such a good soul into this world."

"It is a pleasure to meet the leader of such a wonderful group of people. Maggie has told me all about ye."

They walked as Maggie showed her mother around.

"What brings you out?" Mingan asked.

"We are sending supplies into town for our neighbors who are in need because of the war, but we want to make sure you are well stocked for the winter before we do."

Mingan waved his hand. "Our bounty was plentiful thanks to you. We have more than enough."

"Good!"

Mingan scratched his chin. "How is John?"

"He is well."

"I miss having him around to talk to."

Maggie cringed. "Have things calmed down any?"

"Yes, and whatever ill will is left will be forgiven when the babies are born."

"Babies?" asked Ana.

"Yes. Maggie's blessing, along with John's short time here, now has three previously barren women with child. Our tribe has been truly blessed by Spirit."

Maggie stopped. "Three?" she exclaimed. "John got three women pregnant?"

Mingan grinned. "Yes, and the women could not be more pleased. Will you tell him the good news?"

"Oh, I will tell him alright," grumbled Maggie.

They visited for a little while longer before going back home.

That afternoon, Maggie and Ana were having drinks in the drawing room when the men returned.

"Everything is all packed up and ready to go," proclaimed Duncan and came over to kiss her.

"What are you ladies up to?" asked Gabe.

Maggie looked down at her drink. "We were trying to figure out something and maybe one of you will know the answer."

"What is it?" asked John, pouring a drink and taking a sip.

Maggie narrowed her eyes at John. "Are condoms a thing yet?"

John nearly spat out his whisky.

"Condoms?" questioned Duncan.

"Yeah, although they may be called something else now."

"No, that's what they are called," answered Gabe, the corners of his mouth twitching up.

Quinn looked at him strangely.

"Sheaths for— you know."

"Oh!" acknowledged Quinn when he realized what he meant.

"Ye mean the ones they sell at the whorehouses?" inquired Duncan.

Maggie blinked her eyes at her husband. "How would you know about them?"

Duncan flinched. "So I have heard— from Reade and Evan," he mumbled and downed his drink, a guarded look on his face.

"There is actually a shop in London that sells them for disease prevention. From what I understand, they do a fine job of custom making them." said Gabe.

"Custom made?" Ana giggled. "Ye mean, they actually measure and *fit* them?" She and Maggie looked at each other and burst into laughter.

"Wait!" said Maggie holding up her hand, at a loss. "They fit them for only one use?"

"One use?" asked Gabe, confused. "No! You get many uses out of one."

"Ye reuse them?" questioned Ana, incredulously. "In the future, ye use one and throw it away."

"Yuck!" Maggie gasped. "Are they washable, at least?"

Ana leaned back, her hands to her stomach, laughing even harder. "I wonder what the setting on the washer for that is!"

Maggie covered her face, tee-heeing. "Oh, we are going to London and finding this shop." Maggie now laughed so hard she had to wipe tears from her eyes.

"Why do *ye* want to know?" demanded Duncan, "Because, if ye think I am using one, think again!"

"Oh no!" She pointed with her finger. "Not you, but I think John needs to pay them a little visit to make a purchase."

"Me?" he asked and sat down. "Why in the world would I do something like that?"

"Well, considering you already have THREE babies on the way."

John's face paled and he froze, paused mid-sip. Maggie stood and placed her hand on his shoulder.

"Congratulations! You successfully knocked up three women at the tribe."

John sat dumbfounded and paralyzed, as Duncan, Gabe, and Quinn began to chuckle, toning it down when they saw John's true reaction.

"You are going to make a wonderful father," said Gabe reassuringly.

"Aye, ye will," added Duncan. "I could not be any happier for ye. Sleep while ye can and, remember, they vomit on everything."

"Are— you — certain?" stuttered John to Maggie.

"Mingan confirmed it. That is what happens when you ask the Goddess of Fertility for help, you know?" she scolded.

"You— you— you— should have known better than to give me that," he argued.

"You— you— you—," she parroted, wagging her finger, "are a grown man and I have no say over who you choose to sleep with," she stated firmly. "Who you are with is your own business, and it is not my place to tell you what you should and shouldn't do." She squeezed his shoulder and looked over at her mom, who gave her an 'I'm proud of ye' look.

"What am I supposed to do?" he asked.

"I think ye have already done it," teased Quinn.

"John," Duncan was serious, "children are a gift and ye should consider yourself fortunate to be blessed with them. Once ye get used to the idea, ye will see that."

"Three!" he whispered. "Three?"

"Look at it this way," Gabe could hardly keep a straight face, "you have almost caught up with Maggie and Duncan."

"Good point!" Maggie grinned. "Now the real question is— are you going to try to outdo us?"

John shook his head vigorously back and forth before he looked up at Gabe. "Where did you say that shop was located?"

Maggie was in bed waiting for Duncan later that night.

"How's John?" she asked, propped up on her elbow watching him undress.

"Better, I think. I sat down with him and we had a long talk about fatherhood. He will be fine once the shock wears off and he gets used to the idea."

"Thank you for talking to him."

Duncan laid his belt on the nightstand. "I am curious about one thing."

"Condoms in the future?" she chuckled.

"Make that two things," he corrected. "The first one being — why did ye ask *me* to talk to John? Usually ye do that."

Maggie chewed on her lip. "Two reasons. The first one being, that I can think of no one better than you to give him advice. You are the most amazing father that ever was and, if John is even half the father you are, he will be fine."

"And the other reason?" he asked as he removed the rest of his clothes.

Maggie sighed. "Mom pointed out something to me today. I may be unintentionally keeping John from finding someone to be with. I just want to make sure he has the chance to find the one to make him as happy as you do me. I don't want to hold him back."

Duncan smiled and pushed back the covers to slip into bed. "I am very happy to hear ye say that." He kissed her and stretched out. Biting his lip, he turned on his side to face her smiling a wicked smile.

"Something on your mind?" she asked, playfully.

"Aye, actually," he said, rolling over on top of her, pushing himself up on his knees, straddling her. "A little payback."

"For what?"

"For binding my hands during that 'lap dance'. I thought I might return the favor." He pulled his belt off the table, pushed her arms above her head, and hooked them in the belt loop as she giggled.

"Oh! Lucky me!"

"Now, keep them above your head and no touching," he said, mimicking her, and kissed her.

Maggie moaned as he took the time to touch every part of her body with his tongue before moving to where she craved it the most.

John heard them upstairs as he finished his drink. They would be occupied the rest of the night and no one would miss him. He had been practicing his shimmering, and Ana was right, the more you used the abilities, the sharper they became. He closed his eyes and envisioned his destination. When he opened them, he was right where he wanted to be, and she was peacefully sleeping. He quickly undressed and slipped underneath the covers. Waking instantly when he kissed the back of her neck, she sighed softly as he placed his hand on her thigh. She rolled over and smiled before he kissed her thoroughly.

"I have missed you," he said and pushed a stray strand of hair out of her eyes.

"It's been a few days."

"I know. I haven't been able to get away, and there are some other matters I need to deal with," he looked down, his expression troubled.

She pressed her finger to his lips. "It doesn't matter. We both agreed one did not owe the other anything outside of this room. We are just taking comfort from each other."

"That's what I love about this," he said before leaning over to nibble on her neck. "We understand each other."

Pushing him back, the woman rolled over on top of him. He lifted her shift over her head and tossed it to the floor. Splaying her hands over his chest, she closed her eyes and inhaled his scent, feeling herself near the edge from just smelling him. She swayed forward and pressed her lips to his as he cupped her buttocks and her orgasm hit.

"I have barely touched you, woman!" He laughed softly.

He lifted her slightly and positioned her over his erection before slowly lowering her and another spasm overtook her. "Oh God, John! What is it that ye do to me!"

"Shhhh!" he said quietly. "The others will hear."

They moved together until they both found a simultaneous release.

She leaned toward him, exhausted as he rolled her underneath him, never removing himself, already working her up again, taking her until they both lay sated. She was barely awake, a satisfied smile on her face when he pulled out and kissed her.

"I have to go," he said. "I am not sure when I can come back."

"No expectations!" she reminded him as he dressed. "Good night, John."

He smiled and touched her face, before kissing her one final time. "Sleep well, my dearest Aurnia."

Maggie was sitting in the drawing room, sipping a glass of rum when John shimmered back in. He didn't notice her until she spoke.

"You are out very late, young man," she said, in her best parental voice.

Startled, he jumped slightly when he heard her. "Oh Maggie, I didn't see you there." He moved to get a drink. "What are you doing down here?"

"I couldn't sleep. In fact, I am beginning to wonder if we are supposed to sleep. Remind me to ask Mom." She waved her glass at him as he sat down. "Where were you?"

"Oh, I…um," he ran his index finger around the rim of his glass, "…just needed some fresh air to clear my head."

Maggie took a good look at him. It was obvious he had just left the bed of a woman. "How are you handling all of this new information?"

"I am not quite sure yet, but Duncan and I had a good talk. He helped to allay many of my concerns."

"He's pretty good at that." Maggie smiled. "I hope one of these days you will find someone for yourself like I did with him."

"You're the only woman for me," he teased.

"I hope that's not true," she said seriously. "I want you to be happy, John."

"Don't worry about me, Maggie."

"But I do, and more than you will ever know."

"You worry too much," he said and rose. "I am going to bed, and you should try getting some sleep yourself." He leaned down and kissed her on the cheek. "Good night, Maggie."

"Good night, John." She watched him leave, her smile fading as he left.

John smelled like sex and something else. Maggie frowned. She had caught a faint whiff of a distinct lavender soap, one she recognized, and she knew exactly where from. She sat there, her mind running wild, knowing she would not rest that night.

The following afternoon, while the men were out of the house, Maggie found her mother in the drawing room, reading.

"Can we talk?" she asked, pulling the doors closed.

"Of course, sweetheart." Ana closed the book and laid it on the side table.

Maggie grabbed a bottle of rum and two glasses, before she came to sit next to her on the sofa. She poured and handed one to Ana.

"What's on your mind?"

Maggie sighed. "You know how you said I should let John live his own life and try to find someone? Well, I found out the other night he has been seeing someone, and I really wish I hadn't."

"Is it because you have more feelings for him than ye realized?"

"No!" She shook her head. "It is because it is someone we know very well, and if word got out, it would be devastating for all concerned."

Ana frowned. "What does John say about it?"

Maggie sipped from her glass. "He doesn't know I know. He shimmered in the other night, and I smelled her scent on him, a very distinct one, I instantly recognized."

Ana furrowed her brow. "I don't understand. Is she married?"

"No! She is an older widow."

Ana scratched her head. "Then, what is the problem?"

Maggie blew out a deep breath. "It's Duncan's mother."

"Lady Aurnia?" whispered Ana, more than a little surprised. "Are ye sure?"

"Yeah, and if Duncan finds out, he will lose his shit, Mom. I mean, he is jealous and protective over me and his horse, but that is nothing compared to how he is over his mother. He accepted John and I were once together, begrudgingly, because he had no choice in that matter, and John goads him to no end over it. They keep it good-natured, for now, but it is a fine line they walk. I don't know what to do. If Duncan finds out, with the two of them being gods — they very well may level Virginia."

"That *is* a predicament."

Maggie topped off their drinks. "You should have seen how he was when he found out Quinn was gay. I had to step in to keep him from beating Gabe to death."

"But he did come around."

"Only after I threatened to withhold sex from him," she muttered. "I firmly believe that man would internally combust if he were cut off."

Ana laughed. "He is a man after all, and the Dagda does have a healthy appetite for that sort of thing."

"Don't I know it?"' Maggie looked down into her glass. "What should I do, Mom?"

"Truthfully, baby? I think ye should stay out of John's business. Aurnia and John are consenting adults and if they choose to do what they are doing, that is between the two of them and is none of your concern."

"Maybe you are right." Maggie leaned her head over on her mother's shoulder. "Do you have any idea how much I have missed this? How many times over the years I have just wanted to sit down and talk to you about everything?"

Ana took her hand. "Probably about as many times as I wished ye were there to crawl into bed with me and watch crappy TV while your father was absorbed in grading papers, or having ye beside me when I was cooking, or rather burning, dinner and ordering pizza."

"I am so glad you are here now," said Maggie, "I need your advice now more than ever."

Two days later, Maggie knocked on John's door. "Got a minute?"

"For you? Always!" he said and waved her in. She sat down in one of the chairs, placing a small box on her lap while he took the chair across from her.

"You look very solemn," he remarked. "Is something wrong?"

"No," and shook her head. "I actually brought you something. I shimmered to London and did a little 'after hours' shopping." She handed him the gift. "I hope it fits," she half-smiled.

John accepted the box, watching her curiously as he removed the top, looking down. "A condom —with a red bow?'"

"Apparently, that is how you keep them on in the eighteenth-century before the rubber ones are invented."

John laughed softly. "It may be a little late for this."

Maggie's face became serious. "Well, if you are going to have a dalliance with my mother-in-law, you can at least be safe about it."

John's amusement faded and he sucked in a deep breath.

"I smelled her scent on you the other night and, while I may not approve of who you choose to have these brief one or two night affairs with, this is my way of saying — I am minding my own business."

Placing the top back on the box, John cast his eyes downward. "It's not like that," he whispered. "I actually care for Aurnia a great deal."

"So, the two of you are together, exclusively?"

"No," he said and placed the box on the side table, "but, not by my choice."

"I don't understand."

John exhaled sharply. "*She* is the one who does not want anything more with *me*."

"Oh!" said Maggie, softly, sympathetically. "I see."

He stood and went to get a bottle of whiskey and two glasses from his desk. He poured and handed Maggie one.

"We began spending time together on our last trip to Scotland," he explained as he took his seat. "Everyone was so busy with everything else, no one even noticed. We spent our first night together the night of Logan's wedding. I guess there was something in the air. I had hoped it was the beginning of something special, but she made it clear that it was nothing more than taking some enjoyment from each other. I have, however, found myself unable to stay away."

"I'm sorry, John." She legitimately felt bad for him because he was obviously disappointed.

"Does Duncan know?" he asked as he looked down at the floor.

"No."

"Are you going to tell him?"

"I am not."

John looked to her questioningly.

She leaned forward and placed her hand on his knee. "Again! This is me, minding my own business. Who you are with is none of my concern." She took his hand and squeezed it. "I do, however, love you very much, and I am here if you need me, even if it is only to listen."

He gripped her hand tightly and grinned. "You want to hear about me being with other women?"

"Well, I don't, but I will, because that is what friends do for each other."

"Thank you." He looked to the box and frowned. "'After hours shopping'?"

Maggie rolled her eyes. "I wasn't going to a condom shop in broad daylight. With my luck, Georgie would have popped around the corner and seen me. I did leave money, if that is what concerns you," she said and leaned back in the chair. "I am no thief."

"I am more concerned you may not have gotten a big enough size," he bragged with a devilish smirk on his lips.

Maggie scoffed. "I am fairly certain I judged it close, and besides, that is what the ribbon is for. It gives a whole new meaning to the saying, 'tied up with a big red bow'. Mom helped me, too."

John choked on his drink. "You took your mother with you to the condom shop to pick out one for me?"

"Well, yes. It's the first shopping trip we have had together since she got here, and it was just too good an opportunity to pass up."

"Exactly *how* did you pick a size?" he asked, extremely curious, his eyes twinkling.

"We just held up several to compare, and I have a good memory!" She grinned. "We actually had a great time. I don't think I have ever laughed so hard."

John covered his face with his hand. "I can't believe you took Ana with you to do that?"

Maggie beamed. "My mother is awesome— I can talk to her about anything and nothing embarrasses her." She pointed to the box. "I know one thing— I am glad Duncan doesn't need one of those. I am fairly sure none of them are 'ribbed for her pleasure' in the eighteenth-century."

16 Chapter Sixteen

October 2, 1781
New York

Elijah MacCray was on his second tankard of ale, waiting. It had been three months since that fateful day. He always thought his old granny daft for her stories of the old ones and most especially that of the banshee — until he laid eyes on one for himself. The high-pitched wail still echoed in his ears every time he closed his eyes, and the sight of what she did haunted his dreams each night.

He had never seen anything like it before and prayed to God he never would again. His granny's description of the creature was dead on — dressed in white, pale as a ghost with long flowing hair down her back, eyes swollen and red from weeping, and blood stains soaking her dress. He shuddered, remembering her mournful howl and how it shook the very ground beneath them that day as she killed a dozen men without laying a finger on them.

Pennington was a fool for murdering an innocent man, and that demon had taken her revenge. He had no idea why she spared him that day, wanting to credit the old Gaelic prayer he had uttered as he looked on in horror, but somehow, he didn't entirely believe that was enough to stop something as powerful as she was. She told him to go, to warn others not to come there, and he had run, getting as far away from that place as he possibly could, being more afraid of her curse than of the British army finding him a deserter. He would hide, and he only knew of one place they would never look for him.

The front door of the tavern opened and the man he had sent word to came through the doorway. He waved the barkeep for an ale before removing his hat and taking a seat next to him.

"Are you MacCray?" he whispered.

"I am."

"I understand you wish to defect, and you have intelligence that would serve us well to prove your loyalty."

"I do, sir. I will do whatever ye ask of me as long as I never have to defend the Crown again."

"Why would you betray the Crown to come and join us?"

MacCray lifted his chin. "I served under a man who murdered the innocent, and my conscience tells me God is not with them. I have seen how the devil punishes the unrighteous and I will not be dragged to Hell for someone else's misdeeds. I will gladly give ye all the information I have if ye take me in."

The newly arrived man sipped from the fresh tankard that had been set before him. "How do I know you are not a spy for them?"

The man ran his hand over the satchel strap across his shoulder. Pennington had given it to him that day to hold onto while he brutally beat MacGregor, before putting the noose around the man's neck and finally putting him out of his misery. It was still on his shoulder when he scrambled away for his life. He took it off and gave it to the man.

"There should be enough here to convince ye. It belonged to a major of intelligence."

"Where is he now?"

MacCray took a long drink. "He is dead, along with all of his men. I was the only one who survived."

"How did you manage that?"

MacCray shook his head. "Truthfully? I don't know. The Lord must have a higher purpose for me to let me be the only one to walk away from evil that day."

"I see." The man accepted the bag and nodded. "If I can verify the information here, I will welcome your service. I will return tomorrow if I find it useful."

"Of course." MacCray watched the man finish his ale and rise from his seat to leave. "I didn't catch your name, sir."

The man turned and put on his hat. "Major Benjamin Tallmadge, at your service."

Ben rode back to camp, and that evening, he sat down at his desk to go through the contents of the bag. He examined some of the correspondence and there appeared to be some valuable information —if it was indeed the real thing. The bag apparently belonged to one Major Jackson Pennington, a man in intelligence working for the British army. He was trying to decide if the information was a plant, when he ran across a letter and a copy of a report containing Maggie's name, catching his attention. It was about that God-awful man, Gerald Wilson, and the events in Oyster Bay.

Why would this man have a copy of this?

Ben sifted through some of the other things until he came across a letter from Wilson to Pennington. He read it and leaned back in his chair.

Son of a bitch! They were brothers!

He pulled out the stack dated last—July 1781.

He flipped through until he found something that made his blood run cold. It was an arrest and execution order for Duncan MacGregor for the murder of Captain Wilson. It also stated he had freely confessed.

Oh my God! Maggie!

Wait!

Remembering something else, he got up and pulled a pile of letters from another place. He looked for a recent one from Washington and reread it. Washington wrote of taking young Wyatt along and having dinner with Maggie and Duncan at their estate. It was dated September, which meant Duncan was alive at that time.

The informant said the owner of all of this was dead. He needed to speak with the man again.

Snatching up the report and stuffing it in his coat pocket, he went out to find his horse. He rode straight to the tavern and got the room information from the owner. Rushing upstairs, he banged on the door until the man opened it.

"Major?" he asked, wiping the sleep from his eyes.

"I need a word, now!"

MacCray made sure no one else was in the hall before motioning him in.

"I must know one thing," demanded Ben. "When did the owner of this bag die?"

MacCray paled a little.

"I need to know!"

"July 5th."

Ben let out the breath he had been holding. "Are you certain?"

MacCray nodded. "I was there. I watched him die."

Ben visibly relaxed. It made sense. The last thing written was that warrant, and it was dated July 5th. There was nothing past that. He took a closer look at the man. In the past few years, he had developed a knack for knowing when people were lying and when they were telling the truth. Everything in him told him this man spoke the truth. "Alright, MacCray, I am willing to take a chance on you, but if I find out you are not who you say you are, I will kill you on the spot."

"I give you my word, Major. Ye will not regret this."

When Ben returned to camp, he went straight back to his desk. He knew Wilson was dead; Maggie informed him Duncan had taken care of him after he attacked her in Tappan, and according to MacCray, so was Pennington. He was inclined to believe him, otherwise a fellow man in intelligence would be tearing up the countryside looking for his satchel. The fact Duncan was still alive and on the estate was further proof of it, which meant Maggie was safe and the only thing that connected her to the two men was what was in front of him.

Ben leafed through all the papers until he was sure that he found everything that mentioned Maggie, before taking the stack over to the fire and tossing it all in, watching it burn. She would be safe and that was all that mattered.

17 Chapter Seventeen

October 31, 1781

Maggie awoke that morning with Duncan's body and lips on hers, kissing her greedily. She moaned, returning the favor. "Good morning," she sighed, her lips still pressed to his.

"Good morning, my love," he said and moved his kiss down to her neck.

"Today is definitely off to a good start," she purred, lightly stroking his back. "What did I do to deserve this?"

He looked up. "Three years ago, today, ye made me the happiest man in the world, or did ye forget?"

"Oh no," she teased. "I always remember our anniversary because it falls on my favorite holiday."

"Samhain?" he asked, rolling over on his side so he could prop himself up.

"No! Halloween! What's Samhain?"

Duncan scoffed. "Some Fae queen ye are. Samhain is the festival marking the end of the harvest. It is also the time when the boundary between this world and the next is the thinnest, allowing spirits and Fae to pass through the easiest."

"Oh! Well, I guess it was a good day to get married!" she said with a grin and turned on her side to face him.

"What's Halloween?"

Maggie raised up on her elbow. "Halloween is the best holiday ever. People dress up in costumes and try to scare each other while all the children go around to different homes getting chocolate. It's called 'trick or treat'. If the house doesn't give candy, they might get toilet paper in their trees."

"What's that?"

"Oh, my dear Duncan, toilet paper is something I miss a great deal. It is this really soft stuff you wipe your butt with when you go, and we take it so for-granted in the twenty-first century, that if they don't get candy, kids use it to throw into trees as a joke."

"Sounds more like a treat than a trick."

"It would be now," she said, sarcastically — and somewhat longingly.

"I think our anniversary beats them all."

"Oh, I agree," she said and wrapped her arms around his neck. "So, what shall we do today?"

He ran his hand down the length of her body. "I have a special surprise for ye after dinner."

"You do?" she asked excitedly. "What is it?"

"It's a *SURPRISE,*" he reiterated and grinned. "Now, come on, let's go have some breakfast. Ye are going to need your strength later.

When they walked into the dining room, the rest of the family was there to congratulate them and wish them 'happy anniversary'.

Hettie came over and hugged Maggie. "I am making a special dinner to celebrate."

And she did— Hettie made all their favorites and several desserts to top it off. After dinner, Duncan looked to Ana. "Everything taken care of?"

"The babies are in good hands," she assured.

"Quinn and I are staying to lend a hand, as well," added Gabe.

"What are you talking about?" asked Maggie.

"Your surprise," he said and rose from his chair to help her up. "Now, tell everyone 'goodbye' until tomorrow."

"But the babies—"

"The wet nurses are already here," said Ana. "Ye two go have fun."

Duncan pulled her out of the dining room and into the drawing room. He wrapped his arms around her and kissed the top of her head. "Close your eyes."

When she opened them, they were at the springs in Scotland where they had spent their honeymoon. The tent had been resurrected, so they could recreate their magical wedding night.

"Oh Duncan, this is perfect," she said looking around.

"Aye," he said, running his hands over her body, "ye are."

He picked her up, carried her into the tent, and spent the rest of the day and night making love to her."

The next morning, they reluctantly dressed to leave.

"Do ye mind if we pop in and say 'hello' to Mother? She helped me set this up."

"Sure!"

A few minutes later, they shimmered into the library and located Lady Aurnia.

"Happy anniversary, ye two," she said as Duncan kissed her cheek.

"Thank ye for your help, Mother."

"Yes, thank you," added Maggie.

"It was my pleasure!"

"Where is everyone?" asked Duncan when he noticed how quiet the house was.

"Training day. Logan and Shanley are leading the men together now, with Reade and Evan's assistance, and Rozem and Enid are hanging some herbs out to dry."

"Logan and Shanley leading *together*?" Duncan laughed. "I have to see this for myself." He kissed Maggie. "I will be back in a bit," he said on his way out.

"Can I get ye something, Maggie?" asked Lady Aurnia.

"No, I'm good, thanks." Maggie chewed on her lip and sat down, staring into the fire.

"Are ye alright?" asked Lady Aurnia. "Ye seem disturbed by something."

"Oh, I'm fine!"

"Are ye sure? I am always happy to listen if ye need to talk."

Maggie hesitated, wondering if she should even say anything. She glanced towards the window warily to make sure Duncan was still outside. "I know about you and John," she blurted out.

"Oh! I see!" said Lady Aurnia, quietly. "Did he tell ye?

Maggie shook her head. "I smelled your lavender herb soap on him the other night. It wasn't hard to put two and two together."

"I take it Duncan doesn't know."

Maggie shook her head again. "No, and he won't hear it from me. Whatever is going on is between you and John, and I think it is best it stays that way."

"I appreciate that," she half-smiled, "Ye know how unreasonable my boys can be."

"I must say, I was a little surprised to find out John has feelings for you, but I think the two of you might be good for each other."

Lady Aurnia looked at Maggie strangely. "Nay! He does not have feelings for me— he cannot."

"He does," Maggie winced, "he told me."

"Oh, God!" Lady Aurnia stood up, a look of distress on her face. She went and poured two glasses of whisky. "It wasn't supposed to be like that." She handed Maggie one of the drinks. "I was just— we were just— enjoying each other, or so I thought."

Maggie sighed, a little disappointed. "Oh! I thought maybe— well, anyway, I leave that to the two of you. I am remaining out of it for the sake of my marriage, my friendship with John, and the wonderful relationship I have with my mother-in-law. I just don't want to see anyone get hurt. I would hate to see anything come between the family we have created, if you take my meaning."

Lady Aurnia smiled behind her glass. "I understand, and I am sorry that ye had to learn that information the way ye did. I was hoping to keep it between him and I, and the last thing I ever want to do is upset the relationship all of ye have with each other."

Maggie opened her mouth to say something, then closed it.

"Oh, say it," coaxed Lady Aurnia. "No need to hold back now."

Setting her glass on the table. Maggie took her mother-in-law's hand in her own. "Not that it is any of my business, but John *is* a good man and I think you would be doing yourself a great disservice if you didn't give some consideration to a relationship with him."

Lady Aurnia squeezed her hand. "I will give it some thought."

They hugged as Duncan came back inside, laughing. "It didn't take long for Shanley to whip Logan into shape."

Maggie grinned. "It's easy once you get a man hooked. They will do anything for some good loving!"

"Will they now?" he asked, playfully, pulling her up from her chair and wrapping her in his arms.

"Oh yes, I have it on good authority, especially those MacGregor men," teased Maggie. "They are easy-pickings."

He looked over at Lady Aurnia. "We will see ye soon, Mother," and they shimmered out and back into their bedroom.

"Thank you for a wonderful anniversary," Maggie said, kissing him.

"Nay, thank ye for the best three years of my life," he said as he kissed her neck on the right side, "and for the triplets," he moved to the left side, "and for the twins," he moved back up to her lips, "and for being the love of my life for all of eternity."

18 Chapter Eighteen

Spring 1783

Maggie stood in the doorway of the drawing room watching John. He had been quiet, withdrawn for days, and she had not had a chance to speak to him alone until now. The shipping company was growing by leaps and bounds with the rebuilding, and they were all having to pitch in with the extra workload.

"I finally got you all to myself," she said and walked over to him.

"It has been a little busy around here, hasn't it?" He handed her the glass he was sipping and stood to get another one.

"Want to talk about it?" she asked, gripping the glass.

"Talk about what?"

"You have not been yourself the past few days." She sat down on the sofa and made room for him. "What's going on with you? Are your boys alright?"

The three women John had impregnated at the tribe all gave birth to healthy baby boys the year before. John spent time with them whenever he could.

"The children are fine," he sat down next to her, "but Aurnia and I have decided it is best we do not see each other anymore."

Maggie took his hand. "I'm sorry. I know the two of you had been off and on again for the past year or so, but you had been together for a while this last time, and I was hoping things were going to work out."

"So was I," he said, "but, it is for the best. We don't have to worry about getting caught anymore."

"What can I do?" she asked.

John raised an eyebrow. "Well, if you really want to comfort me…"

Maggie smacked at him and laughed. "You're incorrigible."

He chuckled softly. "I know." A tinge of sadness crossed his face, tugging at Maggie's heart.

Maggie rubbed her temple with one finger, and a thought crossed her mind. "Why don't you get out of here for a few days and get your mind off things? I have some business that needs handling up in the northern part of Virginia and you can go in my place. Gabe and I have been talking, and we think it is time to bring you in on the business anyway."

John blinked. "You want me to have a part in the shipping company?"

Maggie nodded. "Yes! You deserve an income of your own, and we need the help, not to mention, you have earned it. What do you say?"

"I don't know what to say—thank you."

"You're welcome. Captain Russell is leaving in the morning with a few of the men, and he can break you in since I have a sneaking suspicion he will be wanting to retire soon. Besides, there are plenty of taverns between here and there, and you will have a good time with the men on the road."

"That sounds like a plan. I will go pack." He kissed her on the cheek and got up to leave.

A week later, after the shipping company business was completed, John decided to secure a private room at the local tavern; the rest of the men and Captain Russell preferring to camp out, while he was hoping for a peaceful night alone to drink himself into oblivion. The business trip had been a welcome distraction, but thoughts of *her* would catch him unexpectedly, especially at night, invading his dreams. He had avoided women at the brothels on the trip there, because he had forgotten to pack the condom Maggie had so graciously gifted him — at least that is what he told himself. He had not needed it with Aurnia since she was well past the point of being able to conceive, and he had been with no other since she had been in his bed. He could have shimmered back to retrieve it, but the truth of the matter was he had not wanted to be with any other woman as of late.

He located the nearest respectable establishment he could find and made his way inside. "Have any private rooms for the night?" he asked the man at the bar.

"If you have money," he replied, without looking up from drying a tankard.

John produced a small pouch from his pocket and shook it.

The man tossed his towel over his shoulder and smiled, his full attention now on John. "Will you be needing supper and ale, sir?"

"Supper and a bottle of your strongest whisky. Also, may I please have a bath brought up?" He tossed a few coins down.

"Right away, sir," said the owner with an agreeable look on his face, laying his hand over the money and sliding it into his apron pocket. He turned to look around until his eyes fell upon a dark-haired young woman. "You, girl! Fetch up a bath for our guest and let him know when it is ready. Have Janey bring the man some supper."

When the young woman caught sight of John, her expression went from annoyed to interested rather quickly. She smiled coyly and made a small curtsey. "I will be happy to," she said, looking him up and down.

The keep pulled a bottle from a shelf and set it in front of John along with a glass.

John took the glass and bottle before occupying a nearby table as Janey placed a bowl of stew before him. He ate his supper and had nearly downed the whole bottle by the time the young woman came to his table.

"Your bath is ready. If you will follow me, I will show you to your room."

"Thank you." John stood, stumbling slightly as he moved from behind the table. She held out her hand and he caught it to steady himself. They did not speak as John followed her up the stairs. She led him to the room at the far end of the hall, opened the door, and followed him inside.

"Thank you," he said, leaning against the bedpost, feeling the effects of the whisky that had been much stronger than he anticipated.

"Can I assist you, sir?" she asked.

He shook his head. "I will manage."

She stepped forward and touched his chest, gently untying his shirt for him. "You have had a great deal to drink. Why don't you let me help you with your bath?"

"That is really not necessary," he said, wobbling slightly. "I am sure you have better things to do."

"But I really *want* to," she replied, and finished loosening his shirt.

John sat back on the bed and she removed his boots. "What's your name?"

"Lucy —Lucy Hanks," she said, setting his boots by the door. "What's yours?"

"My name is John. Is the tavern owner your father?" he asked, trying to focus his cloudy mind.

"No," she walked back over to him, "I do odds and ends here to help out for extra money. Where are you from?" She pulled his shirt over his head.

"I live on an estate in Williamsburg. I am here on business."

She folded his shirt and laid it on a chair before turning and slowly touching his chest, sliding her fingers lightly across it as she let out a sigh.

John laid his hand over on hers to stop her. "That is not a good idea," he whispered. "I wouldn't be very good company."

She lifted her chin, took his face in her hands, and kissed him softly on the lips. "I think I have to disagree with you, sir."

John licked his lips, his mouth dry from the alcohol. Taking her hand, he kissed her palm. "You should go home," he murmured.

"I would rather stay," she said and kissed him harder, dropping her free hand down the front of his body, finding her target, and rubbing him until his body responded.

"It is late, I am drunk, and you are very young," he said, trying to send her away, but she moved her hands to undo his breeches.

"I'm old enough to know what I want."

John leaned back on the bed and closed his eyes while she finished undressing him and then herself. She lay down beside him, kissing his chest and lips as she moved up to look in his eyes. "Please," she begged, "I really want to be with you tonight."

John opened his eyes and took a good look at her. God Almighty, this girl looked so much like *she* must have looked at that same age. His mind was just numb enough from the alcohol to allow her to pass for her.

"Are you sure?" He pushed a strand of hair back from her face. "You need to understand, I can offer you nothing beyond this night."

She responded by crawling atop him and lowering herself onto his erection.

He groaned as she moved up and down; she was lost in the euphoric bliss of having him inside her. Managing to roll her over, he buried his face into the pillow and rammed into her, both building to a peak before reaching a delightful release. After he spilled his seed, John shifted over on his back and began to drift into oblivion, while she curled against him.

"Good night, John," she said and kissed his chest.

"Good night, Maggie, my sweet," he mumbled before passing completely out.

Lucy raised up. "Who is Maggie?" she asked but received no answer to her question.

The next morning, John awoke alone, half dressed, the previous night somewhat of a blur. He propped himself up on his elbows, bits and pieces of the evening's activities starting to come back to him — memories of a woman, her long dark hair, losing himself in her, how much she looked like— Maggie.

He covered his face with his hand and lay back down. The girl from the night before made him realize what his heart had always known — as much as he had cared for Aurnia and would have been content with her, she had not been the woman he truly loved and wanted to be with, only the one he could actually have at the time.

"Oh dear God," he mumbled, "what have I done?" Guilt started to fill his heart.

John dressed, wrapped up the final loose ends in town, and joined the men for the trip home. Once they returned, John and Gabe sat down to go over the business transactions from the trip while the rest of the family was elsewhere for the day.

Gabe looked over the paperwork. "I would say you did very well on your first excursion."

"Captain Russell is a wealth of information," John said as they moved to the armchairs with their drinks. "Maggie did well hiring him all those years ago."

"He has been a lifesaver on more than one occasion," replied Gabe, sitting down and taking a good look at his old friend. "I see your trip didn't do much to improve your mood."

"Hmm?" asked John.

Gabe leaned back in his chair, concerned. "John, what's going on with you? You weren't yourself before you left, and you are even less so now. We have known each other a long time, old friend, and I have never seen you like this. Please, talk to me. I am more worried about you than you know."

John sat silent for a moment. "I was seeing someone before I left, and we decided to part ways."

"I'm truly sorry, John!"

"Yes, well, such is life." He downed his drink and poured another.

"Was it anyone I know?" fished Gabe.

John looked down. "It doesn't matter now. It's over."

Gabe leaned forward. "Why do I have the feeling there is more to this story than you are telling?"

John shrugged and hid behind his glass.

"John, you can talk to me about anything and it will remain between the two of us. You have my word. It might help to get whatever it is off your chest."

Stroking his forehead with his fingers, John tried to decide if he should say anything.

"On my word, John. I will be the soul of discretion— you know that."

John sucked in a deep breath, glancing back at the door to make sure they were alone. "Gabe, I am afraid I suffered a grievous lapse in judgement while I was away and did something I should not have done."

Gabe raised his hand to his chin, giving his full attention. "Go on," he said encouragingly.

John raked his hand through his hair. "I spent the night with a young woman at the tavern before we returned. I had far too much to drink, and she was extremely persistent. I let my guard down when I shouldn't have."

Gabe held up his hand. "John, you do that all the time. What makes this different?"

John swallowed hard. "The following morning, I came to a moral realization which greatly disturbed me and has been weighing on my conscience ever since. I am not sure if it was the alcohol, or just me, but the entire time I was bedding her, I was imagining she was someone else."

"This woman you had been seeing?"

John shook his head slowly and closed his eyes, shame and guilt filling his face.

Drawing his own conclusion, Gabe tapped the arm of his chair with his fingers and looked up at the ceiling, shaking his head. "Maggie," he whispered. "You were imagining you were with Maggie."

John leaned over, his elbows on his knees with his face in his hands. "God help me, Gabe. I know my place, and I know Maggie and Duncan are meant to be together. I would never do anything to interfere with that because I know she is happy with him and that is all that matters. The thought of her cutting me out of her life if I confess this to her, is more than I could ever bear, especially since forever is very real for us — but I can't help how I feel. I didn't realize how deep those feelings went until this other woman and I stopped seeing each other, which makes things even worse because now I feel like I just used her as a substitute. I guess I was, unknowingly, hoping she would fill some sort of void within me I didn't even know existed."

Gabe reached over and touched his shoulder. "I'm sorry, John. I know how you feel about Maggie. You have been in love with her since the day I first introduced her to you as my fiancé in Philadelphia. It has to be hard seeing them together the way they are after what the two of you once shared, and it cannot be easy living under the same roof."

"You have no idea, old friend. What do I do?"

"Nothing!" Gabe reclined back, crossing his legs. "The real question is— 'how are you going to handle these feelings?' If you don't find some sort of way to deal with them, they will eat you alive."

John downed his drink. "I will continue to do it the same way I have always done— plenty of alcohol and trips to the whorehouses. Fortunately for me, shimmering makes that much easier because I can go anywhere in the world whenever I want." He offered a weak smile.

"Will it be enough?"

"It will have to be." He stood, patting Gabe on the back. "Don't worry, Gabe, I will sort through this and be back to my old self soon enough."

Gabe looked up at John with a great deal of concern, not convinced it would be that easy.

Maggie returned a few hours later to find Gabe still in the drawing room.

"How did John make out on his business trip?" she inquired and leaned down to kiss him on the cheek.

"Very well. Everything is in order and Captain Russell has him well on his way."

"Good!" She plopped down in a chair and let out a sigh. "How is he?" she asked seriously.

"Still a little quiet," he replied, glancing over at her.

Maggie frowned. "I was hoping that trip would cheer him up a little."

"You know what might help with that? Perhaps it's time for John to have a house of his own. I mean, it is getting a little crowded around here with the children growing up, and John does like to entertain the ladies. He could do with a little freedom."

"Did he say something about not wanting to live here?" she asked and straightened up.

"No, not at all. It just occurred to me he may need a place to call his own. He is a single man, and the main house is busy at all times."

"What are you not saying, Gabe?"

He paused to find the right wording. "Did it ever occur to you that maybe John might not *want* to live with you, your husband, your mother, and your five children? You didn't marry *him*, after all."

Maggie wrinkled her nose. "I guess I never looked at it that way. We were so worried about keeping him safe after Tappan, and after things didn't work out with the tribe, I just never considered he might want to be somewhere else."

"He might appreciate the privacy. Why don't you bring it up to him and see what he says?"

Maggie nodded. "Maybe, you're right."

Maggie was lost in thought as she undressed for bed that night. She looked over at Duncan who was already there, propped up on some pillows. "Gabe thinks we should offer John a house of his own."

"I think that is an excellent idea," he said and adjusted himself to face her, peeling back the covers for her.

"Do you really?" she asked as she crawled into bed.

"Aye, I do. A man needs his own domain to rule over, and, truthfully, John has been here a great deal longer than I expected. I can't imagine he wants to live with us forever, and 'forever' is a relative term around here.

Besides, it isn't exactly normal for a man to put a roof over the head of his wife's ex-lover."

Maggie settled in against him. "I thought you were past that," she said quietly.

"Oh, I am," he replied, putting his arms around her. "I'm not so sure John is."

She raised up. "What do you mean by that?"

"Maggie, can ye not see how much in love he still is with ye?"

"I am sure he has moved on. He was seeing someone up until very recently."

"Who?"

Maggie shrugged in response, pretending not to know, and hoped he could not see right through her. "I just know he was very serious about her, more so than she was about him apparently."

Duncan narrowed his eyes, knowing she indeed knew 'who', but decided to let it pass. "That doesn't mean that he is not still in love with ye."

"Then, why do you let him stay here?"

Duncan sighed. "I like John— he is family to us. He is also an honorable man and he respects what we have. I know he would never interfere with that in any way, but it cannot be easy for him to see the woman he loves with another every day and night of his life. We are also responsible for him, because by saving him, we took him away from everyone and everything he ever knew, but if he were to ever forget his place when it comes to ye…"

"He won't," she interrupted and assured.

"I also know how much he means to ye," he said and kissed the top of her head. "Ye know I would do anything for ye."

"I will speak to David Percy about deeding him some property of his own."

"Good morning," said John, entering the dining room the next day to join them for breakfast. The dining room table was covered with a large map of the estate. "What's all this?' he asked as he poured himself a cup of coffee.

"The time has come for ye to leave this house," replied Duncan gruffly, leaning back in his chair with his arms folded, glaring at John.

John stopped with his cup halfway to his mouth, glancing over at Gabe, who had a slight smirk on his face.

"What he means to say," clarified Maggie, standing and pulling him closer, "is we think maybe it is time you had a place of your own."

"I don't understand."

Duncan waved his hand over the map. "We are giving ye land and having a house built for ye as our gift. Ye just have to pick out where ye want it to be."

"You can't be serious," he said and looked around.

"Having some privacy might make life a little easier on you," said Gabe with a nod, "for entertainment purposes," he added for the benefit of everyone else.

"Ye can build between here and the tribe," suggested Quinn pointing on the map. "It would be nice to be closer to your boys."

Maggie rubbed his back. "And we will still see you every day just like we do Gabe and Quinn."

John stared at the drawing. "That's quite a gift."

"Think of it more as taking care of one of our own," said Duncan.

"I'm not sure what to say. Thank you."

Three days later, after dinner, John excused himself for the rest of the day, saying he had some matters to attend and shimmered into the shadier side of London. He located the place he was looking for and pushed the door open. Women of all shapes and sizes were in various stages of undress with clients, their eyes all turning to him when he stepped inside. He completely relaxed, freeing the 'lust-dust' he had been reigning in, and as soon as he did, the entire place felt it. He smiled to himself, feeling the power rush throughout his body—and the women began to flock to him, like lambs to the slaughter. The madam of the establishment pushed one woman after another aside as she came over to greet him. "What can I do for you this evening, sir?" she asked running her hand over his arm, up to his shoulder.

"I need company for the night."

The madam waved her hand. "Take your pick, and I will be happy to join in myself —no extra charge," she whispered behind her hand.

John smiled and looked around while the women waved, showing off their wares in hopes they would be picked. He located a pretty young one with long dark hair, taking her hand and kissing it. She smiled back and reached up to touch his face. "I will take a room with this girl and a few bottles of whisky," he said. "I don't want to be disturbed until the morning."

"As you wish!" and she led him to their finest accommodations.

Once they were alone, John looked her over. He turned the bottle up before slowly running the back of his hand over her shoulder, down her arm, admiring her. She started untying his breeches, but he caught her hand. "Slow down. We have all night."

She stepped back and smiled, pushing back what little there was of her silk robe, letting it fall to the floor in a pool, now standing completely naked before him.

John reached out and touched her hip as his eyes swept over her. "You are so beautiful." He tipped up her face and gently kissed her lips.

John sat down on the bed, drinking as she took her time undressing him. He slid back to rest against the headboard and she followed, sprawling out in front of him, lowering her head to take him in her mouth. He sighed, running his fingers through her hair, appreciating the softness of it as he closed his eyes, pretending she was Maggie as she performed.

She moved up to kiss him on the mouth, positioning herself over him.

"Wait," he said and reached into the pocket of his coat lying on the bed next to him, "use this," he said, handing her the condom. "I don't want to take any chances on fathering any more children."

She slipped it over his cock and tied it before she lowered herself upon him. Once she was positioned, he bit his lip and slid one hand across her breast, stopping to tease her nipple with his thumb. She looked surprised, almost climaxing from his touch.

John laughed softly as he fisted his hand in her hair in one hand and used the other to steady and guide her as she rode him. Just as he was about to come, he suddenly wrapped both arms around her, raising up to kiss her, pumping into her hard and fast, forgetting about everything and everyone for a few brief moments.

She cried out as she exploded around him; John tossed his head back and laughed as he came hard. The woman splayed her hands across his chest, trying to catch her breath. "I have never felt anything like that before," she whispered, her face red from the stimulation. "Do it again and I won't even charge you."

John took her hand and kissed it. "You look a little worn out and I am only just getting started." He rubbed her behind gently. "Go tell your madam I will be needing a few more girls for the night and make sure they are all well rested."

That morning, John dressed and went downstairs, deciding he would go out, find an empty corner and shimmer back to Virginia. At the bottom of the stairs, the madam took him by the arm as they walked.

"I trust your night was enjoyable."

"Yes, it was," he said, taking a small bag of coins out of his pocket and pressing it into her hand, making her smile. "Thank you for being so accommodating."

"I should be thanking you. My girls can't stop talking about you and morale is definitely up. To hear them speak, you are some sort of god in the bedroom. There are even rumblings of working for free."

John patted her arm. "I wouldn't want to put you out of business." A thought occurred to him and he stopped. "I don't suppose you would be willing to rent out a private room upstairs, strictly for my own personal use for whenever I pop in? I would be willing to pay a premium price for that privilege, of course."

The madam's face lit up. "That is something I would be happy to arrange."

"Good," he said, pleased. "I will return in a few days and there are few upgrades for the room I will be needing. I will bring a list on my next trip, along with my 'preferences' for the type of women I will be wanting to keep company with."

"I will have everything ready for you— I didn't catch your name."

"Oh, it's John —just John. I think it is best if we stick to given names."

"Well, John, my name is Renee, and I look forward to doing business with you."

John was at the desk in the drawing room, working on correspondence for the business, when Gabe came in.

Gabe closed the pocket door behind him and took the chair on the other side. "Did it help?"

John laid down the quill he was using. "Did what help?"

"I am assuming you missed supper last evening because you went to a whorehouse, did you not?"

Sighing, John reclined back with his hands interlocked behind his head. "I did indeed."

"And?"

"It helped tremendously."

"Good!" Gabe smiled. "You keep doing that to keep your mind occupied.

John rubbed his chin. "I am actually making arrangements to keep a permanent, private room there."

"Oh really?" asked Gabe, somewhat surprised.

"I think it will be a good thing. I will have somewhere to go if it gets to be too much, and I won't have to worry about running into anyone who might recognize me. This way, I don't have to be concerned about expectations from other women."

"I agree," said Gabe. "Whatever it takes to get you through."

"Was the house your idea?" asked John unexpectedly.

Gabe bobbed his head. "I simply pointed out to Maggie you might enjoy a place of your own and that this house was getting a little crowded. I hope you don't take offense to it. I just thought it might make things easier on you, knowing how you feel. I didn't tell her anything else."

John nodded. "I appreciate you thinking of me, and perhaps you are right about that. I will never stop loving her, and I have to find a way to live with that because I know I can never have her."

Gabe offered him a sympathetic look. "I am always here for you, John. If there is anything I can do, or even if you just want to talk, don't hesitate to come to me."

"Thank you, Gabe. I may have to take you up on that offer."

"Anytime," he said, standing and opening the doors. "You know where to find me."

John watched him leave, grateful for his old friend's understanding.

19 Chapter Nineteen

Six months later, the men were absorbed in finishing the construction of John's house when Maggie realized there was some paperwork that urgently needed handling in Hampshire County. She let Duncan know she was going to shimmer up there and take care of things. No shipment was involved, and no one would pay attention to her comings and goings.

She was gathering her papers when her mother came in.

"What are ye up to?" Ana asked.

"I have to pop up north for a bit and take care of some business. It shouldn't take me long; I should be back before supper. I have found shimmering comes in extremely handy in the eighteenth-century."

"Mind if I tag along? I have been feeling a little cooped up lately."

"That is a wonderful idea," said Maggie. "This only requires a few signatures, and we can stop at one of the taverns for dinner afterward. Just let me tell Hettie, Rowe, and Noni we will be out for the afternoon."

After her work was concluded, they found the finest tavern in town. Taking a table, they sat chatting as a young woman came over to bring them drinks.

"Will you be having dinner?" she asked.

"Yes," replied Maggie. "Two of your finest meals."

She returned a short time later with two plates and when she set them down, Maggie smiled. "Are you excited?"

"About what, ma'am?"

Maggie nodded toward her swollen belly. "The baby!"

"Oh," she said, rubbing her rather large stomach, "I am more nervous than anything."

"Ye will be fine," assured Ana. "All expectant mothers feel the same way. Your husband must be excited."

The woman cast her eyes downward. "I am not married; the baby's father is gone," she said quietly.

Maggie's face softened. "Oh, I am so sorry. I am sure you will manage fine on your own."

"That's very sad," she whispered to her mother, watching the young woman walk away. "I know I was scared to death when I thought I was going to be a single mother, and she is so much younger than I was at the time. Thank God I had Gabe."

"Hopefully, she has family to help her," said Ana. "I know you feel bad for her, but there really isn't anything ye can do?"

Maggie tapped her fingers on the table. "Maybe there is a little something I can do." When they were finished and were ready to depart, Maggie called her server over. "I know being alone with the baby is going to be hard on you, but I hope this will help." She pressed a large bag of coins into her hand.

The woman looked down, dumbfounded. "What's this?"

"Just a little money to help get you started."

"I can't take this." The woman tried to give it back.

Maggie closed her hand around it with her own. "Yes, you can, and you will, for the baby's sake."

"Oh, ma'am, I don't know how to thank you." Tears spilled down her face.

"Just take care of that little one," she said and hugged her, "and tell me your name, so I can check on you the next time I am up this way?"

The woman wiped her face. "It's Lucy— Lucy Hanks."

"Well, Lucy, my name is Maggie, and this is my mother, Ana. We want to wish you the best of luck." Maggie held out her hands indicating she wished to touch her. "May I?" she asked. "I can tell you if it is a boy or a girl, if you would like to know. I have a sort of gift for this kind of thing."

Lucy smiled and nodded.

Maggie gently laid her hands on her swollen belly— and suddenly pulled back, looking rather surprised.

Ana took notice. "Maggie?"

"Is something wrong with my child?" Lucy pleaded for an answer anxiously.

Maggie composed herself. "No, not at all. It is a healthy baby girl." She smiled reassuringly.

Lucy grasped her by the hand and laughed. "A girl? Thank you, ma'am —for everything."

Once they were outside, Maggie hooked her arm around her mother's while they walked.

"Is something wrong with that baby?" asked Ana. "I saw your reaction."

"No. I just hadn't done that before and the information hit me so fast it caught me off guard."

"Oh, of course," said Ana. "That was very sweet of ye, what ye did back there."

Maggie glanced back at the tavern. "I can't explain it, but I felt a certain connection to her."

"I never knew I could actually feel another soul brooding until today," said Duncan from the doorway. He had just finished a bath and was standing with a towel around his waist, raking his fingers through his wet mane. When Maggie didn't respond, he walked up behind the chair she was sitting in and shook his wet hair all over her.

"Hey!" she exclaimed, holding out her hands, brushing off the water. "What did you do that for?"

"Because ye weren't paying attention to me," he replied, leaning down to kiss her shoulder, "and I am a very needy husband."

"I'm sorry. What were you saying?"

He came around to stand in front of her, picked her up and sat her back down on his lap. "I said that I can actually feel how ye are feeling, and it's rather disturbing. What has upset ye so much?"

When she didn't reply he used his finger to tip her chin up. "What is it? This isn't like ye."

"Mom and I went up to handle that business and we stopped off at a tavern for dinner. There was a young woman there, incredibly young and heavy with child. She said she had no husband and basically was alone. I felt bad for her because I knew exactly how she felt once upon a time."

Duncan intertwined his fingers in hers as she continued.

"I gave her some money, hoping it would help, and asked if I could lay hands on her belly, so I could let her know if she was having a boy or a girl, but when I touched her, I was hit by something I wasn't expecting."

"What was it?"

Maggie looked deep into his eyes. "That child she is carrying has Fae blood.

Duncan's face clouded over. "Ye are certain?"

"As certain as I am our children carry it."

"How? Who?" he asked. Suddenly, his body tensed. "Surely ye don't think I—"

"No! No!" she shook her head vigorously. "I know you and I are completely faithful to each other, my love. That thought never even occurred to me. I do, however, know who *that* child belongs to."

Duncan tilted his head to the side, quizzically.

"I spoke with Captain Russell. John took a room at that same tavern when they were there six or seven months ago."

"I see!" Duncan blew out a deep breath and sat quietly for a moment. "He needs to know."

"Does he?" she whispered.

He stared at her in disbelief. "He has a right to know, Maggie. She carries his bairn."

Maggie slipped off his lap and walked over to the fireplace. "Why? He will not marry her. He will have nothing to do with that child." She turned around to face him. "If he goes to her, she will get her hopes up and he will crush them when John does what John always does."

"He is a good father to the children at the tribe," Duncan argued.

"He is a good father when it is convenient for him. The mothers of his children there had no expectations from him when they lay with him; they were just thrilled to be able to have children of their own. Duncan, I love John, and it pains me more than you know to say this, but he will not do the right thing by this girl. Deep down, you know it as well as I do."

Standing, Duncan went to her.

"I made a huge mistake granting him fertility, and I bear the responsibility for this situation."

Duncan shook his head. "Nay, ye do not! John does. No one forces him to have relations with all these women."

"He would not have the ferocious appetite for them had I not made him the God of Sex and Lust."

Duncan took her by the shoulders. "I will not allow ye to blame yourself for this."

"Too late," she said, "and it's time I cleaned up my mess. I looked a few things up in the books in the collection room. I can take back the fertility I granted to him, making him sterile again. At the very least, he will not be populating half the countryside with his antics."

"I thought the world needed more Fae blood in its children," he said.

"Not like this—impregnating young women and leaving them to try to survive with no means in a country still recovering from a devastating war? It's not right, Duncan. It's not meant to be this way. Children should be conceived in love by parents who love and want them. Life is hard enough when the odds are *in* your favor."

He took her in his arms. "Ye are right."

"I will take it back without letting him know. It's obvious he is not taking any precautions."

"And the young mother?"

"I don't know," she sighed against his chest. He felt her body shake; she was softly crying, the events of the day becoming overwhelming.

"Shh!" he soothed. "I will see to the girl."

"What do you mean?" She leaned back slightly, and he wiped her tears.

"I will pay a visit, and make sure she has everything she needs. She and the child will want for nothing."

"Promise me you will not tell him," she implored, "for the sake of Lucy Hanks and her daughter."

"I don't agree with that action, Maggie," he frowned, "I can't imagine having one of my children kept from me."

"Duly noted, but I am making this decision for all concerned, and I will bear the responsibility for it. Promise me."

He hesitated, but reluctantly gave in. "Ye have my word."

Maggie was restless that night, so she went down to the collection room after everyone went to bed and selected a bottle from the endless supply of alcohol Finn had gifted them.

She heard him call from behind her chair. "Couldn't sleep?"

"A lot on my mind," she replied, biting her tongue when she caught a whiff of a woman's perfume wafting on the air. Shaking her head to herself, she turned up her glass, knowing full well he had just come from yet another's bed. "What are you doing up?" she asked, curious as to what his answer would be.

"Same!" and he poured his own beverage. "The house will be finished soon, and I was working on a list of items I am going to need —decided to take a break," he lied. He looked over at her as he sat down, his expression becoming serious. "You are noticeably quiet this evening. Is something bothering you?"

She shook her head. "I have just been busy, and I find myself rather weary."

Watching her intently, "Are you sure that's all it is?"

"I actually wanted to talk to you," she said, looking away.

"That's a coincidence," he said, touching his tongue to his top lip, "there is a delicate matter I wanted to discuss with you as well. I was waiting until we were alone to broach the subject."

Maggie waited for him to continue.

"I was wondering about something. The ability to sire children you gave me —is that something you can remove?"

"Why do you ask?" she inquired.

John's face became solemn. "I have decided I do not wish to have any more children. While I am beyond grateful for the three wonderful boys I have been blessed with, I think I have had enough. When Aurnia and I were together, I was not concerned because she was well past the age of conceiving, and I was with no one else, but now that we are finished —well, it's something I don't want to have to worry about. No offense, but that condom you gave me isn't very comfortable."

"So, you are done? No more? Are you sure you don't want to have a girl or two?"

John smiled. "I don't believe so. I love Morgan, Alanna, and Kat as if they were my own, and I think I will be content to just play the doting uncle. I am not sure I would be a particularly good father to a daughter anyway, especially since I know how men are."

Any doubts that Maggie had of keeping the information about Lucy Hanks from John, and making him sterile again, disappeared at that very moment.

"I can do that," she said, setting her glass down and standing. She walked over to stand in front of him, placing both her hands on his face. She closed her eyes, focused, and felt the energy leave his body, the same as it had entered. Maggie opened her eyes, sighed and kissed him on the forehead. Turning to go back to her chair, he firmly grasped her by the hand to hold her in place.

"Please tell me what's wrong," he implored, his eyes searching hers, "It breaks my heart to see you like this. It always has."

"I'm fine," she assured.

"Have you and Duncan had a disagreement?" he prodded.

"No," she whispered, "I have just had some difficult decisions to make, and they have been weighing me down, but I feel better now that I have made them."

He nodded, still holding her hand. "What was it you wanted to talk to me about?"

She forced a smile, touching his face with her free hand. "I was just wondering if you needed me to order anything for your house."

"Oh!" he said, a look of relief filling his eyes. "Thank you for asking, but I think I have it all under control."

Maggie patted his face. "I am going to bed. It has been a long day. Good night, John."

"Good night," he called, watching her leave.

That Saturday, Duncan slipped away from the house and shimmered into town. He took a table in the back corner of the tavern, trying to figure out the best way to handle the situation before him. He wrestled with his conscience, torn between the belief John had a right to know about the child and the promise he made to his wife, and while he had given his word to not tell John, there was nothing stopping the girl from telling him herself. He spotted Lucy serving ale to another table — the young woman was hard to miss in her condition.

"Christ, she is young," he said to himself. "What were ye thinking, John?"

Duncan caught the attention of the owner and waved him over.

"What can I do for you this fine day, sir?"

Duncan laid several coins on the table. "I need to speak with that young lady without being interrupted," he said, indicating the one with his eyes. The man looked down at the coins, a gleam in his eye, then back at Lucy before he laid his hand over the money.

"That can be arranged. Take all the time you need."

He walked over to her, spoke, and sent her to Duncan's table.

"What can I do for you?" she asked, wiping her hands on her apron.

He stood and pulled out a chair. "Ye can sit so we may talk for a bit."

"I shouldn't," she said looking over her shoulder at the bar keep.

"It's alright, I have already spoken to him."

"It would be nice to sit down," she said and sighed heavily.

Duncan helped her settle in before taking his own seat, looking very awkward. "My wife was fairly miserable her last couple of months, as well. It must be difficult working like this in your condition."

"I have no choice, sir. I have a child coming into this world and she will need to be provided for. What can I do for you—what was your name?"

"Duncan MacGregor, at your service." He looked down at the table and rubbed the back of his head. "Aye, well— there is no simple way to say this, so I am just going to come out with it. I know this is none of my business, and please forgive me for being so personal, but I have reason to believe my cousin is the father of your child."

Lucy stared back at him in disbelief. "What makes you think that?"

Duncan winced. "I can't go into a great deal of detail, but he was here on business from Williamsburg about six or seven months ago, and I know he stayed here for one night. He is the type of man who tends to attract the attention of women. His name is John MacGregor."

Lucy paled a little. "So, that is his family name."

"He never told ye his name?" asked Duncan, more than a little disturbed by that fact.

Lucy shook her head as she looked down, obviously upset.

Duncan leaned in close as a horrific thought crossed his mind. "Did he force ye to lay with him?"

Lucy's eyes went wide. "No! No! Not at all. He was truly kind to me. I wanted to be with him, more than he wanted to be with me, if you must know. I had no idea I would become with child. You didn't tell him, did you?" she asked, worried.

"No, I didn't. It is not my place, but don't ye think ye should tell him that ye carry his bairn?"

She looked around to make sure no one could hear. "I didn't know his name or how to find him."

"Now, ye know his name, and I can tell ye where he is," he encouraged. "Ye need only send him a letter."

She raised her chin. "I won't do it."

"Why not? Why would ye not want him to know? He has means, and he can provide for ye."

"Because, I may not have much, but I have my pride, and I will not have a man beholden to me who is in love with another."

Duncan blinked, confused. "Maybe, ye should explain to me what ye mean by that."

Lucy leaned her arms on the table. "That night, he had a great deal to drink. So much so, I had to help him to his room where I had prepared a bath for him. He was in no condition to even undress himself, so I did it for him."

She closed her eyes. "I could not help myself. I was overcome with a desire for him unlike anything I have ever known before, and I was sure that feeling was so strong, he must have felt the same. He tried, more than once, to stop me," she confessed, "but I was determined to be with him, no matter what. When he realized that fact, he gave in, but he made it clear he could promise me nothing beyond that night."

Damn it! I thought he finally had that under control.

"When we were done, as I lay against him, he drifted off to sleep, but before he did," she paused, "he called me by another's name, and I knew in that moment I had been terribly mistaken. He was so drunk that night he thought I was this other woman."

Duncan blew out a long breath. "I'm terribly sorry this happened to ye. I can only imagine how it must have made ye feel, but there *is* a child about to come into this world."

"A daughter I will raise myself. I'd rather eat scraps from the trash than have a man in my life who despises me and my child for not being the one he genuinely loves."

Duncan realized he could not argue with her logic and that it would be pointless anyway. This woman may be young, but her mind was made up.

"Very well," he said, "but I will not let ye and your child suffer because of this. Your daughter is special, whether ye know it or not." Duncan pulled out a leather satchel. "There is a great deal of money in this, and it should provide a comfortable life for the two of ye. There is also a calling card in here with the name of an attorney —David Percy. If ye need anything at all, contact him and he will see to it, or let me know so I can. He is very discreet, and your wish for John not to find out will be honored."

She brushed her fingers over the bag, stunned. "I don't know what to say. Thank you."

"Ye don't have to thank me, but I do have one request. Will ye write to me from time to time and let me know about the child's welfare and where ye are? She is a part of *my* family, after all."

"I will!" she promised. "You have my word."

Duncan stood, and touched her arm as he went to leave. Curiosity got the better of him, recalling John had been seeing someone before all of this happened, and he stopped. "I do have one more question," he said. "What was the name of the woman he called ye by?"

"Maggie," she whispered. "The name he called out was Maggie."

Duncan turned on his heel and trudged out of the establishment, stopping once he was outside to process what she had just said. He knew John loved Maggie, but he had no idea how much until that very instant, and the knowledge of it did not sit well with him.

Maggie was in the kitchen with Hettie and felt the instant Duncan returned. He sent her a message.

Upstairs! We need to talk.

"I will be back later," she said to Hettie, before going up to the bedroom.

She found Duncan pacing in front of the fireplace, his shirt and boots strewn across the floor as if he had taken them off in a fit of rage.

"I am almost afraid to ask how it went," she muttered, looking around, wincing when she noticed how agitated he was.

"COME HERE TO ME!" he ordered gruffly.

She slowly approached, unsure of what to expect from him in his current mood. He abruptly took her face in both hands, forcibly kissing her and demanding her full, uninterrupted attention. Something animalistic filled his face as he stared deep into her eyes, searching them, as he spoke from his very soul, "I do not want ye to ever forget ye belong to me and no one else. Ye are my entire world, Maggie MacGregor. I have never, and will never, love another as I do ye. No woman should ever wonder, or doubt, how the man who claims her body feels about her inside his heart." He kissed her again fervently, in desperate need of proving how impassioned his feelings were, moving his hands down to remove her dress. Deciding it was taking entirely too long, he ripped the gown and her shift clean in half down the front with his bare hands and shoved it back off her shoulders, allowing it to fall to the floor, until she stood bare before him.

"Duncan..." she started to say, but he cut her off by covering her mouth with his, sucking her breath in with such force, she thought she might suffocate. Wrapping his arms around her, he laid her on the floor in front of the hearth, his mouth still on hers as he freed himself from his own clothing constraints.

Maggie felt something unlike anything she had ever felt before, on a level surely not of this world —on fire, as if she were about to internally combust—and he was the only accelerant she would ever desire to feed that searing flame.

He fell upon her, asserting his claim with his body; she gasped for air as he readied for their joining. She moaned, biting and clawing his shoulders as he rubbed the tip of his erection against her entrance, both overcome with insurmountable desire. "I love ye!" he hissed through his teeth before filling her completely— taking her with one powerful, all-claiming massive thrust.

She cried out, tears spilling down her face— taken aback by the shock of it, amazed by the indescribable feeling of it, and overcome by the sheer amount of love she felt for this glorious man.

Stilling his movement, Duncan rested inside of her, the sincerity in his beautiful eyes the only thing she could see as he brushed back the hair from her face. "Never doubt my love for ye," he whispered, before starting to move his hips, pulling almost all the way out and then pushing back in deeply, perfectly, with slow, agonizing strides, making her feel on the verge of an orgasm each time he moved; she whimpered with each stroke. He stopped, moving to suckle on her breasts, one after the other, taking his time, pausing his assault, making her even more insane with lust.

"Who do ye belong to now and for all eternity?" he asked gutturally.

"You!" she answered, breathily, her chest heaving. "It has, and always will be, ONLY you!" She took his face in her hands and pulled it up to look at him. "I love you more than anything in this world, the next, and the one after that! Now, will you just fuck me already!"

He tossed his head back and laughed. "Whatever my love desires, she shall have."

Bracing himself, taking the time to graze his teeth across her shoulder, Duncan pressed his forehead to hers, before slamming into her at a merciless speed, the sound of flesh upon flesh the only sound filling the room.

Maggie came so hard and fast, her sight actually darkened for a few seconds. More tears flooded her face as her emotions overwhelmed. Clinging to him, she sobbed against his chest as Duncan spilled himself deep inside of her.

Overcome as well, he found himself unable to form thoughts or words. Duncan closed his eyes, the sound of his heart pounding in his ears the only thing he could hear. He kissed away the tears from her face before resting his cheek on her breast. Finally, after being able to muster a bit of strength, he rolled over. They lay side by side, silent, drenched in sweat and gasping for air.

Maggie had no energy or desire to move— her limbs simply refused to obey. Mumbling, she asked, "Not that I am complaining in the least, but what the hell was that, and why have you never done it before?"

Duncan chuckled and slipped his hand in hers. "The only thought in my mind was I wanted ye to feel how much I love ye, and for ye to never be able to forget it. I guess ye aren't the only one who can wish up things."

"Mission accomplished," she laughed softly as he lifted her hand and kissed it. "Although, someone may have to scrape me off this floor in a day or so. I can't move any part of my body at all."

"Allow me, my love," he said and rolled over, kissing her shoulder before picking her up and carrying her to their bed. He poured a glass of rum from a bottle on the nightstand and sat down next to her, lifting the glass to her lips, helping her. "Drink!"

She obeyed.

He downed one for himself then crawled onto the bed to lay beside her. Slipping his arm underneath her, he gently adjusted so she rested upon his chest.

They heard a knock at the door, followed by the sound of voices belonging to people who had apparently gathered in the hall.

Gabe cleared his throat. "Everything alright in there?" he called out.

"Knock twice if ye need help," added Quinn— he and Gabe began to snicker.

"Leave them alone, ye two," they heard Ana order, along with the sounds of her shooing them away. "For goodness sakes, never interrupt a girl getting banged like that. We should all be so lucky. Why don't ye boys make yourselves useful and go clean up the ceiling dust off the floor downstairs?"

Maggie and Duncan leaned into each other laughing.

"Go away! We are having a private discussion," yelled Duncan in response.

"And the topic?" pressed Gabe.

"Unwelcome house guests who eavesdrop, and how to get rid of them!" he responded.

They heard an uproar of laughter erupt from the hallway and it slowly started to fade as the group departed.

Maggie stroked his chest with her finger. "Seriously!" she said. "What brought this little session on? Surely, you are not insecure about us."

"Nay, I am not," he sighed, "Lucy Hanks —I went to see her today, as we talked about doing. She told me John was drunk that night and he thought she was someone else while they were together. She wants nothing to do with him, saying she would rather eat out of the trash than have a man in her bed in love with someone else." He kissed the side of her head. "I don't want ye to EVER question or be uncertain of my love for ye."

"I don't, Duncan," she assured. "I won't! I never have and I never will. You and I are truly one soul, and nothing will ever come between us or change that." She grinned. "Although, I wouldn't hate a reminder like this every now and then."

"I will keep that in mind," he laughed, "Anyway, Lucy and the child are all set up, and she has David's information if she needs anything. I also asked her to write and keep us informed as to the welfare of the child."

"Good," she said and kissed his chest. "I do have one question though. What made Lucy think John thought she was someone else?"

Duncan hesitated. "He called out someone else's name while they were together."

Maggie made a face. "Ouch! That must have hurt. Whose name did he call out?" she asked, warily, afraid it might have been Aurnia's.

"She didn't say," he lied. "She only said she did not want him to know about her condition. After speaking with her, I must say I have to agree with that; it may be for the best and the least we can do is respect her wishes."

"I think it is the right call. There is something else I need to tell you. John asked me to make him sterile again."

Duncan looked down, surprised. "Did he really?"

"He said he didn't want any more children, and he felt as if he wouldn't want any daughters anyway."

Duncan huffed. "Well, that's his loss. I would not trade the world for my girls."

"We need to keep an eye on him, Duncan. I am afraid, given his human personality combined with this Fae power, he may be close to becoming out of control. I am personally responsible for all things Fae unleashed on this world."

"Ye mean, *we* are responsible," he said. "Don't worry about John. I am making it my business to keep a very watchful eye on him from now on." He rolled over on her, kissing her slowly, thoroughly, while caressing her body with his hands.

"Take a nap before supper. I have some things to see to and ye will need your strength for later," he teased, smacking her rear playfully. He went over to find his clothes. Picking up what was left of what she had on, he held it up and inspected it. "Remind me to take ye shopping. I owe ye a gown."

Maggie turned on her side to face him. "Small price to pay for an afternoon like that," she grinned. "I'll happily sacrifice my entire wardrobe."

He dressed, then kissed her once more before going downstairs where he found Gabe, Quinn, and Ana. They all stopped to give him an amused look when he came in.

"Where's Maggie?" asked Gabe.

"She is resting," he replied, as he poured a whisky and downed it.

"The poor woman may not be able to walk for days," teased Quinn.

Duncan cut his eyes over at him good-naturedly, attempting to give him a harsh look, but the satisfied expression on his face gave him away.

"Lucky girl!" Ana complimented Duncan and raised her glass in his direction.

He turned so she was the only one who could see his face, smirked and winked.

Ana fanned herself with her hand and laughed.

"Where's John?" he asked.

"I...umm...believe he had some matters to attend to. I don't expect we will see him for supper," replied Gabe, looking away.

"As do I," said Duncan. "Please let Maggie know I will be back later," he smiled to himself, "to finish what we started."

20 Chapter Twenty

Duncan stood outside the whorehouse in London shaking his head. Ana had been right about their powers growing with time. He had been studying the Dagda's book, learning a few tricks of his own, one of them being how to focus his mind and feel where the others were at any given time —his search for John leading him to this spot.

Waving his hand over his face, he disguised himself as an old man, giving him the ability to move around unnoticed —the gift of being a magician and part of being the Dagda. Pushing open the door of the brothel, he stepped inside, pretending to have a hard time moving. One of the working girls, wearing a thin robe, open from the waist up with her breasts on full display, met him as he came inside. Looking him over, she scratched the back of her head with a disinterested expression on her face.

"What sort of services are you looking for tonight?" she asked, with a frown.

"Oh, I just want to sit down by the fireplace and warm these old bones," he replied.

"That's all?" she asked, rather annoyed. "We don't run a charity 'round here, you know!"

"Oh, I have money." Duncan stuck his hand in his pocket, pretending to fish around, taking his sweet time. The woman tapped her foot impatiently. Duncan produced a few coins, more than most of the women made in an entire week and held them up. "Will this buy me a chair and maybe a little something to drink?"

Her face lit up and she smiled at him. "It'll buy you more than that, sweetie," she said, snatching the money and holding it up before slipping the robe back a little further on her shoulders and shaking her chest. She took him by the arm and led him to a small table, pulling out a chair and pushing him down in it before climbing on his lap.

"My name is Vera. What's your pleasure tonight?" She ran her hand around to the back of his head and forcefully pulled his face to her chest, planting his nose right in her cleavage. "Go on," she encouraged, "you are welcome to have a taste. I have been told I have the 'best tits' in London."

Maggie is going to kill me.

Duncan pulled back, going out of his way not to put his hands on her.

"No, I don't think so," he said, his eyes wide. "I don't really like— 'tits'," he lied.

"Suit yourself." She reached down and started undoing his breeches. He caught her by the wrists. "What are ye doing there, missy?"

"I am going to suck your cock."

"No! No! Ye are not!" he said, shaking his head back and forth. "That's really not what I want either."

She stood up and put her hands on her hips. "Look old man, you have paid me a great deal of money, and I work for my coin, so you are getting something for it, whether you like it or not."

Oh, Jesus Christ.

"Ye see—" he stuttered, "I—more like to—observe people."

"Well, why didn't you say so in the first place?" she asked, and playfully tapped his chest. "Hey Molly! We got a watcher!" she called over her shoulder.

Molly was in the corner, bouncing up and down on the lap of another man. "Give me a minute. I'm almost done," she replied before turning back to face her customer. "Oh, you have the biggest cock I have ever had. You are the best! Oh! Oh! Oh!" she said to him with no emotion or enthusiasm in her voice, simply going through the motions. Resting her hand on the wall, she examined one of her fingernails while the transaction was taking place. When he was finished, Molly patted his cheek and climbed off. "See you next week, Bob," she said.

"Have a good week, Molly!" The man pulled his pants up and went on his way.

Molly stopped to wash herself with a rag that had been soaking in a pot of rose water before coming over to join them. "So, you like to watch, do you?" she asked, drying herself off. "Has he got money?" she asked Vera, who leaned over and whispered in her ear. Molly looked over at Duncan with a renewed interest. "For that price, you can have us in a private room for the night. We'll do whatever you please," she offered with a wide grin.

"He doesn't like 'tits'," whispered Vera, behind her hand.

Molly frowned and looked Duncan up and down. "Not a cock lover, are you? Because we can't help you there. There's another place up the street…"

Duncan groaned inwardly. "Nay, I am not," he cut her off. "I meant, I just want to sit down, have a drink and watch the others around me. I don't want anything else. I am a married man, and I won't ever lay with another woman."

Molly and Vera exchanged looks and nodded at each other in understanding.

"She's hard to look at?" inquired Vera sympathetically. "And you need a little 'help' getting it up for her?"

"Face of a dog, but you truly love her?" asked Molly, her hand flying to her heart, touched by his love.

"Aye, that's it," surrendered Duncan. "It's our anniversary, and she's expecting me home later to perform my 'husbandly duties'. Being an old man, things don't work as well as they used to."

Molly and Vera smiled at each other.

"You are a good man," said Molly as she waved one of the other girls for a bottle and a glass. "You just sit right there, enjoy your drink, and watch whatever you like. Find Vera and me when you are ready and will work you up real good before you go home."

"We'll help you to give her a night to remember," promised Vera.

Duncan let out a sigh of relief as she poured a glass for him. He downed it in one gulp.

I know I'll never forget this night.

"Thank ye, ladies. Don't mind me. I will be over here in the corner, minding my own business."

Once they left, he poured another glass and sucked down the inferior alcohol, feeling a strong burn as it hit the back of his throat. He pulled his chair around to be in a better position to see what was going on around him. Vera and Molly each took on new customers, making sure to 'perform' in full sight so he could see. He would occasionally smile and nod when they waved at him.

He waited.

About an hour later, John came down the stairs, a dreamy look on his face, his clothes askew, with three very satisfied looking women on his arm. When he reached the bottom of the stairs, the madam of the establishment went to join them. She pulled him over to a table not far from where Duncan was. John took a seat as two of the women each took a leg and sat down on his lap. He took turns kissing them as they giggled.

"I trust these girls met your expectations?" the madam asked him.

"Renee," he said after nibbling on the bare breast of one of the women, "your choices are exceptional, and the room you furnished is exactly how I wanted it. You could only please me more if you found a few more beauties like these for me."

"Your tastes are very specific, John," she claimed. "For the time being, they are all I have to offer, unless you wish a little variety. It is the spice of life, after all. Take Vera over there," she pointed, "she has the 'best tits' in London."

John leaned over for a look. "They are very nice indeed, but she is a blonde, and I only want dark-haired girls."

Duncan stole a glance at the three women who were on John's arm and a stunning realization slammed him in the gut. All three of those women looked a great deal— like Maggie. He searched his memories. Lucy Hanks could have easily passed for a younger version of Maggie. He felt a little bile rise in the back of his throat. John was only bedding women who looked like his wife. He sat back in his chair, trying to process this new information and what it meant.

"Why don't you send Vera over to the old-timer?" he heard John say. "He looks a little lonely."

Duncan looked up and noticed John was speaking directly to him. He cast his eyes downward into his glass, pretending not to hear. John rose and came over to his table, laying a few coins down.

"You look like you could use a good time," he said to Duncan. "Have some fun, on me tonight."

"He likes to watch." Molly had come over.

"Does he now?" asked John. "Allow me," he said and pulled one of the dark-haired girls over to him, kissing her, then lifting her and placing her on Duncan's table. He proceeded to bury his face in her breasts, licking and teasing with his tongue, glancing over at Duncan every now and then. He smirked as he moved his hand down on her, working his fingers in and out of her until she gripped the edge of the table and cried out in delight.

John leaned down next to Duncan and whispered, "I have already satisfied her, and now I am happy to let you enjoy her for a little while before I take her back later — as long as you don't mind the fact I had her first." John slapped him on the back. "Have fun, old man," he laughed and turned, heading for the door with a little something extra in his step, "while you can, that is."

The woman flipped over on her stomach and tugged on his shirt, smiling. "We can go upstairs if you are shy."

Duncan pushed her hand away. "Not tonight." He stood up and walked out of the brothel, stopping to look back at the door once he was outside. He flicked his hand and returned to his true form, before shimmering back to the collection room at the house in Virginia.

Duncan was so lost in his own thoughts when he arrived, he did not even notice that Gabe and Quinn were sitting in the chairs just to his left. He stood there for a moment, quiet and unmoving, until suddenly, he let out a great, grievous roar and punched the solid gold altar table, breaking it completely in half. The entire room shook violently.

"Duncan, what the hell are ye doing?" shouted Quinn, he and Gabe springing to their feet, looking around.

Duncan was still staring down at the table, breathing hard, a murderous expression filling his face. Once Quinn noticed his condition, he approached him cautiously, holding out a hand to gingerly touch him on the shoulder. "Brother?"

Duncan closed his eyes and swallowed hard as he tried to get himself under control.

"What's going on?" Quinn asked gingerly.

Clearing his throat, he turned his head in their direction, his eyes still looking down. "NOTHING!" he growled.

"Doesn't look like 'nothing'," mumbled Gabe.

"Tell us what the matter is, Brother."

Maggie and Ana appeared at the top of the stairs looking worried.

"Everyone alright down here?" Maggie called over the top rail.

"We're fine," said Gabe, eyeing Duncan warily.

"Is everything good upstairs? The children?" asked Quinn, glancing back at Gabe.

"Yes, everyone's fine," she replied, and they came down the staircase. "I just wasn't expecting an earthquake tonight."

"Oh no," Ana saw the table, coming over to examine it, "the earthquake did this?"

Gabe and Quinn both turned their focus to Duncan.

"Aye," Duncan finally answered. "It was all very strange and happened rather quickly. I will see to it that it gets repaired."

John appeared in front of the fireplace, surprised to see the others standing there.

"Did I miss something?" he asked.

"An earthquake apparently," replied Maggie. "Didn't you feel it? Where were you?"

"I was at the shipping office working on some paperwork."

"This late?" asked Maggie.

"Ye know John," alluded Duncan, "always completely absorbed in his endeavors, no matter what they might be."

Quinn cocked his head to one side. "What exactly is an 'earthquake'?"

"Oh!" Maggie frowned and looked down at the pieces, pushing them with her toe. "It's something that happens, though not usually in Virginia. The world has fault lines in different areas and when the ground shifts, it causes everything to shake like that, although now that I think about it, there is a fault line north of here. They can carry a great distance and cause quite a bit of devastation."

"That must have been it," Duncan half-smiled and took Maggie by the hand, pulling her to him.

"It looks like the only damage is this one table," Maggie frowned, "Which *is* a little odd."

"Isn't that our specialty around here?" remarked Gabe dryly.

"I suppose it is." She turned her attention to Duncan. "I hope this won't interrupt our plans for the night."

"Of course not," he replied, brushing her hair back from her shoulders. "Nothing will keep me from that, my love," his eyes fell upon John as he continued, "I will never let ye forget ye are mine, and why ye chose *me alone* to be in your bed for all eternity." He smiled, embraced her tightly, kissed the top of her head and they disappeared.

Ana walked around the heap of rubble on the floor, examining it closely. "This doesn't look like it was caused by a quake. Looks more like something with a great deal of force split it right down the middle," stealing a suspicious look at Gabe and Quinn, "Ye boys wouldn't know anything about it, would ye?"

Quinn raked his hand back through his hair, glancing at Gabe before cracking a smile at Ana. "I am afraid Maggie and Duncan's earlier activities inspired us. We may have gotten a little out of control."

Gabe stepped behind Quinn, putting his arms around him, resting his chin upon his shoulder. "Quinn is right. It seems we didn't know our own strength."

Ana stared at them trying to decide if she believed them. She looked down and grinned. "At today's rate, there won't be any house left by the end of the week."

"Seems I missed a great deal today," said John.

Ana took him by the arm. "Come on, I will fill ye in over drinks upstairs. We'll give these two some privacy. Try not to break anything else, boys."

John patted her hand, and they departed.

"Ana," called Gabe as they reached the top landing, "maybe it is best if we don't tell Maggie about this. She would never let us live it down."

"Your secret is safe with me," she said before leaving. "Have fun!"

Once she was gone, Quinn spoke. "What do ye think upset Duncan so badly?"

"I don't know, but whatever it was, let's hope Maggie can calm him down. I don't care to see him like that ever again."

A week later, Maggie sat with chin in palm, her elbow propping it up, absentmindedly tapping a letter on her desk.

"You look rather pensive," remarked Gabe as he came into the room.

"I am trying, and failing, to remember something from history."

"What might that be?" he inquired curiously.

Maggie sighed. "I think Ben should have met the woman he is supposed to marry by now, but I just got a letter from him, and it is obvious he has not." She screwed up her face. "I think it may be time to intervene."

"In what way?"

"In a way Duncan isn't going to like." She got up and went over to Gabe's side. "Has Duncan seemed a little 'off' this week to you?"

Gabe thought back to the table in the collection room. "Now that you mention it, maybe a tad. Is there something on his mind?"

"I don't know. If there is, he isn't saying, and he is not letting me pick up on it. He can do this trick where he makes me forget stuff when we are —*you know*—and I have forgotten a great deal this past week. Come to think of it, it's a wonder I even remember my own name."

"We are all very aware," he noted dryly.

"Yeah," she replied, a smile spreading across her face while she chewed on her lip. "It's been —well, there are no words. I could barely walk this morning— had to shimmer into the bathroom."

"That's entirely too much information, Mags!" Gabe grimaced while taking a seat and waving his hand. "You were speaking of Ben."

"Oh yes! I think I might need to make a little trip up north and arrange an introduction."

"How do you plan on doing that?"

"With this," she said, handing him an invitation, "One of the storekeepers we supply in New York, and one we helped out a great deal when he was having a hard time, is having a party to celebrate the victory over the British. He was gracious enough to invite us. If we can get Mary Floyd and Ben under the same roof and introduce them with one of Quinn's love potions, we can get things on track."

"You're right, Duncan is going to hate this idea."

"Which is why we are not telling him. If you and Quinn can keep him busy for a few hours, John can help me, and Ben can get his happily ever after."

"How are you getting them to the same party?"

"I have already sent a letter to her father, along with the invitation, explaining how wonderful it would be if he and his family would grace this event with his presence, and how it might behoove his future political career."

"You know her father?"

Maggie shook her head and chuckled. "No, but I signed it 'General Washington'. Who can refuse an invitation like that?"

Gabe rolled his eyes. "Who indeed? And Ben?"

"I will just send him a note informing him I am in town and to meet me there. He will come." Maggie heard John in the hall speaking to Noni. She called him in. "I need your assistance."

"Anything for you," he said. "What can I do?"

She explained her plan.

"I'm in," he readily offered. "I'm dying for a party and a little excitement anyway."

21 Chapter Twenty-One

December 1783
New York

Maggie and John peered out from behind the heavy, blue velvet curtains. The room was packed with people celebrating the American victory over the British. The war had officially ended on September 3rd, but the celebrations had continued for months.

"Which one do you think she is?" asked Maggie.

"Your guess is as good as mine," replied John. "Are you sure he is going to be here?"

"Yes! I sent him a note and asked him to meet me here tonight. He will come."

"Duncan is not going to be happy about this," he whispered.

"Well, if Gabe and Quinn are doing their part, he will never know."

Maggie gave John a little push. "Now, get out there and go find her."

She grabbed him by the shoulders. "Wait! Don't get distracted and make sure Ben doesn't see you. He will recognize you instantly."

"What's he going to do? Hang me?" he asked sarcastically.

"No, but I will if you get caught," she said, and shoved him out into the group.

"How do I let you talk me into these things?" he mumbled, moving into the crowd.

"Oh, you love it," she retorted.

He responded with a wink and a mischievous smile over his shoulder for her to see.

Maggie shook her head and watched the women flock to him. Ever since he had become the God of Lust and Sex, women could not keep their hands off him. He dripped sex appeal everywhere he went.

Maggie watched John work his way through the crowd. She rolled the potion bottle back and forth in her hands, hoping this was not the worst idea she had ever had.

"Boo!" whispered a voice in her ear.

Maggie jumped, startled, turning to see Duncan standing behind her, his arms folded with a scolding look on his face. "Just what the hell do ye think ye are doing?"

Damn it!

"Who ratted me out?" she demanded.

"Ye forget. Quinn is my little brother. He cannot keep secrets from me. I have been worming information out of him since he came into this world."

Maggie rolled her eyes. "He kept the fact he preferred men from you forever, but he couldn't keep his mouth shut about this for one stinking day?"

Duncan scrunched up his face. "Exactly, what *are* ye doing?"

Maggie wrinkled her nose at him. "Giving Ben his happy ending. He has not been able to move on from what happened between us, and I cannot in good conscience continue to let him be alone. He deserves to be happy after all he has done for this country."

Sighing, Duncan took her in his arms. "Aye, he does. What can I do to help?" He kissed her before they turned to face the crowd.

"Help John find Mary Floyd. She is the woman Ben is destined to marry." She held up the bottle. "We are just going to help it along a little bit to make sure it sticks…literally."

"What is that?"

Maggie grinned. "A love potion Quinn brewed up from one of the books. That, along with a little 'lust dust' from John, should put things right back on course."

"I hope ye know what ye are doing," he said cautiously.

"You and me both," she mumbled. She nodded her head to her left. "Why don't you ask around over there and see if we can figure out which one she is?"

"Whatever ye say," he said and headed off.

Maggie caught sight of John, who now had seven women surrounding him, liking it a little too much. She waved until she got his attention, pointing around the room to remind him of the business they were there for. He grimaced and turned his focus back to the ladies. She could see him asking them questions.

Duncan had taken up with a couple of the men near the fireplace trying to get information out of them. She was so absorbed in the scene before her, she never noticed his approach.

"It looks like you are hiding over here."

She turned and smiled. "Hello, Ben."

He leaned over and kissed her cheek. "Hello, Maggie."

The stress of the war did not show on him. He looked older, yes, but in a handsome, rugged way.

"I must say, I was surprised to get your note," he said. "I had no idea you were in New York."

"Yes, I just had some business to attend to and how could I resist a celebration like this?"

"It has been a long, hard road, one we would have never succeeded at if not for your help."

"Ben, you give me far more credit than I deserve. There are many others who did a great deal more than I did and they are the ones who deserve the praise."

"Are you here alone?" he asked.

"No, Duncan is here, and an old friend is with us."

"I...um...should like to *officially* meet him," he said, and looked down.

Maggie noticed John headed her way with a broad smile on his face. As soon as he saw Ben, he made an abrupt U-turn and went back the way he came.

Duncan sent Maggie a silent message. *She is by the refreshment table, in a blue dress.*

Maggie smiled at Ben and patted his chest. "I think it is past time the two of you met." He offered his arm and she accepted.

"What will you do now?" she asked as they walked.

Ben shrugged. "I'm not sure. I have given some thought to opening a store in Litchfield —maybe live the quiet life for a while."

"Settle down? Marry?" she asked hopefully.

"I don't think so," he replied softly.

We'll see.

Nearing the table, Ben picked up two glasses from a tray, and handed one to Maggie.

"Good evening," said Maggie to Mary, as they approached. "I don't believe we have met. I am Maggie MacGregor, and this is my friend, Major Benjamin Tallmadge."

"Actually, it's 'Colonel' now," he smiled sheepishly, "I was promoted."

"Congratulations," she said, holding up her glass.

"Yes, congratulations. I am Mary Floyd."

"It is a pleasure to make your acquaintance," he said and bowed.

Maggie downed her drink. "I think I need a refill," she said as she went to take Ben's glass, "and I will top yours off too while you keep Miss Floyd company for a moment."

Ben looked down. "My glass is still full."

Maggie took it out of his hand and downed it in one shot. "Not anymore," she said, shaking her head from the rush. "I will be right back, and I will get one for Miss Floyd, as well, so she can celebrate with us."

Ben gave her a puzzled look, but his manners stopped him from asking what was going on in front of Mary.

Maggie turned to see John had joined Duncan and was giving him instructions and a potion bottle. She took the glasses over to the table with the drinks; Duncan met her there.

"Are you sure about this?" He made a drink for Mary with the potion.

"Not really," she said and made one for Ben with the bottle she had. She poured two more for her and Duncan, then took a swig from a nearby bottle.

"You take that one to Mary and DON'T mix the glasses up. The last thing I need is you and Ben falling in love," she chuckled.

Duncan shook his head and laughed. "That would be unfortunate."

"I love you," she said as she gazed at him.

"I love ye too," he replied.

They went back to Ben and Mary, handing them their respective drinks.

"Allow me to officially introduce my husband, Duncan. This is Miss Floyd, and this is Ben."

Ben nodded before slowly holding out his hand to shake Duncan's. "It is a pleasure to finally meet you, sir."

Duncan returned the handshake with a warm smile. "The pleasure is all mine."

Maggie held up her glass for a toast. "Here is to the end of the war and to new beginnings. You never know what the future holds."

They all clinked glasses, Maggie watching anxiously.

Ben and Mary took a sip, their eyes met, and it was if they had just seen each other in that very instant.

Maggie smiled when she saw the looks on their faces— and knew they were in love.

John, with a woman on his arm, walked up behind Ben, lightly touching his back, giving him a little touch of desire. His body shivered slightly, as if he had gotten a chill —and he stepped to the side to 'adjust' himself.

Maggie smirked at Duncan, who was using his hand to cover the amusement on his face. She touched his back. "I'm sorry, Ben, but we must go."

"So soon?" Ben was disappointed. "We haven't had time to catch up."

"There will be plenty of time for that in the future," she said, and squeezed his hand. "It was good to see you, Ben."

"And you too, Maggie."

Maggie hugged him and whispered in his ear. "Be happy!"

He nodded. "You too, and don't be a stranger."

"You never know where I may turn up." She kissed his cheek, smiled, and turned to Duncan.

Ben and Mary were already lost in each other's gaze.

"Time to go home, my love." Duncan took her hand in his and squeezed, smiling.

John kissed two women 'goodbye' before he came to join them. "How did it go?"

"I would say 'mission accomplished'," replied Maggie, and they stepped outside into the garden and then into the fog, arriving back at their home in Virginia in a matter of moments.

MacCray enjoyed a glass of punch and exchanged pleasantries with some of the other men celebrating the end of the war. After Tallmadge had taken him in, he had devoted everything within his power to winning the conflict —and they had. This night was a time to commemorate and bask in their glory.

Stepping aside to welcome another gentleman to the conversation, someone else caught his attention —a stunningly beautiful woman standing near a curtained window, obviously searching the room for a particular person.

Lucky man.

He noted she looked familiar, but he could not for the life of him place her —until HE appeared just behind her, seemingly out of nowhere. The face of a dead man and one he would not forget for as long as he lived.

But it couldn't be him because that man was murdered on that fateful day in Virginia. His gaze shifted back to the woman —and his heart pounded loudly against his chest as the recognition set in. It wasn't possible, but there she stood.

She looked vastly different this evening from the last time he'd seen her —happy and laughing—nothing like the demon who came to drag men to Hell. He watched as they separated and the man came over to join some others by the fireplace, introducing himself. He took a step closer to hear what the man was saying.

"Duncan MacGregor, at your service."

The glass in MacCray's hand started to tremble and his blood ran cold; he felt his limbs go weak and numb.

Dear God, it *was* him— and he was very much alive.

MacCray was just about to maneuver himself even closer to the conversation when he saw something that made his knees literally start to shake. The woman, the banshee, was speaking to Tallmadge and it was obvious they were extremely familiar with one another. He set down his drink and slipped back towards the next room, hoping to not be seen, afraid the woman might recognize him and make good on her promise. He made his way out into the garden, dropped to his knees, and planted his hands flat on the ground, the fear he experienced causing him to vomit.

Once his stomach had fully relieved itself of its contents, he turned so he could sit with his bottom on the ground and tried to make some sort of sense of what he had just witnessed. How could this man be alive? Who was this woman —or rather *what*— was she? He remained there for what had to be a quarter of an hour, in the darkness and the shadows, lost in thought, his mind trying to somehow piece together the puzzle.

MacCray's concentration was broken when he heard laughter from the doorway and saw a trio come outside, happily chatting as a strange mist filled the air around them. As soon as he recognized them as the banshee and the dead man, along with one more, he scrambled to the nearest dark wall to conceal himself —and watched as they disappeared into thin air. He felt the breath leave his body, his head swimming, making him feel faint. The stories of the 'old ones' his Granny had told him about suddenly flooded his mind.

Could it be possible? Could they be real? And if they were, how could he protect himself and others?

January 1784

Duncan had spent the past few weeks trying to figure out what to do about John's little obsession with Maggie. He had told no one else, and the thought of letting things go just would not settle with him. Something had to be done. Duncan waited until John excused himself for the day after dinner, as he always did on those afternoons, claiming to have some business to attend. This time, Duncan was onto him, and managed to shimmer into John's private room at the whorehouse before he arrived. He was sitting in a chair by the fireplace when John stumbled in, entangled in the arms of yet another woman who looked like Maggie.

"Leave us!" ordered Duncan.

The woman looked to John, who nodded. Once she had left, John poured a glass of whisky and kicked back in the chair across from Duncan.

"What are you doing here?" asked John.

"I should be asking ye that."

John shrugged. "The same thing all men do in whorehouses. How did you know where I was anyway?"

"I sensed it, and I followed ye."

"Hmmm— and I thought I was being discreet."

"What are ye doing putting in requests for women who look like my wife?"

John stopped mid-sip, slowly lowering the glass. "What can I say? I like dark-haired women."

"Who look a great deal like Maggie?"

John cast his eyes downward, silent, unsure of what to say. "Does she know?" he finally asked.

"Nay, no one else does. She does not need to know because it would upset her, and I will not have that." Duncan leaned forward. "I am only here as a reminder. I can't fault ye for loving her because it's hard not to. Maggie cares a great deal for ye and so do I —ye are part of our family, but, if ye step an inch out of line, even once, I will put an end to ye, I give ye my word. Fuck all the dark-haired whores ye can manage to find— do whatever ye need to do to get it out of your system. I don't really care how ye satisfy your urges, but know ye will NEVER have my wife."

"So that's the end of it?" asked John. "You find out I am bedding women who remind me of Maggie, and you are going to just let it go so easily?"

"As far as I am concerned, as long as ye remember yourself, it is life as usual." Duncan stood and tossed a few coins on the table on his way out. "The next one's on me. I suggest ye try a blond. Variety is the spice of life, after all, and ye may find your tastes have changed."

Duncan left through the door as to not arouse suspicion, leaving John sitting alone.

John stared straight ahead until the madam knocked on the door and cracked it open. "Everything alright, John? Did you not like the girl?"

"She's fine," he called out. "Send her back in with another like her, and Renee, I may need a couple more before the morning."

He sucked down his drink, tapping his fingers on the arm of the chair while he waited, wondering what had prompted Duncan's unexpected visit. The thought of getting under Duncan's skin *that* much pleased him more than he cared to admit, and he wondered why a man as secure in his marriage as Duncan claimed to be, felt the need to pay him a visit at all —he smiled.

Maggie sat, leaning back against the headboard, with her knees up, sipping a glass of rum, and reading a book, when Duncan shimmered in.

"Where have you been?" she asked, startling him.

"Oh, I had something that needed tending," he said and came over to kiss her.

She held up her hand, stopping him in his tracks, when she caught a whiff of the cheap perfume on him. "What sort of 'something'?" she demanded. "You smell like you have been in a whorehouse."

Duncan scrunched up his face.

"You HAVE been in a whorehouse?" she asked, shoving him away. "What the hell? The Dagda is no longer satisfied by his wife? Does he need more than one woman to meet his needs now?" she spat, on the verge of being enraged.

"Of course not," he scoffed. "You are the only woman I desire."

"Then what were you doing there?"

Duncan rolled his eyes. "I needed to have a word with John, and that is where he was at the time."

Maggie waved her hand around. "We have a drawing room and a secret collection room downstairs. You couldn't speak with him in one of those places?"

Duncan raked his hand through his hair. "John and I needed to come to an understanding."

"What sort of understanding?"

He sat down on the edge of the bed, trying to figure out what to tell her without saying the real reason. "John has been frequenting these types of places a great deal as of late. I was concerned that, by choosing one in London, he might be recognized as John André. I felt it best to head him off, so to speak."

"Again, I ask, why couldn't you do that here?"

Duncan reached out to take her hand, but she pulled back. He grasped her hand firmly, determined, and kissed it. "I thought it would make a bigger impact if I showed up in the place he thought he was keeping secret from everyone, and I did not want ye to have one more thing to concern yourself with. Ye have plenty without adding this to it."

"How did you know where he was?" she asked, calming a bit.

"I sensed it. It is something I can do now, just as ye can," he replied, before taking one of her fingers inside of his mouth, grazing it with his teeth playfully.

Maggie eyed him suspiciously.

He let out a deep sigh. "Maggie, I am sorry I did not tell ye what I was planning in advance." Reaching over, he cupped her face. "My love, we are of one heart and one soul, and I would never let anyone, or anything, come between us, least of all a woman from a whorehouse, even if she does have the 'best tits' in London."

"Even if she— what?" Maggie narrowed her eyes at him. "How would you know which woman has the 'best tits' in London?" She picked up a pillow and slammed it into him.

He tossed the pillow away and smiled. "I wouldn't, but a woman there told me she did, and I did not wish to argue with her, especially since I knew I was coming home to the finest ones in the world."

Maggie snorted, but her face split into a grin, his doing the same. She pressed her forehead to his. "You really JUST went to speak to John?"

"I swear it on the lives of our children," he said and kissed her.

She ran her hands over his chest, and he started untying her gown.

"Now, if ye will permit me the honor of gazing upon those fine tits, I will make sure ye do not regret it," he vowed with a smirk.

"How can I possibly refuse an offer like that?" she smiled and pulled him to her.

February 1784

Duncan handed the letter he received from Lucy Hanks to Maggie. "She gave birth to a healthy baby girl on February 5th in Hampshire County. She named the bairn Nancy."

Maggie skimmed over the post. "Does she need anything?"

"Nay," he replied. "David and I have seen to her. I just thought ye would want to know."

"Good," she sighed. "We will keep a close eye on them to make sure they are taken care of." She stepped closer to the fireplace and tossed the letter into the flames.

"Aye, we will," he said, embracing her from behind and they watched it burn together.

May 1784

Duncan was coming in from the stables when he chanced upon David Percy tying his horse to a hitch in front of the house.

"Morning, David!" he called.

"Oh, good morning, Duncan," said David and opened his saddlebags. "I have come to bring the weekly books up for Maggie."

"How are things looking?" asked Duncan, helping him as they walked towards the house.

"Very well. I have to say, Maggie has the best head for business I have ever seen. It's as if she knows exactly what the future holds and where to put all the best efforts."

"Something like that!" Duncan grinned as he opened the door. "How's your boy?"

"Into everything," David laughed, "but I don't have to tell you about that."

Cora had given birth to a baby boy almost nine months to the day after Maggie laid hands on the couple. Young Davey was about to turn two.

Once they had placed the ledgers on the desk, David looked around to make sure they were alone. "I am actually glad to have a moment with no one else around. I have something for you." David pulled a letter from the satchel across his shoulder and handed it to Duncan. "News from Miss Hanks."

"Ah!" replied Duncan with a nod. "I trust she and the child are comfortable."

"They are, and I will make sure they continue to be."

"Thank you, David. Maggie and I appreciate your discretion with this matter."

"It is my pleasure," he smiled. "A minor repayment for all the kindness this family has done for me and mine." He pointed at the correspondence. "If you wish to respond to that, just let me know, and I will ensure it is delivered safely."

Duncan held it up. "Maggie and I will take a look at this and let ye know."

"Very good," said David as he turned to leave. "You know where to find me."

Duncan broke open the seal of the letter addressed to him as he sat down in the chair behind the desk and read—

I write this letter to make you aware the child and I are both doing exceptionally well. She is healthy, happy, and well cared for thanks to the support you continue to provide to us. I am obliged to keep you informed as to her welfare, per our agreement, but I must ask you would be so kind as to provide some sort of reassurance in the case, God forbid, some great tragedy should befall me. Becoming a mother has given me pause to consider not only my future, but that of my child's as well. I want to know she would be cared for in such an event, and I ask, should that happen, she comes to live with you where she will be among family of her own blood. Mr. Percy has assured me, if that should occur, a story can be invented to explain her unexpected and unusual appearance as he has promised to make sure her true identity as the daughter of a MacGregor of Williamsburg is not to be revealed. I trust you will do the honorable thing and see my wishes are respected in that regard.

I know this situation is not ideal for anyone given the circumstances, but I think the way we have approached it is for the best given the fact her father's heart obviously belongs to another.

L.H.

He leaned back, looking over the words once more, mulling her request when John appeared at the doorway.

"I need a drink," said John and went to the cabinet. "Want one?" he called over his shoulder.

Duncan waited for his back to be turned, then quickly slipped the page into one of the ledger books David Percy had just left for Maggie to go over, meaning to take the letter up to her later to read for herself.

"Why not?" he responded.

John brought over two glasses, handing Duncan one before sitting down across from him.

"How are things with the new house?" asked Duncan, after taking a sip.

"Wonderful! I think everything has a place now, and it's nice to have a little privacy."

"Makes entertaining women easier, one would think," pressed Duncan.

John looked down. "I would not bring any of them here. I am doing my best to be discreet," he replied softly.

"As long as ye aren't thinking about my wife when ye do, have at it," mumbled Duncan.

"Duncan?" called Hettie from the foyer.

"In here," he answered.

Hettie slowly made her way inside. "Quinn is looking for you. Said something about needing some help with a thing he is working on," she called, grimacing as if she were in pain.

Duncan rose and went to her side. "Are ye alright, Hettie?"

"Oh," she waved, "my knee has been giving me a fit the past few days. Things just don't work like they used to."

Taking her by the arm, he helped her over to the sofa. "Ye sit down and rest. I will get Quinn to take a look at it for ye. He makes a good salve for that sort of stuff."

"I have work to do," she protested.

"Sit!" he ordered. He glanced back at John, then leaned close to her ear. "Keep an eye on John. Lord knows he needs someone looking out for him to keep him out of trouble." Duncan kissed her on the cheek. "Rest!"

He stopped as he passed John on his way out. "Make sure she stays put for a while," he whispered and touched him on the back.

John nodded an acknowledgement, before taking Duncan's glass over to Hettie, sitting down next to her. "Drink this. It will help."

She eyed it longingly. "Well, maybe just a little sip— for my knee."

"Yes, for your knee," John winked.

Three glasses later, Hettie was comfortably snoring as John smiled over at her. He pulled forward a blanket hanging over the back of the sofa and used it to cover her. Remembering Gabe had asked him to check one of the ledgers, he carefully got up, so as not to wake her, and went over to the desk, finding the book he needed on the top of the pile.

John opened it and was just about to go over the numbers when he found the loose letter. He flipped it over to see it had been addressed to Duncan, then back over again, the first line catching his attention just as he was about to set it off to the side. He looked around to make sure no one else was around, before reading the rest of it. When he was done, he leaned back, stroking his chin. He studied it closer, taking in every word, his mind working overtime putting the pieces together.

Why would a woman send a letter like this to Duncan, unless...?

John blew out a long, deep breath, the contents of the letter the only thing on his mind as he looked down at it for a third time. Duncan had been with another woman, and a child had come from the union; a child he supported using David Percy as his agent, and one he had to be concealing from Maggie. Duncan must have slipped the letter in the book to hide it when he came in.

Dear God! How dare he sit on his high horse and criticize me for taking women to bed when he has been unfaithful to his own wife and sired a child outside of the marriage bed to boot. How could he do that to Maggie? Something like this will destroy her!

He quickly refolded the letter and tucked it into his coat pocket when he noticed Hettie starting to stir. He carefully put the book back on the top of the stack where he found it. He needed time to consider what to do with the information he had just learned and, if he decided to tell her, Maggie would need proof of her husband's adultery.

After Duncan finished assisting Quinn, he went back to the drawing room, remembering he had tucked the letter away. He found the book, but when he opened it, the letter was gone. He tapped the desktop with his fingers, looking around. He concluded Maggie must have already come in and found it and made a mental note to speak with her about it later.

Towards the end of dinner later that afternoon, Maggie, Gabe, and John were discussing business while Quinn and Ana were having their own conversation about medicinal herbs.

Duncan was more interested in the fact Maggie had on her trousers that day, having taken Onyx out for a ride earlier. Her hair was plaited back in a long braid and she wore one of those things she called a 'bra' under her top, the outline of it making him hungry for more than dinner. He ate, with his fork in one hand, pretending to be interested in their discussion, but instead slipped his free hand down her leg and started sliding it up the inside.

She slyly cut her eyes over at him when she felt his fingers inching up her inner thigh.

Gabe was asking her a question about expanded purchases from some other countries on the side when Duncan reached his mark. Her back arched and she moaned slightly, nodding her head as if she were focused on Gabe's words and the sound she made was in response to his question.

Duncan smirked when he felt her muscles clench around his hand, only encouraging him. He rubbed his fingers against her crotch, the tightness from the leather creating a maddening friction making her crazy with need.

She bit her lip and spread her legs wider so Duncan would have more room to work, the tablecloth covering their shenanigans. Maggie let one of her hands casually fall to her side, using her fingers to inconspicuously loosen the corset-like ties on her trousers. Once there was enough room, Duncan slipped his hand inside and continued his assault, only now he could feel how much she really wanted him. She glanced over at him and winked. He laid down his fork and picked up his glass, taking a sip of wine as he sent her a message.

Guess what I am having for dessert?

Keep that up and you are going to have dessert on this table sooner than you think.

I think I like that idea.

He started moving his fingers, working her up at a rapid pace.

She placed her hand over his, guiding him as she started rhythmically moving her hips against his touch.

"What do you think, John?" she asked, propping her elbows on the table, trying to maintain the dialogue while all of this was going on, after noticing John was being rather quiet.

John knew exactly what was happening and the thought of Duncan's boldness, on many fronts, irked him to no end. He had just received a letter stating another woman had given birth to his child, and here he was, having his way with Maggie at the dining room table.

He looked over at Duncan. "I think there is a great deal to be said for staying with the ones on the home front. You wouldn't want those who currently depend on us for their livelihood to think they suddenly don't matter anymore."

"Why would they think that?' asked Duncan, leaning back against his chair for better access. "It's not like ye would be ending things with them. There is always room for diversity."

"There is also a lot to be said for loyalty," snarked John.

Maggie covered her mouth, closing her eyes and sighing as Duncan finished her off. Resting her hand over on his lap, she felt his own need had grown exponentially.

"What say you, Maggie?" asked Gabe.

"I say we move this conversation to the drawing room. Why don't all of you go ahead? Duncan and I need to have a little discussion of our own first."

Ana looked over and took note of the sudden blush on Maggie's face. "Quinn, why don't ye take me to the garden and show me that herb ye were speaking of?"

"Now?"

"Aye. Let them talk about their boring business."

"Alright," he said, sliding back his chair and standing, offering his arm to Ana, who closed the door behind them on the way out.

"Come on," said Gabe to John, rising from his chair, "I will show you the proposal I have put together while they chat."

John threw down his napkin in disgust and hastily departed with Gabe following behind him.

"Close the door, please," called out Maggie.

Gabe eyed her suspiciously but did as she asked.

As soon as everyone was gone, Duncan used his arm to push all the dishes to the side, roughly grabbing Maggie around the waist and laying her across the table. He yanked her trousers off completely in one move, tossing them to the side, then pulled her top off, leaving her in only her bra. Thankfully, he had worn his tartan that day, so he merely lifted it and sunk himself deeply inside her, letting out a relieved moan. His lips went to the top of her breasts, pulling them out of the bra cup with his hand as he hungrily devoured one and then the other. Kissing her fervently while moving in and out, faster and faster, he groaned as he let go. Maggie lay back on the table, panting as he kissed her stomach and chest tenderly. Pulling her to a sitting position, he took her face between both his hands and kissed her tenderly.

"I needed that," he growled.

"Anytime I can be of assistance," she laughed and ran her hands over his chest. She kissed him and hopped off the table to grab her trousers.

As she bent over, his hands firmly grasped her hips, kissing her back.

She glanced over her shoulder and grinned when she felt him pressing himself against her, ready to take her again. "So soon?"

He ran his hands over her backside. "What can I say? Ye have the finest arse in the world, in addition to the finest tits, and it does things to me." He shifted her so she was bent over the table and he could easily take her from behind. "I'll be quick," he whispered in her ear.

Bracing herself, she bit her lip in anticipation. "Don't rush on my account. Everyone else can wait as far as I am concerned."

He rubbed himself against her before pushing in smoothly, the path already laid. Moving slowly, he reached around to knead her breasts until he worked her up to the edge, waiting for her so they could climax together. They both collapsed forward when they were done.

"We don't have dessert nearly enough," she laughed.

Duncan straightened up, helping her to turn around before kissing her. "I think we should start having it with every meal," he teased and reached for her clothes, helping her dress.

Once she was presentable, she embraced him and smacked him on his behind. "Off with you. I can't think about business when you are around."

"Alright," he sighed, "I need to see to Gavina at the stables while ye go attend to that, but remember, supper is coming, and I am already looking forward to dessert."

After their business was concluded, Maggie took the children out on the side lawn to play. The triplets were now four, and the twins would be three in July, all healthy, strong, and much faster than their nannies. Kat, who was almost six, and Alastair, now twelve, came out to join them. The children were enjoying a rousing game of tag with their fathers as Maggie and Ana watched from the blanket they were sitting on.

"Enjoy your wee 'chat' with Duncan after dinner?" asked Ana, leaning in close.

"There's nothing 'wee' about that man," Maggie grinned behind her hand.

"I hope ye know what a lucky woman ye are, my dear."

"He does his best to remind me on a daily basis."

Ana glanced around. "Where is John?"

"I am not sure. He was incredibly quiet at dinner and at our meeting after. Duncan said he has been spending a great deal of time at a brothel in London."

Ana raised her eyebrows. "I suppose that explains where he disappears off to. How do ye feel about that?"

"I try not to think about it," she said, and waved at the children. "I have enough of John's messes to clean up without looking for more."

Ana was just about to ask what she meant when Duncan raced over to them, Morgan under one arm and Alanna under the other, both giggling loudly as he spun around with them.

"Again! Again!" the girls squealed when he stopped.

He sat them down. "I can't. I think it is your mother's turn."

"Yes!" clapped Alanna.

"Spin Mother!" cheered Morgan.

"Oh no!" exclaimed Maggie, waving her hands.

"Oh, yes!" Duncan laughed devilishly, reaching down and pulling her to her feet.

As soon as she was upright, she dashed away from him.

Duncan followed, quickly overtaking her, scooping her up as she shrieked, and swinging her over his shoulder while twirling her around. They both shook with laughter when they fell to the ground, happily embraced in each other's arms. As they kissed, all the children ran over and piled atop them, joining in the fun as Maggie and Duncan gathered them closer to tickle them while covering them with kisses.

John watched from the window of the drawing room, still trying to make sense of what he read and what would drive Duncan to be foolish enough to risk all he had to take another woman to bed. His stomach was tied up in knots, wondering what he should do with the information he held close. On one hand, ignorance was bliss —

Maggie did love the man and their family more than anything. They were her world. On the other hand, she had a right to know he had fathered a child with another woman. He had broken a sacred vow to the woman he promised to love, honor, and be faithful to for all eternity.

If he were to tell Maggie, she would be heartbroken, and so would the children who adored their father. Maggie and the babies did not deserve to be treated this way.

John walked away from the window, back to the desk and collapsed in the chair. He picked up the feather quill, fiddling with it and using the soft side to stroke his jaw as he considered the ramifications.

"What are you thinking, John?" he said aloud and threw the pen to the desk in disgust. "Can you honestly do that to her? Break her heart that way?" He didn't want to, but he couldn't let Duncan make a fool out of her either.

Noni appeared at the doorway. "Pardon me, John, but there is a gentleman here looking for Maggie and Gabe. Should I bring him in while I fetch them?"

"Of course," he said, rising from his chair. He was more than a little surprised to see Martin, Gabe's stepfather come into the room.

"Martin!" He went to greet him.

"John!" The man extended his hand.

"What are you doing here? Gabe didn't mention you were coming for a visit."

"He didn't know I was coming. I am afraid…" he was cut off when the family started making their way in.

"Martin! What an unexpected pleasure," exclaimed Maggie, and kissed him on the cheek.

"We weren't expecting you," said Gabe and they embraced. "Where's Mother?"

Martin let out a deep breath and gripped Gabe's shoulders. "That's why I am here. I have come to bring you some bad news."

Maggie called for Noni and Rowena to come take the children upstairs as Martin motioned for Gabe to sit down.

Quinn and Duncan exchanged wary looks as Quinn moved to Gabe's side.

"What news?" asked Gabe softly, as if he already knew.

"I am very sorry to have to tell you your mother has passed."

Gabe closed his eyes, nodding as Quinn kneeled in front of him.

Taking Gabe's hand, Quinn asked the question. "How?"

"She developed an infection in her lungs. It all happened very quickly, in a matter of days. I knew there was nothing to be done, so I kept her as comfortable as I could, making sure she was in no pain. Georgie was in my arms when she...." Martin stopped to wipe a few tears that had leaked from his own eyes. "I didn't have the heart to just send a letter; I wanted to tell you in person."

Gabe stared down at the floor. "I appreciate that more than you know," he finally said.

Maggie curled into Duncan's chest and he enveloped her with his arms.

"I'm so sorry," whispered Quinn, "for both of ye."

Clearing his throat, Gabe squeezed Quinn's hand tightly. "When did this happen?"

"It was seven weeks ago. She was buried at the church next to your father. Thankfully, Robert was able to handle everything; I was certainly in no shape to do it."

Maggie broke away from Duncan and went to stand behind Gabe, hugging him from behind, then came around to do the same for Martin, offering her condolences.

"What can we do?" she asked Gabe.

"There is nothing to be done." He addressed Martin. "Thank you for taking care of her and for loving her. You made her happier than I had ever seen. She was lucky to have you."

"I was the lucky one. I miss her very much."

Maggie could sense Gabe on the verge of breaking down and decided it was best for him and Quinn to have some private time alone.

"Martin, you must be tired. Let's find you a room and get you settled."

Martin stood, placing his hand comfortingly on Gabe's back as he passed.

Maggie escorted him into the foyer, Duncan, John, and Ana following closely behind.

Martin smiled at Ana. "I don't believe we have met."

"Oh no! You haven't," said Maggie. "Martin, this is Ana Bishop, my mother."

"Your mother?" he asked, taken aback.

"Mom, this is Martin Barnes."

Martin bowed slightly. "A pleasure, although I wish it were under better circumstances. Forgive my confusion, I thought Maggie's mother was no longer of this world."

Ana tilted her head. "We mistakenly believed each other gone, but recently found out otherwise. I am deeply sorry for your loss."

"Thank you."

Maggie got Martin to his room, then went back to peek in on Gabe and Quinn. Gabe was weeping on Quinn's shoulder with Quinn comforting him.

Duncan came up behind her.

"All of these Fae powers and there was nothing we could do," she whispered.

Her husband kissed the side of her head. "I am afraid it is something we are going to have to get used to, my love. We cannot save those destined to pass into the next life. It is only our job to see to them while they are here." He turned her around to face him. "How are ye? I know ye and Georgie were very fond of each other."

"Better than Gabe. I know they had their issues, but they loved each other very much and he is going to have a difficult time with this."

John came down the stairs carrying Kat in one arm, his other hand on Alastair's shoulder. "I told the children. It might be good for Gabe to see them right now."

Maggie nodded, took Alastair's hand and led them into the drawing room. John set Kat down just inside the door, and she immediately ran to Gabe, crawling onto his lap.

Gabe hugged her tightly and she patted his back, while Alastair went over to hug him as well. He shot Maggie a grateful look.

She and John stepped out of the room, pulling the pocket doors closed behind them.

"What can we do?" asked John.

Maggie blotted her face with her palm. "There isn't anything we can do except be here for him."

Late that evening, after everyone was asleep, Maggie shimmered into Gabe and Quinn's home, knowing he would be awake and half-way through a bottle by now. She found him sprawled out on the sofa, sitting alone in the darkness.

"Mind some company?" she asked.

He waved his hand in response.

"How are you doing?" she asked and sat down beside him.

"I suppose I am still in a bit of shock. I mean, I knew this day would come, I just didn't realize how hard it would be when it actually did."

"Kind of like Georgie herself," agreed Maggie. "You knew she was coming —you just didn't know how powerful the punch would be until she actually slammed into you."

Gabe covered his mouth with the back of his hand and smiled. "That's exactly how it is— and how she was."

"Your mother was definitely one of a kind." Maggie snapped her fingers, making a full glass appear in her hand.

"Is this what it is going to be like?" he whispered. "All of us watching the ones we love die, one right after the other, while not being able to do anything to stop it."

"So, it would seem," she replied quietly, looking down into her glass. "It is the price we must pay for immortality. I try not to think about it, but every now and then it creeps into the back of my mind. Hettie, Harm, Martin, even my own mother— one day, in the not-too-distant future— they will all be gone from us and we will be left to carry on without them. It is a dismal thought."

"It's all a bit unnatural as well, isn't it?" he pondered aloud. "You know, I always thought I would go before she did, because dying at an early age was something I accepted when I entered into the service of the Crown, expected it even. In some ways, I think it would have been much easier."

She pulled him over to her. Resting his head upon her breast, he wrapped his arm around her waist. They sat that way silently for at least an hour before Gabe eventually drifted off to sleep. Shortly thereafter, Quinn stepped out of the shadows. "I'll get him to bed," he whispered.

"Don't disturb him. Let him rest and go get some sleep yourself. We're fine."

Quinn left the room and returned with a blanket, placing it around Gabe and across Maggie's lap. He kneeled and placed a light kiss on his husband's forehead, before moving to kiss Maggie on the top of the head. "Let me know if ye need anything."

At some point in the middle of the night, after she had dozed off, she felt Gabe tucking the blanket around her, whispering 'thanks Mags', in her ear and felt him kiss her cheek. She woke up the next morning, stretched out on the sofa with her head on Duncan's lap.

Her eyes fluttered open. "When did you get here?"

He lightly brushed the hair back from her face. "A couple of hours ago."

"Where's Gabe?"

"Quinn is taking care of him in the way only he can."

Duncan gently slipped his arms around her and picked her up before he shimmered them back to their bedroom and onto their bed. "Go back to sleep," he whispered, wrapping himself around her, embracing her tightly.

Martin enjoyed the following day with the family, especially his time with the children.

"Do you have any of your own?" Ana asked Martin after Rowe and Noni took the children up to the nursery.

"Not unless you count Gabe and his brothers, who are mostly older than me," he chuckled softly.

"I am very sorry about your wife," said Ana sympathetically. "I still miss Maggie's father every day."

"My condolences to you as well. I must say, I was more than a little shocked when Maggie introduced us yesterday. I thought Maggie had no family left."

"Yes, well, we mistakenly thought each other dead, but were pleasantly surprised to find we were both wrong. I cannot tell ye how beside myself I was when I discovered she was very much alive and had blessed me with five beautiful grandchildren. I just wish Steven was around to see them."

"It's strange, isn't it?" Martin sighed. "Being without them after being together for so long, I mean."

"It is. Some mornings I wake up and forget he is no longer, and it's like losing him all over again when I come to my senses."

"Georgie and I only had a few short years together, but I don't remember what life was like before her."

Ana reached over and laid her hand on his. "I wish I could tell ye it gets easier, but I'm not sure if it ever does."

Martin was still gripping her hand when Maggie and Duncan came through the doorway. Maggie stopped short and turned her head sideways, bewildered by the scene before her.

Duncan followed her gaze and quickly looked away, pretending not to notice. "Did the children wear ye out?"

Martin released Ana's hand and turned. "They do keep you on your toes, don't they?"

"That's putting it mildly," said Maggie. "What are you two up to?" she asked, folding her arms.

"Commiserating over lost spouses," replied Ana.

"Oh," said Maggie quietly.

The rest of the day passed uneventfully, and after breakfast the following morning, the family gathered in the drawing room.

"Gabe, when you are feeling up to it, there are some matters regarding your mother we need to discuss," said Martin.

"What sort of matters?"

"Your mother's will and estate need to be settled."

"Martin, I am sure she made her wishes clear to you, whatever they were, and I am equally as certain that Robert will see everything is taken care of. My advice is not needed in that regard."

"It's not that. It's about what she left you in her will."

Gabe scoffed. "Let me guess, her wedding ring in hopes it would find its way to some lovely woman's hand someday." His tone was slightly more than sarcastic.

Martin bobbed his head back and forth. "Among other things."

"What else would she leave me?"

Martin held out his hands, palms up. "She left you everything."

Gabe slowly turned his head. "What do you mean by that?"

"She left it ALL to you. The house, her share of the law business, and the bank accounts."

Gabe paled. "Why on Earth would she do something like that?"

"According to her will, she was afraid you might starve to death being a simple partner in a merchant business in this God-forsaken place called America." Martin grinned, amused. "She wanted to ensure you had enough to provide for Kat, and for a wife, in the event you decided to marry, and yes, she specifically did leave her, and your father's wedding rings, to that purpose. She felt all of your brothers had provided well enough for themselves and thought you could use it the most."

"Oh dear God," mumbled Maggie, stifling a giggle. "The woman will not let it go, not even in death. Georgie Ashton Barnes, matchmaking from beyond the grave."

Gabe stared at Martin in disbelief. "I don't want any of that. That should all go to you, Martin, especially the house."

"No, not me," he retorted. "That was your father's home, and it should stay in the family."

"But Martin, you ARE family! As much as anyone who carried her blood. You deserve to have it."

"I appreciate you saying that Gabe, but the truth of the matter is, I cannot bear to go back to that house. There are too many memories, while all good, they overtake me whenever I am there alone, which is the other reason I came to deliver the news in person. I have no intention of returning to London."

"You're not?" Maggie was truly shocked. "What about your practice?"

"I handed off my patients to another physician and closed the office."

"What will ye do?" asked Duncan.

"Start over somewhere new, although I have not decided where yet. I will figure things out once I have been to see Wyatt. I wanted to tell him the news in person, as well."

Maggie looked around the room at the others. "I think I speak for all of us when we say we would love to have you here."

"Absolutely!" added Gabe.

"We'll see," said Martin. "I am in no rush to make any long-term decisions just yet. I am too busy trying to focus on getting through each day. At any rate, I have all the paperwork for you to look over whenever you like."

"Well, ye are welcome to stay as long as ye like," offered Duncan. "We are more than happy to have ye."

"Maggie, a word?" asked Martin, later that day when she found him in the drawing room alone.

She sat down next to him.

"Georgie left something for you in her will." He reached in his coat pocket, pulled out a key and a letter, and handed it to her.

"For me?"

"Yes. There is a small trunk I had sent up to your room this key unlocks. She wanted you to have it."

"I don't know what to say. What's in it?"

"Honestly, I have no idea. She made me promise not to open it, and to make sure it came directly into your hands, so whatever it is, she wanted it to remain between the two of you. She also requested you open it alone. I have to admit, I am curious, but I will abide by her wishes."

"Well, now so am I."

Maggie sat down in the bedroom and made herself comfortable before breaking the seal on the letter.

My Dearest Maggie,

If you are reading this, I have passed into the next life, preferably after a long night of making love to my handsome husband. I have asked Martin to bring this to you in the event of my death. You are the only one I trust with the contents. You will understand when you open it. Some of the items will be self-explanatory; once you see them, you will know why. In addition, there are a few other things I need to explain. The first is a ring Gabe's father gave to me on the day he was born. It is a beautiful sapphire with diamonds around the edges. I ask that you give this to Kat when she is old enough. I had hoped to be around to see her grow up, but I know this will not likely happen. I know I do not need to ask, but please help Gabe with her. While he may be able to charm the ladies, he has never seen the likes of a young girl when her monthly courses come. Be there for both of them—he will need your advice and she will need a woman around. The second thing is a set of two diamonds. I wish for you to put them aside in the event Gabe finds someone who makes him happy and he wishes to spend the rest of his life with. I truly hope that day will come, and, if and when it does, please have them set into an appropriate piece of jewelry to celebrate their love. I know you will be the best judge of that person. The third is one of my favorite pieces of jewelry, a ruby necklace I purchased for myself just because I loved the look of it. It made me feel like the most beautiful woman in the world when I wore it, and I happened to be wearing it the night I met Martin when my world changed for the better. Only a confident woman who knows herself well can carry it off—it will be perfect for you.

Please, keep check on Martin for me. He will be heartbroken in the beginning, but in time, encourage him to move on and find someone else to love. His heart is too big to be alone for the rest of his life.

Gabe will need you in the days to come, so I ask you look out for him as well. Remind him, even though he would become angry and frustrated with my ways, I always did what I did out of my deep, enduring love for him. He has been one of my biggest blessings in this life, and I have wanted nothing but the best for him.

And lastly to you, I hardly know what to write. You are one of the few people in my life who truly understood me, and for that, I am beyond grateful. I love you as one of my own. You are the daughter I never had but prayed to come into my life. Thank you for that.

Look after everyone for me and never let them forget how much I loved them.

All my love,
Georgie

P.S. If things don't work out between you and Duncan, I still think you would make the perfect wife for Gabe. You know I had to give it one last try.

"Oh Georgie, I am going to miss you."

Maggie set the letter aside, slid the key into the lock and turned the tumble. Lifting the top, she found three velvet bags, containing the jewelry from the letter. The sapphire ring for Kat was beyond stunning. The diamonds for Gabe's love were lovely stones about a half a carat each, flawless and perfect in every way. Finally, Maggie held up the ruby necklace she was gifted. It was large, beautiful, and as vibrant as Georgie herself— and it made Maggie smile.

Setting it to the side to see the rest of the contents, she found a stack of letters tied together. Maggie slipped one out of the bundle and was more than a little astonished to read the words. It was a rather graphic letter from Gabe's father, writing of all the things he imagined doing to her once he returned home from an extended business trip.

Maggie dropped the letter as if it were covered in thorns. "Let's just save those for later, shall we," she said to herself, gingerly picking them up, holding them away from her body, and moving them to the table.

Turning back to the task at hand, she found the rest of the trunk filled with books. Maggie shifted them around and flipped through the titles, wondering why Georgie felt the need to conceal them and leave them specifically to her. She opened the first one her hand touched and began to read a bit. Her hand flew to her mouth when she saw why. She grabbed another, only to find that it was much of the same. All the books had one common theme— Georgie Asheton Barnes had bequeathed Maggie her entire collection of erotic novels.

Maggie burst into laughter, leaning back in the chair, holding her stomach, and tee-heeing until tears rolled from her eyes.

Duncan opened the door and peered around the corner when he heard her from the hall. "Find something amusing?" He closed the door behind him.

She waved him over. "My inheritance! Come and see!"

He cocked his head to one side and sat down next to her on the small sofa.

She handed him one.

He looked at her oddly. "Books?"

"Open one up and take a gander at the contents."

Duncan's face transformed from a solemn frown, to eyes wide with shock, to a little embarrassed, then finally, entertained as he began to chuckle. "Are they all like this?"

"Uh-huh!" she replied and straightened the stack on the table. "Seems Georgie had quite the collection."

Duncan snapped the book shut. "I can see why she didn't want anyone else to see them. They might tarnish her reputation as a 'proper lady'."

"Why do you suppose she sent them to me?"

He tossed the book over his shoulder and pulled her over onto his lap. "I can't imagine," he growled, tipped her back, and kissed her.

She stretched out, wrapping her arms around his neck as his lips fell to her neck. As she did, her foot accidentally caught the small trunk, knocking it over onto the floor.

"Shit!" she exclaimed and pushed Duncan away to pick it up.

"That can wait," he grumbled and pressed against her. "I cannot!"

"Just give me a minute," she said. "There are two small diamonds for Gabe I don't want to lose."

She knelt on the floor and gathered all the jewels and the books that had spilled out, but when she went to put them back in, she noticed something unusual.

"What is this?" she asked and looked closer. The box had revealed a false bottom, one that had popped open when it fell. She reached down, removing it to find another bundle of letters. She held them up. "I wonder what this is all about?" She sat back, cross legged on the floor.

Duncan pushed up on his elbow. "Something that is going to take more than a minute, I'm guessing," he teased.

Maggie scrunched up her face at him and untied the bundle, opening the first letter. She read it over, then set it to the side and opened the next one. Her pace became more frantic with each new letter and her focus intensified.

Duncan rolled off the sofa and crawled over to her. "Did Georgie take up writing her own stories?"

She shook her head. "Oh no, she did much more than that."

Duncan picked up the first letter, reading the graphic details for himself.

"Love letters? This can't be!" he exclaimed. "Nay, not her!"

"She did!" Maggie lifted her head. "Georgie had an affair with another *woman*."

Maggie held up the last letter. "They were all in order by date. The woman's name is Holly. It looks like they were 'together' for about two years. It seems it ended the year before she and Martin met when Holly decided to marry a merchant by the name of 'Masters' from the Colonies. It also appears that they were very much in love, which is probably why she couldn't bring herself to dispose of them."

Propping her elbow up on her thigh, she rested her cheek in her palm. "All this time, Gabe has hidden his true self from his mother because he didn't think she would understand, when she was probably one of the few people who actually would. Look at all the time they wasted, all the arguments they could have avoided, if they had just stopped keeping secrets from each other."

"Secrets will tear a family apart faster than anything. Are ye going to tell him? Or Martin for that matter?"

"Not Martin. It would serve no purpose and the man has enough to deal with, but with Gabe —it's a little different story with him." Maggie looked back down at the stack of letters. "What would you do?"

"That's a tough one. I am not sure what I would do."

She gathered them up, carefully put them back in order and tied them before placing them back in the trunk, along with everything else. "I need to give this some thought."

The following Saturday at dinner, Martin decided it was time to make a move.

"Maggie, can you make arrangements on one of the ships for me to get to New York to see Wyatt?"

"You can take our personal ship whenever you like. It is at your disposal," she replied.

"That is very generous. Thank you."

"When will ye go?" asked Ana.

"I think the sooner, the better. I wouldn't want word to reach him before I did."

"I should go with you," volunteered Gabe. "Wyatt may be more upset than you realize."

Quinn laid his hand over on Gabe's. "Then I will go as well."

"Why don't we all go?" suggested Maggie. "We could use a change of scenery and it would be good to see Wyatt, especially all grown up. We can check on some of the business while we are there."

"Has he really pulled himself together?" asked Martin.

"General George Washington himself bragged on him while he was here," Gabe smiled. "He truly has found his calling."

"What about the children?" asked Ana.

Maggie looked over at Duncan. "Let's leave them here. We have enough nannies to keep watch and none of us really get any adult time with each other. Besides, we won't be gone that long. A quick trip up and back."

"Where have I heard that before?" mumbled Gabe.

22 Chapter Twenty-Two

After three days at sea, they arrived in New York late that afternoon. With the help of some of the residents, they managed to locate Wyatt at his house on the edge of town. It housed a small office built off to the side, with a bell above the door that rang when someone came in.

"I will be right with you," called Wyatt from the back.

"I hope you won't keep us waiting too long," replied Gabe.

A surprised Wyatt poked his head around the doorway wiping his hands on a towel. "Uncle Gabe? Martin?" he went over to greet them. "Aunt Maggie!" he kissed her cheek. "What are you all doing here?"

"We came to speak with you about an important family matter," answered Martin.

Wyatt pointed over his shoulder. "Let me finish up with my patient and we can visit. Come on back."

Wyatt had been interrupted while in the process of lancing a boil on a man's neck.

"Where are the others?" he asked, as he went back to work.

Maggie scrunched up her face, repulsed by the task he was performing. "Duncan, Quinn, John, and my mother are securing rooms for us."

Wyatt slowly looked up, perplexed. "Your mother?"

"Yes, it's a long story, but she is living with us now."

Maggie cringed, opened her mouth and gagged a bit when the boil erupted, spilling pus down the man's chest.

"AHH!" exclaimed the patient, relief washing over him.

Gabe turned his head, focusing his attention on the label of a bottle on the nearby table, while Martin watched Wyatt, a look of pride on his face.

"All done, Mr. Kane," he said and cleaned up the wound. "That should be feeling better in no time."

"Thank you, Wyatt," said a grateful Mr. Kane and got up. "I'll have the wife send over your supper for the rest of the week." Once clothed, the man waved and bid them farewell.

Wyatt gathered his medical tools and began to clean them. "To what do I owe the pleasure of this visit?"

Gabe looked to Martin, then back at Wyatt. "I am afraid we have some bad news to give you and we wanted to tell you in person. Your grandmother has passed."

The young man slowly set the instrument in his hand back down on the table, his face drawing a blank. "I see. What happened?"

"A lung infection. I did all I could, but it was not enough." Martin's voice was filled with sad remorse. "I made her as comfortable as possible until the very end."

Wyatt nodded his head. "Of course you did, Martin!" He stepped next to his step-grandfather and placed his hand comfortingly on his shoulder. "Grandmother lived a long, eventful life. We were fortunate to have her for the time we did, and she was blessed to have you. I'm sorry for your loss." he turned his head, "and for yours, Uncle Gabe."

"Thank you, Wyatt!"

Maggie looked at the almost unrecognizable person before her, utterly amazed at how much he had transformed in such a short amount of time. The childish boy she sent off to war had grown into quite a responsible, mature man.

"Let me close up here, and we can have a drink at the tavern."

As they walked up the street, Maggie slipped her arms into Wyatt's. "Who are you and what have you done with my favorite miscreant?" she teased.

"Oh, he still manages to rear his ugly head every now and again," he quipped, "but nothing makes you grow up faster than watching a man die on a battlefield," he added dolefully and patted her arm.

"You seem to enjoy being a physician," she remarked.

"I truly do, and I owe you a debt of gratitude. Being sent to Nathaniel was the best thing that could have ever happened to me. Learning the skills that enabled me to save a human life helped me to find the road I was meant to take."

Maggie pulled him tightly and leaned her head on his shoulder. "I am so glad to hear I have done at least one thing right."

He smiled warmly. "Oh, I know for a fact you have done a few more than one."

Duncan, Quinn, John, and Ana were seated at a table when they entered the tavern. After a round of 'hellos' and hugs, and after introducing Ana, they sat down and ordered.

They spent the next hour exchanging amusing stories about Georgie, sharing a few good laughs before Wyatt held up his tankard. "A toast to Grandmother, may she rest in peace."

"And a toast to the poor bastards she is ordering around in the next world as we speak," added Gabe.

"Hear, hear!"

"So, you have a practice here?" Martin asked Wyatt.

"A thriving one since I am the only physician in town. The last one passed away a few months ago, and I have more patients than I know what to do with. I finally moved into a place with an office because the other residents of the boarding house where I was staying got tired of being woken up nearly every night for some emergency."

"You are *that* busy?"

"Doctors are in short supply in the entire area, and there are many in need."

As they continued their conversation, a rather shapely woman walked by, lingering to drag her hand along Wyatt's back. She stopped and leaned down, "Hello, Wyatt. I have missed you. Come and see me soon," she whispered before continuing along.

He watched her go with a wide, wicked smile on his face, the others giving him a quizzical look.

Clearing his throat and straightening up soberly, "One of my patients," he explained, before glancing to John with a roguish smirk.

John lifted his chin and shifted in his seat for a better look at the woman sashaying away. "I wouldn't wait too long. The poor thing appears to be on her deathbed," he winked causing Maggie to roll her eyes.

Some things never change.

They decided to have an early supper, and before retiring for the night, Gabe, Quinn, and Martin decided to go back to Wyatt's house so he was not alone after finding out the news.

After dinner the next day, Martin and Ana went to visit Wyatt at his office while the rest of the group made their way up the street. A sudden ruckus from behind caught their attention, and they all turned to see what was happening.

A horse, with an attached wagon, had been spooked and was barreling down a path in their general direction. A young woman, who had stepped from inside a building while fiddling with her purse string, found herself about to be trampled to death. A look of horror crossed her face and she froze, unable to move out of fear.

Gabe was closest, so he rushed the woman, tackling her and taking her to the ground out of the path of danger, landing with a 'thud' off to the side.

Maggie closed her eyes and willed the horse to stop just as it made it to the edge of town

"Quinn and I will make sure everyone is alright," Duncan called out as they hurried up the street.

Maggie and John rushed to Gabe's side, who was already helping the young woman to her feet.

"Are you hurt?" he asked.

The poor thing was still in shock, unable to speak, and only shook her head.

"Here's the tavern," said John, holding out his hand, "I think the lady is in need of something to soothe her nerves."

They escorted her inside the establishment; Maggie called for the strongest drink they had. After receiving their order, Gabe held the glass up to her. "Drink this. It will help."

She obeyed and finally calmed down enough to form words. "I don't know how to thank you. I was fairly certain I was about to meet my maker."

"Gabe is pretty quick on his feet," Maggie smiled and took a glass for herself. "What's your name?"

"Holly Masters," she replied, her voice still a little shaky.

Maggie's eyes widened as she became strangled on her drink, smacking the table and coughing. John patted her on the back.

"Are you alright, Maggie?"

"Went down the wrong way," she muttered and motioned with her index finger.

Gabe looked at her oddly, then back to Holly, who was taking another long sip. "Well, Ms. Masters, this is Maggie MacGregor, John MacGregor, and I am Gabe Asheton."

It was Holly's turn to choke on her drink, gasping and sputtering, her eyes wide, looking bewildered. "Asheton, you say?" she finally croaked.

John looked back and forth between Maggie and Holly, suspecting there was something the rest of them did not know.

"You wouldn't happen to be Gabe Asheton whose family owns the law office in London, would you?" she squeaked.

"I am," he replied. "My father established the business. How would you know about that?" He suddenly became extremely curious.

"I am —from London. Your family is well known there," she covered.

"Ah!" Gabe nodded.

"Known to some better than others," mumbled Maggie and waved the tavern keep for more alcohol.

"What was that?" asked Gabe.

"I just said— "small world". Your family is obviously well known from all over."

Duncan and Quinn came in to join them, accepting drinks from the server.

"No one was hurt, and the damage is minimal," stated Quinn.

Maggie rested her cheek on her palm, wiggling her other index finger in Holly's direction for Duncan as he lifted the tankard to his lips, "Allow me to introduce the lovely young woman Gabe saved —meet Mrs. Holly Masters— from London," she said, pressing her lips together in a line and lifting her eyebrows.

It was Duncan's turn to be taken completely off guard. He spat out his drink and wiped his mouth with his hand; everyone turned their eyes to him.

Gabe peered down into his cup before setting it aside. "Is there something wrong with the alcohol here? Should we not be drinking it?"

"It was just a little more than I was expecting," replied Duncan, before downing the rest in one gulp.

"Quinn and Duncan MacGregor," presented Gabe before turning back to face the young woman. "Are you sure you are not hurt?"

"I am fine," she said, having composed herself. "Thank you. I am in your debt, but I must return home."

"Please, allow me to escort you," offered Gabe and they both stood. "You have had quite a fright."

"And ye are bleeding," pointed out Quinn, standing and reaching for her arm to examine where the encounter had scuffed her up. "This cut needs cleaning and bandaging right away. Ye seem to have a few other injuries that need tending as well."

"Quinn is a healer, and my nephew is the town physician. Let us take you to him."

She looked down at the large gash on her arm to see it was indeed bleeding profusely. "I suppose?"

"Why don't I take her?" suggested Maggie. "She may be more comfortable with another woman?"

"Of course," agreed Gabe, taking her meaning.

Maggie took her by the arm, led her outside, and they chatted as they walked.

"Have you lived in town long?"

"A few years— my husband and I moved here after we married. Have all of you just relocated here?" asked Holly. "It's a small town and everyone knows each other."

"No, we live in Virginia. We came to see Gabe's nephew to bring news of the passing of…" Maggie paused and watched for her reaction, "…Gabe's mother, Georgie."

The color drained from Holly's face and she stopped short. Remembering herself, she continued on, slowly. "You have no idea how very sorry I am to hear that," she whispered, looking away, overcome with a wave of sad emotion. "What happened to her, if I may ask?"

"An infection in her lungs. She was married to a physician, but there was nothing he could do but keep her comfortable."

"Married?"

Maggie nodded. "She and Martin wed a few years ago. They were incredibly happy together in the short time they had."

"That is very good to hear —when a woman has a good marriage, I mean."

"Do you have one?" inquired Maggie.

"I do," she smiled. "I love my husband very much; he is a good man."

When they reached the office, Maggie pushed open the door.

"Maggie!" exclaimed Ana as they came inside.

"I brought you a patient."

Martin and Wyatt popped their heads around the corner.

"This is Holly Masters. Gabe saved her from being trampled by a runaway wagon, but she has some cuts that are bleeding."

"Oh my dear, come in," said Martin and helped her to a chair. "We will get you fixed right up."

"Holly, this is Wyatt, Gabe's nephew and Gabe's stepfather, Martin." Maggie watched for a response, one that resulted in Holly looking Martin up and down, her mouth agape. "And this is my mother, Ana Bishop."

"Nice to meet you," mumbled Holly, still carefully studying Martin.

As Wyatt cleaned her wounds, she turned her attention to him. "I thought your name was 'MacGregor'?"

Wyatt flinched. "It is actually Asheton, but using MacGregor was safer during the war. I just never corrected anyone afterwards. I hope Aunt Maggie and Uncle Duncan don't mind."

Holly looked to Maggie, confused.

"He is not our nephew by blood, but we treat him like one. His Uncle Gabe and I have been close friends for many years."

"Oh, I see!"

When they had finished up, Wyatt placed something in a glass bottle. "Take this and mix it in a bit of whisky when you get home. It is one of Quinn MacGregor's finest remedies. You seem very on edge, and rightly so. It will calm your nerves and let you rest."

"Thank you," she said gratefully.

"May I escort you home?" offered Martin.

"No, but I do appreciate the offer. I live close by. Thank you all for your help," and quickly departed.

"I guess Gabe isn't the only one who likes them young," remarked Duncan when Maggie found him in their room later.

"Must run in the family. What are the chances we encounter her here?"

"Slim to none, I would expect. Will ye tell him?"

Maggie sighed. "Maybe it is a sign we should."

After the tavern settled down for the night, Maggie and Duncan knocked on Gabe and Quinn's door. Maggie held up two bottles, shaking them in the air when Gabe answered.

"Oh God!" mumbled Quinn, hanging his head. "What's wrong now?"

"Might want to find some glasses," said Duncan, slapping his brother on the back.

Maggie handed one of the bottles to Gabe. "We have some news that is going to require a great deal of whisky. I'm sure this won't be enough, but lucky for you, I can wave my hand and refill the containers."

"Is this two or four-bottle news?" asked Gabe.

Duncan winced. "Probably more like nine or ten."

"Lovely," muttered Quinn as he set four glasses on the table

Duncan pulled all the chairs in the room together around it.

Gabe opened the first bottle and poured. "What's going on? You two look far too serious."

"Sit down," said Duncan to Gabe and Quinn, who both looked at Maggie questioningly, but did as they were told.

She downed a full glass and slammed it down on the table. "Look, I am not sure how to broach this rather delicate subject, so I am just going to lay it all out on the line for you." Maggie exhaled sharply. "Georgie left me a trunk with some of her personal items. I learned a great deal more about your mother than I ever knew or needed to know, and I think it is time you did as well. It seems, the two of you were more alike than you ever knew."

Gabe furrowed his brow. "What exactly did she leave you?"

Duncan pulled the stack of letters from his pocket and handed them to Gabe, who set down his drink and took them for a closer inspection.

Quinn looked over. "What are these?"

"Letters I discovered in a false bottom of that box she left me." Maggie chewed on her thumbnail. "Your mother had a lover a few years before she met Martin."

"She —what? No —that's not right," stuttered Gabe in disbelief. "She said she had not had another man in her bed before Martin, not since my father died."

Maggie scratched the bridge of her nose. "Well, *technically*, she wasn't lying."

"Well, if she wasn't with another man…" Gabe's face clouded over when her words sank in and his jaw dropped, rendered speechless. He slowly looked down at the parcel of letters in his hands. "What exactly are you saying? Are you trying to tell me…" he finally forced out, "…my mother was with...another *woman*?"

"Georgie?" asked an astonished Quinn. "Nay!"

"I am afraid it's all true." Duncan pointed to the stack in his hand. "Maybe, ye should just read the letters."

Gabe dropped them to the table in a dramatic form. "Why don't you just give me the abbreviated version instead?"

Maggie and Duncan exchanged looks.

"She had a relationship with a young woman she loved a great deal. Those letters graphically detail their relationship right up until the other woman married and moved to America." Maggie scrunched up her face. "Which brings me to the rest of it."

"There's more!" groaned Gabe, wiping the beads of perspiration from his forehead. He downed his glass and refilled it. "Go on."

"The woman she was seeing married a merchant by the name of— 'Masters'."

"Masters?" He crushed the letters with his hand and his eyes closed. "Not a very common family name, is it?" he whispered. "Let me guess —her lover's name was— Holly?"

"I don't normally believe in coincidences, but it seems this might be one of them," she replied.

Gabe's breathing started to come on faster; Quinn rubbed his back in a calming manner.

"This can't be right. Why would she push me to get married all these years if she herself..."

Maggie laid her hand over on his. "Because you never *told* her you preferred men. She just assumed you were alone because of what happened with Penny and Samuel. The thought never occurred to her that you just didn't want to be with women. If you had, chances are, she would have been more than a little understanding. Gabe, your mother just wanted you to be happy, and I daresay, if she had known about you and Quinn—how much you two love each other— she would have approved."

"Oh God!" he choked and dropped his head. "All the time we spent butting heads, disagreeing, and she..."

Maggie squeezed his hand. "I know it is a lot to process, but I thought you should know."

"It seems my mother had a whole other side I had no idea existed."

"A little more than you know," she smiled. "Georgie left me a few other things as well, including some very steamy letters from your father and her erotic book collection. If you wish to have a look, you are welcome to, but I must tell you, there is some stuff in there so scandalous even Duncan and I would not attempt it."

Duncan shook his head and grinned before mouthing to her. "Not true!"

Maggie lifted her finger to her lips, silently shushing him, amused.

Gabe slowly raised his head to meet her gaze. "I find it hard to believe there isn't anything you two wouldn't try."

Duncan shrugged. "The man knows us well."

One by one, each person began to laugh until the tension in the room finally started to lift.

After they finished off the second bottle, Gabe leaned back in his chair. "I can't believe this, and Holly, she is so much younger than Mother."

"Like mother, like son," teased Quinn while squeezing his leg.

Gabe laughed softly. "Oh, right!"

"It's probably more common than you think," said Maggie. "I mean, I guess it would spice up some of those boring afternoon tea parties."

"Did the letters say how they met?"

Maggie looked down into her glass. "Boring afternoon tea party," she mumbled.

Gabe emptied another glass and pointed. "Fill it up."

Maggie waved her hand until his glass overflowed. "Gabe, Georgie was unlike any woman I have ever met before. To be honest, this doesn't surprise me now that I think about it."

"It doesn't? Because it sure as hell does me."

"Georgie was a woman all her own. She was strong-willed and lived her life on her own terms. Don't think badly of her for following her heart; she wouldn't have faulted you for it." Maggie pushed back her chair. "Duncan and I should be going." She went over and kissed Gabe on the cheek, then Quinn. "I love you both!"

"We love you too, Mags!"

After a night of unexpected revelations, Gabe was still awake early the next morning, so he decided to take a walk to clear his head. The sun had just come up and the town was still quiet, only a few people out and about. He walked to the far end of town and was so lost in his thoughts; he didn't notice her sitting on the porch.

She set down her cup and went down the steps to stop him on the street as he reached the front of the house.

"You look very far away," she called out.

He looked up to see Holly smiling back at him. "Oh, I didn't see you there," he said and bowed, his eyes fixated on her when he straightened up. "How are you feeling?" he asked.

"Very well, thank you. Your nephew took exceptionally good care of me."

"I am glad to hear that."

"May I offer you some tea?" she asked, wringing her hands. "It's the least I can do since you saved my life."

Gabe hesitated, then finally nodded. "I would like that. Thank you."

He followed her onto the porch and took a seat as she called for her servant to bring a tray. "I should have sought you out sooner to express my gratitude. Please forgive my dreadful manners, but the past few days have been upsetting, to say the least."

"Not at all," he said after she joined him, and he accepted the cup she offered. After taking a sip, he closed his eyes and smiled. "I have not had tea like this since I left London."

"My husband ensures I am well stocked, knowing my affinity for it." She took in a deep breath. "I am very sorry for the loss of your mother."

Gabe's entire body tensed. "Thank you."

"I actually knew your mother very well."

"Oh?" he asked, setting his cup back on the saucer, his heart beating a little faster.

"I met her during a difficult time in my life. I had lost my own mother and was feeling very alone in the world when she befriended me at the local teahouse. I was sitting by myself when this beautiful soul pulled up a chair, planted herself right in it, and extended out her hand to introduce herself. She said something unexplained compelled her to come over to my table. We spent that entire afternoon talking and getting to know one another. It was the first time I had laughed since my mother's passing. Georgie was a special woman and this world just became a little dimmer without her in it."

Gabe casually brushed a tear from his eye. "It sounds like you cared for her a great deal."

"More than you will ever know," she whispered. Holly sipped her tea and regarded him. "She spoke of you often, of how proud she was of you for going off to be your own man."

"Mother and I always seemed to disagree over my life choices. Surely you have me mixed up with one of my brothers."

"No, I do not. She always had a certain gleam in her eye whenever she mentioned your name. Georgie once told me she thought you were the most like her out of all her boys— never one to follow the crowd, but one to carve your own path in this world. Between the two of us, I think you were secretly her favorite."

"My own path— I suppose that is why she was always trying to marry me off," he said dryly.

"She was worried about you being alone. Your mother wanted you to have someone to love and to share your life with. She felt you deserved it more than anyone after your wife and son passed."

The sound of little feet running towards them made them both look up. A beautiful little girl, with bouncing blond curls, around the age of five came running to them. Holly happily embraced her. "Allow me to introduce my little ray of sunshine— Georgianna."

Gabe's eyes widened, becoming misty, and he looked down. He lifted his hand to his face, swallowing hard, before smiling. "It is very nice to meet you, young lady," he said.

The little girl climbed onto her mother's lap and buried her face against her breast, just as the nanny came looking for her.

Gabe slowly rose from his seat. "I should be going. Thank you for the tea and the conversation. It meant more to me than you will ever know."

When he stepped off the porch, Holly called out to him, "Did you? Find someone, I mean?"

He turned. "I did, and we are very much in love."

"Georgie would be pleased," she affirmed.

"I hope so," he replied before sniffling and walking away.

"I have an announcement to make," said Martin, at dinner the day before they were to depart. "I have decided to stay here."

"What?" asked Gabe.

Maggie frowned. "I don't understand."

Wyatt grinned. "Martin is going to be my new partner in the medical practice."

"I think it will be a good fit, especially since I do not wish to return to London —even though we may need a bigger office."

"I think that is wonderful news!" exclaimed John.

Gabe rubbed his jawline. "I thought you were going to stay closer to us."

"I will be of more use here," he replied. "We will only be a few days apart as opposed to a few weeks. Besides, I like the town a great deal, and I think it will be a good place for a new start."

"America is not London," cautioned Gabe. "It will be an enormous adjustment."

"I think a big change is exactly what I need. At least here, I won't have some memory of Georgie on every corner."

Ana placed her hand on his back comfortingly. It was Gabe's turn to take notice of the gesture, and Quinn's turn to pretend he didn't see.

"We are going to miss you," said Maggie. "Hopefully, you will come to visit more often?"

"Nothing will keep me away!"

After a late supper, Wyatt and John excused themselves, claiming to want to go have a drink and catch up. Judging by the mischievous looks on their faces, they would be 'catching up' at the small tavern just outside of town known for its large breasted barmaids.

Martin went to deliver his things to Wyatt's house and settle in until he could find a place of his own, so Ana decided to turn in early, leaving Maggie, Duncan, Gabe, and Quinn to drink in the privacy of their room.

"She named her daughter Georgianna?" asked a stunned Maggie.

Quinn took Gabe's hand. "They must have meant a great deal to each other if she did something that special."

"She also told me some things that made me see my mother in a whole new light. I just wish I could have a chance to say a proper 'goodbye', to let her know that I am happy, and that she didn't need to worry about me."

"I expect she knows," a sudden thought occurred to Maggie, "or you could tell her now."

Gabe looked up questioningly.

"Visiting Penny and Samuel's graves seemed to help you a great deal before and it might just help now."

"I think that is a wonderful idea," said Quinn.

"We can shimmer over. It will be late there, and no one else will be around," added Duncan.

"What do you say, Gabe?"

"Yes! Let's do it."

They all joined hands and shimmered to the cemetery at the churchyard where Georgie had been laid to rest.

Maggie and Duncan slipped away to give Gabe and Quinn some time alone, walking towards the church. It was just before dawn in London, and they were surprised to find the door unlocked. Pushing it open, Maggie cautiously put one foot across the threshold, testing the way. When nothing happened, she moved the rest of her body inside, making a face as she pulled Duncan in with her. "Oh good, we didn't burst into flames! That's a bonus!"

"Always a good sign!" Duncan smirked.

They held hands and worked their way to the front, Maggie lazily touching each pew as she went. Taking a seat in the front, her gaze fell to the pulpit and she became lost in her own memories. She had not stepped foot in a church since they had become Fae, and she missed the simple beauty and peace that came with being inside one.

"My parents were never overly religious, but my father was raised in the Catholic Church, and he would take me along, on occasion, when he felt the need to unburden his soul for some reason or another. I was always amazed by the difference seeing him after confessional, the transformation from the lifted weight clearly evident on his face. It was something he needed to do for his own mind and soul's sake. I imagine these visits to the graveside are much the same for Gabe."

"They say confession is good for the soul." Duncan put his arm around her, lightly stroking her back. "I suppose there is a great deal of truth in that."

When they returned, they found Gabe kneeled between his mother's and his father's stones, saying a prayer as Quinn gripped his shoulder tightly.

23 Chapter Twenty-Three

The next day, before they bid farewell to Martin and Wyatt, Gabe pulled Martin off to the side, and handed him some paperwork. "I hope this will help. I am signing over Mother's bank accounts to you."

"Gabe, I can't accept this! Your mother wanted you to have all of it."

"I don't want it, Martin. I would rather you and Wyatt use it to invest in your practice and your new life. I can think of no better way for the money to be spent."

"What about you?"

Gabe laughed. "Contrary to Mother's belief, I am far from being destitute or on the verge of starvation. We are just fine."

"I don't know what to say."

Gabe embraced him. "Say you will be happy, and you won't spend the rest of your life grieving my mother. Promise me you will move on and not be alone for too long, because time is fleeting."

"I will miss you, Gabe."

"I will miss you too, Martin."

They returned home, and the following Saturday, Maggie was at her desk, writing down some notes when her mother came into the room late that afternoon. "What are ye doing?"

Maggie pushed the hair back from her face with both hands. "Paying bills, going over receipts, making orders —you name it, I'm doing it."

Ana folded her arms, "Huh!"

"What?" asked Maggie.

"Oh nothing, except I was just thinking that the Queen of the Fae might have better things to do with her time than paying bills."

Maggie leaned back in her chair and steepled her fingers. "What do you *propose* I should be doing?"

Ana shrugged and sat down across from her. "Queenly Fae things?"

"Mom, I have a husband, five children, and a whole estate of people who depend on me to do menial things, like paying the bills. I don't exactly have time for 'other' things."

"And that is the problem. Maggie, ye are the Queen of the Fae, but you have not embraced it and that greatly concerns me. I thought when we were back in Scotland and ye married Logan and Shanley, ye had begun, but once we returned here, ye fell right back into this humanly rut. It's time ye step up and become who ye are meant to be."

Maggie laid her arms on the desk. "I don't know how to be a queen, much less a Fae one. I didn't exactly know what I was signing up for."

"Well, my dear, ye can start by letting someone else deal with all of these tedious business affairs."

"Mom! If I don't bring in money, the people here don't eat."

Ana rolled her eyes. "There ye go thinking like a human again." Her mother picked up a piece of parchment from the tabletop. "What is this? What do ye see?"

"A piece of paper."

Ana shook her head. "Nay! Ye see money."

Maggie made a face, picked it up and shook it. "Paper."

Ana snatched it. "In your mind, see it as something else, then touch it."

"Okay, Mom. It's a bag full of coins!" she said mockingly and took it back, only this time it was so heavy, it fell from her hand, hitting the desktop hard. The paper had turned into a pouch full of gold.

"Huh?" Maggie picked it up, weighing it in her hand.

Her mother smiled. "Ye are the most powerful creature walking this Earth. Accept it, let it become a part of ye, and be who ye are meant to be." Ana reached across and touched her daughter's face before getting up to leave. "Be the Queen of the Fae!"

Maggie took out one of the gold coins and examined it closely while thinking about what her mother said. She was still lost in thought when Hettie came in. "You need anything, Maggie?" she asked.

"No, I'm fine, thank you." She took a good look at Hettie. "You look like you are feeling better. How's your knee?"

Hettie smiled. "It's much better. As a matter of fact, I haven't felt this good in years. Quinn rubbed some of that salve of his on my leg and it ain't hurt a bit since then. Harm can't even keep up with me."

"That's good to hear. I am going out for a bit. Please let Noni and Rowe know."

Hettie waved her hand. "Shoot, I might let them have the afternoon off and just chase those young'uns myself."

Maggie laughed and watched Hettie leave. As soon as she was out of sight, Maggie shimmered out and found herself at the waterfall. Stripping off her clothes, she stepped into the water, tipping her face up so the spray spilled down her cheeks. She moved into the deeper part of the pool, lying on her back so she was floating in the water, looking up at the white, wispy clouds in the sky.

After about an hour, she made her way out. Realizing she had nothing to dry off with, she closed her eyes and imagined a large towel and a spread-out blanket on the ground. When she opened them, both were there. She dried off, tossed the towel to the side, then stretched out on her stomach with her face turned to the side, closing her eyes and enjoying the warmth of the sun on her back.

"What are ye doing out here all by yourself?" she heard him ask.

"Contemplating my life," she said without moving.

He sat down next to her and used his finger to trace down her back. "Not rethinking your choice of husbands, I hope."

"No, I think I'll keep the one I have. He's pretty good in bed," she grinned, her eyes still closed.

"That's a relief!" He stretched out beside her, and lightly kissed her shoulder. He stopped. "Wait! *Pretty* good?"

She laughed and opened her eyes, propping up on her elbow and reached out to touch his chest. "I just needed a quiet place to think about something my mother said."

"What was it?" he inquired, running his hand down the length of her body.

"Something about embracing my Fae Queen status. She seems to think I should be doing things the Fae way instead of the human way, but if I don't do things like an actual person, it will bring attention to us and put the people on the estate in danger. I can't just go around waving my hands, making things appear out of thin air."

"Your mother was born a Fae, then became human. The circumstances are a little different, and it may be harder for her to see that. I think ye are doing a fine job. Besides, we are raising children who need to know how to live in a human world, not in a world of magic."

Maggie rolled over on her back. "We still have so much to learn. Today, she had me turn a sheet of paper into a bag of gold and it was far easier than I ever thought it would be. I am finding the more I open myself up to it, the more like second nature magic is becoming. I have got to keep a tight grip on it for the safety of everyone around us."

Duncan slid his hand over her midsection. "I have complete faith in my queen," he smiled and leaned over to kiss her. "Now, I think the Dagda must redeem himself, since his wife thinks he is only 'pretty good' in bed," he said playfully.

"What did you have in mind?" she teased and slipped her arms around his neck.

"I am sure I can figure something out," he said before moving over her, kissing his way all the way down to the perfect spot.

"I think you are off to a very good start," she moaned, biting her lip and running her fingers through his hair.

Maggie returned from the waterfall alone, looking very refreshed.

"You are in a good mood," remarked John when he saw her descending the staircase.

"After a few hours like the ones I just had with my husband, I can't help but be," she grinned. "He is very good to me."

John's smile faded and he looked down, remembering the letter he still carried. He touched the breast of his coat where he kept it.

"Maggie, there is something I need to speak with you about," he said, taking her by the hand, leading her into the drawing room. His face showed signs of strain, obviously greatly troubled by something.

"Okay," she said and let him guide her to the sofa. As she sat, he did as well. Slipping his arm over the back of the couch, he turned so he could look her directly in the eyes.

"What's going on?" she asked.

John laid his hand on her lap. "I have something extremely difficult to tell you and it is going to come as a great shock to you. For the record, I take no pleasure in this."

"In what?"

John closed his eyes. "Duncan has...done something... you deserve to know about," pausing to search for the words.

"What has he done?" she asked. "What are you talking about?" Her body clenched when she saw the look of pity appear in John's eyes.

Maggie's face paled and her stomach lurched. "Just say it."

He stared back at her. "Duncan has had an affair."

"What?" she asked, stunned, dumbfounded. "You are mistaken. He wouldn't!"

John gripped her hand tightly. "I am afraid he would, and he did."

"No!" she shook her head vigorously. "He would never!"

"There's more, Maggie," he said, stroking her arm. "There's a child."

Maggie pulled her hand from his and stood, turning away. "He wouldn't do that to me." She turned back to face John, her voice cracking. "You're lying! Why would you lie to me like this?"

"I wouldn't make this up. I could never do that to you. It's killing me to have to tell you this." He rose and pulled the letter from his pocket. "I have proof. It is a letter I found he was attempting to conceal." He held it out for her. "He has provided for the child, Maggie. Why would he do that if it wasn't his?"

Maggie snatched the letter from him, her hands shaking so badly she could barely open it. She stepped off to the side and read it.

"What the hell is going on here?" shouted Duncan from the doorway. "What have you done to upset my wife? I could feel her pain from the other side of the estate."

"You have no one to blame but yourself," spat John, stepping between Duncan and Maggie. "She has the proof in her hands that you were unfaithful to her and impregnated another woman with your child."

"Have ye lost your mind!" roared Duncan. "I have done no such thing. I don't take women to bed indiscriminately the way ye do."

"Oh, but you did, didn't you, producing a child you are hiding from everyone?"

Duncan rushed at John, knocking over chairs and tables to pin him against the wall, punching him as the entire house shook from the encounter. "I will not allow ye to come between me and my wife with these lies!"

John shoved him back and was just about to launch at him when Maggie planted herself between them.

"STOP!" she shouted, her voice coming out in a deep, dark tone, the floors buckling from the sheer force of it.

She turned to John. "Duncan has not been unfaithful to me. I know all about this situation, and this letter isn't about HIS child."

John narrowed his eyes at her, trying to comprehend. "Surely not Quinn's?"

"Nay, ye fool," bellowed Duncan. "The child belongs to YE!"

John blinked, his face void of all emotion. "That's impossible. I am sterile."

Maggie covered her mouth. "It happened before I took that back from you. This occurred when you went to Hampshire County with Captain Russell on that first business trip."

John shook his head, searching his memories. "No! No! No!"

"Does the name Lucy Hanks ring a bell?" Duncan mocked and turned, pacing with his hands behind his head, still vibrating from his anger.

John took two steps to the side and slowly sat down on the edge of the sofa. "If this is true, why would she not tell me? Why would she not send word?"

"You didn't tell her your family name, for one thing, ye fecking fool!" replied Duncan. "And she wanted nothing to do with ye when ye called her 'Maggie' in the throes of passion, as I am sure ye do all of the whores ye specifically request to look exactly like my wife at the brothel ye keep a permanent room at," he blurted out before realizing his words.

Maggie spun around to Duncan. "He WHAT?"

Duncan's eyes widened and he wiped his mouth with his hand.

"MY name was the one he called out to Lucy...and he is taking.... whores who look...like me?" She stepped to Duncan and shoved him. "How could you keep something like that from me?"

"I didn't want to upset ye, my love."

"YOU FAILED!" she growled.

Turning to John, "You called that girl by my name while you were...knocking her up...and whores...like me..." Maggie covered her face with both hands, finding it hard to form words. "John, what the hell?" she screamed. "How could you do something like that?"

"I was drunk, too drunk to know what I was doing. She undressed me and before I knew it, we had..." he whispered, still shell-shocked. "I was drinking myself into oblivion after Aurnia and I stopped seeing—"

Duncan's head snapped up. "After ye stopped WHAT?" he demanded.

John stared down at the floor, his mind racing.

Duncan closed the gap between them in seconds and snatched him by the collar. "Did ye bed my mother?"

John closed his eyes, his silence answering the question.

Duncan roared at the top of his lungs and he slammed John into the floor, falling upon him, pummeling his face with his hands.

Maggie tried to pull him away but was unable to.

Gabe and Quinn rushed into the room, moving to break them up, taking the strength of them both to separate the pair. They got Duncan to the other side of the room, holding him back as he fought against them, shouting over their shoulders. "I swore I would kill ye if ye ever touched my mother!"

Quinn and Gabe both looked over their shoulders at John, stunned and horrified, as he sat up on his elbows, his wounds already healing, and Maggie stooping down to help him up.

"Calm yourself, Duncan!" she commanded.

"I will not! That bastard seduced my mother!"

"He did NOT!" she barked back.

Duncan's face darkened as he stared at Maggie. "Ye knew!" he stated, angrily. "Ye knew he was sleeping with my mother, and ye said nothing!"

Maggie moved to stand in front of him. "I did and I had my reasons." She started to reach for him, but he jerked back.

Rage engulfed Duncan's entire body as the floor began to tremble. "My own wife betrayed me by keeping secrets from me."

"Don't pretend you didn't keep a few of your own from me," she fired back.

Duncan's face contorted — he waved his hand and disappeared.

Maggie turned to see John had shimmered out as well.

Ana appeared at the door looking around the room at the mess, including the two new cracks and the hole in the wall that much resembled the outline of a body that had been pressed into it. "I am afraid to ask," she called as she made her way in.

"Are the children alright, Mom?" asked Maggie.

"Aye, they are fine. They even managed to sleep through all of this," she replied, stopping to set a table back up, "and thankfully, all of the mortals had vacated the house for the day."

"Just what exactly happened?" asked Gabe.

Quinn folded his arms. "Please tell me John didn't bed my mother."

Maggie stepped over to the liquor cabinet that had collapsed in the ruckus, managing to fish out a couple of unbroken bottles, as Gabe and Quinn righted the chairs. "Sit down and let's get everything out in the open."

24 Chapter Twenty-Four

Maggie explained what had led up to the confrontation. "I knew John had taken a room at the whorehouse in London," admitted Gabe, an expression of detest on his face, "but I certainly had no idea he was doing THAT, or that he had gotten that girl with child!"

Clearly upset he had been kept in the dark, Quinn turned to face his husband, "Ye knew and ye didn't tell me? Why would ye keep something like that from me?"

"Or me?" demanded Maggie.

Gabe laid his hand on Quinn's leg. "I'm sorry. I gave John my word I wouldn't mention it to anyone else, especially since the matter was so delicate."

"What do ye mean by 'delicate'?" asked Ana.

Gabe looked over at Maggie.

"Oh, just spit it out!" she said, before turning up the bottle, rubbing her left temple. "I don't think anything else is going to shock me tonight."

"First of all," he said to Quinn apologetically, "I knew he had been seeing someone, but I had no idea it was your mother. I would not have kept something as important as that from you."

Maggie threw her hands up in the air. "Oh good, *I* am officially the worst spouse in the room. Yay me!" She took another swig from the bottle while her mother rubbed her back and indicated Gabe should continue.

"After his night with the girl, he felt truly horrible. He came to the realization it wasn't Aurnia he was really in love with, but another," Gabe turned his gaze to Maggie, "John was using the whorehouse as a way to keep himself in check. He knew you would never choose him over Duncan, and he didn't want to lose the relationship you have now over his feelings. Had I known he was looking for women who only looked like you, I would have stepped in and set him straight immediately, but he really was trying to do the right thing, in his own sordid way."

"He is also the God of Sex and Lust. He is what he is," defended Ana. "The fact he was trying to channel it is encouraging. John has had a more difficult time than the rest of ye with his new life."

Quinn leaned forward. "What of this relationship with my mother? Maggie, surely ye understand why Duncan is upset?"

"I do," she sighed, "but he does not have all the facts. Quinn, your mother initiated the relationship. She was also the one who wanted it to not be serious and for the rest of you to not know about it. I only found out by accident. John really did have feelings for her, or at least he thought he did.," she smiled, "I think your husband can fill you in on lonely mothers and the things they will do."

Gabe scoffed. "Just be grateful you didn't find out by walking in on your mother straddling John, riding him like a seasoned horse— or another woman for that matter."

"Ugh!" Quinn shrank back and made a face, the image obviously now in his mind.

"Another woman?" asked Ana, confused.

"Apparently, my mother kept a female lover for a while."

"Really? How interesting! Seems there have been quite a few secrets floating around." Ana turned her attention to Maggie. "Where are Duncan and John now?"

Maggie shrugged. "They shimmered off."

Ana patted her arm. "Give them some time to calm down. It's all ye can do."

Gabe looked over at the damage. "How are you going to explain the holes in the wall?"

Maggie flipped her hand nonchalantly. "What holes?" And they disappeared.

Ana tilted her head, pleased. "Ye are getting very good at this stuff, ye know?"

"Let's see if I can fix the other damage that easily," she said, and closed her eyes, focusing in on Duncan's location.

She found him at the waterfall, destroying the longhouse they had spent so many hours making love in.

"Stop!" she ordered and stormed over to him. "Don't do this!"

He turned, his face full of rage. "Ye need to leave!"

"We need to talk!" she countered.

"NAY!" his voice full of venom, "I cannot bear the sight of ye right now."

"What?" she asked, stunned and hurt by his words.

"Ye lied to me. Ye broke our trust!" he howled, picked up a large boulder and threw it.

"I wasn't the only one," she shouted back. "You kept things from me as well, so don't pretend you are the perfect one here."

"Ye took his side over mine!"

"I took no one's side! I was trying to mind my own business and stay out of John's. I thought that would please you."

He spun around. "Do I look pleased?" he bellowed.

She stepped closer and reached out for him, but he backed away, and held up his hands. "Nay! Don't touch me!"

"Duncan," she said softly.

He shook his head, sneering, and shimmered away.

Maggie stood completely motionless. For the first time since they'd met, she seriously wondered if she would ever see him again.

Maggie was wide awake that night, hoping Duncan might return home soon, but when he didn't, she decided it was time to take a few matters into her own hands. By God, she was the Queen of the Fae— it was high time she started acting like it.

Closing her eyes, she focused in on John, and shimmered to his location, landing outside of the entrance to the brothel. Steeling herself, she charged right in. It was early morning, and most of the downstairs was deserted. Maggie made her way up the staircase and knocked on the door of the room she sensed him in.

"I don't need any girls tonight, Renee," he called.

"How about a friend without benefits?" she snarked and cracked open the door.

"Maggie?"

He laid on the bed alone, his back against the headboard with his legs sprawled out, the smell of alcohol wafting in the air. Closing the door behind her, she went to the side of the bed. "Mind sharing?" she asked.

"All I have is yours for the asking," he said with a wave.

"Scoot over," she said and lightly smacked the side of his arm with the back of her hand. Starting to crawl into bed next to him, she stopped suddenly. "Are these sheets clean?"

He chuckled softly. "Freshly laundered each day, and no one else has been in this bed today, save me."

She made herself comfortable next to him; he handed her the glass he was drinking from and she took a sip. "Ugh! What is this?"

"I am not sure, though I imagine it is a lot like what piss tastes like," he replied, wrinkling his nose.

Maggie tossed the liquid in the chamber pot by the bed, then waved her hand over the glass, making something else appear. She took a taste.

"Much better!" She handed it back to him. "One of the more useful tricks I learned from Finn."

John sipped it. "Indeed! Here's to actual *useful* Fae tricks."

Maggie nodded. "Are you okay? Any injuries that didn't heal?"

"I'm fine," he said quietly.

"I owe you an apology, John. Keeping the news about Lucy from you was my idea."

"Why didn't you want to tell me?"

Maggie sighed. "It was at the same time you asked me to make you sterile again. If you recall, I asked if you wanted any daughters and you emphatically said 'no'.

However, the ultimate and final decision was made by Lucy herself. She did not want a man around her only there out of a sense of obligation, especially when she knew you desired another."

"And that brings us to the bigger issue. I have a confession to make, one I should have made a long time ago." He laid his hand over on hers and swallowed hard. "I love you, Maggie. I have since the day I first met you. Don't tell Gabe, but that night I was already scheming, planning to steal you away from him," he grinned. "When you came to Oyster Bay and told me you had married, I was beside myself. I have to admit, I seriously considered letting Duncan rot away in that jail just to get him out of the picture."

Maggie cut him a sideways look.

"Then, I saw how much in love you were with him, and I knew I could never intentionally cause you that kind of pain, so I kept my feelings to myself. You became pregnant shortly after, and I knew my chance with you had passed. When Aurnia and I were together, I thought we might be happy until I realized she wasn't you. I think somewhere deep down, she knew it too, which is why she kept me at arm's length." He kissed her hand. "There, I have finally divulged my feelings. I know the only way I can be in your life is as a friend, and that WILL be enough for me, if you will allow me to stay. I can't imagine Duncan will want me around though, and I will abide your wishes."

"I wouldn't know what Duncan wants. He has not seen fit to come back," she revealed, "and I am not sure he ever will."

"Maggie, I am sorry!" and hung his head shamefully. "This is all my fault."

Maggie turned to face him. "No, it is not, John, I am responsible for all of this," frowning as she took note of her surroundings. "Well, not the room in the whorehouse, that's all on you, but it was my decision to save you from the hangman's noose. It was also my choice to make you a Fae god, though I did not suspect it would be the God of Lust and Sex, and I was the one who decided it was best to not tell you about Lucy's baby. Duncan actually argued for you to be told, but I bear more responsibility for the matters around us than anyone. I am the Queen of the Fae, the most powerful being on the planet, and it's well past time I started acting like it."

"What do you mean by that?" he questioned, his voice full of concern.

"I mean, it's time I took control of the situation and the ones around me."

Maggie blew out a long breath and traced the outline of his face. "I love you, John, and I need you in my life. I also cannot continue to let you suffer because of your feelings for me when I have the power to do something about it."

She tipped up his chin and moved her face slowly to his. Watching her intently, he was uncertain of what was happening— until he felt the touch of her lips brush against his. She kissed him tenderly, which he fervently returned, placing his hand on the back of her head, pulling her closer. He sighed, happier than he had ever been, lost in a moment designed to sustain him through all eternity, no matter what the future might bring. She pulled back slowly, smiling at him. "How do you feel?"

His eyes fluttered open and he lifted his fingers to his lips. The man appeared befuddled. "I feel —different. What did you do to me?"

"I took away your feelings of desire for me, leaving only the family love between us. You will never pine for me, or what might have been, ever again. I have cleared your heart to be open to someone else."

"What about my yearning for other women?" he asked, suddenly in a bit of a panic.

Maggie rolled her eyes. "I only took away your proclivity for me. You will continue to chase all other women like a dog in heat, as per usual."

He smirked. "I may have to test that theory."

"Knock yourself out," she chuckled and slapped his thigh.

"What about Duncan?" he asked solemnly. "He will not forgive me for his mother, and he will not want me to remain on the estate."

Patting his face, "You leave him to me."

She started to get up, but John stopped her.

"What should I do about the child?"

Maggie frowned. "Honestly? I think you should leave it to me."

"What? You don't want me to take responsibility?"

"John," she sat back down, "what would you do? Would you marry her? Be a good and faithful husband? What's the point? You know as well as I, she has no true feelings for you."

He sat silent.

"Truthfully, I think it is better for all concerned if she continues to believe you do not know. Lucy deserves to find someone who wants to be with her because he loves her, not someone who will be with her out of a sense of obligation. That is a recipe for disaster and regret. Lucy and the baby are being provided for and will want for nothing. For the time being, let it go. If you want to check in, or be there for the child, we can figure out a way to do it without involving Lucy."

"It's not right for you to have to bear responsibility for what I did," he whispered. "You have enough to deal with."

"So, what's one more thing?" Maggie stopped and kissed him on the forehead. "Give me a few days to sort Duncan out, if I can, before you come home."

"Thank you, Maggie."

She went to the door and out into the hall. She caught a woman by the arm who was passing on the landing, stopping to admire the goods she had on display. Maggie did a double take. "Your breasts are spectacular," she complimented.

"Thank you, sweetie," said the woman. "I have been told I have the 'best tits' in London."

Maggie laughed. "I believe you just might, and it just so happens," she led her towards John's door, "I have a friend in this room who needs a little consoling." Maggie closed her hand into a fist, then opened it, producing a solid gold coin, handing it to the woman. "Make sure he is well taken care of, will you?"

The woman's eyes widened at the sight of the currency. "I'll take care of both of you, if you like," she winked with a wicked smile.

Maggie bobbed her head. "As tempting as that sounds, just make him really happy for as long as that will buy."

"Whatever you say, love," she said, pushed up her breasts and headed into John's room.

Maggie went down the stairs and out onto the street before shimmering back to the house.

Gabe was waiting for her when she returned.

"Shouldn't you be getting some sleep?" she asked.

"I was about to say the same to you."

"I found John."

"And?"

"And— I sorted him out. He no longer desires me in that way."

Gabe regarded her and folded his arms. "How the bloody hell did you manage that?"

Maggie held out her hands. "I am embracing being the Queen of the Fae and all of the power that goes with it. I was able to remove it from him, so it is not an issue anymore."

"Just like that?" he asked.

"Yep!" she nodded. "You would be amazed by what I can do since I have opened myself up to it." She pulled up a chair to sit in front of him. "Now, you and I need to have a chat."

"I'm not getting the paddle, am I?" he teased.

"Do you *want* the paddle?" she quipped. "I can have one made up and give it to Quinn if you are into that kind of kinky thing, or maybe some of your mother's books will give you some ideas."

"I think I will pass," he grimaced, "I have enough excitement as of late."

"Don't knock it until you try it," she insisted and smiled.

Maggie took his hand. "You are my oldest and dearest friend. We have always had each other's back— come lovers, come husbands, come Georgie Asheton Barnes, and come hell or high water. You and I need to agree to not keep things from each other, no matter how much we think it might hurt."

"You're right," he agreed. "I didn't tell you because I thought John was taking care of his needs in a better way. I was wrong, and I truly had no idea he was asking for women who looked like you."

"I know. Our family has grown by leaps and bounds the past few years, and I feel like we aren't as close as we once were. I think it's time to remedy that."

"Agreed," he smiled, "I have missed our time together."

Maggie took both his hands. "From now on, once a week, you and I have a dinner date, just the two of us, to tell each other everything. I need to have that time with you again for my own sanity. The best part being, we can go anywhere in the world for it."

"I like the idea of that!"

Maggie leaned forward and kissed him on the lips. "Good. We start as soon as I get everyone around here sorted out."

"How are you going to do that?"

She shrugged. "I dunno. I am just going to wing it. Where's Quinn?"

"He went to pay a visit to his mother. I think it's best he hears her side of things about this business with John from her."

"That is actually an excellent idea! Where are Kat and Alastair?"

"Upstairs asleep. Where's Duncan?"

She plopped back in the chair. "Stewing in his own juices. I don't know if I can fix this, Gabe. I mean, he has been upset with me before, but never like this. He wouldn't let me get near him."

"He just needs to cool off."

She shook her head gravely. "I am just afraid of what he might do before then. He is not thinking clearly." Maggie scratched her head. "Why don't you shimmer over to the stronghold and lend a little support to your husband while he is talking to Aurnia?"

He nodded, leaned forward, and kissed her cheek before shimmering out.

Maggie held out her hand until a glass of whisky appeared in it. After taking a sip, she called over her shoulder, "How am I doing so far?"

Ana leaned against the doorway with her arms folded, smiling. "Very well, I'd say. Allowing yourself to accept the power ye were born to wield certainly has made a difference." She came over to her daughter and Maggie waved her hand, producing a glass for her mother. "Thank ye," she said, touching Maggie on the shoulder on her way to the chair.

"Not sure even I am powerful enough to save my marriage," she whispered gravely.

"Duncan loves ye, sweetheart, and ye will figure out a way to work this out."

"How, Mom? He is so angry with me, not that I am too thrilled with him at the moment myself."

"Your love is the stuff of legends. Ye will find a way to overcome this," assured Ana. "I have no doubt. I am going to bed and I will make sure the children are looked after. Take all the time ye need." She rose and kissed Maggie's head on her way out of the room.

Duncan found himself in Paris for some odd reason, the product of not thinking clearly and wanting to be as far away from Maggie as possible. He walked until he happened upon a tavern. Going inside, he took a table and ordered. A smiling, redheaded barmaid brought over a bottle and a glass, lightly brushing against him as she sat it in front of him. As he downed his first shot, he noticed an older man, peering over the top of his spectacles, watching the woman walk away and partaking of the view. "I think she likes you," he said. "I bet she would make fine company for the evening."

"I am not looking for company," barked Duncan.

"Ah, a Scotsman," the man said and pulled his chair closer, "and if you aren't interested in her, would you mind terribly sending her my way."

Duncan looked at the man strangely and poured himself another glass.

The man studied him. "Let me guess, woman troubles? Or should I say, problems with the wife, judging by that wedding ring on your hand."

"I'm really not in the mood for talking," he mumbled.

"Me either," said the man, holding up his glass. "Here's to drinking and watching large-bottomed women bend over," craning his neck for a better look at one of the ladies. He waited for one to come by. "Watch this," he whispered. Tossing a coin on the floor, he announced loudly, "Oh moi, j'ai laissé tomber une pièce et je ne peux pas l'atteindre car mon vieux dos ne veut pas plier!" (translating loosely to— "Oh me, I have dropped a coin and I cannot reach it because my old back won't bend!")

One of the women rushed over to pick it up, the old man stealing a glimpse down the front of her dress as she did.

"Un autre," he pointed under a table, shaking his finger.

She got down on all fours to look for it. The old man leaned forward and smiled wickedly as he adjusted his spectacles. "Dear God, I love women!"

Duncan laughed at the dirty minded old man despite his own sour mood.

He sipped from his glass, turning his attention back to Duncan. "Look at you —big, handsome, and strong. You can have every woman in this place, and you sit here fretting over one you are forced to look at every day. What is wrong with you— or her? Does she have the face of a horse?"

"Nay!" refuted Duncan. "My wife is a beautiful goddess, and I love her more than life itself!"

"Then why are you here drinking with me instead of being back home, dipping your wick in her blessed feminine folds?"

"She betrayed me." Duncan downed a third glass.

"What's good for the goose is good for the gander, I say. She didn't happen to be unfaithful to you, did she?"

"Nay! She would never do that, but she did keep a secret from me."

"Is that all?" The man waved him off with a scoff. "Women keep secrets. It's part of their allure, and besides, where's the fun in knowing everything about them? If we did, we would be bored out of our minds."

As one of the barmaids walked by, the man grabbed her by the hand and pulled her onto his lap. He fished a coin from his coat and held it up.

The woman smiled as she snatched it, casually slipped it in her shoe, and put her arm around his neck.

Duncan watched the exchange and finished off the bottle, a sudden realization hitting him. "Oh, for Christ's sake, is this a brothel?"

"Of course it is," replied the man, pushing his round-rimmed glasses up on his nose, engrossed in the woman's ample cleavage. "What did you think it was?"

"I thought it was just a tavern."

"Not in Paris, my dear boy," he said and grabbed the arm of the woman who was smiling at Duncan earlier, guiding her towards him. "Might as well enjoy yourself while you are here. Say, what did you say your name was?"

"I didn't—it is Duncan MacGregor."

"Well, it is nice to meet you. My name is Benjamin Franklin. I would shake your hand, but as you can see, both of mine are quite full." He laughed and wrapped his arms around the shapely woman on his lap.

The other woman went over to Duncan and ran her hands across his shoulder.

He tried to shrug her off, but she was persistent. "I just want a room," he said and tried to stand, but stumbled because the exceptionally potent alcohol hit him hard. Holding up his hands, he repeated. "Just a room."

"Une chambre pour l'homme," said the old man before burying his face between his date's breasts, happily lost between the mountains.

The other woman nodded, then took Duncan by the hand, and led him to the staircase. They were alone in the room, and before he knew what was happening, the woman had taken off his shirt, and pushed him back on the bed.

"No!" he said as they toppled over. He flipped over on his stomach, wanting to just lay still for a bit, hoping the room might stop spinning, but she took the opportunity to draw closer to him, splaying her hands across his backside and kissing his back.

"NO!" he shouted when he felt her lips upon him, rolling back over, so she would fall off to the side. "GO!" he ordered and pointed to the door.

The woman cursed at him in French.

He took a few coins from his pocket and held them up. "Just go!" He pointed at the door again.

She snatched the money, then stormed out.

Duncan covered his face with his hands. "What the hell am I doing?"

Maggie sat there for an hour before deciding it was time to deal with the issue head on. She focused in on Duncan and willed herself to his location. She was surprised, and somewhat disheartened, to find herself in Paris in front of a rather seedy looking establishment.

She could feel he was alone, so she shimmered into his room. He sat on the side of the bed, his face in his hands, his shirt off, reeking of alcohol. Maggie's heart sank when she noticed the red splotch on his back in the shape of a woman's lips.

"One fight and you run off here to take comfort with another?" she asked softly, her eyes becoming watery as she looked away.

He rubbed his face with his hands. "I was not unfaithful to ye."

"That lipstick on your back says different," she retorted.

"I had a great deal to drink and one of the barmaids who had been flirting with me brought me up here, but when she touched me, your face was the only one I could see. She took my shirt off and kissed my back before I knew what was happening, but it felt so foreign, so wrong, because she wasn't ye. I stopped her, sent her away, and paid her to leave me alone for the rest of the night. I could not take another woman if my very soul depended on it."

Maggie let out the breath she had been holding, moving to sit down next to him. "I'm sorry I did not tell you about your mother, but she did not want you to know."

He continued to look down at the floor. "That bastard seduced my mother, and ye did nothing to stop him. Ye chose him over me by protecting him."

"No," she said, shaking her head, still not touching him. "It was not like that. Your mother *wanted* to be with him."

"Because his 'lust-dust' affected her," he snapped.

"For the record, John cared a great deal about your mother, but she was the one who did not want a relationship, was the one that wanted it kept secret, and the one who ended it. I only found out by mistake."

"That's not possible!" he growled.

"If you are so sure, then go ask her yourself. Get her side of the story before you pass judgement on anyone else. She will tell you the truth of the matter."

"My WIFE should have told me the truth of it."

Maggie turned her gaze upward, leaning back on her arms. "The same way my husband should have told me about the obsession John had with me, which, by the way, if you had, I could have moved sooner to do something about, before it became such a problem."

"I did not want to upset ye," he stated, abrasively.

"You mean the same way I didn't want to upset you by telling your mother's business—and it is HER business, whether you like it or not. If you think mothers don't have needs like that, I suggest you go talk to Gabe and let him set you straight," she said sarcastically. "We both had a lapse in judgement and made the wrong choices for what we thought were the right reasons."

Duncan's body tensed. "What do ye mean by ye moved to do something about John?"

"I took away his desire for me."

Duncan turned to face her. "Ye what?"

Maggie stood and walked over to a small basin of water and wrung out a rag that was hanging next to it, her back to him. "I have discovered the abilities Finn left me with are a great deal more powerful than I could have ever imagined. I am able to do things I never thought possible and I was able to do that for John," she turned, "The only feelings he has left for me are the ones he has for a close family member. He will never desire me in that way again."

Duncan stared at her in disbelief.

Holding up the rag, "May I please wash that woman's lip rouge off you?"

His face relaxed a bit and he nodded curtly.

Moving to the other side of the bed, she crawled up behind him and lightly touched his back. After gently washing the makeup off, she tossed the rag onto the floor before gingerly laying her hands on him and leaning close to his ear. "That's better." Maggie pressed her lips to his neck and moved her hands around to his chest, but he caught her by the wrists, preventing her from going any further. Stunned by the rebuff, she froze.

"Don't," he said softly. "I can't."

Maggie pulled back, his words cutting her to the bone causing tears to well in her eyes. She moved off the bed, and over to the window to look out, wiping the wetness from her cheek. "Go talk to your mother," she advised before shimmering out.

He turned in that direction, immediately regretting his refusal of her. "Maggie," he called longingly, but she was already gone.

Duncan found himself at the stronghold in Scotland, Quinn and Gabe still there when he arrived.
"Mother, I have come…"

She abruptly cut him off. "I know exactly why ye have come!" she shouted. "Sit your arse down and let me tell ye what I just explained to your brother."

He did as he was told, catching a glimpse of Quinn and Gabe who were sitting quietly, eyes wide, afraid to move, while Lady Aurnia paced, enraged. She wagged her finger at Duncan. "Ye are a damned fool!"

"What?" he asked, affronted.

"Ye heard me! Aye, John and I had an affair. I was the one who desired him in my bed. He did not seduce me, he did not force me, it was MY choice. I am a grown woman and if I want to lay with every fecking man in Scotland, it is none of my children's concern. It's not like any of ye consulted with me when ye had your way with all of those women ye thought ye were hiding from me over the years —like I couldn't smell them on ye every time ye came home after being with one."

"But Mother, John of all people?"

"Do I sound like I am finished?" she bellowed.

Duncan opened his mouth to say something but thought better of it and snapped it shut.

"Quinn tells me ye accused Maggie of betraying ye for not telling ye."

Duncan glared at Quinn who mouthed 'sorry' to him.

"I did not want any of ye to know for this exact reason and she kept that confidence for me. Ye will not blame her for my actions, and I will not allow ye to take out your frustrations on her. That woman loves ye more than life itself. She accepted becoming the Fae Queen just to save your life, gave ye five beautiful children, has done more for this family than anyone can imagine, and ye thank her by treating her this way. Do ye have any idea the kind of responsibility that poor woman bears upon her shoulders? And here ye are, not supporting her like a husband should, but instead giving her grief for trying to do right by the people around her. I am ashamed of the misguided, foolhardy way ye are behaving."

"But Mother— John?"

"Aye, John! Why the bloody hell *not* John? He's a handsome, desirable man and he can do things to curl a woman's toes unlike anything I have ever experienced in my entire existence, even with your father," she recalled wistfully, a sly smirk crossing her face.

"STOP!" he cringed. "I don't want to know this!"

"Then tend to your own damned business and quit worrying about mine!" she admonished.

Duncan threw up his hands in defeat, before collapsing into a chair. "Ye are right. I *am* a damned fool. I kept something from her as well, so I have no room to speak. I should have apologized instead of brushing her off in Paris."

"Paris?" Gabe's head snapped up. "Why were you in Paris?"

Lady Aurnia walked over to her son, leaned down, and caught a whiff of rose water rolling off him. Her eyes widened and she smacked the back of his head hard.

"OW! Why did ye do that?" he asked, his hand flying to cover that spot.

"I can smell the cheap perfume all over ye, and Maggie does not wear cheap perfume. Ye were with another woman." She popped him again.

"Were ye, Brother?" demanded Quinn incredulously.

"Aye, I was," he muttered, cutting his eyes up at his mother, "but I was not unfaithful to Maggie."

"Then, why were you there?" asked a suspicious Gabe

"It's a long story, but I did not break my vows."

"But did she find ye there?" questioned Lady Aurnia.

"Aye!"

She smacked him a third time.

"For Christ's sake woman, will ye stop that?" he exclaimed.

"Nay! Not until I can knock some sense into that thick head of yours. Ye need to go find her, get down on your knees, and beg for her forgiveness. Where did she go?"

Duncan sighed, closing his eyes to sense her. His eyes flew open, worry lines creasing his face. "I don't know where she is. I can't feel her."

"Try again!" ordered Lady Aurnia.

He did and still felt nothing.

"Has that ever happened before?"

"Nay, never! We are always able to reach each other," he said, standing, a dreadful expression on his face.

"She is probably at home," said Quinn, and he and Gabe stood. "We should go see!"

—but Duncan was already gone.

Lady Aurnia grasped Quinn's arm. "Let me know what is happening and make sure he doesn't do anything stupid."

Duncan paced the floor frantically.

"Are ye sure she has not been back here?" he asked Ana for the third time.

"No, she has not. What is going on?"

He pounded his fist on the mantle. "She found me, and I refused her. She thinks I won't forgive her."

"Will ye?"

"I already have," he whispered, "but she doesn't know that. I need to find her."

"Can't ye sense her?"

He shook his head. "I cannot— and that is what frightens me."

Gabe and Quinn appeared.

"Is she here?" asked Gabe.

"Nay, she is not," responded Ana.

"Maybe she is with John?" suggested Quinn.

Duncan looked up, focusing in on him. "He is at the brothel in London. I will go and see. The two of ye check your own house and the tribe. If ye find her, bring her home and don't let her leave."

Duncan pushed open the door of John's room at the brothel to find John with a woman atop him.

Duncan averted his eyes. "Ye are needed— Maggie is missing."

John stopped what he was doing and gently slid the woman off him. "Go!" he said to her and pushed back the covers before reaching for his breeches.

"What do you mean she is 'missing'?"

"Missing!" he emphasized. "We can't find her—*I* can't find her—or feel her."

"Where was she last seen?" he asked, dressing in a hurry.

Once the woman was gone, Duncan faced him. "She found me at a place in Paris. We had words and she left."

"What kind of place?" John leaned in and smelled him, cursing under his breath. "Please tell me you did not take another woman," groaned John as he pulled on his boots.

"I did not!"

"Then, why do you smell like you have been with a whore?"

Duncan sat down next to John on the bed. "I was drinking when one of the barmaids—" he paused, "—I would never bed another woman."

"Does Maggie know that?"

"Aye, but I also pulled away from her, and she left me when I did."

"Are you still angry with her?" asked John, reaching for a bottle by the bed and handing it to Duncan.

"Nay," he replied quietly before taking a swig and glancing over at John, "and, I am not angry with ye anymore either."

"What changed your mind?"

Duncan exhaled sharply. "Mother put me in my place and told me to tend to my own business, which apparently I am not doing a very good job of."

John took back the bottle. "Your mother is an extraordinarily smart woman. I still find it sometimes hard to believe you are her son," he said sarcastically. "And you are an idiot for letting Maggie walk away from you."

"Don't press your luck," warned Duncan. "And indeed, I am an idiot. We need to find her."

"You know you won't be able to locate her unless she wants to be found," pointed out John gravely.

"I know."

Maggie sat on the beach looking out over the water, the light from the full moon dancing across the waves. It had been almost twenty years since she woke up in this exact spot —and her world had changed forever.

Closing her eyes, she listened to the sound of the waves crashing on the shore, wondering if it was about to change again. She had blocked Duncan from being able to find her, needing some time alone to think. A gentle nudge against the back of her neck reminded her some things would never change— and there was one who would always be by her side when she needed him.

She smiled and twisted around to rub Onyx's muzzle. "Here we are again, old friend —right back where we started from, just the two of us." She lay back in the sand and looked up at the stars. "Who knew waking up in the year 1765 would be the easy part?"

Onyx dropped his head to lick her forehead, making her giggle.

Duncan was frantically pacing the floor as the others looked on. They had searched everywhere for Maggie, to no avail, and Duncan was becoming more panicked with each passing moment.

"Duncan, sit down!" ordered Quinn. "Ye are making yourself insane, not to mention, the rest of us."

"Maggie will come back," assured Gabe. "She would never leave the children."

Duncan slammed his hand on the nearest table. "She could slip in, take them away, and we would never know. She is more powerful than all of us combined."

John shook his head. "She would not do that to you, or to them."

Sitting down, Duncan raked both hands through his hair. "And I never thought I would recoil from my wife's touch or find another woman's lips on my body, yet here we are."

Everyone stopped to stare at him. "Ye forgot to mention *that* little detail, Brother," chided Quinn.

Gabe's eyes widened with concern. "Did Maggie happen to see it?"

Duncan nodded, ashamed of himself.

"Damn it!" cursed Gabe before turning to Quinn and mouthing, "She may not come back!"

Quinn bobbed his head in agreement.

"Stop it!" fussed John when he saw the exchange. "She WILL come back, Duncan. She loves you too much not to. Don't worry."

Gabe squinted at John. "She really did do it, didn't she? She removed your desire for her."

"She did indeed," he replied, "and, I must say, my head is much clearer now, in more ways than one."

"It's strangely disconcerting," remarked Duncan, "I also no longer feel the desire to wring your neck."

"Ye are not picking up on those feelings because they are not there," pointed out Quinn. "The bone of contention is gone."

"Doesn't mean I won't rib you every now and then, if it makes you feel any better," John winked.

Duncan was about to pop back with a witty response when he felt her. Snapping his head up, he exclaimed, "I've got her!" and shimmered out.

He saw her silhouette, illuminated by the full moon, about thirty paces away, sitting with her back to him, her hair loose and blowing from the ocean breeze.

"Oh thank God!" he muttered, relieved. He took a step towards her, when Onyx appeared, smoke rolling from his snout, his eyes glowing red, pawing at the ground.

The big horse slammed his head into Duncan's chest with such force, it caused Duncan to take a step back. The beast was obviously enraged and not afraid to let him know it. He continued to back Duncan away from Maggie, blowing and snorting, giving the man a piece of his mind.

Finally, Duncan stopped and held his ground. "Aye, I am an idiot, I know. Ye are not the first one to tell me that tonight, but I have come to take my wife home, and no one will keep me from her," he said, stating his intent.

Onyx glared at him, meeting him eye for eye.

Duncan held up his hands in a nonthreatening way. "I love her, and I need to tell her. Please, let me by."

Onyx stood unmoving, not preventing him, but growled a warning, and snapped at him as he passed.

Duncan jumped. "Watch it, beast!"

Onyx huffed at him in disgust and went to stand beside Maggie protectively.

"I was afraid I might never see ye again," he said softly.

"Funny, I was thinking the same thing about you."

"I'm sorry— for everything," he said, his voice full of remorse. "I was acting like a childish fool and I am begging ye to forgive me. When I could not feel ye, I feared ye had left me forever and the thought terrified me. Maggie, I can never be without ye. Ye are my life and my world."

Maggie nodded, turning slightly towards him. "I should have told you about your mother. I'm sorry too."

"Nay, ye were right not to. Mother made it clear her personal life was none of my business and that I was to steer clear of it. Besides, I fear she may use the books to find a way to end me if I were to tell her that I lost ye."

Maggie snorted into her hand. "Still afraid of your mother?"

"Damn right," he chuckled. "I have never seen her as angry as she was this night when she thought I had pissed off her favorite daughter-in-law. My head still hurts where she bopped me so many times."

They both laughed.

"At any rate," he said, reaching out for her, "it doesn't matter. Just say ye will forgive me and ye will let me make it up to ye."

Maggie leaned into his touch. "Under one condition— no more secrets of any kind. We need to tell each other everything."

"Ye are right," he agreed. "Ye have my word, no more secrets."

After they kissed, Maggie nestled against his chest.

"What is this place?" he asked, looking out.

"The Outer Banks of North Carolina, the exact spot where I woke up nineteen years ago and my world changed forever."

"It's beautiful here. What's this place like in the future?" he asked.

"Much the same, but there are homes and hotels, which are like really big taverns, all up and down the shore. It's a little strange to see it like this now, so empty with no lights, but I like it. It's very calming."

"It's also very private," he noted playfully. "Looks like the perfect place to makeup and watch the sunrise."

"I am not so sure about that," she said, wrapping her arms around his neck. "Sand in the wrong places can get rather uncomfortable."

"I can fix that. Ye are not the only one who has been practicing," he said and kissed her.

Snapping his fingers, a rather large bed of blankets and deerskins appeared on the shore, along with several lit lanterns around the pallet, creating an ethereal glow. "I must keep my queen happy," he smirked, gathering her up and carrying her over to it.

They made love until dawn, watching the rising sun entangled with one another, talking, laughing, and loving before dozing off.

Seven exhausted, bone weary travelers arrived at their intended destination just south of Edinburgh a little before dawn, after using the cover of darkness to conceal their movements. Griffin and Samer hid the horses in the nearby woods while the others helped their injured brother, Lawrence, into the abandoned, dilapidated abbey. Once everyone was gathered inside, they barred the doors.

"We are all that is left," muttered the old man before collapsing into a nearby pew, holding his left side, fresh blood spilling from between his splayed fingers, his wound reopened by the hard ride.

"What are we going to do?" asked the youngest man, called Richard, as he pushed the hood back from his face and went over to one of the windows to look outside, ensuring they weren't followed.

"We cannot let the treasure we protect fall into the wrong hands, and the church does not deserve any of it after what they did to our leader, Jacques de Molay. I, for one, will die before I hand one piece of that over to the Pope who turned on us, his very own protectors, like

a venomous viper in a nest," spat Sebastian, helping Lawrence drink from one of the skins he carried.

"There is one thing we can do," suggested a handsome, young dark-haired knight, leaning against the wall with his arms folded, deep in thought. "The 'old ones' never failed us. WE were the ones who turned our backs on them, not the other way around. Perhaps, if we beg their forgiveness and ask for their help..."

"You speak blasphemy, Blade!" coughed Lawrence, whose strength had begun to ebb. "Have you forgotten your vows and your sacred duty to our one true God?"

"I speak the truth!" he retorted. "We did our duty and look at how we have been treated by the ones we swore loyalty to and sacrificed our lives for; they repaid us by allowing us to be hunted down like animals, slaughtered like sheep in a pasture, giving the luckiest of our kind quick deaths, while others were tortured in barbaric ways for countless days, years even. We did what we believed to be right and now we are all that is left of our brotherhood. A price on our heads is the only thing we have to show for it. I, for one, am sick to death of it, and I want to survive." The young man looked around. "What say the rest of you?"

"But we have hunted and killed so many of THEIR kind," said Porter, who had sat down on the cold, stone floor. "Why would they ever help us?"

"I know," replied Blade, as he walked over and gripped his shoulder. "But, right now, I don't see any other options. We don't have homes to go to and there is nowhere for us to hide. If anyone else has any better ideas, speak now!"

His request was answered by silence.

Blade looked around. "Alright, let's put it to a vote. Who agrees we take a chance, beg for mercy, and ask the old gods for their help?"

One by one, each man slowly nodded an acknowledgement until the old man was the only one left.

Lawrence looked down at the blood on his hands, knowing he was not long for this world and his journey would soon be over anyway. He closed his eyes before lifting his head and agreeing as well.

Blade walked to the front of the abbey, located an altar plate, and placed it on a nearby table. He produced a small medallion from his pocket, one he had always kept hidden away, passed down through his family for generations. He kissed the image of the Goddess Danu, and carefully laid it on the plate. Taking his dagger from his belt, he pulled the blade against his palm until the blood flowed freely, closed his hand into a fist, and let it drip onto the ancient charm as he spoke,

"Old ones hear my plea. We have been abandoned by the ones we served and left to die by the ones we swore to protect. We beg for your mercy and we will swear allegiance to be obedient only to you, and to do your bidding."

They waited, the silence becoming deafening for what seemed like an eternity.

"It was worth a try," said Porter sadly and leaned forward to rest his head on his knees. It was then he noticed a strange mist forming around his feet. He looked up and was just about to say something as a strong fog rushed under the cracks of the doors they had bolted and started to form a pattern.

The men clambered to their feet and formed a back to back circle in a defensive position just as Finn, the King of the Fae and Ana, his daughter who was also known as Danu, the Goddess of Fertility, appeared at the back of the chapel.

"Ye rang?" asked Finn sarcastically.

The startled men fell to their knees, one by one, and bowed their heads. Finn and Ana started to the front of the church to address the one who had summoned them. As they reached the men, Ana caught sight of the old man in the pew, blood pooling around him. She went over and knelt beside him. "Ye are dying," she said compassionately and brushed a few long strands of white hair away from his aged, wrinkled face, looking into his deep, green eyes.

"I am an old man," he swallowed hard, "my life does not matter anymore."

"That's not true. Each and every life in this world matters whether ye acknowledge it or not," she whispered before rejoining her father. She touched his arm and tilted her head in Lawrence's direction.

Finn looked over and patted her hand, a look of understanding passing between them.

"We need your help," said Blade, cautiously rising with his head still bent out of respect and motioned for the others to do the same.

"Aye, I know," said Finn. "Your kind is scattered to the wind. Ye are all that is left, betrayed by the one ye served, and here ye are, calling on us, the creatures ye have hunted and driven into the darkest recesses of the world, to save ye. Some might call that poetic justice. Why would we ever help ye?"

"We will do your bidding, be loyal only to you, if you help us prevent what we protect from falling into the hands of those who denied us," he replied nervously.

"Oh, my dear boy, ye need us for far more than that," scoffed Finn as he stepped closer to the young man. "Ye were the one who summoned us, so ye know we lived peacefully with mankind before your religion took over. We weren't hurting anyone, doing far more to help man than your Pope ever did. Granted, we had one or two who got out of hand, but our good deeds far outweighed our bad."

Blade nodded. "You are correct. Things have been done badly on both sides, but this is a chance to make some of those things right. Use us to take your revenge."

Finn looked down and rocked on his heels. "Revenge is not what we seek and honestly, ye have nothing to offer us for your protection. I am afraid ye have wasted your time— and ours."

Ana strolled over to, and around, the young man, taking a better look at him. She turned and looked over the rest of the men behind him before working her way back around to her father. "Maybe we COULD use them," she whispered, leaning close to his ear while tapping her lips with her index finger.

"What are ye talking about, Ana?" asked Finn, calling her by the nickname he had given her.

She took him by the shoulder and guided him off to the side. "We have four MacGregor women in desperate need of husbands. To be honest, the choice of men has been extremely slim pickings in the Highlands as of late."

"Is it really that bad?" he asked. "Are these truly the best we can come up with?"

Ana shrugged, then nodded. "Think of it this way— these men are warriors and, combined with the Fae blood carried by the MacGregor women, we would have *strong, not to mention, loyal children for generations to come." Ana leaned her head to the side and smiled. "Besides, it's not like they are hard to look at."*

Finn inconspicuously glanced over his shoulder. "Ye may have a point," he agreed, before turning back around, his arms folded. "On second thought, perhaps we can be of assistance to each other."

"What do you propose?" asked the burly red-headed Samer.

"We may be in need of some help from a few good men, and we would be willing to return the favor."

The men all looked around at each other, questioningly.

"Look!" said Finn. "Your leader, Jacques de Molay is dead, betrayed by your precious Pope and the King of France. Our numbers have been decimated by your kind for the behavior of a few wayward Fae, who went against their own king, namely me. Seems we are all victims of circumstance. Perhaps, if ye are willing to help us store some of our own treasure, we will be able to help ye protect yours." He stepped closer to the group. "Ye are hiding a great deal underneath this church, are ye not?"

The men looked at each other uneasily.

"We do not want YOUR treasure, for the record, but we can see it is kept safe," clarified Ana. "We are immortal and our kind will always be around in some form, and as long as your kind stops hunting us and gives us a little assistance instead, we can help watch over your precious cargo for much longer than any of ye will be alive."

"Why do you need us? Why can't ye hide your own?" asked the old man, now coughing up blood.

Finn turned to face him. "Our treasure is more of a bloodline that needs to endure. We need our Fae blood to continue in this world for generations to come, and we need the keepers of our history to be loyal to a fault. Ye scratch our backs and we will scratch yours, so to speak."

"A bloodline?" Lawrence huffed. "We have no women of our kind to lay with yours and give you children?"

"Oh, we have women," Ana smiled, "We need your men to lay with them. They are part of a family already sworn only to us. It seems, the current generation that is of age, are all women who need husbands, men who will promise to be true to the ones the family serves and are willing to take on THEIR family names. It is the perfect way to hide ye from those who would seek to destroy ye. In return, those children ye sire will be extraordinary, bringing a strength to that family line unlike anything the world has ever seen. They will have the ability to heal the sick, provide bounties and protect your new family with the strength of ten men. We also have a few other gifts we are offering as well."

"We have taken vows of celibacy," argued Richard.

"How are those vows working out for ye?" asked Finn. "Surely the urge to bed a woman has not completely left ye..." Finn looked in the direction of the man's groin, "...or did they cut your cocks off when they signed ye up?"

"Father!" scolded Ana, before looking back at the men. "Take what we offer and ye can live in peace, unbothered by those who hunt ye, because we will place ye somewhere safe and give your precious Order of Solomon's Temple a chance to endure, as well. While ye might never be able to return to your former glory as knights, ye can go underground, quietly grow your numbers and perhaps reemerge under another name in the years to come, while continuing to pursue your

'endeavors'— only now ye will have the power of the Fae to back ye."

"Make a new pact here to be our allies and we will sweeten the pot, so to speak," offered Finn.

"How?" asked Blade.

Finn looked over at the blood spilling from the old man's mouth. He stepped over, touched the man on the forehead and healed him in an instant.

"I will avenge your fallen leader by fulfilling his final request spelled out in his last words. I will ensure King Philip IV of France and Pope Clement V follow him to the grave within the year and the king's descendants will pay the piper as well."

The men's eyes widened.

"Go talk amongst yourselves," Finn shooed them to a corner, "We'll wait back here." He pointed to the last pew, and walked back, sitting down with his hands clasped behind his head as Ana joined him.

"Think they will agree to it?" she asked.

"They would be daft not to," he replied. "They will make far better friends than enemies and once their men are joined with MacGregor women, none of them will ever dare make a move against one of our kind again. Besides, now that they have set aside their vows, my guess is, their one of celibacy is the first one they will be wanting to break."

After an hour of deliberation, the men rejoined Finn and Ana, and Blade gave them their answer.

"We accept your offer but need some reassurances."

"Oh, my dear man," said Finn, "after our history together, so do we. We will make a blood pact to ensure everyone keeps their vows. Once your men are joined with our women, ye will all pledge to never harm another *who carries our blood and to protect our secrets, lest your entire order and their generations to come will forfeit their lives. In return, should anyone with Fae blood refuse to help one of your kind when asked, they will do the same. Our two families will be joined for all eternity."*

"How many of us do you need?" asked Griffin.

"There are four MacGregor women, all beautiful I might add," replied Ana. "We will need the four youngest of ye."

"Very well," agreed Blade, holding out his hand still covered in his own blood from the summoning. "Let the deal be made."

Finn turned. "Maggie, the pact must be upheld no matter what —or our kind will go extinct."

Maggie sat straight up, breathing hard, her heart pumping fast.

Duncan raised up. "What is it?"

"It was a dream," she said, panting, lifting her hand to her breast.

"Must have been some dream," he said and touched her back.

"It was." She raised her hand to shield her eyes as the sun's brightness blinded her. "As much as I hate to say it, we should be getting home."

Duncan looked out over the water. "Only if we can come back and bring the children sometime. I think they would like it here."

"Deal!" she said and kissed him. They dressed slowly before shimmering back into their bedroom and heading downstairs for breakfast.

"I take it ye two made up?" Ana smiled and sipped her coffee.

"We did!" said Maggie looking around. "Everybody good? Anybody got anything they need to get off their chest or can we go back to what passes for somewhat normal around here?"

"Please!" begged Gabe.

Quinn grinned. "I am not sure which is harder on the foundation of the house —your fighting or your making up."

"Definitely, their making up!" Ana laughed. "I'm not ashamed to admit I am a little jealous."

"I could help you with that," teased John, winking at Maggie, who wagged her finger at him good naturedly.

As things started to settle down over the next couple of days, Maggie's strange dream nagged at the back of her mind. She decided to ask her mother about it.

"Aye, it did happen," said Ana, motioning Maggie to sit.

"What about it is so familiar?" she asked.

"Ye know the Order of Solomon's Temple by another name—the Knights Templar."

"What? The Templars?" Maggie was completely stunned.

"Ye remember how the Fae were driven underground? The Order was a big part of that," explained Ana. "Their main directive was escorting followers to and from the Holy Land, but another part of their mission was to rid the world of us, a job they took very seriously. They even managed to kill a few of my brothers and sisters before driving the others into hiding. They got a hold of one of our spell books somehow and tortured a follower who could read it into translating it, giving them far too much knowledge about us. It is why we gave the books to the MacGregors for safekeeping to begin with. Father and I kept a watchful eye on them, staying just far enough ahead of them to not be threatened by them. When their own turned on them, they summoned us for help. By binding them to the MacGregors and to Fae blood, we ensured they would never be a threat to us again."

"They took MacGregor wives?"

"They did. Oh, don't worry, we made sure they had happy marriages, even if their starts were a little rocky."

"How so?"

Ana laughed. "Four young men sworn to be celibate. They weren't exactly 'excited' for their honeymoons."

Maggie covered her mouth to muffle her laugh. "If the MacGregor women are anything like their men, I am guessing the 'virgin grooms' didn't stand a chance."

"Not at all!" Ana giggled. "Of course, we did have to help them along a little."

"Do tell!" said Maggie, settling in her chair.

"Let's just say that Father had to give them 'the talk'. They may have been fierce on the battlefield, but they were terrified in the bedroom."

"Who was terrified in the bedroom?" asked Duncan.

He and the rest of the men filed into the room.

"Your ancestors, apparently," replied Maggie.

He looked at her strangely and Maggie explained her dream to everyone in the room.

"What I wouldn't have given to be a fly on those walls that night," John smirked.

"At any rate, it all worked out," said Ana.

"So, why did I dream about something that happened so long ago?"

Her mother shrugged. "I have no idea. Perhaps it is part of your expanding abilities?"

"Why do I have a feeling there is more to it than that?" mumbled Maggie.

Late that night, after the house was quiet, Maggie went down to the collection room, taking out the book that recorded the family line of the MacGregors. She flipped the pages until she found what she was looking for.

Indeed, in the year 1314, four MacGregor women were married on the same date and went on to have several children, Duncan's earlier ancestors. Only the men's given names were listed, having taken the MacGregor name, but each one had a small red cross beside them.

"What are ye doing down here?" asked Duncan.

"I couldn't sleep, so I came down to look through the MacGregor book of lineage."

"Find any new long-lost relatives we should be concerned about?" He wiped the sleep from his eyes.

"No. I was just curious about the dream I had and look—I found them." She pointed to the names.

"So ye did," he said and leaned over her shoulder. "Keeping the family records updated was always a priority. Which reminds me, should we add John's new addition now that he knows about her?"

"I suppose we should. She carries Fae blood, and we need to keep track of everyone who does. I will do it later." She closed the book.

"I can't figure out what triggered this dream," she said, pushing it away. "I didn't wish for it; I didn't even know about it. The thought of Templars mingling with Fae never even occurred to me, but I do remember one thing from that dream that bothers me. The last thing I heard before I woke up was Finn's voice saying the pact must be upheld or we would go extinct. The whole thing was so crazy, it didn't occur to me that the dream was something that actually happened until I asked Mom. Now, I am worried about what may be coming down the line."

Duncan took her hands and pulled her over to him. "One day at a time, my love. We will take things as they come."

Maggie knocked on the door of Gabe and Quinn's house.

"Knocking now, are we?" asked Gabe, leaning against the door, smiling.

"I didn't want to interrupt anything," she grinned and kissed him on the cheek.

Quinn came from the kitchen, wiping his hands on a towel and went over to kiss Maggie. "What brings ye out?"

"A final request from Georgie."

Gabe and Quinn eyed her warily, but they sat down, waiting for her to explain.

"Your mother asked me to do something for you. She sent two small diamonds and asked, that should you find the love of your life, to have them set into an appropriate piece of jewelry, leaving the judgement and the approval of the person up to me." She pulled out a small box and handed it to them. "I more than approve, and I hope you like them."

Gabe opened the top and looked down to find two gold bands, a diamond in the center of each, outlined by the same Fae design her own wedding band contained.

"Oh, Mags, these are magnificent."

Quinn took out the other. "They really are. How did ye do this?"

Maggie waved her hand. "The Queen of the Fae has all sorts of nifty tricks at her disposal. I think it is time the two of you had true wedding bands, and I think Georgie would approve."

Gabe covered his mouth and his eyes started to water. "I like to think so too," he choked and pulled Maggie to him. "I love you, Mags," he said, wiping his face as he sat back. "Thank you."

"Aye, thank ye," added Quinn.

"You're welcome." She pulled out the letter. "This is what Georgie wrote to me. I thought you might like to read it." She handed him the paper and stood. "Oh, and you are welcome to read her collection of novels —when I am finished with them, that is." She winked and shimmered out.

Epilogue

July 1806
(22 years later)

"There is news from Lucy Hanks about her daughter, Nancy," said Duncan, sitting down.

"What does it say?" asked Maggie as she brushed her hair.

"It looks like she has married a man by the name of Thomas Lincoln."

"Oh, that's nice." Maggie stopped and slowly turned around. "Wait! Did you say Lincoln? She is now 'Nancy Lincoln'?" Maggie searched her memories from a long ago visit to a civil war museum her father had taken her to in Illinois, and a spark of recognition slammed into her.

"Holy fuck! Nancy Lincoln is the name of the mother of —holy fuck!"

"Who?" demanded Duncan.

"Abraham Lincoln, future American president." She turned. "No! It couldn't be—could it?"

Tempie W. Wade

ABOUT THE AUTHOR

Tempie W. Wade is an author of historical fiction that incorporates elements of fantasy and the supernatural. She uses real-life events and timelines to make her stories more real, while encouraging the audience to take a step back into history, and to research the lives of those who played such an important part in the founding of America for themselves.

She is a long-term resident of Williamsburg, Virginia.

www.TempieWade.com

Tempie W. Wade

The Timely Revolution Book Series
(In Order)

More to come....

www.ingramcontent.com/pod-product-compliance
Lightning Source LLC
Chambersburg PA
CBHW051545250626
47157CB00001B/188